Richard Chenevix ꓕꓤꓰꓠꓞꓧ

English Past and Present

Richard Chenevix Trench

English Past and Present

Reprint of the original, first published in 1871.

1st Edition 2022 | ISBN: 978-3-36812-454-0

Verlag (Publisher): Outlook Verlag GmbH, Zeilweg 44, 60439 Frankfurt, Deutschland
Vertretungsberechtigt (Authorized to represent): E. Roepke, Zeilweg 44, 60439 Frankfurt, Deutschland
Druck (Print): Books on Demand GmbH, In de Tarpen 42, 22848 Norderstedt, Deutschland

ENGLISH,

PAST AND PRESENT.

EIGHT LECTURES

BY

RICHARD CHENEVIX TRENCH, D.D.,

ARCHBISHOP OF DUBLIN.

SEVENTH EDITION.
REVISED AND IMPROVED.

NEW YORK:

CHARLES SCRIBNER AND COMPANY,

1871.

PREFACE

TO

THE FIRST EDITION.

A SERIES of four lectures which I delivered
last spring to the pupils of King's College
School, London, supplied the foundation to this
present volume. These lectures, which I was obliged
to prepare in haste, on a brief invitation, and under
the pressure of other engagements, being subsequently
enlarged and recast, were delivered in the autumn
somewhat more nearly in their present shape to the
pupils of the Training School, Winchester; with only
those alterations, omissions and additions, which the
difference in my hearers suggested as necessary or
desirable. I have found it convenient to keep the
lectures, as regards the persons presumed to be addressed, in that earlier form which I had sketched
out at the first; and, inasmuch as it helps much to
keep lectures vivid and real that one should have
some well-defined audience, if not actually before

one, yet before the mind's eye, to suppose myself
throughout addressing my first hearers.   I have supposed myself, that is, addressing a body of young
Englishmen, all with a fair amount of classical knowledge (in my explanations I have sometimes had
others with less than theirs in my eye), not wholly
unacquainted with modern languages ; but not yet
with any special designation as to their future work ;
having only as yet marked out to them the duty in
general of living lives worthy of those who have England for their native country, and English for their
native tongue.   To lead such through a more intimate knowledge of this into a greater love of that,
has been a principal aim which I have set before myself throughout.

ITCHENSTOKE : *Feb.* 7, 1855.

CONTENTS.

ENGLISH

PAST AND PRESENT.

LECTURE I.

THE ENGLISH VOCABULARY.

' A VERY slight acquaintance with the history of
our own language will teach us that the
speech of Chaucer's age is not the speech of Skelton's,
that there is a great difference between the language
under Elizabeth and that under Charles the First,
between that under Charles the First and Charles the
Second, between that under Charles the Second and
Queen Anne ; that considerable changes had taken
place between the beginning and the middle of the
last century, and that Johnson and Fielding did
not write altogether as we do now. For in the course
of a nation's progress new ideas are evermore mount-
ing above the horizon, while others are lost sight of
and sink below it : others again change their form and
aspect : others which seemed united, split into parts.
And as it is with ideas, so it is with their symbols,
words. New ones are perpetually coined to meet the

demand of an advanced understanding, of new feelings that have sprung out of the decay of old ones, of
ideas that have shot forth from the summit of the tree
of our knowledge ; old works meanwhile fall into disuse and become obsolete ; others have their meaning
narrowed and defined ; synonyms diverge from each
other and their property is parted between them ; nay,
whole classes of words will now and then be thrown
overboard, as new feelings or perceptions of analogy
gain ground.   A history of the language in which all
these vicissitudes should be pointed out, in which the
introduction of every new word should be noted, so
far as it is possible—and much may be done in this
way by laborious and diligent and judicious research
—in which such words as have become obsolete
should be followed down to their final extinction, in
which all the most remarkable words should be
traced through their successive phases of meaning,
and in which moreover the causes and occasions of
these changes should be explained, such a work
would not only abound in entertainment, but would
throw more light on the development of the human
mind than all the brainspun systems of metaphysics
that ever were written.'

These words are not my own, but the words of a
greatly honoured friend and teacher, who, though we
behold him now no more, still teaches, and will teach,
by the wisdom of his writings, and the remembered
nobleness of his life.   They are words of Archdeacon
Hare.   I have put them in the forefront of my
lectures ; anticipating as they do, in the way of

masterly sketch, all or nearly all which I shall attempt
to accomplish ; and indeed drawing out the lines of
very much more, to which I shall not venture to put
my hand. At the same time the subject is one which,
even with my partial and imperfect handling, will, I
trust, find an answer and an echo in the hearts of all
whom I address ; which every Englishman will feel of
near concern and interest to himself. For, indeed,
the love of our native language, what is it in fact, but
the love of our native land expressing itself in one
particular direction ? If the noble acts of that nation
to which we belong are precious to us, if we feel
ourselves made greater by the greatness, summoned
to a nobler life by the nobleness of Englishmen, who
have already lived and died, and have bequeathed to
us a name which must not by us be made less, what
exploits of theirs can well be worthier, what can
more clearly point out their native land and ours as
having fulfilled a glorious past, as being destined for
a glorious future, than that they should have acquired
for themselves and for us a clear, a strong, an harmonious, a noble language ? For all this bears witness to corresponding merits in those that speak it, to
clearness of mental vision, to strength, to harmony,
to nobleness in them who have gradually shaped and
fashioned it to be the utterance of their inmost life
and being.

    To know concerning this language, the stages which
it has gone through, the sources from which its riches
have been derived, the gains which it has made or is
now making, the perils which are threatening it, the
losses which it has sustained, the capacities which

may be yet latent in it, waiting to be evoked, the points in which it transcends other tongues, the points in which it comes short of them, all this may well be the object of worthy ambition to every one of us. So may we hope to be ourselves guardians of its purity, and not corruptors of it ; to introduce, it may be, others into an intelligent knowledge of that, with which we shall have ourselves more than a merely superficial acquaintance : to bequeath it to those who come after us not worse than we received it ourselves. ' Spartam nactus es ; hanc exorna,'—this should be our motto in respect at once of our country, and of the speech of our country.

Nor is a study such as this alien or remote from the purposes which have brought us hither. It is true that within these walls we are mainly occupied in learning other tongues than our own. The time we bestow upon it is small as compared with that bestowed on those others. And yet one of our main objects in learning them is that we may better understand this. Nor ought any other to dispute with it the first and foremost place in our reverence, our gratitude, and our love. It has been well and worthily said by an illustrious German scholar, ' The care of the national language I consider as at all times a sacred trust and a most important privilege of the higher orders of society. Every man of education should make it the object of his unceasing concern, to preserve his language pure and entire, to speak it, so far as is in his power, in all its beauty and perfection. . . . . A nation whose language becomes rude and barbarous,

must be on the brink of barbarism in regard to everything else. A nation which allows her language
to go to ruin, is parting with the best half of her intellectual independence, and testifies her willingness
to cease to exist.'*

But this knowledge, like all other knowledge which
is worth attaining, is only to be attained at the price
of labor and pains. The language which at this day
we employ is the result of processes which have been
going forward for hundreds and for thousands of
years. Nay more,—it is not too much to affirm that
processes modifying the English which we now write
and speak, have been operating from the first day that
man, being gifted with discourse of reason, projected
his thought from himself, and embodied and contemplated it in his word. Which things being so, if we
would understand this language as it now is, we must
know something of it as it has been ; we must be able
to measure, however roughly, the forces which have
been at work upon it, moulding and shaping it into
the forms, and bringing it into the conditions under
which it now exists.

At the same time various prudential considerations
must determine for us how far up we will endeavour
to trace the course of its history. There are those

* F. Schlegel, *History of Literature, Lecture* 10. Milton :
Verba enim partim inscita et putida, partim mendosa et per-
peram prolata, quid si ignavos et oscitantes, et ad servile quid-
vis jam olim paratos incolarum animos haud levi indicio de-
clarant ? I have elsewhere quoted this remarkable passage in
full (*Study of Words*, 12th edit. p. 83).

who may seek to trace our language to the forests of
Germany and Scandinavia, to investigate its relation
to all the kindred tongues that were there spoken ;
again, to follow it up, till it and they are seen de-
scending from an elder stock ; nor once to pause, till
they have assigned to it its proper place not merely in
that smaller group of languages which are immediately round it, but in respect of all the tongues and languages of the earth.   I can imagine few studies of a
more surpassing interest than this.   Others, however,
must be content with seeking such insight into their
native language as may be within the reach of all who,
unable to make this the subject of especial research,
possessing neither that vast compass of knowledge,
nor that immense apparatus of•books, not being at
liberty to yield to it that devotion almost of a life
which, followed out to the full, it would require, have
yet an intelligent interest in their mother tongue, and
desire to learn as much of its growth and history and
construction as may be fairly within their reach.   To
such I shall suppose myself to be speaking.   I assume
no higher ground than this for myself.

   I know, indeed, that some, when invited at all to
enter upon the past history of the English language,
are inclined to answer—'To what end such studies
to us ?   Why cannot we leave them to a few anti-
quaries and grammarians ?   Sufficient to us to know
the laws of our present English, to obtain an acquaintance as accurate as we can with the language
as we now find it, without concerning ourselves with
the phases through which it has previously passed.'

This may sound plausible enough ; and I can quite understand a real lover of his native tongue, who has not bestowed much thought upon the subject, taking up such a position as this. And yet it is one which cannot be maintained. A sufficient reason why we should occupy ourselves with the past of our language is, that the present is only intelligible in the light of the past, often of a very remote past indeed. There are in it anomalies out of number, which the pure logic of grammar is quite incapable of explaining ; which nothing but an acquaintance with its historic evolutions, and with the disturbing forces which have made themselves felt therein, will ever enable us to understand ; not to say that, unless we possess some such knowledge of the past, we cannot ourselves advance a single step in the unfolding of the latent capabilities of the language, without the danger of doing some outrage to its genius, of committing some barbarous violation of its very primary laws.*

The plan which I have laid down for myself in these lectures will be as follows. In this my first I shall invite you to consider the language as now it is, to decompose some specimens of it, and in this way

---

* Littré (*Hist. de la Langue Française*, vol. ii. p. 485) : Une langue ne peut être conservée dans sa pureté qu'autant qu'elle est étudiée dans son histoire, ramenée à ses sources, appuyée à ses traditions. Aussi l'étude de la vieille langue est un élément nécessaire, lequel venant à faire défaut, la connaissance du langage moderne est sans profondeur, et le bon usage sans racines. Compare Pellissier, *La Langue Française*, p. 259.

to prove, of what elements it is compact, and what functions in it these elements severally fulfil. Nor shall I leave this subject without asking you to admire the happy marriage in our tongue of the languages of the North and South, a marriage giving to it advantages which no other of the languages of Europe enjoys. Having thus before us the body which we wish to submit to scrutiny, and having become acquainted, however slightly, with its composition, I shall invite you in my next to consider with me what this actual language might have been, if that event, which more than all other put together has affected and modified the English language, namely, the Norman Conquest, had never found place. In the lectures which follow I shall seek to institute from various points of view a comparison between the present language and the past, to point out gains which it has made, losses which it has endured, and generally to · call your attention to some of the more important chànges through which it has passed, or is at this present passing.

I shall, indeed, everywhere solicit your attention not merely to the changes which have been in time past effected, but to those also which at this very moment are going forward. I shall not account the fact that some are proceeding, so to speak, under our own eyes, a sufficient ground to excuse me from noticing them, but rather an additional reason for so doing. For, indeed, these changes which we are ourselves helping to bring about, are the very ones which we are most likely to fail in observing. So many causes ´

contribute to withdraw them from notice, to veil
their operation, to conceal their significance, that,
save by a very few, they will commonly pass wholly
unobserved. Loud and sudden revolutions attract
and even compel observation ; but revolutions silent
and gradual, although with issues far vaster in store,
run their course, and it is only when their cycle is
nearly or quite completed, that men perceive what
mighty transforming forces have been at work un-
noticed in their very midst.

Thus, in this matter of language, how few aged
persons, even among those who retain the fullest
possession of their faculties, are conscious of any
serious difference between the spoken language of
their early youth, and that of their old age ; are aware
that words and ways of using words are obsolete now,
which were usual then ; that many words are current
now, which had no existence at that time. And yet it
is certain that so it must be. A man may fairly be assumed to remember clearly and well for sixty years
back ; and it needs less than five of these sixties to
bring us to the age of Spenser, and not more than
eight to set us in the time of Chaucer and Wiclif.
No one, contemplating this whole term, will deny the
immensity of the change within these eight memories.
And yet, for all this, we may be tolerably sure that,
had it been possible to interrogate a series of eight
persons, such as together had filled up this time, intelligent men, but men whose attention had not been
especially awakened to this subject, each in his turn
would have denied that there had been any change

worth speaking of, perhaps any change at all, during his lifetime. It is not the less sure, considering the multitude of words which have fallen into oblivion during these four or five hundred years, that there must have been some lives in this chain which saw those words in use at their commencement, and out of use before their close. And so too, of the multitude of words which have sprung up in this period, some, nay, a vast number, must have come into being within the limits of each of these lives.*

---

* See on this subject the deeply interesting chapter, the 23rd, in Sir C. Lyell's *Antiquity of Man,* with the title, *Origin and development of Languages and Species compared.* I quote a few words : 'Every one may have noticed in his own lifetime the stealing in of some slight alterations of accent, pronunciation, or spelling, or the introduction of some words borrowed from a foreign language to express ideas of which no native term precisely conveyed the import. He may also remember hearing for the first time some cant terms or slang phrases, which have since forced their way into common use, in spite of the efforts of the purists. But he may still contend that "within the range of his experience" his language has continued unchanged, and he may believe in its immutability in spite of minor variations. The real question, however, at issue is, whether there are any limits to this variability. He will find on further investigation, that new technical terms are coined almost daily, in various arts, sciences, professions and trades, that new names must be found for new inventions ; that many of these acquire a metaphorical sense, and then make their way into general circulation, as "stereotyped" for instance, which would have been as meaningless to the men of the seventeenth century as would the new terms and images derived from steamboat and railway travelling to the men of the eighteenth.'

Nor is it hard on a little reflection to perceive how
this going and coming have alike been hid from their
eyes. In the nature of things, words which go excite
little or no notice in their going. They drop out of
use little by little, no one noticing the fact. The
student, indeed, of a past epoch of our literature finds
words to have been freely used in it which are‚not
employed in his own ; and these, when all brought
into a vocabulary, by no means to be few in number.
But it was only one by one that they fell out of sight,
and this by steps the most gradual ; were first more
seldom used, then only by those who affected a somewhat archaic style, and lastly not at all. And as with
the outgoers, so in a measure also is it with the
incomers. The newness and strangeness of them,
even where there is knowledge and observation sufficient to recognize them as novelties at all, wears off
very much sooner than would be supposed. They are
but of yesterday ; and men presently employ them as
though they had existed as long as the language itself.
Nor is it words only which thus steal out of the
language and steal into it, unobserved in their coming
and their going. It is the same with numbers, tenses,
and moods, with old laws of the language which
gradually lose their authority, with new usages which
gradually acquire the force of laws. Thus it would
be curious to know how many have had their attention drawn to the fact that the subjunctive mood is at
this very moment perishing in English. One who
now says, ' If he *call*, tell him I am out '—many do
say it still, but they are fewer every day—is seeking

to detain a mood which the language is determined to get rid of. The English-speaking race has come to perceive that clearness does not require the maintenance of any distinction between the indicative and subjunctive moods, and has therefore resolved not to be at the trouble of maintaining it any more. But the dropping of the subjunctive, important change as it is, goes on for the most part unmarked even by those who are themselves effecting the change. On this matter, however, I shall have by and by something more to say.

With these preliminary remarks I address myself to our special subject of to-day. And first, starting from the recognized fact that the English is not a simple but a composite language, made up of several elements, so far at least as its vocabulary is concerned, as are the people who speak it, I would suggest to you the profit to be derived from a resolving of it into its component parts—from taking, that is, some passage of English, distributing the words of which it is made up according to the sources whence they are drawn ; estimating the relative numbers and proportion which these languages have severally lent us ; as well as the character of the words which they have contributed to the common stock.

Thus, suppose the English language to be divided into a hundred parts ; of these, to make a rough distribution, sixty might be Saxon ; thirty Latin (including of course the Latin which has come to us through the French) ; five perhaps would be Greek. We should in this way have allotted ninety-five

parts, leaving the other five to be divided among all
the other languages which have made their several
smaller contributions to the vocabulary of our English
tongue. It is probable that, all counted, they would
not amount to this five in the hundred. They certainly would not, unless we include in this list words
which we owe to languages closely allied to the
Anglo-Saxon, but which are not found in the Anglo-
Saxon vocabulary. I refer to those, Scandinavian
we may call them for convenience, for which we are
mainly indebted to the Danish settlements in the
north of England. Let me speak first of these. It
would be idle to attempt an exhaustive enumeration
of them ; but a small selection will show of how
serviceable a character they are, and what an important part of our every-day working English they form.
Thus take these nouns, 'bag,' 'bole,' 'booty,' 'brag,'
'brink,' 'bull,' 'cake,' 'cripple,' 'dairy,' 'earl,'
'fell,' 'fellow,' 'fool,' 'froth,' 'gable,' 'gill,' 'gin,'
'hustings,' 'keg,' 'kid,' 'leg,' 'muck,' 'odds,'
'puck,' 'rump,' 'root,' 'sark,' 'scald,' 'scull,' 'skill,'
'sky,' 'sleight,' 'tarn,' 'thrum,' 'tyke,' 'windlass,'
'window ;' or, again, these verbs, 'to bask,' 'to clip,'
'to cuff,' 'to curl,' 'to daze,' 'to droop,' 'to dub,' 'to
flit,' 'to grovel,' 'to hale,' 'to hug,' 'to lurk,' 'to
ransack,' 'to scrub,' 'to skulk,' 'to thrive.' Then
too there are Dutch words, especially sea-terms, which
have found their way into English, as 'boom,' 'dog-
ger,' 'hoy,' 'lubber,' 'schooner,' 'skates,' 'skipper,'
'sloop,' 'smack,' 'stiver,' 'tafferel,' 'yacht,' 'to luff,'
'to smuggle.'

But to look now farther abroad. We have a certain number of Hebrew words, mostly, if not entirely, belonging to religious matters, as 'amen,' 'caba-
la,' 'cherub,' 'ephod,' 'gehenna,' 'hallelujah,' 'ho-
sanna,' 'jubilee,' 'leviathan,' 'manna,' 'Messiah,'
'sabbath,' 'Satan,' 'seraph,' 'shibboleth,' 'talmud.'
The Arabic words in our language are more numerous; we have several arithmetical and astronomical
terms, as 'aldebaran,' 'algebra,' 'almanach,' 'azi-
muth,' 'cypher,'* 'nadir,' 'talisman,' 'zenith,' 'zero;'
and chemical no less; for the Arabs were the chem-
ists, no less than the astronomers and arithmeticians
of the middle ages; as 'alcohol,' 'alembic,' 'alkali,'
'elixir.' Add to these the names of animals, plants,
fruits, or articles of merchandise first introduced by
them to the notice of Western Europe; as 'amber,'
'antimonium,' 'apricot,'† 'arrack,' 'artichoke,' 'bar-
ragan,' 'bournous,' 'camphor,' 'carmine,' 'coffee,'
'cotton,' 'crimson,' 'endive,' 'gazelle,' 'giraffe,'
'henna,' 'jar,' 'jasmine,' 'lake,' (lacca) 'laudanum,'
'lemon,' 'lime,' 'lute,' 'mattress,' 'mummy,'
'musk,' 'popinjay,' 'saffron,' 'senna,' 'sherbet,'
'sirup,' 'shrub,' 'sofa,' 'sugar,' 'sumach,' 'talc,'
'tamarind;' and some further terms, 'admiral,' 'al-
cove,'‡ 'alguazil,' 'amulet,' 'arsenal,' 'assassin,'
'barbican' 'caliph,' 'caffre,' 'carat,'§ 'caravan,'

---

* But see J. Grimm, *Deutsche Mythologie*, p. 985.
† See Mahn, *Etymol. Untersuch.* p. 49.
‡ See Mahn, p. 156.
§ This is the Greek χεράτιον, which, having travelled to

'dey,' 'divan,' 'dragoman,'* 'emir,' 'fakir,' 'feluc-
ca,' 'firman,' 'hanger,' 'harem,' 'hazard,' 'hegira,'
'houri,' 'islam,' 'koran,' 'magazine,' 'mamaluke,'
'marabout,' 'minaret,' 'monsoon,' 'mosque,' 'muf-
ti,' 'mussulman,' 'nabob,' 'otto,' 'quintal,' 'razzia,'
'sahara,' 'salaam,' 'scheik,' 'simoom,' 'sirocco,'
'sultan,' 'tarif,' 'vizier;' and I believe we shall have
nearly completed the list. Of Persian words we have
these : 'azure,' 'bazaar,' 'bezoar,' 'caravanserai,'
'check,' 'chess,' 'dervish,' 'jackal,' 'lilac,' 'necta-
rine,' 'orange,' 'pagoda,' 'saraband,' 'sash,' 'scar-
let,' 'sepoy,' 'shawl,' 'taffeta,' 'tambour,' 'turban ;'

---

the East, has in this shape come back to us, just as δηνάριον
has returned in the ' dinar ' of the *Arabian Nights.*
  * The word hardly deserves to be called English, yet in
Pope's time it had made some progress towards naturalization.
Of a real or pretended polyglottist, who might thus have served
as an universal *interpreter*, he says :

  ' Pity you was not *druggerman* at Babel.'

' Truckman,' or more commonly ' truchman,' familiar to all
readers of our early literature, is only another form of this,
which probably has come to us through ' turcimanno,' an
Italian form of the word. Let me here observe that in Clarendon's *History of the Rebellion,* b. i. § 75, there can be no
doubt that for ' trustman,' as it is printed in all editions which
I have been able to consult, we should read ' truchman.'
Prince Charles at the time of his visit to Spain not speaking
Spanish, the king, we are told, summoned the Earl of Bristol
into the coach with them ' that he should serve as a *trustman,*'
—a word yielding no kind of sense ; or rather no word at all,
but only the ignorant correction of some scribe or printer, to
whom ' truchman ' was strange.

this last appearing in strange forms, 'tolibant' (Put-tenham), 'tulipant' (Herbert's *Travels*), 'turribant' (Spenser), 'turbat,' 'turbant,' and at length 'turban;' 'zemindar,' 'zenana.' We have also a few Turkish, such as 'bey,' 'caftan,' 'chouse,' 'fez,' 'janisary,' 'odalisk,' 'tulip,' 'xebek.' Of 'civet,' 'mohair,' and 'scimitar' I believe it can only be asserted that they are Eastern. 'Bamboo,' 'cassowary,' 'gong,' 'gutta-percha,' 'orang-utang,' 'rattan,' 'sago,' 'upas,' are Malay. The following are Hindostanee : 'avatar,' 'banian,' 'bungalow,' 'calico,' 'chintz,' 'cowrie,' 'jungle,' 'lac,' 'loot,' 'muslin,' 'punch,' 'rajah,' 'rupee,' 'toddy.' 'Tea,' or 'tcha,' as it was once spelt, with 'bohea,' 'hyson,' 'souchong,' is Chinese ; so too are 'junk,' 'hong,' 'nankeen.'

To come nearer home—we have a certain number of Italian words, as 'ambuscade,' 'bagatelle,' 'bal-cony,' 'baldachin,' 'balustrade,' 'bandit,' 'bravo,' 'broccoli,' 'buffoon,' 'burlesque,' 'bust' (it was 'busto' at first, and therefore from the Italian, not from the French), 'cadence,' 'cascade,' 'cameo,' 'canto,' 'caricature,' 'carnival,' 'cartoon,' 'case-mate,' 'casino,' 'catafalque,' 'cavalcade,' 'charlatan,' 'citadel,' 'concert,' 'conversazione,' 'corridor,' 'cu-pola,' 'dilettante,' 'ditto,' 'doge,' 'domino,' 'fiasco,' 'filagree,' 'fresco,' 'gabion,' 'gazette,' 'generalis-simo,' 'gondola,' 'gonfalon,' 'grotto' ('grotta' in Bacon), 'gusto,' 'harlequin,' 'imbroglio,' 'inamo-rato,' 'influenza,' 'lagoon,' 'lava,' 'lavolta,' 'laza-retto,' 'macaroni,' 'madonna,' 'madrepore,' 'madri-gal,' 'malaria,' 'manifesto,' 'maraschino,' 'masquerade' ('mascarata' in Hacket), 'mezzotint,' 'motett, 'motto,' 'moustachio' ('mostaccio' in Ben Jonson), 'nuncio,' 'opera,' 'oratorio,' 'pantaloon,' 'parapet,' 'pedant,' 'pedantry,' 'piano-forte,' 'piaster,' 'piazza,' 'porcelain,' 'portico,' 'protocol,' 'proviso,' 'regatta,' 'rocket,' 'ruffian,' 'scaramouch,' 'sequin,' 'seraglio,' 'serenade,' 'sirocco,' 'sketch,' 'solo,' 'sonnet,' 'stanza,' 'stiletto,' 'stucco,' 'studio,' 'terrace,' 'ter-racotta,' 'torso,' 'trombone,' 'umbrella,' 'vedette,' 'vermicelli,' 'violoncello,' 'virtuoso,' 'vista,' 'vol-cano,' 'zany.' Others once common enough, as 'becco,' 'cornuto,' 'fantastico,' 'impresa' (the ar-morial device on shields), 'magnifico,' 'saltim-banco' (= mountebank), are now obsolete. Sylves-ter has 'farfalla' for butterfly, but, so far as I know, this use is peculiar to him.

If this is at all a complete collection of our Italian words, the Spanish in the language are nearly as numerous ; nor would it be wonderful if they were more ; for although our literary relations with Spain have been slight indeed as compared with those which we have maintained with Italy, we have had other points of contact, friendly and hostile, with the former much more real than we have known with the latter. Thus we have from the Spanish, 'albino,' 'alligator' ('el lagarto'), 'armada,' 'armadillo,' 'barricade,' 'bastinado,' 'bolero,' 'bravado,' 'buf-falo' ('buff' or 'buffle' is the proper English word), 'cambist,' 'camisado,' 'cannibal,' 'caracole,' 'cara-vel,' 'carbonado,' 'cargo,' 'carrack,' 'cartel,' 'cigar,' 'cochineal,' 'commodore,' 'creole,' 'desperado,' 'don,' 'duenna,' 'eldorado,' 'embargo,' 'fandango,' 'farthingale,' 'filibuster,' 'flotilla,' 'gala,' 'garotte,' 'grandee,' 'grenade,' 'guerilla,' 'hackney,' 'hooker,'* 'indigo,' 'infanta,' 'jennet,' 'junto,' 'maravedi,' 'maroon,'† 'merino,' 'molasses,' 'mosquito,' 'mulatto,' 'negro,' 'olio,' 'ombre,' 'palaver,' 'parade,' 'paragon,' 'parasol,' 'parroquet,' 'peccadillo,' 'picaroon,' 'pintado,' 'platina,' 'poncho,' 'punctilio' (for a long time spelt 'puntillo' in English books), 'quinine,' 'reformado,' 'sarsaparilla,' 'sassafras,' 'sherry,' 'soda,' 'stampede,' 'stoccado,' 'strappado,' 'tornado,' 'vanilla,' 'verandah.' 'Caprice' too we obtained rather from Spain than Italy; it was written 'capricho' by those who used it first. Other Spanish words, once familiar, are now extinct. 'Punctilio' lives on, but not 'punto,' which is common enough in Bacon. 'Privado,' a prince's favourite, one admitted to his *privacy* (frequent in Jeremy Taylor and Fuller), has disappeared; so too have 'quirpo' (cuerpo), a jacket fitting close to the *body;* 'quellio' (cuello), a ruff or *neck*-collar; 'matachin,' the title of a sword-dance; all frequent in our early dra-

---

* Not in our dictionaries; but a kind of coasting vessel well known to seafaring men, the Spanish 'urca ;' thus in Oldys' *Life of Raleigh:* 'Their galleons, galleasses, gallies, *urcas*, and zabras were miserably shattered.'

† A 'maroon' is a negro who has escaped to the woods, and there lives wild. The word is a corruption of 'cimarron,' signifying wild in Spanish. In our earlier discoverers it still retains its shape (Drake writes it 'symaron '), though not its spelling. See *Notes and Queries*, 1866, p. 86.

matists ; and ' flota,' the constant name of the trea-
sure-fleet from the Indies. 'Intermess,' employed
by Evelyn, is the Spanish ' entremes,' though not recognized as such in our dictionaries. 'Albatross,'
'gentoo,' ' mandarin,' 'marmalade,' 'moidore,' 'pa-
lanquin,' 'yam,' are Portuguese.

Celtic *things* for the most part we designate by
Celtic words ; such as 'bannock,' 'bard,' ' bog,'
'brogues,' ' clan,' 'claymore,' 'fillibeg,' ' kilt,' 'pi-
broch,' 'plaid,' ' reel,' ' shamrock,' ' slogan,' ' usque-
baugh,' 'whiskey.' The words which I have just
named are for the most part of comparatively recent
introduction ; but many others, how many is yet a
very unsettled question, which at a much earlier date
found admission into our tongue, are derived from
this same quarter.*

Then too the New World has given us a certain
number of words, Indian and other—'anana' or
'ananas' (Brazilian), ' cacique' ('cassiqui,' in Raleigh's *Guiana*), 'caiman,' ' calumet,' ' canoe,' ' cari-
bou,' 'catalpa,' 'caoutchouc' (South American),
' chocolate,' ' cocoa,' ' condor,' 'guano ' (Peruvian),
' hamoc' ('hamaca' in Raleigh), 'hominy,' ' inca,'
' jaguar,' 'jalap,' ' lama,' ' maize' (Haytian), 'ma-
nitee,' ' mocassin,' ' mohawk,' ' opossum,' 'pampas,'
' pappoos,' ' pemmican,' 'pirogue,' ' potato ' ('ba-
tata' in our earlier voyagers), ' puma' (Peruvian),
' raccoon.' ' sachem,' ' samp,' ' savannah ' (Haytian),

---

* See Kock, *Hist. Gram. der Englischen Sprache*, vol. i.
p. 4.

'skunk,' 'squaw,' 'tapioca,' 'tobacco,' 'tomahawk,'
'tomata' (Mexican), 'wampum,' 'wigwam.' If
'hurricane' was originally obtained from the Carib-
bean islanders,* it should be included in this
list.

We may notice, finally, languages which have bestowed on us some single word, or two perhaps, or
three. Thus 'hussar' is Hungarian; 'hetman,'
Polish; 'drosky,' 'ukase,' Russian; 'caloyer,' Ro-
maic; 'mammoth,' of some Siberian language;
'taboo,' 'tattoo,' Polynesian; 'caviar,' and 'steppe,'
Tartarian; 'gingham,' Javanese; 'assegai,' 'chim-
panzee,' 'fetisch,' 'gnu,' 'kraal,' 'zebra,' belong to
various African dialects; but 'fetisch' has reached us
through the channel of the Portuguese.

Now I have no right to assume that any among
those to whom I speak are equipped with that knowledge of other tongues, which shall enable them to
detect at once the nationality of all or most of the
words which they meet—some of these greatly disguised, and having undergone manifold transformations in the process of their adoption among us; but
only that you have such helps at command in the
shape of dictionaries and the like, and so much diligence in the use of these, as will enable you to trace
out their birth and parentage. But possessing this
much, I am confident to affirm that few studies will
be more fruitful, will suggest more various matter of

* See Washington Irving, *Life and Voyages of Columbus*,
b. viii. c. 9.

reflection, will more lead you into the secrets of the
English tongue, than an analysis of passages drawn
from different authors, such as I have just now proposed. Thus you will take some passage of English
verse or prose—say the first ten lines of *Paradise Lost*
—or the Lord's Prayer—or the 23rd Psalm; you will
distribute the whole body of words which occur in
that passage, of course not omitting the smallest, according to their nationalities—writing, it may be, A
over every Anglo-Saxon word, L over every Latin,
and so on with the others, should any other find room
in the portion submitted to examination. This done,
you will count up the *number* of those which each
language contributes; again, you will note the *character* of the words derived from each quarter.

Yet here, before passing further, let me note that
in dealing with Latin words it will be well further to
mark whether they are directly from it, and such might
be marked L¹, or only mediately, and to us directly
from the French, which would be L², or Latin at
second hand. A rule holds generally good, by which
you may determine this. If a word be directly from
the Latin, it will have undergone little or no modification in its form and shape, save only in the termination. 'Innocentia' will have become 'innocency,'
'natio' 'nation,' 'firmamentum' 'firmament,' but
this will be all. On the other hand, if it comes
through the French, it will have undergone a process
of lubrication; its sharply defined Latin outline will
in good part have disappeared; thus 'crown' is from
corona,' but through 'couronne,' and in itself a

dissyllable, 'coroune,' in our earlier English ; 'treasure' is from 'thesaurus,' but through 'trésor;'
'emperor' is the Latin 'imperator,' but it was first
'empereur.' It will often happen that the substantive
has thus reached us through the intervention of the
French ; while we have only felt at a later period our
need of the adjective as well, which we have proceeded to borrow direct from the Latin. Thus 'people' is 'populus,' but it was 'peuple' first, while
'popular' is a direct transfer of a Latin vocable into
our English glossary ; 'enemy' is 'inimicus,' but it
was first softened in the French, and had its Latin
physiognomy in good part obliterated, while 'inimi-
cal' is Latin throughout ; 'parish' is 'paroisse,' but
'parochial' is 'parochialis;' 'chapter' is 'chapitre,'
but 'capitular' is 'capitularis.'

Sometimes you will find a Latin word to have been
twice adopted by us, and now making part of our
vocabulary in two shapes : 'doppelgänger' the Germans would call such. There is first the older word,
which the French has given us ; but which, before it
gave, it had fashioned and moulded ; clipping or
contracting, it may be, by a syllable or more, for the
French devours letters and syllables ; and there is the
younger, borrowed at first hand from the Latin.
Thus 'secure' and 'sure' are both from 'securus,'
but one directly, the other through the French ;
'fidelity' and 'fealty,' both from 'fidelitas,' but one
directly, the other at second hand ; 'species' and
'spice,' both from 'species,' spices being properly
only *kinds* of aromatic drugs ; 'blaspheme' and

'blame,' both from 'blasphemare,'* but 'blame,'
immediately from 'blâmer.' Add to these 'granary',
and 'garner;' 'captain' (capitaneus) and 'chieftain;'
'tradition' and 'treason;' 'rapine' and 'ravin;'
'abyss' and 'abysm;' 'phantasm' and 'phantom;'
'coffin' and 'coffer;' 'regal' and 'royal;' 'legal'
and 'loyal;' 'cadence' and 'chance;' 'balsam'
and 'balm;' 'hospital' and 'hotel;' 'digit' and
'doit;' 'pagan' and 'paynim;' 'captive' and 'caitiff;' 'persecute' and 'pursue;' 'aggravate' and
'aggrieve;' 'superficies' and 'surface;' 'sacristan'
and 'sexton;' 'faction' and 'fashion;' 'particle'
and 'parcel;' 'redemption' and 'ransom;' 'probe'
and 'prove;' 'abbreviate' and 'abridge;' 'dormi-
tory' and 'dortoir' or 'dorter'(this last now obsolete,
but not uncommon in Jeremy Taylor); 'desiderate'
and 'desire;' 'compute' and 'count;' 'fact' and
'feat;' 'esteem' and 'aim;' 'major' and 'mayor;'
'radius' and 'ray;' 'pauper' and 'poor;' 'potion'
and 'poison;' 'ration' and 'reason;' 'oration' and
'orison;' 'penitence' and 'penance;' 'zealous'
and 'jealous;' 'respect' and 'respite;' 'fragile' and
'frail;' 'calix' and 'chalice;' 'fabric' and 'forge;'
'tract,' 'treat,' and 'trait.'† I have, in the instancing

* This particular instance of 'dimorphism' as Latham calls
it, 'dittology' as Heyse, recurs in Italian, 'bestemmiare' and
'biasimare;' and in Spanish, 'blasfemar' and 'lastimar.'

† Somewhat different from this, yet itself also curious, is the
passing of an Anglo-Saxon word in two different forms into
English, and now current in both; thus 'drag' and 'draw;'
'desk' and 'dish,' both the Anglo-Saxon 'disc,' the German

of these, named always the Latin form before the
French ; but the reverse has been no doubt in every
instance the order in which the words were adopted
by us ; we had 'pursue' before 'persecute,' 'spice'
before 'species,' 'royalty' before 'regality,' and so
with the others.*

'tisch ; ' 'beech' and 'book,' both the Anglo-Saxon 'boc,'
our first books being *beechen* tablets (See Grimm, *Woerterbuch*,
s. vv. 'buch,' 'buche ') ; 'girdle' and 'kirtle,' the German
" gürtel ; ' already in Anglo-Saxon a double spelling, 'gyrdel,'
'cyrtel,' had prepared for the double words ; so too 'shell,'
'shale,' and 'scale ; ' 'skiff' and 'ship ; ' 'tenth' and
'tithe ; ' 'shirt' and 'skirt ; ' 'school' and 'shoal ; ' 'glass'
and 'glaze ; ' 'swallow' and 'swill ; ' 'wine' and 'vine ; '
'why' and 'how ; ' 'kill' and 'quell ; ' 'beacon' and
'beckon ; ' 'flesh' and 'flitch ; ' 'black' and 'bleak ; '
'pond' and 'pound ; ' 'whit' and 'wight ; ' 'deck and
'thatch ; ' 'deal' and 'dole ; ' 'weald' and 'wood ; ' 'dew'
and 'thaw ; ' 'wayward' and 'awkward ; ' 'dune' and
'down ; ' 'hood' and 'hat' ; ' 'evil' and 'ill ; ' 'hedge'
and 'hay ; ' 'waggon' and 'wain ; ' 'heathen ' and 'hoyden ; ' 'ant' and 'emmet ; ' 'spray' and 'sprig ; ' 'thew'
and 'thigh ; ' 'bow ' and 'bay,' as in *bay* window. We
have, let me add, another form of double adoption. In
several instances we possess the same word, first in its more
proper Teutonic shape, and secondly, as the Normans, having
found it in France and made it their own, brought it with
them here. Thus 'wise' and 'guise ; ' 'wed,' 'wage,' and
'gage ; ' 'wile' and 'guile ; ' 'warden' and 'guardian ; '
'warranty' and 'guarantee.'

* We have double adoptions from the Greek ; one direct,
one modified in passing through some other language ; thus,
'adamant' and 'diamond ; ' 'monastery' and 'minster ; '
'paralysis' and 'palsy ; ' 'scandal' and 'slander ; ' 'theriac'

The explanation of this more thorough change which the earlier form has undergone, is not far to seek. Words introduced into a language at a period when as yet writing is rare, and books are few or none, when therefore orthography is unfixed, or being purely phonetic, cannot properly be said to exist at all, have for a long time no other life save that which they live upon the lips of men. The checks therefore to alterations in the form of a word which a written, and still more which a printed, literature imposes are wanting, and thus we find words out of number altogether reshaped and remoulded by the people who have adopted them, so entirely assimilated to *their* language in form and termination, as in the end to be almost or quite undistinguishable from natives. On the other hand a most effectual check to this process, a process sometimes barbarizing and defacing, even while it is the only one which will make the newly brought in entirely homogeneous with the old and already existing, is imposed by the existence of a much written language and a full-formed literature. The foreign word, being once adopted into these, can no longer undergo a thorough transformation. Generally the utmost which use and

and 'treacle ;' 'asphodel' and 'daffodil,' or 'affodil' (see the *Promptorium*), as it used to be ; 'presbyter' and 'priest ;' 'dactyl' and 'date,' the fruit so called deriving its name from its likeness to a 'dactyl' or finger ; in Bacon it is still known as a 'dactyl ;' 'cathedral' and 'chair.' 'Cypher' and 'zero,' I may add, are different adoptions of one and the same Arabic word.

familiarity can do with it now, is to cause the gradual dropping of the foreign termination ; not that this is unimportant ; it often goes far to make a home for a word, and to hinder it from wearing any longer the appearance of a stranger and intruder.*

---

* The French language in like manner 'teems with Latin words which under various disguises obtained repeated admittance into its dictionary,' with a double adoption, one popular and reaching back to the earliest times of the language, the other belonging to a later and more literary period, 'demotic' and 'scholastic' they have been severally called ; on which subject see Génin, *Récréations Philologiques*, vol. i. pp. 162–166 ; Littré, *Hist. de la Langue Française*, vol. i. pp. 241–244 ; Fuchs, *Die Roman. Sprachen*, p. 125 ; Mahn, *Etymol. Forschung.*, pp. 19, 46, and passim ; Pellissier, *La Langue Française*, p. 205. Thus from 'separare' is derived 'sevrer,' to separate the child from its mother's breast, to wean, but also 'séparer,' without this special sense : from 'pastor,' 'pâtre,' a shepherd in the literal, and 'pasteur' the same in a tropical, sense ; from 'catena,' 'chaine' and 'cadène ;' from 'fragilis,' 'frêle' and 'fragile ;' from 'pensare,' 'peser' and 'penser ;' from 'gehenna,' 'gêne' and 'géhenne ;' from 'captivus,' 'caitif,' 'chétif,' and 'captif ;' from 'nativus,' 'naïf,' and 'natif ;' from 'immutabilis,' 'immutable' and 'immuable ;' from 'designare,' 'dessiner' and 'désigner ;' from 'decimare,' 'dîmer' and 'décimer ;' from 'consumere,' 'consommer' and 'consumer ;' from 'simulare,' 'sembler' and 'simuler ;' from 'sollicitare,' 'soucier' and 'solliciter ;' from 'adamas,' 'aimant' (lodestone) and 'adamant ; from the low Latin 'disjejunare,' 'dîner' and 'déjeûner ;' from 'acceptare,' 'acheter' and 'accepter ;' from 'homo,' 'on' and 'homme ;' from 'paganus,' 'payen' and 'paysan ;' from 'obedientia,' 'obéissance' and 'obé-

But to return from this digression. I said just now that you would learn much from making an inventory of the words of one descent and those of another occurring in any passage which you analyse ; and noting the proportion which they bear to one another. Thus analyse the diction of the Lord's Prayer. Of the seventy words whereof it consists only the following six claim the rights of Latin citizenship—the noun 'trespasses,' the verb 'trespass,' 'temptation,' 'deliver,' 'power,' 'glory.' Nor would it be very difficult to substitute for any one of these a Saxon word. Thus for 'trespasses' might be substituted 'sins ;' for 'trespass' 'sin ;' for 'deliver' 'free ;' for 'power' 'might ;' for 'glory' 'brightness ;'

dience ;' from 'monasterium,' 'moûtier' and 'monastere ;' from 'strictus,' 'étroit' and 'strict ;' from 'scintilla,' 'étincelle' and 'scintille ;' from 'sacramentum,' 'serment' and 'sacrement ;' from 'ministerium,' 'métier' and 'minis-tère ;' from 'parabola,' 'parole' and 'parabole ;' from 'natalis,' 'Noël' and 'natal ;' from 'rigidus,' 'raide' and 'rigide ;' from 'sapidus,' 'sade' and 'sapide ;' from 'pere-grinus,' 'pèlerin' and 'péregrin ;' from 'factio,' 'façon' and 'faction,' and it has now adopted 'factio' in a third shape, that is, in our English 'fashion ;' from 'pietas,' 'pitié' and 'piété ;' from 'paradisus,' 'parvis' and 'paradis ;' from 'capitulum,' 'chapitre' and 'capitule,' a botanical term ; from 'causa,' 'chose' and 'cause ;' from 'movere,' 'muer' and 'mouvoir ;' from 'ponere,' 'poser' and 'pondre ;' while 'attacher' and 'attaquer' only differ in pronunciation. So too, in Italian we have 'manco,' maimed, and 'monco,' maimed *of a hand ;* 'rifutare,' to refute, and 'rifiutare,' to refuse ; 'dama' and 'donna,' both forms of 'domina.'

which would only leave 'temptation,' about which there could be the slightest difficulty; and 'trials,' though now employed in a somewhat different sense, would exactly correspond to it. This is but a small percentage, six words in seventy, or less than ten in the hundred; and we often light upon a still smaller proportion. Thus take the first three verses of the 23rd Psalm :—'The Lord is my Shepherd; therefore can I lack nothing; He shall feed me in a green *pasture*, and lead me forth beside the waters of *comfort;* He shall *convert* my soul, and bring me forth in the paths of righteousness for his Name's sake.' Here are forty-five words, and only the three in italics are Latin ; for each of which it would be easy to substitute one of 'home' growth; little more, that is, than the proportion of seven in the hundred; while in five verses out of Genesis, containing one hundred and thirty words, there are only five not Saxon,—less, that is, than four in the hundred ; and, more notably still, the first four verses of St. John's Gospel, in all fifty-four words, have no single word that is not Saxon.

Shall we therefore conclude that these are the proportions in which the Anglo-Saxon and Latin elements of the language stand to one another? If they are so, then my former proposal to express their relations by sixty and thirty was greatly at fault ; and seventy to twenty, or even eighty to ten, would fall short of adequately representing the real predomi-. nance of the Saxon over the Latin element in the lan-

guage. But it is not so ; the Anglo-Saxon words by
no means outnumber the Latin in the degree which
the analysis of those passages would seem to imply.
It is not that there are so many more Anglo-Saxon
words, but that the words which there are, being
words of more primary necessity, do therefore so much
more frequently recur. The proportions which the
analysis of the *dictionary*, that is, of the language *at
rest*, would furnish, are very different from those
instanced just now, and which the analysis of *sentences*,
or of the language *in motion*, gives. Thus if we
analyse by aid of a *Concordance* the total vocabulary
of the English Bible, not more than sixty per cent of
the words are native ; but in the actual translation the
native words are from ninety per cent in some passages to ninety-six in others.* The proportion in
Shakespeare's vocabulary of native words to foreign is

---

* See Marsh, *Manual of the English Language*, Engl. ed.,
p. 88, *sqq.*

It is curious to note how very small a part of the language
writers who wield the fullest command over its resources, and
who, from the breadth and variety of the subjects which they
treat, would be likely to claim its help in the most various
directions, call into active employment. Set the words in the
English language at the lowest, and they can scarcely be set
lower than sixty thousand ; and it is certainly surprising to learn
that in our English Bible somewhat less than a tenth of these,
about six thousand, are all that are actually employed, that
Milton in his poetry has not used more than eight thousand
words, nor Shakespeare, with all the immense range of subjects
over which he travels, more than fifteen thousand.

much the same as in the English Bible, that is, about
sixty to forty in every hundred ; while an analysis of
various plays gives a proportion of from eighty-eight
to ninety-one per cent of native among those in actual
employment.   Milton gives results more remarkable
still.   We gather from a *Concordance* that only thirty-
three per cent of the words employed by him in his
poetical works are of Anglo-Saxon origin ; while an
analysis of a book of *Paradise Lost* yields eighty per
cent of such, and of *L'Allegro* ninety.   Indeed a vast
multitude of his Latin words are employed by him
only on a single occasion.

The notice of this fact will lead us to some important conclusions as to the *character* of the words
which the Saxon and the Latin severally furnish ; and
principally to this :—that while English is thus compact in the main of these two elements, their contributions are of very different characters and kinds.
The Anglo-Saxon is not so much what I have just
called it, one element of the English language, as the
basis of it.   All the joints, the whole *articulation*, the
sinews and ligaments, the great body of articles,
pronouns, conjunctions, prepositions, numerals, auxiliary verbs, all smaller words which serve to knit
together and bind the larger into sentences, these,
not to speak of the grammatical structure, are Saxon.
The Latin may contribute its tale of bricks, yea, of
goodly stones, hewn and polished, to the spiritual
building ; but the mortar, with all which binds the
different parts of it together, and constitutes them a

house, is Saxon throughout. Selden in his *Table
Talk* uses another comparison; but to the same
effect : ' If you look upon the language spoken in the
Saxon time, and the language spoken now, you will
find the difference to be just as if a man had a cloak
which he wore plain in Queen Elizabeth's days, and
since, here has put in a piece of red, and there a piece
of blue, and here a piece of green, and there a piece
of orange-tawny. We borrow words from the French,
Italian, Latin, as every pedantic man pleases.' Whe-
well sets forth the same fact under another image :
' Though our comparison might be bold, it would be
just if we were to say that the English language is a
conglomerate of Latin words bound together in a
Saxon cement; the fragments of the Latin being
partly portions introduced directly from the parent
quarry, with all their sharp edges, and partly pebbles
of the same material, obscured and shaped by long
rolling in a Norman or some other channel.'

   This same law holds good in all composite languages; which, composite as they are, yet are only
such in the matter of their vocabulary. There may
be a motley company of words, some coming from
one quarter, some from another; but there is never
a medley of grammatical forms and inflections. One
or other language entirely predominates here, and
everything has to conform and subordinate itself to
the laws of this ruling and ascendant language. The
Anglo-Saxon is the ruling language in our present
English. This having thought good to drop its

genders, the French substantives which come among us must in like manner leave theirs behind them ; so too the verbs must renounce their own conjugations, and adapt themselves to ours.*   'The Latin and the French deranged the vocabulary of our language, but never its form or structure.'†   A remarkable parallel to this might be found in the language of Persia, since the conquest of that country by the Arabs.   The ancient Persian religion fell with the government, but the language remained totally unaffected by the revolution, and in its grammatical structure and organization forfeited nothing of its Indo-germanic character. Arabic vocables, the only exotic words found in Persian, are found in numbers varying with the object and quality, style and taste of the writers, but pages of pure idiomatic Persian may be written without employing a single word from the Arabic.

---

* W. Schlegel (*Indische Bibliothek*, vol. i. p. 284) : Coëunt quidem paullatim in novum corpus peregrina vocabula, sed grammatica linguarum, unde petitæ sunt, ratio perit.

† Guest, *Hist. of English Rhythms*, vol. ii. p. 108. 'Languages,' says Max Müller, ' though mixed in their dictionaries, can never be mixed in their grammar. In the English dictionary the student of the science of language can detect by his own tests Celtic, Norman, Greek, and Latin ingredients ; but not a single drop of foreign blood has entered into the organic system of the English language. The grammar, the blood and soul of the language, is as pure and unmixed in English as spoken in the British Isles, as it was when spoken on the shores of the German Ocean by the Angles, Saxons, and Jutes of the Continent.'

At the same time the secondary or superinduced language, though powerless to force its forms on the language which receives its words, may yet compel that other to renounce a portion of its own forms, by the impossibility which is practically found to exist of making these fit the new comers ; and thus it may exert, although not a positive, yet a negative, influence on the grammar of the other tongue. It has proved so with us. ' When the English language was inundated by a vast influx of French words, few, if any, French forms were received into its grammar : but the Saxon forms soon dropped away, because they did not suit the new roots ; and the genius of the language, from having to deal with the newly imported words in a rude state, was induced to neglect the inflections of the native ones. This for instance led to the introduction of the *s* as the universal termination of all plural nouns, which agreed with the usage of the French language, and was not alien from that of the Saxon, but was merely an extension of the termination of the ancient masculine to other classes of nouns.'*

If you wish to make actual proof of the fact just now asserted, namely, that the radical constitution of the language is Saxon, try to compose a sentence, let it be only of ten or a dozen words, and the subject entirely of your own choice, employing therein none but words of a Latin derivation. You will find it

---

J. Grimm, quoted in *The Philological Museum*, vol. i. p. 667.

impossible, or next to impossible, to do this. Which-
ever way you turn, some obstacle will meet you in
the face. There are large words in plenty, but no
binding power; the mortar which should fill up the
interstices, and which is absolutely necessary for the
holding together of the building, is absent altogether.
On the other side, whole pages might be written, not
perhaps on higher or abstruser themes, but on familiar matters of every-day life, in which every word
should be of Saxon descent; and these, pages from
which, with the exercise of a little patience and ingenuity, all appearance of awkwardness should be
excluded, so that none would know, unless otherwise
informed, that the writer had submitted himself to
this restraint and limitation, and was drawing his
words exclusively from one section of the English
language. Sir Thomas Browne has given several
long paragraphs so constructed. Here is a little
fragment of one of them : 'The first and foremost
step to all good works is the dread and fear of the
Lord of heaven and earth, which through the Holy
Ghost enlighteneth the blindness of our sinful hearts
to tread the ways of wisdom, and lead our feet into
the land of blessing.' * This is not stiffer than the
ordinary English of his time.†

---

* *Works*, vol. iv. p. 202.
† What Ampère says of Latin as constituting the base of the
French (*Formation de la Langue Française*, p 196), we may
say of Anglo-Saxon as constituting the base of English : Il ne
s'agit pas ici d'un nombre plus ou moins grand de mots fournis

But because it is thus ·possible to write English,
foregoing altogether the use of the Latin portion of
the language, you must not therefore conclude this
latter portion to be of little value, or that we should
be as rich without it as with it. We should be very
far indeed from so being. I urge this, because we
hear sometimes regrets expressed that we have not
kept our language more free from the admixture of
Latin, and suggestions made that we should even now
endeavor to restrain our employment of this within
the narrowest possible limits. I remember Lord
· Brougham urging upon the students at Glasgow that

à notre langue ; il s'agit de son fondement et de sa substance.
Il y a en français, nous le verrons, des mots celtiques et
germaniques ; mais le français est une langue *latine*. Les
mots celtiques y sont restés, les mots germaniques y sont
venus ; les mots latins n'y sont point restés, et n'y sont point
venus ; ils sont la langue elle-même, ils la constituent. Il ne
peut donc être question de rechercher quels sont les éléments
latins du français. Ce que j'aurai à faire, ce sera d'indiquer
ceux qui ne le sont pas. Koch, in some words prefixed to his
Historic Grammar of the English Language, has put all this
in a lively manner. Having spoken of the larger or smaller
contingents to the army of English words which the various
languages have furnished, he proceeds : Die Hauptarmee,
besonders das Volkheer, ist deutsch, ein grosses französisches
Hilfs- und Luxuscorps hat sich angeschlossen, die andern
Romanen sind nur durch wenige Ueberläufer vertreten, und
sie haben ihre nationale Eigenthümlichkeit seltener bewahrt.
Ein stärkeres Corps stellt das Lateinische ; es hat Truppen
stossen lassen zum Angelsächsischen, zum Alt- und Mittel-
englischen, und sogar noch zum Neuenglischen.

they should do their best to rid their diction of long-tailed words in 'osity' and 'ation.' Now, doubtless, there was sufficient ground and warrant for the warning against such which he gave them. Writers of a former age, Samuel Johnson in the last century, Henry More and Sir Thomas Browne in the century preceding, gave beyond all question undue preponderance to the learned, or Latin, element in our language ; and there have never wanted those who have trod in their footsteps ; while yet it is certain that very much of the homely strength and beauty of English, of its most popular and happiest idioms, would have perished from it, had they succeeded in persuading the great body of English writers to write as they had written.

But for all this we could *almost* as ill spare this Latin portion of the language as the other. Philosophy and science and the arts of an advanced civilization find their utterance in the Latin words which we have made our own, or, if not in them, then in the Greek, which for present purposes may be grouped with them. Granting too that, all other things being equal, when a Latin and a Saxon word offer themselves to our choice, we shall generally do best to employ the Saxon, to speak of 'happiness' rather than 'felicity,' 'almighty' rather than 'omnipotent,' a 'forerunner' rather than 'precursor,' a 'forefather' than a 'progenitor,' still these latter are as truly denizens in the language as the former ; no alien interlopers, but possessing the rights of citizenship as

fully as the most Saxon word of them all. One part
of the language is not to be unduly favoured at the ex-
pense of the other ; the Saxon at the cost of the Latin,
as little as the Latin at the cost of the Saxon. ' Both,'
as De Quincey, himself a foremost master of English, has well said, ' are indispensable ; and speaking
generally without stopping to distinguish as to subject,
both are *equally* indispensable. Pathos, in situations
which are homely, or at all connected with domestic
affections, naturally move by Saxon words. Lyrical
emotion of every kind, which (to merit the name of
lyrical) must be in the state of flux and reflux, or,
generally, of agitation, also requires the Saxon element
of our language. And why ? Because the Saxon is
the aboriginal element ; the basis and not the super-
structure : consequently it comprehends all the ideas
which are natural to the heart of man and to the
elementary situations of life. And although the Latin
often furnishes us with duplicates of these ideas, yet
the Saxon, or monosyllabic part, has the advantage of
precedency in our use and knowledge ; for it is the
language of the nursery whether for rich or poor, in
which great philological academy no toleration is
given to words in "osity" or "ation." There is
therefore a great advantage, as regards the consecra-
tion to our feelings, settled by usage and custom upon
the Saxon strands in the mixed yarn of our native
tongue. And universally, this may be remarked—that
wherever the passion of a poem is of that sort which
uses, presumes, or *postulates* the ideas, without seeking

to extend them, Saxon will be the "cocoon" (to speak
by the language applied to silk-worms), which the
poem spins for itself. But on the other hand, where
the motion of the feeling is *by* and *through* the
ideas, where (as in religious or meditative poetry—
Young's for instance or Cowper's), the pathos creeps
and kindles underneath the very tissues of the thinking,
there the Latin will predominate ; and so much so
that, whilst the flesh, the blood, and the muscle, will
be often almost exclusively Latin, the articulations
only, or hinges of connection, will be Anglo-Saxon.
On this same matter Sir Francis Palgrave has expressed
himself thus : 'Upon the languages of Teutonic origin
the Latin has exercised great influence, but most
energetically on our own. The very early admixture
of the *Langue d'Oil*, the never interrupted employment
of the French as 'the language of education, and the
nomenclature created by the scientific and literary
cultivation of advancing and civilized society, have
Romanized our speech ; the warp may be Anglo-
Saxon, but the woof is Roman as well as the em-
broidery, and these foreign materials have so entered into the texture, that were they plucked out,
the web would be torn to rags, unravelled and
destroyed.'*

We shall nowhere find a happier example of the
preservation of the golden mean than in our Authorized Version of the Bible. Among the minor and

---

* *History of Normandy and England*, vol. i. p. 78.

secondary blessings conferred by that Version on the
nations drawing their spiritual life from it,—a blessing
only small by comparison with the infinitely greater
blessings whereof it is the vehicle to them,—is the
happy wisdom, the instinctive tact, with which its
authors have kept clear in this matter from all exag-
geration.   There has not been on their parts any
futile and mischievous attempt to ignore the full rights
of the Latin element of the language on the one side,
nor on the other any burdening of the Version with so
many learned Latin terms as should cause it to forfeit
its homely character, and shut up large portions of it
from the understanding of plain and unlearned men.
One of the most eminent among those who in our
own times abandoned the communion of the English
Church for that of the Church of Rome has expressed
in deeply touching tones his sense of all which, in
renouncing our Translation, he felt himself to have
foregone and lost.   These are his words: 'Who will
not say that the uncommon beauty and marvellous
English of the Protestant Bible is not one of the great
strongholds of heresy in this country ?   It lives on the
ear, like a music that can never be forgotten, like the
sound of church bells, which the convert hardly knows
how he can forego.   Its felicities often seem to be
almost things rather than mere words.   It is part of
the national mind, and the anchor of national serious-
ness. . . . . The memory of the dead passes into it.
The potent traditions of childhood are stereotyped in
its verses.   The power of all the griefs and trials of a

man is hidden beneath its words. It is the representative of his best moments, and all that there has been about him of soft and gentle and pure and penitent and good speaks to him for ever out of his English Bible. . . . . It is his sacred thing, which doubt has never dimmed, and controversy never soiled. In the length and breadth of the land there is not a Protestant with one spark of religiousness about him, whose spiritual biography is not in his Saxon Bible.' *

Certainly one has only to compare this Version of ours with the Rhemish, at once to understand why he should have thus given the palm and preference to ours. I urge not here the fact that one translation is from the original Greek, the other from the Latin Vulgate, and thus the translation of a translation, often reproducing the mistakes of that translation ; but, putting all such higher advantages aside, only the superiority of the diction in which the meaning, be it correct or incorrect, is conveyed to English readers. Thus I open the Rhenish Version at Galatians v. 19, where the long list of the 'works of the flesh,' and of the 'fruit of the spirit,' is given. But what could a mere English reader make of terms such as these— 'impudicity,' 'ebrieties,' 'comessations,' 'longani-

---

* In former editions of this book I used language which seemed to ascribe these words to Dr. Newman, whose I supposed they were. They indeed occur in an Essay by the late Very Rev. Dr. Faber, on '*The Characteristics of the Lives of the Saints,*' prefixed by him to a *Life of St. Francis of Assisi,* p. 116.

mity,' all which occur in that passage ? while our
Version for 'ebrieties' has 'drunkenness,' for 'comessations' has 'revellings,' for 'longanimity' 'long-
suffering.' Or set over against one another such
phrases as these,—in the Rhemish, 'the exemplars of
the celestials' (Heb. ix. 23), but in ours, 'the patterns
of things in the heavens.' Or suppose if, instead of
what *we* read at Heb. xiii. 16, 'To do good and to
communicate forget not; for with such sacrifices God
is well pleased,' we read as in the Rhemish, 'Benefi-
cence and communication do not forget ; for with
such hosts God is promerited' !—Who does not feel
that if our Version had been composed in such Latin-
English as this, had been fulfilled with words like these
—'odible,' 'suasible,' 'exinanite,' 'contristate,' 'pos-
tulations,' 'coinquinations,' 'agnition,' 'zealatour,'
'donary,'—which all, with many more of the same
mint, are found in the Rhemish Version,—our loss
would have been great and enduring, such as would
have been felt through the whole religious life of our
people, in the very depths of the national mind ? *

There was indeed something deeper than love of
sound and genuine English at work in our Translators,
whether they were conscious of it or not, which
hindered them from presenting the Scriptures to their
fellow-countrymen dressed out in such a semi-Latin
garb as this. The Reformation, which they were in

* There is more on this matter in my book, *On the Authorized Version of the New Testament*, pp. 33-35.

this translation so effectually setting forward, was just a throwing off, on the part of the Teutonic nations, of that everlasting pupilage in which Rome would fain have held them ; an assertion at length that they were come to full age, and that not through her, but directly through Christ, they would address themselves unto God. The use of Latin as the language of worship, as the language in which alone the Scriptures might be read, had been the great badge of servitude, even as the Latin habits of thought and feeling which it promoted had been most important helps to the continuance of this servitude, through long ages. It lay deep then in the essential conditions of the conflict which they were maintaining, that the Reformers should develope the Saxon, or essentially national, element in the language ; while it was just as natural that the Roman Catholic translators, if they must render the Scriptures into English at all, should yet render them into such English as should bear the nearest possible resemblance to that Latin Vulgate, which Rome, with a wisdom that in such matters has never failed her, would gladly have seen as the only version of the Book in the hands of the faithful.*

---

* Where the word itself which the Rhemish translators employ is a perfectly good one, it is yet instructive to observe how often they draw on the Latin portion of the language, where we have drawn on the Saxon,—thus ' corporal ' where we have ' bodily ' (1 Tim. iv. 8), ' coadjutor ' where we have ' fellow-worker ' (Col. iv. 11), ' prescience ' where we have ' foreknowledge ' (Acts ii. 23), ' dominator ' where we have

Let me again, however, recur to the fact that what
our Reformers did in this matter, they did without ex-
aggeration ; even as they have shown the same wise
moderation in matters higher than this. They gave
to the Latin element of the language its rights, though
they would not suffer it to encroach upon and usurp
those of the other. It would be difficult not to believe,
even if many outward signs did not suggest the same,
that there is an important part in the future for that
one language of Europe to play, which thus serves as
connecting link between the North and the South,
between the languages spoken by the Teutonic
nations of the North and by the Romance nations
of the South ; which holds on to and partakes of
both ; which is as a middle term between them.*
There are who venture to hope that the English
Church, having in like manner two aspects, looking
on the one side toward Rome, being herself truly
Catholic, looking on the other toward the Protestant
communions, being herself also protesting and re-
formed, may have reserved for her in the providence
of God an important share in that reconciling of a

'Lord' (Jude 4), 'cogitation' where we have 'thought'
(Luke ix. 46), 'fraternity' where we have 'brotherhood'
(1 Pet. ii. 17), 'senior' where we have 'elder' (Rev. vii.
13), 'exprobrate' where we have 'upbraid' (Mark xvi. 14.)

   * See a paper, *On the Probable Future Position of the
English Language*, by T. Watts, Esq., in the *Proceedings of
the Philological Society*, vol. iv. p. 207 ; and compare the concluding words in Guest's *Hist. of English Rhythms*, vol. ii.
p. 429.

divided Christendom, whereof we are bound not to despair. And if this ever should be so, if, notwithstanding our sins and unworthiness, so blessed an office should be in store for her, it will be no small assistance to this, that the language in which her mediation will be effected is one wherein both parties may claim their own, in which neither will feel that it is receiving the adjudication of a stranger, of one who must be an alien from its deeper thoughts and habits, because an alien from its words, but a language in which both must recognize very much of that which is deepest and most precious of their own.*

. Nor is this prerogative which I have just claimed for our English the mere dream and fancy of patriotic vanity. The scholar most profoundly acquainted with the great group of the Teutonic languages in Europe, a devoted lover, if ever there was such, of his native German, I mean Jacob Grimm, has expressed himself very nearly to the same effect, and given the palm over all to our English in words which you will not

---

* Fowler (*English Grammar*, p. 135) : The English is a medium language, and thus adapted to diffusion. In the Gothic family it stands midway between the Teutonic and the Scandinavian branches, touching both, and to some extent reaching into both. A German or a Dane finds much in the English which exists in his own language. It unites by certain bonds of consanguinity, as no other language does, the Romanic with the Gothic languages. An Italian or a Frenchman finds a large class of words in the English, which exist in his own language, though the basis of the English is Gothic.'

grudge to hear quoted, and with which I shall bring
this lecture to a close. After ascribing to our language
'a veritable power of expression, such as perhaps
never stood at the command of any other language of
men,' he goes on to say, ' Its highly spiritual genius,
and wonderfully happy development and condition,
have been the result of a surprisingly intimate union
of the two noblest languages in modern Europe, the
Teutonic and the Romance,—It is well known in
what relation these two stand to one another in the
English tongue ; the former supplying in far larger
proportion the material groundwork, the latter the
spiritual conceptions. In truth the English language,
which by no mere accident has produced and upborne
the greatest and most predominant poet of modern
times, as distinguished from the · ancient classical
poetry (I can, of course, only mean Shakespeare),
may with all right be called a world-language ; and,
like the English people, appears destined hereafter to
prevail with a sway more extensive even than its
present over all the portions of the globe.* For in

---

* A little more than two centuries ago a poet, himself
abundantly deserving the title of ' well-languaged,' which a
contemporary or near successor gave him, ventured in some
remarkable lines timidly to anticipate this. Speaking of his
native English, which he himself wrote with such vigour and
purity, though deficient in the passion and fiery impulses
which go to the making of a first-rate poet, Daniel exclaims :

   ' And who, in time, knows whither we may vent
   The treasure of our tongue, to what strange shores

wealth, good sense, and closeness of structure no
other of the languages at this day spoken deserves to
be compared with it—not even our German, which is
torn, even as we are torn, and must first rid itself of
many defects, before it can enter boldly into the lists,
as a competitor with the English.' †   ↢

> This gain of our best glory shall be sent,
> To enrich unknowing nations with our stores ?
> What worlds in the yet unformèd Occident
> May come refined with the accents that are ours ?
> Or who can tell for what great work in hand
> The greatness of our style is now ordained ?
> What powers it shall bring in, what spirits command,
> What thoughts let out, what humours keep restrained,
> What mischief it may powerfully withstand,
> And what fair ends may thereby be attained ?'

† *Ueber den Ursprung der Sprache*, Berlin, 1832, p. 50.
Compare Philarète Chasles, *Etudes sur l'Allemagne*, pp.
12-33.

LECTURE II.

ENGLISH AS IT MIGHT HAVE BEEN.

WE have seen that many who have best right to speak are strong to maintain that English has gained far more than it has lost by that violent interruption of its orderly development which the Norman Conquest brought with it, that it has been permanently enriched by that immense irruption and settlement of foreign words within its borders, which followed, though not immediately, on that catastrophe.   But there here suggests itself to us an interesting and not uninstructive subject of speculation ; what, namely, this language would actually now be, if there had been no Battle of Hastings ; or a Battle of Hastings which William had lost and Harold won.   When I invite you to consider this, you will understand me to exclude any similar catastrophe, which should in the same way have issued in the setting up of an intrusive dynasty, supported by the arms of a foreign soldiery, and speaking a Romanic as distinguished from a Gothic language, on the throne of England.   I lay a stress upon this last point—a people speaking a Romanic language ; inasmuch as the effects upon the language spoken in England would have been quite different, would have fallen far short of those which actually found place, if the great Canute had succeeded in founding a Danish,

or Harold Hardrada a Norwegian, dynasty in England
—Danish and Norwegian both being dialects of the
same Gothic language which was already spoken here,
Some differences in the language now spoken by
Englishmen, such issues,—and one and the other were
at different times well within the range of possibility,—
would have entailed ; but differences inconsiderable by
the side of those which have followed the coming in
of a conquering and ruling race speaking one of the
tongues directly formed upon the Latin.

This which I suggest is only one branch of·a far
larger speculation.   It would be no uninteresting task
if one thoroughly versed in the whole constitutional
lore of England, acquainted as a Palgrave was with
Anglo-Saxon England, able to look into the seeds of
things and to discern which of these contained the
germs of future development, which would grow and
which would not, should interpret to us by the spirit of
historic divination, what, if there had been no successful Norman invasion, would be now the social and
political institutions of England, what the relations of
the different ranks of society to one another, what the
division and tenure of land, what amount of liberty
at home, of greatness abroad, England would at this
day have achieved.   It is only on one branch of this
subject that I propose to enter at all.

It may indeed appear to some that even in this I
am putting before them problems which are in their
very nature impossible to solve, which it is therefore
unprofitable to entertain ; since dealing, as here we
must, with what might have been, not with what

actually has been or is, all must be mere guesswork for
us ; and, however ingenious our guesses, we can
never test them by the touchstone of actual fact, and
so estimate their real worth. Such an objection would
rest on a mistake, though a very natural one. I am
persuaded we *can* know to a very large extent how,
under such conditions as I have supposed, it would
have fared with our tongue, what the English would
be like, which in such a case the dwellers in this
island would be speaking at this day. The laws
which preside over the development of language are
so fixed and immutable, and capricious as they may
seem, there is really so little caprice in them, that if
we can at all trace the course which other kindred
dialects have followed under such conditions as
English would have then been submitted to, we may
thus arrive at very confident conclusions as to the
road which English would have travelled. And there
are such languages ; more or less the whole group of
Gothic languages are such. Studying any one of
these, and the most obvious of these to study would
be the German, we may learn very much of the forms
which English would now wear, if the tremendous
shock of one ever-memorable day had not changed so
much in this land, and made England and English
both so different from what otherwise they would have
been.

At the same time I would not have you set *too* high
the similarity which would have existed between the
English and other Gothic languages, even if no such
huge catastrophe as that had mixed so many new

elements in the one which are altogether foreign to
the other. There are *always* forces at work among
tribes and ·people which have parted company, one
portion of them, as in ·this instance, going forth to
new seats, while the other tarried in the old ; or both
of them travelling onward, and separating more and
more from one another, as in the case of those whom
we know as Greeks and Italians, who, going forth from
those Illyrian highlands where they once dwelt
together, occupied each a peninsula of its own ;
or, again, as between those who, like the Britons of
Wales and of Cornwall, have been violently thrust
asunder and separated from one another by the
intrusion of a hostile people, like a wedge, between
them ; there are, I say, forces widening slowly but
surely the breach between the languages spoken by the
one section of the divided people and by the other,
multiplying the points of diversity between the speech
of those to whom even dialectic differences may once
have been unknown. This, that they should travel
daily further from one another, comes to pass quite
independently of any such sudden and immense revolution as that of which we have been just speaking. If
there had been no Norman Conquest, nor any event
similar to it, it is yet quite certain that English would
be now a very different language from any at the
present day spoken in Germany or in Holland. Different of course it would be from that purely conventional language, now recognized in Germany as the
only language of literature ; but very different too
from any dialect of that Low German, still popularly

spoken on the Frisian coast and lower banks of the Elbe, to which no doubt it would have borne a far closer resemblance. It was indeed already very different when that catastrophe arrived. The six hundred years which, on the briefest reckoning, had elapsed since the Saxon immigration to these shores —that immigration had probably begun very much earlier—had in this matter, as in others, left their mark.

I will very briefly enumerate some of the dissimilating forces, moral and material, by the action of which those who, so long as they dwelt together, possessed the same language, little by little become barbarians to one another.

One branch of the speakers of a language engrafts on the old stock various words which the other does not; and this from various causes. It does so by intercourse with new races, into contact and connection with which it, but not the other branch of the divided family, has been brought. Thus in quite recent times South African English, spoken in the presence of a large Dutch population at the Cape, has acquired such words as 'to treck,' 'to inspan,' 'to outspan,' 'spoor,' 'wildbeest,' 'boor' in the sense of farmer, of which our English at home knows nothing. So too the great English colony in India has acquired 'ayah,' 'bungalow,' 'dunbar,' 'loot,' 'nabob,' 'nautch,' 'nullah,' 'rupee,' 'zeminder,' with many more. It is true that we too at home have adopted some of these, and understand them all. But suppose there were little or no communication between us at home and our colony in India, no

passing from the one to the other, no literature common to both, here are the germs of what would grow
in lapse of years to an important element of diversity
between the English of England and of India. Or
take another example. The English-speaking race
in America has encountered races which we do not
encounter here, has been brought into relation with
aspects of nature which are quite foreign to Englishmen. For most of these it has adopted the words
which it has found ready made to its needs by those
who occupied the land before it, or still occupies it
side by side with itself; has borrowed, for example,
'pampas' and 'savannah' from the Indian; 'bayou,'
'cache,' 'crevasse,' 'levée,' 'portage,' from the
French of Louisiana or of Canada; 'adobe,' 'can-
yon' (cañon), 'chaparral,' 'corral,' 'hacienda,'
'lariat,' 'lasso,' 'mustang,' 'placer,' 'rancho,' or
'ranche,' 'tortilla,' the slang verb 'to vamose' (the
Spanish 'vamos,' let us go), from the Spaniards of
Mexico and California. In like manner 'backwoods-
man,' 'lumberer,' 'squatter,' are words born of a
natural condition of things, whereof we know nothing.
And this which has thus happened elsewhere, happened also here. The Britons—not to enter into the
question whether they added much or little—must
have added something, and in the designation of
natural objects in 'aber' and 'pen' and 'straith,'
certainly added a good deal,* to the vocabulary of

* See Isaac Taylor, *Words and Places*, 2nd edit. p. 193.

the Saxon immigrants into this island, of which those
who remained in old Saxony knew nothing. Again,
the Danish and Norwegian inroads into England were
inroads not of men only but also of words. In all
this an important element of dissimilation made
itself felt.

Then too, where languages have diverged from one
another before any definite settlement has taken place
in the dictionary, out of the numerous synonyms for
one and the same object which the various dialects of
the common language afford, one people will perpe-
tuate one, and the other another, each of them after
a while losing sight altogether of that on which their
choice has not fallen. That mysterious sentence of
death which strikes words, we oftentimes know not
why, others not better, it may be worse, taking their
room, will frequently cause in process of time a word
to perish from one branch of what was once a common
language, while it lives on and perhaps unfolds itself
into a whole family in the other. Thus of the words
which the Angles and Saxons brought with them
from beyond the sea, some have lived on upon our
English soil, while they have perished in that which
might be called, at least by comparison, their native
soil, Innumerable others, on the contrary, have here
died out, which have continued to flourish there. As
a specimen of those which have found English air
more healthful than German we may instance 'bairn.'
This, once common to all the Gothic languages, is
now extinct in all of the Germanic group, and has
been so for centuries, 'kind' having taken its place;

while it lives with us and in the languages of the Scandinavian family. Others, on the contrary, after an existence longer or shorter with us, have finally disappeared here, while they still enjoy a vigorous life on the banks of the Elbe and the Eyder. A vulture is not here any more a 'geir' (Holland), nor a rogue a 'skellum' (Urquhart), nor an uncle (a *mother's* brother) an 'eame,' but ' geir' and 'schelm' and 'oheim' still maintain a vigorous existence there. Each of these words which has perished, and they may be counted by hundreds and thousands, has been replaced by another, generally by one which is strange to the sister language, such as either it never knew, or of which it has long since lost all recollection. ' Languages,' as Max Müller has said, ' so intimately related as Greek and Latin, have fixed on different expressions for son, daughter, brother, woman, man, sky, earth, moon, hand, mouth, tree, bird, &c. It is clear that when the working of this principle of natural selection is allowed to extend more widely, languages, though proceeding from the same source, may in time acquire a totally different nomenclature for the commonest objects.' * There is thus at work a double element of estrangement of the one from the other. In what has gone a link between them has been broken ; in what has come in its room an element of diversity has been introduced.

---

* *On the Science of Language*, 1st Ser. p. 271, *sqq.* See too on this ' divergence of dialects ' of which we are treating, Marsh, *Origin and History of the English Language*, p. 82. *sqq.*

Sometimes even where a word lives on in both languages, it will have become provincial in one, while it keeps a place in the classical diction of the other. Thus 'klei' is provincial in German,* while our 'clay' knows no such restriction of the area in which it moves.

Or where a word has not actually perished in one division of what was once a common language, it will have been thrust out of general use in one, but not in the other. Thus 'ross,' earlier 'hros,' is rare and poetical in German, having in every-day use given way to 'pferd;' while 'horse' has suffered no parallel diminution in the commonness of its use. 'Head' in like manner has fully maintained its place; but not so 'haupt,' which during the last two or three centuries has been more and more giving way to 'kopf.'

Again, words in one language and in the other will in tract of time and under the necessities of an advancing civilization appropriate to themselves a more exact domain of meaning than they had at the first, yet will not appropriate exactly the same; or one will enlarge its meaning and the other not; or in some other way one will drift away from moorings to which the other remains true. Our 'timber' is the same word as the German 'zimmer,' but it has not precisely the same meaning; nor 'rider' as 'ritter,' nor 'hide' as 'haut;' neither is 'beam' exactly the same as 'baum,' nor 'reek' as 'rauch,' nor 'schnecke' (in German a 'snail') as 'snake;' nor 'tapfer' as 'dap-

---

* See Grimm's *Woerterbuch*, s. v.

per,' nor 'deer' as 'thier,' nor 'acre' as 'acker,' nor
'to whine' as 'weinen,' nor 'tide' and 'tidy' as
'zeit' and 'zeitig.' 'Booby' suggests an intellectual
deficiency, 'bube' a moral depravity. 'Lust' in
German has no subaudition of *sinful* desire ; it has
within the last two hundred years acquired such in
English. 'Knight' and 'knecht,' 'knave' and
'knabe' have travelled in very different directions.
Much of this divergence is the work of the last two
or three hundred years, so that the process of estrangement is still going forward. Thus 'elders were
parents in England not very long ago, quite as much
as 'eltern' are parents to this day in Germany (see
Luke ii. 41 ; Col. iii. 20, Coverdale). Our 'shine'
is no longer identical in meaning with the German
'schein ;' but it too once meant 'show' or 'semblance,' as the latter does still.* 'Taufer' in German
is solemn, 'dipper' in English is familiar. The
English of England and the English of America are
already revealing differences of this kind. 'Corn' on
the other side of the Atlantic means always maize,
'grain' means always wheat. We know nothing
here of these restrictions of meaning. Nay, the same
differences may be found nearer home. A 'merchant'
in Scotland is not what we know by this name, but a
shopkeeper ;† while in Ireland by a 'tradesman' is

---

* Thus Col. ii. 23 (Coverdale), 'which things have a *shine*
of wisdom.

† Κάπηλος, not ἔμπορος.

indicated not a grocer, butcher, or one following other similar occupations, but an artisan, a bricklayer, glazier, carpenter, or the like. Here is another element of divergence between sister languages, evermore working to make two what once had been only one. But further, in the same way as the bulk and sinews of an arm rapidly increase, being put to vigorous use, while other limbs, whose potential energies have not been equally called forth, show no corresponding growth, even so it proves with speech. It is indeed marvellous how quickly a language will create, adapt, adopt words in any particular line of things to which those who speak that language are specially addicted ; so that while it may remain absolutely poor in every other department of speech, it will be nothing less than opulent in this.* It will

---

* Pott (*Etymol. Forschung.* 2nd edit. vol. ii. p. 134) supplies some curious and instructive examples of this unfolding of a language in a particular direction. Thus in the Zulu, a Caffre dialect, where the chief or indeed entire wealth consists in cattle, there are words out of number to express cows of different ages, colours, qualities. Instead of helping themselves out as we do by an adjective, as a *white* cow, a *red* cow, a *barren* cow, they have a distinctive word for each of these. *We* do not think or speak much about cocoa-nuts, and only seeing them when they are full ripe, have no inducement to designate them in other stages of their growth ; but in Lord North's Island, where they are the main support of the inhabitants, they have five words by which to name the fruit in its several stages from the first shoot to perfect maturity. In the Dorsetshire dialect there are distinct names for the four

follow that where races separate, and one group or
both seek new seats for themselves, the industrial
tendencies of the separated groups, as suggested by
the different physical aspects and capabilities of the
regions which they occupy, will bring about a large
development in each of words and phrases in which
the other will have no share. Thus the occupants of
this island became by the very conditions of their
existence, and unless they were willing to be indeed,
what the Latin poet called them, altogether divided
from the whole world, a seafaring people. It has
followed that the language has grown rich in terms
having to do with the sea and with the whole life of
the sea, far richer in these than the dialects spoken
by the mediterranean people of Germany. They, on
the contrary, poor in this domain of words, are far
better furnished than we are with terms relating to
those mining operations which they pursued much
earlier, on a scale more extended, and with a greater
application of skill, than we have done.

There has been a vigorous activity of political life
in England which has needed, and needing has
fashioned for itself, a diction of its own. Germany
on the contrary is so poor in corresponding terms,
that when with the weak beginnings of constitutional
forms in our own day some of these terms became

stomachs of ruminant animals (Barnes' *Glossary*, p. 78). In
Lithuanian there are five different names for five several kinds
of stubble (Grimm, *Gesch. der Deutschen Sprache*, vol. i.
p. 69).

necessary, it was obliged to borrow the word 'bill'
from us. It is true that in this it was no more than
reclaiming and recovering a word of its own, which
had been suffered to drop through and disappear.
The same word will obtain a slightly different pronunciation, and a somewhat more marked difference
in spelling, in the one language and the other.
Where there is no special philological training, a very
slight variation in the former will often effectually
conceal from the ear, as in the latter from the eye,
an absolute identity, and for all practical purposes
constitute them not one and the same, but two and
different. Most of us in attempting to speak a foreign
language, or to understand our own as spoken by a
foreigner, have had practical experience of the obstacles to understanding or being understood, which a
very slight departure from the standard of pronunciation recognized by us will interpose. And quite
as effectual· as differences of pronunciation for the
ear, are differences of spelling for the eye, in the way
of rendering recognition hard or even impossible. It
would be curious to know how many Englishmen who
have made fair advances in German, as usually taught,
have recognized the entire identity of 'deed' and
'that,' of 'fowl' and 'vogel,' of 'dough' and 'teig,'
of 'oath' and 'eid,' of 'durch' and 'through,' of
'dreary' and 'traurig,' of 'ivy' and 'epheu,' of 'death'
and 'tod,' of 'quick' and 'keck,' of 'deal' and 'theil,'
of 'clean' and 'klein,' of 'enough' and 'genug.'
It is only too easy for those who are using the very

same words, to be, notwithstanding, as barbarians to one another.

Again, what was the exception at the time of separation will in one branch of the divided family have grown into the rule, while perhaps in the other branch it will have been disallowed altogether., So too idioms and other peculiar usages will have obtained allowance in one branch, which, not finding favour with the other, will in it be esteemed as violations of the law of the language, or at any rate declensions from its purity. Or again idioms, which one people have overlived, and have stored up in the unhonoured lumber-room of the past, will 'still be in use and honour with the other ; and thus it will sometimes come to pass that what seems, and in fact is, the newer swarm, a colony which has gone forth, will have older idioms than the main body of a people which has remained behind, will retain an archaic air and old-world fashion about the words they use, their way of pronouncing, their order and manner of combining them. Thus after the Conquest our insular French gradually diverged from the French of the Continent. The Prioress in Chaucer's *Canterbury Tales* could speak her French ' full faire and fetishly ;' but it was French, as the poet slyly adds,

> ' After the scole of Stratford atte bow,
> For French of Paris was to hire unknowe.'

One of our old chroniclers, writing in the reign of Elizabeth, informs us that by the English colonists

within the Pale in Ireland numerous words were
preserved in common use,—'the dregs of the old
ancient Chaucer English,' as he contemptuously calls
them,—which were quite obsolete and forgotten in
England itself. Thus they called a spider an 'atter-
cop'—a word, by the way, still in popular use in the
North ; a physician a 'leech,' as in poetry he is still
styled ; a dunghill a 'mixen,'—the word is common to
this day all over England; a quadrangle or base-court a
'bawn;'* they employed 'uncouth' in the earlier sense
of 'unknown.' Nay more, their pronunciation and
general manner of speech was so diverse from that of
England, that Englishmen at their first coming over
often found it hard or impossible to comprehend.
Something of the same sort took place after the Re-
vocation of the Edict of Nantes, and the consequent
formation of colonies of French Protestant refugees
in various places, especially in Amsterdam and other
chief cities of Holland. There gradually grew up
among these what was called 'refugee French,'†
which within a generation or two diverged in several
particulars from the classical language of France ; the
divergence being mainly occasioned by the fact that
this remained stationary, while the classical language

* The only two writers whom Richardson quotes as using
this word are Spenser and Swift, both writing in Ireland and
of Irish matters.

† There is an excellent account of this 'refugee French' in
Weiss' _History of the Protestant Refugees of France._

‡ Lyell (_On the Antiquity of Man_, p. 466) confirms this

was in motion ; this retained words and idioms, which the other had dismissed.* So too, there is, I believe, a very considerable difference between the Portuguese spoken in the old country and in Brazil.

Again, the wear and tear of a language, the using up of its forms and flexions, the phonetic decay which is everywhere and in all languages incessantly

---

* Lyell (*On the Antiquity of Man*, p. 466) confirms this from another quarter :—'A German colony in Pennsylvania was cut off from frequent communication with Europe, for about a quarter of a century, during the wars of the French Revolution between 1792 and 1815. So marked had been the effect even of this brief and imperfect isolation, that when Prince Bernhard of Saxe Weimar travelled among them a few years after the peace, he found the peasants speaking as they had done in Germany in the preceding century, and retaining a dialect which at home had already become obsolete (see his *Travels in North America*, p. 123). Even after the renewal of the German emigration from Europe, when I travelled in 1841 among the same people in the retired valleys of the Alleghanies, I found the newspapers full of terms half English and half German, and many an Anglo-Saxon word which had assumed a Teutonic dress, as "fencen" to fence, instead of umzäunen, "flauer" for flour, instead of "mehl," and so on. What with the retention of terms no longer in use in the mother country and the borrowing of new ones from neighbouring states, there might have arisen in Pennsylvania in five or six generations, but for the influx of new comers from Germany, a mongrel speech equally unintelligible to the Anglo-Saxon and to the inhabitants of the European fatherland.' Compare Sir G. C. Lewis, *On the Romance Languages*, p. 49.

going forward, will go forward at a faster rate in one
branch of the language than in the other ; or, if not
faster, will light not upon exactly the same forms or
the same words ; or, if on the same, yet not exactly
upon the same letters. Thus the Latin ' sum ' and
the Greek εἰμί, the same word, as I need hardly say,
are both greatly worn away,—worn away in comparison with words of rarer use, as sixpences passing
oftener from hand to hand, lose their superscription
faster than crowns,—but they are not worn away in
precisely the same letters ; each has kept a letter belonging to a more primitive form of the word, which
the other has not kept, and lost a letter which the
other has not lost. This too, the unequal action of
phonetic decay, will account for much.

Nor may we leave out of sight that which Grimm
has dwelt on so strongly, and brought into so clear a
light—namely, the modifying influence on the throat
and other organs of speech, and thus on human speech
itself, which soil and climate exercise—an influence
which, however slight at any one moment, yet being
evermore in operation produces effects which are
very far from slight in the end. We have here in
great part the explanation of the harsh and guttural
sounds which those dwelling in cold mountainous
districts make their own, of the softer and more
liquid tones of those who dwell in the plains and under
a more genial sky. These climatic influences indeed
reach very far, not merely as they affect the organs of
speech, but the characters of those who speak, which

characters will not fail in their turn to express themselves in the language. Where there is a general lack of energy and consequent shrinking from effort, this will very soon manifest itself in a corresponding feebleness in the pronunciation of words, while, on the other hand, a Dorian strength will show itself in a corresponding breadth of utterance.

But it would lead me too far, were I to attempt to make an exhaustive enumeration of all the forces which are constantly at work, to set ever farther from one another in this matter of language those who once were entirely at one. These causes which I have instanced must suffice. The contemplation of these is enough to make evident that, even could we abstract all the influences upon English which the Norman Conquest has exercised, it would still remain at this. day a very different language from any now spoken by Old-Saxon or Frisian,* that it would

---

* In the contemplation of facts like these it has been sometimes anxiously asked, whether a day will not arrive when the language now spoken alike on this side of the Atlantic and on the other, will divide into two languages, an Old English and a New. It is not impossible, and yet we can confidently hope that such a day is far distant. For the present at least, there are mightier forces tending to keep us together than those which are tending to divide. Doubtless, if they who went out from among us to people and subdue a new continent, had left our shores two or three centuries earlier than they did, when the language was much farther removed from that ideal after which it was unconsciously striving, and in which, once reached, it has in great measure acquiesced ; if they had not

be easy to set far too high the resemblance whîch
under other circumstances might have existed between

carried with them to their new homes their English Bible, their
English Shakespeare, and what else of worth had been already
uttered in the English tongue ; if, having once left us, the
intercourse between Old and New England had been entirely
broken off, or only rare and partial, there would then have
unfolded themselves differences between the language spoken
here and there, which, in tract of time accumulating and
multiplying, might already have gone far to constitute the
languages no longer one, but two. As it is, however, the
joint operation of these three causes, namely, that the separation did not take place in the infancy or early youth of the
language, but only in its ripe manhood, that England and
America own a body of literature, to which they alike look up
and appeal as containing the authoritative standards of the
language, that the intercourse between the two people has been
large and frequent, hereafter probably to be larger and more
frequent still, has up to this present time been strong enough
effectually to traverse, repress, and check all those forces
which tend to divergence. At the same time one must own
that there are not wanting some ominous signs. Of late, above
all since the conclusion of their great Civil War, some writers
on the other side of the Atlantic have announced that henceforth America will, so to speak, set up for herself, will not
accept any longer the laws and canons of speech which may
here be laid down as of final authority for all members of the
English-speaking race, but travel in her own paths, add words
to her own vocabulary, adopt idioms of her own, as may seem
the best to her. She has a perfect right to do so. The language is as much hers as ours. There are on this matter some
excellent remarks in Dwight's *Modern Philology*, 1st Ser. p.
141, with which compare Whitney, *Language and the Study of
Language*, p. 173. Still for our own sake, who now read so

English and the other dialects of the Gothic stock. For all this we may be certain that they would have resembled one another far more nearly than now they do. Let us endeavor a little to realize to ourselves English as it might then have been; and in view of this consider the disturbing forces which the Norman occupation of England brought with it, and how they acted upon the language; so we shall be better able to measure what the language except for these would have been.

The Battle of Hastings had been lost and won. Whether except for the strange and terrible coincidence of the two invasions of England almost at the same instant the Saxon battle-axes might not have proved a match for the Norman spears we cannot now determine. But the die was cast. The invader had on that day so planted his foot on English soil, that all after efforts were utterly impotent to dislodge him. But it took nearly three centuries before the two races, the victors and the vanquished, who now dwelt side by side in the same land, were thoroughly reconciled and blended into one people.

---

many American books with profit and delight, and look forward to a literature grander still unfolding itself there, for our own sake, that we do not speak of hers, we must hope that 'to donate,' 'to placate,' 'to berate,' 'to belittle,' 'to happify,' 'declinature,' 'resurrected,' 'factatively,' and the like, are not fair specimens of the words which will constitute the future *differentia* between the vocabularies of America and of England.

During the first century which followed the Conquest,
the language of the Saxon population was, as they
were themselves, utterly crushed and trodden under
foot. A foreign dynasty, speaking a foreign tongue,
and supported by an army of foreigners, was on the
throne of England ; Norman ecclesiastics filled all the
high places of the Church, filled probably every
place of honour and emolument ; Norman castles
studded the land. During the second century, a
reaction may very distinctly be traced, at first most
feeble, but little by little gathering strength, on the
part of the conquered race to reassert themselves, and
as a part of their reassertion to reassert the right of
English to be the national language of England. In
the third century after the Conquest it was at length
happily evident that Normandy was forever lost
(1206), that for Norman and Englishman alike there
was no other sphere but England ; this reassertion
of the old Saxondom of the land gaining strength
every day ; till, as a visible token that the vanquished
were again the victors, in the year 1349 English and
not French was the language taught in the schools
of this land.

But the English, which thus emerged from this
struggle of centuries in which it had refused to die,
was very different from that which had entered into it.
The whole of its elaborate inflections, its artificial
grammar, showed tokens of thorough disorganization
and decay ; indeed most of it had already disappeared,
How this came to pass I will explain to you in the

---

excellent words of the late Professor of Anglo-Saxon at Oxford. 'Great and speedy,' he observes, 'must have been the effect of the Norman Conquest in ruining the ancient grammar. The leading men in the state having no interest in the vernacular, its cultivation fell immediately into neglect. The chief of the Saxon clergy deposed or removed, who should now keep up that supply of religious Saxon literature, of the copiousness of which we may judge even in our day by the considerable remains that have out-lived hostility and neglect? Now that the Saxon landowners were dispossessed, who should patronize the Saxon bard, and welcome the man of song in the halls of mirth? The shock of the Conquest gave a deathblow to Saxon literature. The English lan-guage continued to be spoken by the masses who could speak no other ; and here and there a secluded student continued to write in it. But its honours and emoluments were gone, and a gloomy period of de-pression lay before the Saxon language as before the Saxon people. The inflection system could not live through this trying period. Just as we accumulate superfluities about us in prosperity, but in adversity we get rid of them as encumbrances, and we like to travel light when we have only our own legs to carry us—just so it happened to the English language. For now all these sounding terminations that made so handsome a figure in Saxon courts; the –AN, the –UM ; the –ERA, the –ANA ; the –IGENNE and –IGENOUM ; all these, as superfluous as bells on idle horses, were laid aside when the exercise of power was gone.'

But another force, that of external violence, had · been at work also for the breaking up of the grammar of the language. A conquering race under the necessity of communicating with a conquered in their own tongue is apt to make very short work of the niceties of grammar in that tongue, to brush all these away, as so much trumpery, which they will not be at the pains to master. If they can make their commands intelligible, this is all about which they concern themselves. They go straight to this mark ; but whether, in so doing, adjective agree with substantive, or verb with noun, or the proper case be employed, for this they care nothing if only they are understood ; nor is this all ; there is a certain satisfaction, a secret sense of superiority, in thus stripping the language of its ornament, breaking it up into new combinations, compelling it to novel forms, and making thus not merely the wills, but the very speech of the conquered, to confess its subjection.*

Nor was it the grammar only which had thus become a ruin. Those three centuries had made enormous havoc in the vocabulary as well. Rich and expressive as this had been in the palmy days of Anglo-Saxon literature, abundantly furnished as undoubtedly then it was with words having to do with matters of moral and intellectual concern, and in the nomenclature of the passions and affections, it was very far from being richly supplied with them now. Words which dealt with the material interests of every-

---

* Compare Sir G. C. Lewis, *On the Romance Languages.* pp. 21-23.

day life could scarcely help remaining familiar and vernacular ; but those pertaining to higher domains of thought, feeling, and passion and to all loftier culture, either moral or material, had in vast multitudes dropt out of use and been forgotten. Curious illustrations have been given of the destruction which had been wrought in some of the most illustrious and far branching families of words, so that of some of these there did not half a dozen, of others there did not one representative survive.*

The destruction of grammatical forms was, it is true, only the acceleration and the more complete carrying out of what would anyhow have come to pass, although perhaps not so thoroughly, as certainly not at so early a date. For indeed there is nothing more certain than that all languages in their historical period are in a continual process of simplifying themselves, dropping their subtler distinctions, allowing the mere collocation of words in their crude state or other devices of the same kind to do that which once was done by inflection. To this subject, however, I shall have occasion by and by to recur ; I will not therefore dwell upon it here. But the insufficiency of the vocabulary, consequent in part on this impoverishment of it, in part on the novel thoughts and things claiming to find utterance through it, was a less tolerable result of those centuries of depression ; happily too was capable of remedy ; which the perishing of grammatical forms, even if remedy had been looked for, was not.

* Thus see Marsh, *Origin and History of the English Language*, pp. 113, 443.

Two ways were open here.   An attempt might have
been made to revive and recover the earlier words
which had been lost and let go ; and where new
needs demanded expression, to fabricate from the
vernacular words which should correspond to these
new needs.   Now, if the revival of the English
nationality had meant the expulsion of the dominant
Norman race, this would very probably have been the
course taken ; and the reaction would have put under
a common ban language and institutions alike.   But
happily it meant no such thing.   It meant the blend-
ing of the two races into one, the forming of a new
English nation by the gradual coalition of the two, by
the growing consciousness that this England was the
equal heritage of both, the welfare of which was the
common interest of both.   It was not on either side
a triumph, or rather, as are all reconciliations, it was
on both sides a triumph.   But where under these
circumstances should a supply of the new necessities
be so naturally looked for as from the French?   That
was the language of one of the parties in this happy
transaction ; of the one which, in respect of language,
was given up far the most, and which therefore might
fairly look for this partial compensation.   Words of
theirs, few as compared with those which afterwards
found an entrance into the English tongue, but not
few in themselves, had already effected a lodgement
there ; others, if not adopted, had become more or
less familiar to English ears ; not to say that the
language which they spoke was in possession of a
literature far in advance at that time of any other in

modern Europe, a literature eagerly read here as
elsewhere in originals or translations more or less free,
representing, as it did, that new world which was
springing up, and not, as the Anglo-Saxon did, an
old world which was passing or had passed away.

Now it is a very interesting question, and one
which often has been discussed, What proportion do
the French words which then found their way into the
language, or which have subsequently entered by the
door which was thus opened to them, by the declaration then virtually made that their admission was *not*
contrary to the genius of the language, bear to the
original stock of the language, on which they were
engrafted? A recent enquirer, who professes to have
made an inventory of the whole language, has arrived
at this result, namely, that considerably more than
one half of our words, not indeed of those which we
use in writing, still less in speaking, but more than
one half of those registered in our dictionaries, are
Romanic,* are therefore the result of the Norman
Conquest, and but for it with very few exceptions
would not have found their way to us at all.

I believe the proportion which he indicates to be
quite too high, and the data on which his calculation
proceeds to be altogether misleading. But without
entering upon this question, and assuming proportions
which I am persuaded are more accurate, let us suppose that there are in round numbers one hundred

* Thommerel, *Recherches sur la Fusion du Franco-
Normand et de l'Anglo-Saxon.* Paris, 1841.

thousand words in the English language,—it is easy
to make them any number we please, according to the
scheme of enumeration upon which we start, to bring
them up to half as many again, or to reduce them, as
some have done, to less than one half,—and let us
further suppose that some thirty thousand of these
have come to us through that contact with France into
which the Battle of Hastings and its consequences
brought us, and but for these would never have
reached us at all. Let us, I say, assume this; and
a problem the most interesting presents itself to us—
namely, how should we, or whoever else might in that
event have been at this moment living in England,
have supplied the absence of these words? What
would Englishmen have done, if the language had
never received these additions? It would be a slight
and shallow answer; in fact no answer at all, to reply,
we should have done without them. We *could not*
have done without them. The words which we thus
possess, and which it is suggested we might have
done without, express a multitude of facts, thoughts,
feelings, conceptions, which, rising up before a people
growing in civilization, in knowledge, in learning, in
intercourse with other lands, in consciousness of its
own vocation in this world, *must* find their utterance
by one means or another, could not have gone without some words or other to utter them. The problem
before us is, *what* these means would have been ; by
what methods the language would have helped itself,
if it had been obliged, like so many sister dialects, to
draw solely on its own resources, to rely on home

manufactures, instead of importing, as it was able to do, so many serviceable articles ready made from abroad.

To this question I answer first and generally, and shall afterwards enter into particulars, that necessity is the mother of invention, and that many powers of the language, which are now in a great measure dormant, which have been only partially evoked, would have been called into far more frequent and far more vigorous exercise, under the stress of those necessities which would then have made themselves felt. Take, for example, the power of composition, that is, of forming new words by the combination of old—a power which the language possesses, though it is one which has grown somewhat weak and stiff through disuse. This would doubtless have been appealed to far more frequently than actually it has been. Thrown back on itself, the language would have evolved out of its own bosom, to supply its various wants, a far larger number of compound words than it has now produced. This is no mere guess of mine. You have only to look at the sister German language—*half*-sister it is now, it would have been *whole* sister but for that famous field of Hastings —and observe what it has effected in this line, how it has stopped the gaps of which it has gradually become aware by aid of these compound words, and you may so learn what *we*, under similar conditions, would have done. Thus, if we had not found it more convenient to adopt the French 'desert,' if English had been obliged, like the spider, to spin a word out

.of its own bowels, it might have put 'sand-waste' together, as the German actually has done. This and other words I shall suggest may sound strange to you at first hearing, but would have long left off their strangeness, had they been current for some hundreds of years. If we had not the Low-Latin 'massacre,' we might have had 'blood-bath,' which would not be a worse word in English than in German. Soo too, if we had not had 'deluge,' the Latin 'diluvium,' we too might have lighted on 'sin-flood,' as others have done. A duel might have been a 'two-fight' or 'twi-fight,' following the analogy of 'twilight' and 'twibill.' Instead of 'pirate' we might have had 'sea-robber;' indeed, if I do not mistake, we have the word. We should have needed a word for 'hypocrisy;' but the German 'scheinheiligkeit' at any rate suggests that 'shewholiness' might have effectually served our turn. This last example is from the Greek, but the Greek in our tongue entered in the rear of the Latin, and would not have entered except by the door which that had opened.

Let me at the same time observe that the fact of the Germans having fallen on these combinations does not make it in the least certain that we should have fallen upon the same. There is a law of neces-sity in the evolution of languages ; they pursue certain courses on which we may confidently count. But there is a law of liberty no less, and this liberty, making itself felt in this region, together with a thou-sand other causes, leaves it quite certain that in some, and possibly in all these instances, we should have supplied our wants in some other way not travelled in exactly the same paths as they have struck out for themselves. Thus, nearly allied as the Dutch is to the German, and greatly under German influence as it has been, it has various compound words of which the German knows nothing.* Still the examples which I have given sufficiently indicate to us the *direction* which the language would have taken.

But we are not here driven to a region of conjectures, or to the suggesting what *might* have been done. We can actually appeal to a very numerous company of these compound words, which have been in the language ; but which have been suffered to drop, the Latin competitors for some reason or other having, in that struggle for existence to which words are as much exposed as animals, carried the day against it. Now we may confidently affirm that all, or very nearly all, of these would have survived to the present hour, would constitute a part of our present vocabulary, if they had actually been wanted ; and they would have been wanted, if competing French words, following in the train of the conquering race, had not first made them not indispensable, and then wholly pushed them from their places. When I say this I do not mean to imply that these words were all actually born before the Norman Conquest, but only that the Conquest brought influences to bear, which were too strong for them, and in the end cut short their existence.

---

* See Jean Paul, *Æsthetik*, § 84.

Thus, if we had not proverb, 'soothsaw' or 'by-word' would have served our turn ; 'sourdough' would have supplied the place of leaven ; 'wellwill-ingness' of benevolence ; 'againbuying' of redemp-tion ; 'againrising' of resurrection ; 'undeadliness' of immortality ; 'uncunningness' of ignorance ; 'un-mildness' of asperity ; 'forefighter' of champion ; 'earthtilth' of agriculture ; 'earthtiller' of agricul-turist; 'comeling' of stranger ; 'greatdoingly' of magnificently ; 'to afterthink' (still in use in Lan-cashire) might have stood for to repent; 'medeful' for meritorious; 'untellable' for ineffable ; 'dearworth' for precious ; all which are in Wiclif. Chaucer has 'foreword' for promise ; 'bodeword' for prohibi-tion ; and *Piers Ploughman* 'goldhoard' for treasure. 'Tongful' (see Bosworth) would have stood for loquacious ; 'truelessness' for perfidy ; 'footfast' for captive ; 'allwitty' (*Prick of Conscience*) for omniscient; 'witword' for testimony. Jewel has 'foretalk' for preface ; Coverdale 'childship' for adoption, 'show-token' for sign ; 'to unhallow' for 'to profane;' Holland 'sunstead' for solstice ; 'leechcraft' for medicine; 'wordcraft' for logic ; Rogers 'turnagains' for reverses ; as little should we have let go 'book-craft' for literature, or 'shipcraft' for navigation. 'Starconner' (Gascoigne) did service once side by side with astrologer; 'redesman' with counsellor ; 'half-god' (Golding) has the advantage over demi-god, that it is all of one piece ; 'to eyebite' (Holland) told its story at least as well as to fascinate ; 'weapon-

shew' (the word still lives in Scotland) as review ;
'yearday' (*Promptorium*) as anniversary ; 'shrift-
father' as confessor ; 'earshrift' (Tyndale) is only two
syllables, while auricular confession is eight ; 'water-
fright' is preferable to our awkward hydrophobia.
The lamprey (lambens petram) would have been, as
in our country parts it now is, the 'suckstone' or the
'lickstone ;' and the anemone the 'windflower.' For
remorse of conscience we might have had, and it
exactly corresponds, 'ayenbite of inwyt,' being, as this
is, the title of a remarkable religious treatise of the
middle of the fourteenth century ;* in which I observe among other noticeable substitutes for our Latin
words, 'unlusthead' for disinclination. Emigrants
would everywhere have been called what they are
now called in districts of the North, 'outwanderers'
or 'outgangers.' A preacher who bade us to sacrifice
some of our 'neednots' (the word is in Rogers) instead of some of our superfluities, to the distresses of
others, would not deliver his messages less intelligibly
than now ; as little would he do so if he were to enumerate the many 'pullbacks,' instead of the many
obstacles which we find in the way of attaining to
eternal life. It too is a Puritan word.

Then too with the absence from the language of

---

* The *Ayenbite of Inwyt* is, in a philological point of view,
one of the most valuable of the many valuable books which the
Early English Text Society has rendered accessible at an
almost inconceivably low price to all who wish to study the
origins of the English language.

the Latin prefixes, the Saxon would have come far more into play. The Latin which we employ the most frequently, or rather which are oftenest found in words which we have adopted, are ' sub' as in ' subdue, ' subtract ;' ' de' as in ' descendant,' ' deprive ; ' circum' as in ' circumference,' ' circumvent ;' and ' præ' or 'pro as in ' predecessor,' ' progenitor.' Had these been wanting, the Latin words to which they are prefixed would have been wanting too. How would the language have fared without them? Not so ill. They would have left no chasm which it would not have been comparatively easy to fill up. Thus if the speakers of English had not possessed ' subjugate' they would have had ' underyoke,' if not ' subvert,' yet still 'underturn,' and so on with many more now to be found in Wiclif 's Bible and elsewhere. There is not at the present moment a single word in the English language—one or two may perhaps survive in the dialects—beginning with the prefix ' um.' There were once a great many. An embrace was an ' umgripe' or a gripe round (um = ἀμφί), a circuit an ' umgang ;' the circumference or periphery of a circle was the umstroke ;' to surround was to ' umlapp' (*Prick of Conscience*); to besiege on every side ' to um-besiege' (Sibbald, *Glossary*) The last appearance of ' umstroke' is in Fuller, while it would be very difficult to find so late an example of any of the others. We might have had, and probably should have had in the case which I am imagining, a large group of such words, instead of those now beginning with 'circum.' In the absence of 'præ' or 'pro,' 'fore,' which even now enters into so many of our words, as 'foretell,' 'forewarn,' would have entered into more. As we have just seen, for preface we should have had 'foretalk,' or 'forespeech' (*Ayenbite*); for predecessor 'foreganger,' for progenitor 'fore-elder,'—in all this I am not guessing, but am everywhere bringing forward words which existed once in the language.

The prefix 'for,' conveying the idea of privation or deterioration, and corresponding to the German 'ver,' —not therefore to be confounded with 'fore'—to which we already owe several excellent words, 'forlorn,' 'forbid,' 'forgo,' would have yielded us many more, each one of which would have rendered some Latin word superfluous. We can adduce the participles, 'forwandered' (*Piers Ploughman*), 'forwearied,' 'forwasted,' 'forpined' (all in Spenser), 'forwept,' 'forwelked,' and the verbs 'forfaren,' to go to ruin, 'forshapen,' to deform (*Piers Ploughman*), with other words not a few, as samples of much more in this direction, if need had been, which the language could have effected. 'Mis' too, which already does much work, as in 'misplace,' 'mislead,' would have been called to do more; instead of to abuse we should have had 'to miscall;' and the like. 'Out' would have been put to more duty than now it is; thus 'outtake' would have kept the place from which now it has been thrust by 'except,' as 'outdrive' has been by 'expel.' It would have fared the same with 'after.'

Instead of our successors we should speak of our
'aftercomers;' consequences would have been 'after-
comings;' posthumous would have been 'afterborn,'
and a postscript an 'aftertale.' All these too existed
once. 'To backjaw' is current in some of our dialects still, and would have been a vigorous substitute
for 'to retort.'

Something, again, may be concluded of what the
English-speaking race would have been able to effect,
if thrown exclusively upon such wealth as it possessed
at home, by considering the more or less successful
attempts of some who have chosen, without any such
absolute necessity, to travel the paths, which in that
case there would have been no choice but to tread.
Thus Sir John Cheke, in his Version of St. Matthew,
has evidently substituted, as often as he could, Saxon
words for Greek and Latin; thus for proselyte he has
substituted 'freshman,' for prophet 'foreshewer,' for
lunatic 'mooned.' Puttenham in the terms of art
which he employs in his *Art of English Poesy* has
made a similar attempt, though with no remarkable
success. Fairfax, author of a curious and in some
aspects an interesting book, *The Bulk and Selvedge
of the World*, has done better. He too would fain by
his own example show how very rarely even in a
subject of some considerable range it is necessary to
employ any other words than such as are home-
growths; that 'moreness,' for example does its work
as well as plurality, 'findings' as inventions. I ex-
tract a brief passage from the Introduction, at once for

its bearing on the subject which we now have in hand, and also as itself a testimony of the vigorous English which it is. possible under such self-imposed limitations to write : 'I think it will become those of us, who have a more hearty love for what is our own, than wanton longings after what is others', to fetch back some of our own words that have been jostled out in wrong, that worse from elsewhere might be hoisted in ; or else to call in from the fields and waters, shops and workhousen, that well fraught world of words that answers works, by which all learners are taught to do, and not to make a clatter.'

I remember once, this subject being under familiar discussion, and one present vaunting the powers of our Anglo-Saxon tongue to produce words of its own which should thus answer any and every need, and this without being beholden to any foreign tongue, another present put him to the proof, demanding a sufficient native equivalent for 'impenetrability.' The challenge was accepted, and without a moment's delay 'unthoroughfaresomeness' was produced. The word may not be a graceful one, but take it to pieces, and you will find that there is nothing wanting to it. For what is impenetrability ? It is the quality in one thing which does not allow it to be pierced or passed through by another. And now dissect its proposed equivalent ; and first, detaching from it its two pre-fixes, and affixes as many, you have 'fare' or passage for the body of the word ; you have next 'thorough-fare' or place through which there is a passage ; by aid of the suffix 'some' you obtain the adjective 'thoroughfaresome,' or affording a passage through ; the negative prefix 'un' gives you 'unthoroughfaresome,' the negation of this ; and the second suffix 'ness,' 'unthoroughfaresomeness,' or the state which refuses to afford a passage through,—in other words, impenetrability.

We can thus, I think, trace, and not altogether by mere guesswork or at random, some of the paths along which English would have travelled, had it been left to itself, and to its own natural and orderly development, instead of being forced by the stress of external circumstances into paths in part at least altogether new. We can assert with confidence that it would have been no unserviceable, shiftless, nor ignoble tongue ; and this, while we gladly and thankfully acknowledge that it has done better, being what it is, that language in which our English Bible is written, in which Shakespeare and Milton have garnered for the after world the rich treasure of their minds.

Let us, before quite dismissing this subject, contemplate two or three points which broadly distinguish English as it is from English as it would then have been. The language, we may be quite sure, would in that case have been more abundantly supplied with inflections than at present it is. It was, as we saw just now, during the period of extreme depression which followed on the Conquest that it stripped itself so bare of these. I do not of course mean to imply that a vast number of inflections would not, according to the universal law of all languages, have anyhow fallen away. But continuing as it would have done, the language of the Church, the Court, and of literature, it would never have become that mere *torso* which it was, when at length it emerged victorious from its three hundred years of conflict for supremacy on this English soil. We should assuredly have possessed a much more complex grammatical system, probably as complex or nearly as complex as the German possesses at the present day. Foreigners complain that even now English is hard enough to master; it would assuredly have been much harder then. There would have been many more distinctions to remember. Our nouns substantive, instead of being all declined in one way, would have been declined some in one way, some in another; they would probably have had their three genders,—masculine, feminine, and neuter; and have modified according to these the terminations of the adjectives in concord with them; and very much more of this kind, now dismissed, and on the whole happily dismissed, would have been retained.

The language is infinitely richer now in synonyms than but for this settlement of French and Latin in its midst it would have been—in words covering the same, or very nearly the same, spaces of meaning. In cases almost innumerable it has what we may call *duplicate* words; there can be very few languages in

the world so amply furnished with these. The way it
has obtained them is this. It has kept the Saxon
word, and superadded to this the Latin, or the French
derived from the Latin. Thus we have kept 'heavenly,' but we have added 'celestial;' we have not
dismissed 'earthly,' though we have acquired 'terrestrial;' nor 'fiery,' though we have adopted 'igneous;' .
'providence' has not put 'foresight' out of use, nor
'flower' 'bloom,' nor 'reign ' 'kingdom,' nor 'omnipotent' 'almighty.' I might go on instancing
these almost without end, but I have dwelt more
fully on this matter elsewhere,* and here therefore
will not urge it more.

Nor can it be said that this abundance is a mere
piece of luxury, still less that it is an embarrassment.
It gives the opportunity of wearing now a homelier,
now a more scholarly garment of speech, as may seem
most advisable for the immediate need.   Poetry is
evidently a gainer by it, in the wider choice of
expressions which it has thus at command, to meet
its manifold exigencies, now of rhyme, now of melody,
and now of sentiment. And prose is not less a gainer,
demanding as it does rhythm and modulation, though
of another kind, quite as urgently as poetry does, and
having these much more within its reach through this
choice of words than otherwise it would have had.
Thus most of us have admired in .Handel's greatest
composition the magnificent effect of those words

---

* *Study of Words*, 13th edit. p. 229.

from the Apocalypse, 'For the Lord God *omnipotent* reigneth.' Now the word which our Translators have here rendered 'omnipotent,' they have everywhere else rendered 'almighty;' but substitute 'almighty' here, and how manifest the loss. What a sublime variation have they thus found within their reach.*

These are manifest gains; but for all this I would not affirm that everything is gain. Thus if our Saxon had never been disturbed, there would certainly have been in the language a smaller number of what our ancestors called, 'inkhorn terms,' the peculiar pro-

---

* I only know one in modern times, but he is one whose judgment must always carry great weight, Dr. Guest, who in his *History of English Rhythms* takes a less favourable view of the results of the large importation of French and Latin words into the language :—' The evils resulting from these importations have, I think, been generally underrated in this country. When a language must draw upon its own wealth for a new term, its forms and analogies are kept fresh in the minds of those who so often use them. But with the introduction of foreign terms, not only is the symmetry—the *science*—of the language injured, but its laws are brought less frequently under notice, and are the less used, as their application becomes more difficult. If a new word were added to any of the purer languages, such as the Sanscrit, the Greek, or the Welsh, it would soon be the root of numerous offshoots, substantives, adjectives, verbs, &c., all formed according to rule, and modifying the meaning of their root according to well-known analogies. But in a mixed and broken language few or no such consequences follow. The word remains barren and the language is "enriched" like a tree covered over with wreaths taken from the boughs of its neighbour ; which carries a goodly show of foliage and withers beneath the shade.

perty of the scholar, not used and not understood by the poor and the illiterate. More words would be what all words ought to be, and once were, 'thought-pictures,' transparent with their own meaning, telling their own story to everybody. Thus if I say that Christ 'sympathizes' with his people, or even if I say, 'has compassion,' I am not sure that every one follows me ; but if I were to say, He 'fellow-feels,' and the word existed not long ago, as ' fellow-feeling' does still, all would understand. 'Redemption' conveys to our poor the vague impression of some great benefit ; but 'againbuying' would have conveyed a far more distinct one. 'Middler'—this word also is to be found in Wiclif—would have the same advantage over mediator. Even our Authorized Version, comparatively little as we have to complain of there, would itself not have lost, but gained, if its authors had been absolutely compelled to use the store of Saxon vocables at their command, if sometimes they had been shut in, so to speak, to these ; for instance, if instead of 'celestial bodies and bodies terrestrial,' they had had no choice but to write ' heavenly bodies and bodies earthly' (1 Cor. xv. 40). All would have understood them then ; I very much doubt whether all understand them now.

Other advantages too might have followed, if the language had continued all of one piece. Thus in the matter of style, it would not have been so fatally easy to write bad English, and to fancy this bad to be good, as now it is. That worst and most offensive kind of bad English, which disguises poverty of thought, and lack of any real command over the language, by the use of big, hollow, lumbering Latin words, would not have been possible.   It is true that on the other hand the opportunities of writing a grand, sustained, stately English would not have been nearly so great, but for the incoming of that multitude of noble words which Latin, the stateliest of all languages, has lent us. Something not very different indeed, not immeasurably remote from Swift's or Dryden's prose might have existed ; but nothing in the least resembling the stately march of Hooker's, of Milton's, or of Jeremy Taylor's. A good style would have been a much simpler, less complex matter than now it is ; the language would have been an instrument with not so many strings, an organ with fewer pipes and stops, of less compass, with a more limited diapason, wanting many of the grander resonances which it now possesses ; but easier to play on, requiring infinitely less skill ; not so likely to betray into gross absurdities, nor to make an open show of the incapacity of such as handled it badly.

On the whole, then, while that Norman Conquest, in the disturbing forces which it has exerted on the English language, has no doubt brought with it losses no less than gains, we may boldly affirm that the gains very far transcend the losses.   As so many things have wrought together to make England what she is, as we may trace in our 'rough island-story' so many wonderful ways in which good has been educed from evil, and events the most unpromising have left their blessing behind them, not otherwise has it been here. That which brought down our English tongue from its pride of place, stript it of so much in which it gloried, condemned it, as might have seemed, if not to absolute extinction, yet to serve henceforward as the mere patois of an illiterate race of subject bondsmen and hinds, it was even that very event which in its ultimate consequences wrought out for it a complete-ness and a perfection which it would never else have obtained. So strange in their ultimate issues are the ways of Providence with men.

LECTURE III.

GAINS OF THE ENGLISH LANGUAGE.

IT is with good right that we speak of some languages as *living*, of others as *dead*. All spoken languages may be ranged in the first class ; for as men will never consent to use a language without more or less modifying it in their use, will never so far forgo their own activity as to leave it exactly where they found it, there follows from this that so long as it is thus the utterance of human thought and feeling, it will inevitably show itself alive, and that by many infallible proofs, by growth and misgrowth, by acquisition and loss, by progress and decay. This title therefore of living, a spoken language abundantly deserves ; for it is one in which, spoken as it is by living men, *vital* energies are still in operation. It is one which is in course of actual evolution ; which, if the life that animates it be a healthy one, is appropriating and assimilating to itself what it anywhere finds congenial to its own life, multiplying its resources, increasing its wealth ; while at the same time it is casting off useless and cumbersome forms, dismissing from its vocabulary words of which it finds no use, rejecting by a reactive energy the foreign and heterogeneous, **which may** for a while have forced themselves upon it. In the process of all this it may easily make mistakes; in the desire to simplify, it may let go distinctions which were not useless, and which it would have been better to retain ; the acquisitions which it makes are very far from being all gains ; it sometimes rejects as worthless, and suffers to die out, words which were most worthy to have lived. So far as it commits any of these faults its life is not healthy ; it is not growing richer but poorer ; there are here tokens, however remote, of disorganization, decay, and ultimate death. But still it lives, and even these misgrowths and malformations, the rejection of this good, the taking up into itself of that bad, even these errors are themselves the utterances and evidences of life. A dead language knows nothing of all this. It is dead, because books, and not now any generation of living men, are the guardians of it, and what they guard, they guard without change. Its course has been completely run, and it is now equally incapable of gaining and of losing. We may come to know it better ; but in itself it is not, and never can be, other than it was before it ceased from the lips of men. In one sense it is dead, though in another it may be more true to say of it that it has put on immortality.

Our own is, of course, a living language still. It is therefore gaining and losing. It is a tree in which the vital sap is circulating yet ; and as this works, new leaves are continually being put forth by it, old are dying and dropping away. I propose to consider some of the evidences of this life at work in it still.

In my present lecture and in that which follows I shall take for my subject, the *sources* from which the English language has enriched its vocabulary, the *periods* at which it has made the chief additions to this, the *character* of the additions which at different periods it has made, and the *motives* which induced it to seek them.

In my first lecture I dwelt with some emphasis on the fact, that the core, the radical constitution of our language, is Anglo-Saxon ; so that, composite or mingled as it is, it is such only in its vocabulary, not in its construction, inflections, or generally its grammatical forms. These are all of one piece ; there is indeed no amalgamation possible in these ; and whatever of new has come in has been compelled to conform itself to the old. The framework is native ; only a part of the filling in is exotic ; and of this filling in, of these comparatively more recent accessions, I now propose to speak.

The first great augmentation by foreign words of our Anglo-Saxon vocabulary, and that which in importance has very far exceeded all the others put together, was a consequence, although not an immediate one, of the Battle of Hastings. You will have gathered from what I have said already that I am unable to share in the sentimental regrets over the results of that battle in which Thierry has led the way. With the freest acknowledgment of the miseries entailed for a while on the Saxon race by the Norman Conquest, I can regard that Conquest in no other light than as the making of England ; a judgment, it is true, but a judgment and a mercy in one. It was a rough and rude, and yet most necessary discipline, to which the race which for so many hundred years had occupied the English soil was thereby submitted ; a great tribulation, yet one not undeserved, and which could not have been spared ; so grievously relaxed were all the moral energies of Saxon England at the time of the Conquest, so far had all the vigour of those institutions by which alone a nation lives, decayed and departed. God never showed more plainly that he had a great part for England to play in the world's story than when He brought hither that aspiring Norman race. Heavily as for a while they laid their hand on the subject people, they did at the same time contribute elements absolutely essential to the future greatness and glory of the land which they made their own. But it is only of their contributions in one particular direction that we have here to speak.

Neither can it be said of these that they followed at once. The actual interpenetration of our Anglo-Saxon with any large amount of French words did not find place till a very much later day. Some French words we find very soon after; but in the main the two streams of language continued for a long while separate and apart, even as the two nations remained aloof from one another, a conquering and a conquered, and neither forgetting the fact. It was not till the middle of the fourteenth century that French words began to find their way in any very large number into English. Then within a period of

some fifty years very many more effected a permanent
settlement among us than had so done during the
three hundred preceding. In the bringing in of these
too much has been ascribed to the influence and
authority of a single man. Some have praised, others
have blamed,* Chaucer overmuch for his share in this
work. Standing in the forefront of his time, he no
doubt fell in with and set forward tendencies in the
language, yet these such, it is plain, as were in active
operation already. To assume that the greater number of French vocables which he employed had
never been employed before, were strange to English
ears, is to assume, as Tyrwhitt urges well, that his
poetry presented to his contemporaries a motley
patchwork of language, and is quite irreconcilable
with the fact that he took his place at once as the
popular poet of the nation.†
It would be hardly too much to affirm that there

---

* Thus Alexander Gil, head-master of St. Paul's School, in
his book, *Logonomia Anglica*, 1621, *Preface :* Huc usque pere-
grinæ voces in linguâ Anglicâ inauditæ. Tandem circa annum
1400 Galfridas Chaucerus, infausto omine, vocabulus Gallicis
et Latinis poësin suam famosam reddidit. The whole passage,
which is too long to quote, as indeed the whole book, is
curious.

† In his *Testament of Love* he expresses his contempt of
Englishmen who would not be content to clothe their thoughts
in an English garb : 'Let these clerkes endyten in Latyn, for
they have the propertye in science and the knowinge in that
facultye, and lette Frenchmen in their Frenche also endyte
their queynt termes, for it is kyndly to theyr mouthes ; and let
us shewe our fantasyes as we learneden of our dames tonge.'

is quite as large a proportion of Latin words in *Piers
Ploughman* as in Chaucer,—certainly a very remarkable
fact, when we call to mind that *Piers Ploughman* dates
some twenty or thirty years earlier than Chaucer's
more important poems, that in form it cleaves to the
old alliterative scheme of versification, and in substance evidently addresses itself not to the courtier or
the churchman, but claims to find, as we know it
actually found, an audience from the commonalty of
the realm.   Its religious, ecclesiastical, and ethical
terminology is abundant, and with rare exceptions is
Latin throughout—which, when we keep in mind the
opulence in such terms of the earlier Anglo-Saxon,
signally attests the havoc which had been wrought
during the centuries of depression in all the finer
elements of the language.   We meet there with ' ab-
stinence,' 'ampulle,' 'assoil,' 'avarice,' 'benigne,'
'bountée,' 'cardinal vertues,' 'conscience,' 'charitée,'
' chastitée,' 'confession,' 'consistory,' 'contemplatif,'
'contrition,' 'indulgence,' 'leautée,' 'mitigation,'
'monial,' 'recreant,' 'relic,' 'reverence,' 'sanctitée,'
'spiritual,' 'temporaltée,' 'unitée.'   Already we find
in *Piers Ploughman* French words which the English
language has finally proved unable to take up into
itself, as ' bienfait,' 'brocage,' 'chibolles,' 'creaunt,'
'devoir,' 'entremetten,' 'fille,' 'losengerie;' 'mestier,'
'pain' (=bread), 'prest' (=prêt).   The real difference between Langlande and Chaucer is that the
former seems to us, as we read, only to have partially
fused into one harmonious whole the two elements
whereof the language which he writes is composed ;

while the mightier artist,—though he too was a great
one,—has brought them into so perfect a chemical
combination, that we never pause to consider from
what quarter the ore which he has wrought into such
current money was extracted, whether from the old
mines of the land, or imported from other new ones,
opened beyond the sea. But the *Romance of William
of Palerne* supplies evidence more remarkable still.
Madden puts 1350, nearly half a century earlier than
the *Canterbury Tales*, as about the date of this poem.
Here are some of the words which it yields, 'aunter,'
'bachelor,' 'defaute,' 'deraine,' 'digne,' 'duresse,'
'emperice,' 'eritage,'. 'facioun,' 'feyntise,' 'hautein,'
'merciabul,' 'mesurabul,' 'paramour,' 'queyntise,'
'scowmfit,' 'travail,' with very many more of like
kind.

Other considerations will tend to the abating of the
exclusive merit or demerit of Chaucer in this matter.
There were other forces beside literature which at this
time were helping to saturate English with as much
of French as it could healthily absorb. 'It is,' Marsh
says, 'a great but very widely spread error, to suppose
that the influx of French words in the fourteenth
century was due alone to poetry and other branches
of pure literature. The law, which now first became
organized into a science, introduced very many terms
borrowed from the nomenclature of Latin and French
jurisprudence ; the glass-worker, the enameller, the
architect, the brass-founder, the Flemish clothier, and
the other handicraftsmen, whom Norman taste and
luxury invited, or domestic oppression expelled from

the Continent, brought with them the vocabularies of
their respective arts ; and Mediterranean commerce—
which was stimulated by the demand for English
wool, then the finest in Europe—imported from the
harbours of a sea where French was the predominant
language, both new articles of merchandise and the
French designation of them.   The sciences too, medicine, physics, geography, alchemy, astrology, all of
which became known to England chiefly through
French channels, added numerous specific terms to the
existing vocabulary, and very many of the words, first
employed in English writings as a part of the technical
phraseology of these various arts and knowledges,
soon passed into the domain of common life, in
modified or untechnical senses, and thus became incorporated into the general tongue of society and of
books.'

It is true that there happened here what will happen
in every attempt to transplant on a large scale the
words of one language into another.   The new soil
will not prove equally favourable for all.   Some will
take root and thrive ; but others, after a longer or
shorter interval, will pine and wither and die. Not all
the words which Langlande or Chaucer employed, and
for which they stood sponsors, found final allowance
with us.*   At the same time, such an issue as this

---

* Plautus in the same way uses a multitude of Greek words,
which Latin did not want, and therefore refused to absorb :
thus, 'clepta,' 'zamia,' 'danista,' 'harpagare,' 'apolactizare,'
'nauclerus,' 'strategus,' 'drapeta,' 'morus,' 'morologus,'
'phylaca,' 'malacus,' 'sycophantia,' 'euscheme' ($\varepsilon \dot{v} \acute{o} \chi \eta \mu o \varsigma$),

was no condemnation of their attempt. Nothing but
actual proof could show whether the language needed,
and would therefore absorb these ; or, not needing, in
due time reject them. How little in excess Chaucer
in this matter was, how admirable his choice of words,
is singularly attested by the fact—I state it on Marsh's
authority—that there are not more than a hundred
French words used by him, such for example as
' misericorde,' ' malure' (malheur), ' penible,' 'ayel,'
(aïeul), 'tas,' 'fine' (fin·), 'meubles,' 'hautain,'
' gipon,' 'racine,' which have failed to win a permanent place among us. I cannot say how many *Piers
Ploughman* would yield, but we saw just now that it
would yield several ; and Gower in like manner—
such, for example, as ' feblesse,' 'tristésse,' ' mestier,'
'pelerinage.' Wiclif would furnish a few, as for
instance 'creansur,' ' roue,' ' umbre ;' though very
far fewer than either of those other ; for indeed the
non-English element in him, which the language has
finally refused to take up, does not so much consist
of words from the French, as of words drawn by him
directly from his Latin Vulgate, such as had never
undergone a shaping process in their passage through
any intermediate language. Of these the necessities,
or if not the necessities, yet the difficulties, of the case

'dulice ' (δουλικῶς), [so 'scymnus' by Lucretius], none of
which, I believe, are employed except by him ; while others,
as ' mastigia ' and ' techna,' he shares with Terence. Yet
only experience could show that they were superfluous ; and it
was well done to put them on trial.

drove him to employ not a few, as 'simulacre,' 'bilibre,' 'cyconye,' 'argentarie,' 'signacle,' 'eruke' (eruca), 'amfore' (amphora) 'architriclyn,' and others.

It is curious to observe to how late a day some of those adoptions from the French kept their ground ; which, for all this, they have proved unable to keep to the end. Thus 'mel' (Sylvester) struggled hard and long for a place side by side with honey ; 'roy' with king ; this last quite obtaining one in Scotch. It has fared not otherwise with 'egal' (Puttenham) ; with 'ouvert,' 'mot,' 'baine,' 'mur,' 'ecurie,' 'sacre,' 'baston,' 'gite,' 'to cass' (all in Holland) ; with 'rivage,' 'jouissance,' 'noblesse,' 'tort,' 'accoil' (accueillir), 'sell (=saddle), 'conge,' 'surquedry,' 'foy,' 'duresse,' 'spalles' (épaules), 'gree' (gré), all occurring in Spenser ; with 'outrecuidance ;' with 'to serr' (serrer), 'vive,' 'brocage,' 'reglement,' used all by Bacon ; with 'esperance,' 'orgillous' (orgueilleux), 'rondeur,' 'scrimer,' 'amort,' 'maugre,' 'sans' (all in Shakespeare). 'Devoir,' 'dimes,' 'puissance,' 'bruit' (this last used often in our Bible) were English once ; they are not so any longer. The same holds true of 'dulce,' 'aigredoulce' (=soursweat), of 'volupty' (Sir Thomas Elyot), 'volunty' (Evelyn), 'medisance' (Montagu) ' 'pucelle' (Ben Jonson), 'petit' (South), 'aveugle,' 'colline' (both in *State Papers*), of 'defailance' 'plaisance,' 'paysage,' 'pareil' (all in Jeremy Taylor) ; of 'eloign' (Hacket), and of others, more than I can here enumerate.

But to return. With Chaucer English literature had made a burst, which it was not able to maintain. Dreary days were before it still. Our morning star, he yet ushered in no dawn which was at the point of breaking. Chaucer has by Warton been well compared to some warm bright day in the very early spring, which seems to announce that the winter is over and gone ; but its promise is deceitful ; the full bursting and blossoming of the spring-time is yet far off. The long struggle with France, the hundred years' War, which began so gloriously, but which ended so disastrously, even with the loss of our whole ill-won dominion there, the savagery of our wars of the Roses, wars which were a legacy bequeathed to us by that unrighteous conquest, leave a huge gap in our literary history, nearly a century during which very little was done for the cultivation of our native tongue, few important additions to its wealth were made.

The period, however, is notable as that during which for the first time we received a large accession of words directly drawn from the Latin. A small settlement of these, for the most part ecclesiastical, had long since found their home in the bosom of the Anglo-Saxon itself, and had been entirely incorporated with it. The fact that we had received our Christianity from Rome, and that Latin was the constant language of the Church, sufficiently accounts for these. Such were 'monk,' 'bishop,' (it was not as Greek but as Latin that these words reached us), 'priest,' 'provost,' 'minster,' 'cloister,' 'candle,' 'devil,' 'psalter,' 'mass,' and the names of certain foreign animals, as 'camel,' 'lion,' or plants or other productions, as 'lily,' 'pepper,' 'fig;' which are all, with slightly different spelling, words whose naturalization in England reaches back to a period anterior to the Conquest.* These, however, were exceptional, and stood to the main body of the language, not as the Romance element of it does now to the Gothic, one power over against another, but as the Spanish or Italian or Arabic words in it stand to the remainder of the language, and could not be affirmed to affect it more.

So soon, however, as French words were brought largely into it, and were found to coalesce kindly with the native growths, this very speedily suggested the going straight to the Latin, and drawing directly from it; and thus in the hundred years after Chaucer no small amount of Latin had penetrated, if not into our speech, yet into our books—words not introduced *through* the French, for they are not, and some of them have at no time been, French; but yet such as would never have established themselves here, if the French, already domesticated among us, had not prepared their way, bridged over the gulf that would have otherwise been too wide between them and the Saxon vocables of our tongue; and suggested the models on which these later adoptions should be framed.

They were not for the most part words which it was any gain to acquire. The period was one of great

---

* Guest, *Hist. of English Rhythms*, vol. ii. p. 109 ; Koch, *Hist. Gramm. der Engl. Sprache*, vol. i. p. 5.

depression of the national spirit; and nothing sympathizes more intimately with this, rising when it rises, and sinking when it sinks, than does language. Not first at the revival of learning, but already at this time began the attempt to flood the language with pedantic words from the Latin; take as specimens of these ' facundious,' 'tenebrous,' 'solacious,' ' pulcritude,' 'consuetude' (all these occur in Hawes), with a multitude more of the same fashion which the language has long since disallowed; while others which have maintained their ground, and have deserved to maintain it, were yet employed in numbers quite out of proportion to the Saxon vocables with which they were mingled, and which they altogether overtopped and overshadowed. Chaucer's hearty English feeling, his thorough sympathy with the people, the fact that, scholar as he was, he was yet the poet not of books but of life, and drew his best inspiration from life, all this had kept him, in the main, clear of this fault. But it was otherwise with those who followed. The diction of Lydgate, Hawes, and the other versifiers,—for to the title of poets they have little or no claim,—who filled up the interval between Chaucer and Surrey, is immensely inferior to his; being all stuck over with long and often ill-selected Latin words. The worst offenders in this line, as Campbell himself admits, were the Scotch poets of the fifteenth century. 'The prevailing fault,' he says, 'of English diction, in the fifteenth century, is redundant ornament, and an affectation of anglicising Latin words. In this pedantry and use of ''aureate terms'' the Scottish

versifiers went even beyond their brethren of the
south. . . . . When they meant to be eloquent,
they tore up words from the Latin, which never took
root in the language, like children making a mock
garden with flowers and branches stuck in the ground,
which speedily wither.'*   It needs but to turn over a
few pages of the Scotch poetry of the fifteenth and
sixteenth century to find proof abundant of what
Campbell has here observed.

This tendency to latinize our speech received a new
impulse from the revival of learning, and the familiar
re-acquaintance with the master-pieces of ancient
literature which went along with this revival. Happily
another movement accompanied, or followed hard on
this ; a movement in England essentially national ;
and one which stirred our people at far deeper depths
of their moral and spiritual life than any mere revival
of learning could have ever done ; I refer, of course,
to the Reformation. It was only among the Germanic nations of Europe, as has often been remarked,
that the Reformation struck lasting roots ; it found its
strength therefore in the Teutonic element of the national character, which also it in turn further strengthened, purified, and called out. And thus, though
Latin came in upon us now faster than ever, and in a
certain measure also Greek, yet this found redress and
counterpoise in the contemporaneous unfolding of the
more fundamentally popular side of the language.
Popular preaching and discussion, the necessity of

---

* *Essay on English Poetry*, p. 93.

dealing with truths the most transcendant in a way to be understood not by scholars only, but by 'idiots' as well, all this served to evoke the native resources of our tongue; and thus the relative proportion between the one part of the language and the other was not dangerously disturbed, the balance was not destroyed; as it might easily have been, if only the Humanists had been at work, and not the Reformers as well.

The revival of learning, which made itself first felt in Italy, extended to England, and was operative here, during the reigns of Henry the Eighth and his immediate successors. Having thus slightly anticipated in time, it afterwards ran exactly parallel with, the period during which our Reformation was working itself out. The epoch was in all respects one of immense mental and moral activity, and such epochs never leave a language where they found it. Much in it is changed; much probably added; for the old garment of speech, which once served all needs, has grown too narrow, and serves them now no more. The old crust is broken up, and what was obscurely working before forces itself into sight and recognition. 'Change in language is not, as in many natural products, continuous; it is not equable, but eminently by fits and starts;' and when the foundations of the mind of a nation are heaving under the operation of truths which it is now for the first time making its own, more important changes will follow in fifty years than in two centuries of calmer or more stagnant existence. Thus the activities and energies which the Reformation awakened among us, as they made themselves felt far beyond the domain of our directly religious life, so they did not fail to make themselves effectually felt in this region of language among the rest.* The Reformation had a scholarly, we might say, a scholastic, as well as a popular, aspect. Add this fact to that of the revived interest in classical learning, and you will not wonder that a stream of Latin, now larger than ever, began to flow into our language. Thus Puttenham, writing in Queen Elizabeth's reign,†

---

* Some lines of Waller reveal to us the sense which in his time scholars had of the rapidity with which the language was changing under their hands. Looking back at changes which the last hundred years had wrought in it, he checked with misgivings such as these his own hope of immortality :

> ‘Who can hope his lines should long
> Last in a daily changing tongue?
> While they are new, envy prevails,
> And as that dies, our language fails.

> . . . .

> ‘Poets that lasting marble seek,
> Must carve in Latin or in Greek:
> *We* write in sand ; our language grows,
> And like the tide our work o'erflows.’

How his misgivings, which assume that the rate of change would continue what it had been, have been fulfilled, every one knows. The two centuries which have elapsed since he wrote, have hardly antiquated a word or a phrase in his poems. If we care very little for them now, this is owing to quite other causes—to their want of moral earnestness more than to any other.

† In his *Art of English Poesy*, London, 1589, republished

gives a long list of words, some Greek, a few French
and Italian, but far the most Latin, which, as he
affirms, were of quite recent introduction into the
language ; and though he may be here and there
mistaken about some single word, it cannot be
doubted that in the main what he asserts is correct.
And yet some of these it is difficult to understand
how the language could so long have done without ;
as ' compendious,' ' delineation,' ' dimension,' ' figurative,' ' function,' ' idiom,' ' impression,' ' indignity,'
' inveigle,' ' method,' ' methodical,' ' metrical,' ' numerous,' ' penetrable,' ' penetrate,' ' prolix,' ' savage,'
' scientific,' ' significative.' All these he adduces
with praise. Others, not less commended by him, have
failed to hold their ground, as ' placation,' ' numero-
sity,' ' harmonical.' In his disallowance of ' facun-
dity,' ' implete,' ' attemptat ' (attentat), he only anticipated the decision of a later day. Other words which
he condemned no less, as ' audacious,' ' compatible,'
' egregious,' have maintained their ground. These
have done the same : ' despicable,' ' destruction,' ' ho-
micide,' ' obsequious,' ' ponderous,' ' portentous,'
' prodigious ;' all of them by another writer a little
earlier condemned as ' inkhorn terms, smelling too
much of the Latin.'

It is curious to note the ' words of art,' as he calls
them, which Philemon Holland, a voluminous translator at the end of the sixteenth and beginning of the
seventeenth century, counts it needful to explain in

in Haslewood's *Ancient Critical Essays upon English Poets
and Poesy*, London, 1811, vol. i. pp. 122, 123.

a glossary appended to his translation of Pliny's *Natural History.** One can hardly understand how any who cared to consult the book at all would be perplexed by words like these : 'acrimony,' 'austere,' 'bulb,' 'consolidate,' 'debility,' 'dose,' 'ingredient,' 'opiate,' 'propitious,' 'symptom,' all of which as novelties he carefully explains. Certainly he has words in his glossary harder and more technical than these ; but a vast majority present no greater difficulty than those just adduced.† The Rhemish Bible,

---

* London, 1601. Besides this work Philemon Holland translated the whole of Plutarch's *Moralia*, the *Cyropædia* of Xenophon, Livy, Suetonius, Ammianus Marcellinus, and Camden's *Britannia*. His works make a part of the 'library of dulness' in Pope's *Dunciad :*

> ' De Lyra there a dreadful front extends,
>   And here the groaning shelves *Philemon* bends '—

very unjustly ; and Southey shows a far juster estimate of his merits, when he finds room for two of these, Plutarch's *Moralia* and Pliny's *Natural History*, in the select library of *The Doctor*. The works which Holland has translated are all more or less important, and his versions of them a mine of genuine idiomatic English, neglected by most of our lexicographers, wrought with eminent advantage by Richardson ; yet capable of yielding much more than they have yielded yet.

† So too in French it is surprising to find how new are many words which now constitute an integral part of the language. ' Désintéressement,' ' exactitude,' ' sagacité,' ' bravoure,' were not introduced till late in the seventeenth century. ' Renaissance,' ' emportement,' 'sçavoir-faire,' ' indélébile,' ' désagrément,' were all recent in 1675 (Bouhours) ; ' indévot,' ' intolérance,' ' impardonnable,' ' irréligieux,' were struggling

published in 1582, has a table consisting of fifty-five terms 'not familiar to the vulgar reader; among which are 'acquisition,' 'advent,' 'allegory,' 'co-operate,' 'evangelize,' 'eunuch,' 'holocaust,' 'neo-phyte,' 'resuscitate,' 'victim.' More than one of these was denounced by the assailants of this Version, as for instance by our own Translators, who say in

---

into allowance at the end of the seventeenth century, and. not established till the beginning of the eighteenth. 'Insidieux' was invented by Malherbe ; 'frivolité' is wanting in the earlier editions of the *Dictionary of the Academy ;* the Abbé de St.-Pierre was the first to employ 'bienfaisance,' the elder Balzac 'féliciter,' Sarrasin 'burlesque,' Rousseau 'investiga-tion' (see *Guesses at Truth,* 1866, p. 220), the Abbé de Pons 'érudit.' Mme. de Sévigné exclaims against her daughter for employing 'effervescence' (Comment dites-vous cela, ma fille ? Voilà un mot dont je n'avais jamais ouï parler). 'Démagogue' was first hazarded by Bossuet, and counted so bold a novelty that for long none ventured to follow him in its use. Mon-taigne introduced 'diversion' and 'enfantillage,' the last not without rebuke from contemporaries. It is a singularly characteristic fact, if he invented, as he is said to have done, 'enjoué.' Desfontaines first employed 'suicide ;' Caron gave to the language 'avant-propos,' Ronsard 'avidité,' Joachim Dubellay 'patrie,' Denis Sauvage 'jurisconsulte,' Ménage 'gracieux' (at least so Voltaire affirms) and 'proṣateur,' Desportes 'pudeur,' Chapelain 'urbanité,' and Etienne first brought in, apologizing at the same time for the boldness of it, 'analogie,' (si les oreilles françoises peuvent porter ce mot). 'Accaparer' first appeared in the *Dictionary of the Academy* in 1787 ; 'préliber' (prælibare) is a word of our own day ; and Charles Nodier, if he did not coin, yet revived the obso-lete 'simplesse.'—See Génin, *Variations du Langage Français,* pp. 308–319.

their *Preface*, 'We have shunned the obscurity of the Papists in the azims, tunicke, rational, holocausts, prepuce, pasche, and a number of such like, whereof their late translation is full.' It is curious that three out of the six which they thus denounce should have kept their place in the language.

The period during which this naturalization of Latin words in the English language was going actively forward, extended to the Restoration of Charles the Second, and beyond it. It first received a check from the coming up of French tastes, fashions, and habits of thought consequent on that event. The writers whose style was already formed, such as Cudworth and Barrow, continued still to write their stately sentences, Latin in structure, and Latin in diction, but not so those of a younger generation. We may say of this influx of Latin that it left the language vastly more copious, with greatly enlarged capabilities, but somewhat burdened with its new acquisitions, and not always able to move gracefully under their weight; for, as Dryden has happily said, it is easy enough to acquire foreign words, but to know what to do with them after you have acquired, is the difficulty.

Few, let me here observe by the way, have borne themselves in this hazardous enterprise at once as discreetly and as boldly as Dryden himself has done ; who has thus admirably laid down the motives which induced him to look abroad for words with which to enrich his vocabulary, and the principles which guided him in the selection of such, 'If sounding words are not of our growth and manufacture, who shall hinder me to import them from a foreign country? I carry not out the treasure of the nation which is never to return, but what I bring from Italy I spend in England. Here it remains and here it circulates, for, if the coin be good, it will pass from one hand to another. I trade both with the living and the dead, for the enrichment of our native language. We have enough in England to supply our necessity, but if we will have things of magnificence and splendour, we must get them by commerce. Poetry requires adornment, and that is not to be had from our old Teuton monosyllables; therefore if I find any elegant word in a classic author, I propose it to be naturalized by using it myself : and if the public approves of it, the bill passes. But every man cannot distinguish betwixt pedantry and poetry : every man therefore is not fit to innovate. Upon the whole matter a poet must first be certain that the word he would introduce is beautiful in the Latin ; and is to consider in the next place whether it will agree with the English idiom : after this, he ought to take the opinion of judicious friends, such as are learned in both languages ; and lastly, since no man is infallible, let him use this licence very sparingly ; for if too many foreign words are poured in upon us, it looks as if they were designed not to assist the natives, but to conquer them.'*

---

* *Dedication of the translation of the Æneid.* I cannot say that I have observed very many of these words there. 'Irre-

It would indeed have fared ill with the language, if *all* the words which the great writers of this second Latin period proposed as candidates for admission into it, had received the stamp of popular allowance. But happily this was not the case. The re-active energy of the language, enabling it to throw off that which was foreign to it, did not fail to display itself now, as it had done on former occasions; nor is it too much to affirm that in almost every instance during this period, where the Alien Act was enforced, the sentence of banishment was a just one. Either the word violated the analogy of the language, or was not intelligible, or was not needed, or looked ill, or sounded ill; or some other valid reason existed for its exclusion. A lover of his native tongue might well tremble to think what his tongue would have become, if all the innumerable vocables introduced or endorsed by illustrious names, had been admitted to a free course among us on the strength of their recommendation; if 'torve' and 'tetric' (Fuller), 'cecity' (Hooker), 'fastide' and 'trutinate' (*State Papers*), 'immanity' (Shakespeare), 'insulse' and 'insulsity' (Milton, prose), 'scelestick' (Feltham), 'splendidous' (Drayton), 'pervicacy' (Baxter), 'stramineous,' 'ardelion' (Burton), 'lepid,' 'sufflaminate' (Barrow), 'facinorous' (Donne), 'immorigerous,' 'funest' 'clancular,' 'ferity,' 'ustulation,' 'stultiloquy,' 'lipothymy' (λειποθυμία) 'hyperaspist'

---

meable' (*Æn.* vi. 575) is the only one which I could adduce at the instant.

'deturpate,' 'intenerate,' 'effigiate' (all in Jeremy
Taylor), if 'mulierosity,' 'subsannation,' 'coaxation,'
'ludibundness,' 'delinition,' 'sanguinolency,' 'sep-
temfluous,' 'medioxumous,' 'mirificent,' 'palmifer-
ous' (all in Henry More), 'pauciloquy,' 'multiloquy'
(Beaumont, *Psyche*); if 'dyscolous' (Foxe), 'ata-
raxy' (Allestree), 'moliminously' (Cudworth), 'lu-
ciferously,'. 'meticulous,' 'lapidifical,' 'exenteration,'
'farraginous' (Sir Thomas Browne), 'immarcescible'
(Bishop Hall), 'exility,' 'spinosity,' 'incolumity,'
'solertiousness,' 'lucripetous,' 'inopious,' 'eximious,'
'eluctate' (all in Hacket), 'arride' (ridiculed by
Ben Jonson), with hundreds of other births, as monstrous or more monstrous than are some of these, had
not been rejected and disallowed by the sound linguistic instincts of the national mind.

Many words too *were* actually adopted, but not
precisely as they had been first introduced among us.
They were compelled to drop their foreign termination, or whatever else indicated them as strangers, to
conform themselves to English ways, and only thus
were finally incorporated into the great family of English.* Thus of Greek words take the following :
'pyramis' and 'pyramides,' forms often employed by
Shakespeare ('pyramises' in Jeremy Taylor), became
'pyramid' and 'pyramids ;' 'dosis' (Bacon) 'dose ;'

---

* J. Grimm (*Woerterbuch*, p. xxvi.) : Fällt von ungefähr ein
fremdes Wort in den Brunnen einer Sprache, so wird es so
lange darin umgetrieben, bis es ihre Farbe annimmt, und seiner
fremden Art zum trotze wie ein Heimisches aussieht.

'aspis' (Latimer) 'asp;' 'distichon' 'distich' (Holland), 'aristocratia' and 'democratia' (the same)
'aristocracy' and 'democracy;' 'hemistichon'(North)
'hemistich;' 'apogæon' (Fairfax) or 'apogeum'
(Browne) 'apogee;' 'sumphonia' (Lodge) 'sym-
phony;' 'myrrha' (Golding) 'myrrh;' 'prototypon'
(Jackson) 'prototype;' 'synonymon' (Jeremy
Taylor) or 'synonymum' (Hacket), and 'synonyma'
(Milton, prose), became severally 'synonym' and
'synonyms;' 'parallelon' (North) 'parallel;' 'syn-
taxis' (Fuller) became 'syntax;' 'extasis' (Burton)
'ecstasy;' 'parallelogrammon' (Holland) 'parallel-
ogram;' 'programma' (Warton) 'program;' 'epi-
theton' (Cowell) 'epithet;' 'epocha' (South)
'epoch;' 'disenteria' and 'epilepsis' (both in Sylvester) 'dysentery' and 'epilepsy;' 'biographia'
(Dryden) 'biography;' 'apostata' (Massinger)
'apostate;' 'despota' (Fox) 'despot;' 'misanthro-
pos' (Shakespeare, &c., 'misanthropi,' Bacon) 'mis-
anthrope;' 'psalterion' (North) 'psaltery;' 'chasma'
(Henry More) 'chasm;' 'idioma' and 'prosodia'
(both in Daniel, prose) 'idiom' and 'prosody;'
'energia' (Sidney) 'energy,' 'Sibylla' (Bacon)
'Sibyl; 'zoophyton' (Henry More) 'zoophyte;'
'enthouslasmos' (Sylvester) 'enthusiasm;' 'phan-
tasma' (Shakespeare) 'phantasm;' 'paraphrasis' ·
(Ascham) 'paraphrase;' 'magnes' (Gabriel Harvey)
'magnet;' 'cynosura' (Donne) 'cynosure;' 'galax-
ias' (Fox) 'galaxy; 'heros' (Henry More) 'hero.
The same process has gone on in a multitude of
Latin words which testify by their terminations that

they were, and were felt to be, Latin at their first employment; though now they are such no longer. It will be seen that in this list I include Greek words which came to us through the medium of the Latin, and witH a Latin termination. Thus Bacon has ' insecta' for 'insects;' æquinoctia' for 'equinoxes;' 'chylus' for 'chyle ;' Coverdale 'tetrarcha' for 'tetrarch ;' Latimer 'basiliscus' for 'basilisk ;' Frith 'syllogiśmus' for syllogism ;' Bishop Andrews 'nardus' for 'nard ;' Milton 'asphaltus' for 'asphalt ;' Clarendon 'classis' for 'class ;' Spenser 'zephyrus' for 'zephyr.' So too 'dactylus' (Ascham) preceded 'dactyle ;' 'interstitium' (Fuller) 'interstice ;' 'philtrum' (Culverwell) 'philtre ;' 'expansum' (Jeremy Taylor) 'expanse ;' 'vestigium' (Culverwell) 'vestige ;' 'preludium' (Beaumont, *Psyche*) 'prelude ;' 'precipitium' (Coryat) 'precipice ;' 'aconitum' and 'balsamum' (both in Shakespeare) 'aconite' and 'balsam ;' 'idyllium' (Dryden) 'idyl ;' 'heliotropium' (Holland) 'heliotrope ;' 'helleborum' (North) 'hellebore ;' 'vehiculum' (Howe) 'vehicle ;' 'trochæus' and 'spondæus' (Holland) 'trochee' and 'spondee ;' 'transitus' (Howe) 'transit ;' and 'machina' (Henry More) 'machine.' We meet 'intervalla,' not 'intervals,' in Chillingworth ; 'postulata,' not 'postulates,' in Swift ; 'archiva,' not 'archives,' in Baxter ; 'adulti,' not 'adults,' in Rogers ; 'plebeii,' not 'plebeians,' in Shakespeare ; 'helotæ,' not 'helots,' in Holland ; 'triumviri,' not 'triumvirs,' in North ; 'demagogi,' not 'demagogues,' in Hacket ; 'elegi,' not 'elegies,' in Holland ;

'pantomimus' in Lord Bacon and Ben Jonson for 'pantomime;' 'mystagogus' for 'mystagogue,' in Jackson and Henry More; 'atomi' in Lord Brooke for 'atoms.' In like manner, 'ædilis' (North) went before 'edile;' 'effigies' and 'statua' (both in Shakespeare) before 'effigy' and 'statue;' 'abyssus' (Jackson) before 'abyss;' 'postscripta' (*State Papers*) before 'postscript;' 'commentarius' (Chapman) before 'commentary;' 'vestibulum' (Howe) before 'vestibule;' 'symbolum' (Hammond) before 'symbol;' 'spectrum' (Burton) before 'spectre;' while only after a while 'quære' gave place to 'query;' 'audite' (Hacket) to 'audit;' 'plaudite' (Henry More) to 'plaudit;' 'remanent' (*Paston Letters*) to 'remnant;' and the low Latin 'mummia' (Webster) became 'mummy.' The change of 'innocency,' 'indolency,' 'temperancy,' and the large family of words with the same termination, into 'innocence,' 'indolence,' 'temperance,' and the like, is part of the same process of completed naturalization. So too it is curious to note how slowly the names of persons drop their Greek or Latin, and assume an English, form. Aristotle indeed had so lived through the Middle Ages that we nowhere find his name in any but this popular shape; but Ascham speaks of 'Hesiodus,' Bacon of 'Sallustius,' 'Appianus,' 'Livius,' Milton of 'Pindarus,' and this in prose no less than verse. It is the same with places. North writes 'Creta' and 'Syracusæ,' Ascham 'Sicilia;' while our English Bible has 'Palestina,' 'Grecia,' 'Tyrus.'

Spenser speaks of the 'Ilias and 'Odysseis,' and
Dryden, not indeed always of the 'Æneis.'
The plural very often tells the secret of the foreign
light in which a word is still regarded, when the singular, being less capable of modification, would have
failed to do this. Thus when Holland writes 'pha-
langes,' 'bisontes,' 'archontes,' 'sphinges,' 'ideæ,' it
is clear that 'phalanx,' 'bison,' 'archon,' 'sphinx,'
'idea,' had in no sense become English, but continued
Greek words for him ; as was 'rhinoceros' for Purchas,
when he wrote 'rhinocerotes' for the plural ; and
'dogma' for Hammond, when he made 'dogmata'
the plural.* In the same way Spenser using 'heroës'
as a trisyllable,† plainly implies that it is not yet
thoroughly English for him ; indeed, as we have just
seen, the singular was 'heros' half a century later.
'Cento' is no English word, but a Latin one used in
English, so long as the plural is not 'centos,' but
'centones,' as in the old anonymous translation of
Augustin's *City of God;* 'specimen' in like manner
is Latin, so long as it owns the plural 'specimina'
(Howe) ; so too 'asylum,' so long as its plural is
'asyla,' as in Clarendon it is. Pope employing
'satellites' as a quadrisyllable—

---

* Have we here an explanation of the 'battalia' of Jeremy
Taylor and others ? Did they, without reflecting on the matter,
regard 'battalion' as word with a Greek neuter termination?
It is difficult to think so ; yet more difficult to suggest any
other explanation.

   †   'And old *heroes*, which their world did daunt.'

Sonnet on Scanderbeg.

'Why Jove's *satellites* are less than Jove '—

intimates that it is still Latin for him ; just as 'ter-
minus,' which the necessities of railways have introduced among us, will not be truly naturalized till it
has 'terminuses,' and not 'termini' for a plural ;
nor 'phenomenon,' till we have renounced 'phenomena ;' nor 'crisis,' while it makes 'crises.' Sometimes both plurals have been retained, with only the
assignment of different meanings to them, as in the
case of 'indices' and 'indexes,' of 'genii' and
'geniuses,' of 'stamina' and 'stamens' (botanical).
    The same process has gone on with words from
other languages, as from the Italian and the Spanish ;
thus 'bandetto' (Shakespeare), or 'bandito' (Jeremy
Taylor), becomes 'bandit ;' 'porcellana' (so we read
it in Fuller) becomes 'porcelain ;' 'ruffiano' (Coryat),
'ruffian ;' 'concerto' 'concert ;' 'busto' (Lord Chesterfield) 'bust ;' 'caricatura' (Sir Thomas Browne)
'caricature ;' 'princessa' (Hacket) 'princess ;' 'scara-
mucha'.(Dryden) 'scaramouch ;' 'pedante' (Bacon)
'pedant ;' 'pedanteria' (Sidney) 'pedantry ;' 'mascarata' (Hacket) 'masquerade ;' 'impresa' 'impress ;'
'caprichio' (Shakespeare) becomes first 'caprich'
(Butler), then 'caprice ;' 'duello' (Shakespeare)
'duel ;' 'alligarta' (Ben Jonson) 'alligator ;' 'parro-
quito' (Webster 'parroquet.' Not otherwise 'scalada'
(Heylin) or 'escalado' (Holland) becomes 'escalade ;'
'granada' (Hacket) 'grenade ;' 'parada' (Jeremy
Taylor) 'parade ;' 'emboscado' (Holland) 'stoccado,'
'barricado,' 'renegado,' 'hurricano' (all in Shake-

speare), 'brocado' (Hackluyt), 'palissado' (Howell),
these all drop their foreign terminations, and severally
become 'ambuscade,' 'stockade,' 'barricade,' 'renegade,' 'hurricane,' 'brocade,' 'palisade ;' 'croisado'
(Bacon) in like manner becomes first 'croisade'
(Jortin), and then 'crusade ;' 'quinaquina' or 'quin-
quina,' 'quinine.' Other modifications of spelling,
not always in the termination, but in the body of a
word, will indicate its more entire incorporation into
the English language. Thus 'shash,' a Turkish word,
becomes 'sash ;' 'tulippa' (Bacon) 'tulip ;' 'quel-
ques choses,' 'kickshaws ;' 'restoration' was at first
spelt 'restauration ;' and so long as 'vicinage' was
spelt 'voisinage' * (Sanderson), 'mirror' 'miroir'
(Fuller), 'recoil' 'recule,' 'voyage' 'viage,' and
'career' 'carriere' (all by Holland), they could
scarcely be esteemed the thoroughly English words
which now they are.

Here and there even at this later period awkward
foreign words will have been recast in a more
thoroughly English mould ; 'chirurgeon' will become
'surgeon ;' 'hemorrhoid' 'emerod ;' 'squinancy,'
first 'squinzey' (Jeremy Taylor), and then 'quinsey ;'
'porkpisce' (Spenser), or hogfish, will be 'porpesse,'
and then 'porpoise,' as now. Yet the attempt will
not always be successful. 'Physiognomy' will not
give place to 'visnomy,' though Spenser and Shake-

---

* Skinner (*Etymologicon*, 1671) protests against the word
altogether, as purely French, and having no right to be considered English at all.

speare employ this familiar form ; nor 'hippopotamus'
to 'hippodame' at Spenser's bidding ; nor 'avant-
courier' to 'vancurrier' at Shakespeare's.   Other
words also have finally refused to take a more popular
shape, although such was current once.   Chaucer
wrote 'sawter' and 'sawtrie,' but we 'psalter' and
'psaltery ;' Holland 'cirque,' revived by Keats, but
we 'circus ;' 'cense,' but we ' 'census ;' 'interreign,'
but we 'interregnum ;' Sylvester 'cest,' but we
'cestus ;' 'quirry,' but we 'equerry ;' 'colosse' (so
also Henry More), but we 'colossus ;' Golding 'ure,'
but we 'urus ;' 'metropole,' but we 'metropolis ;'
Dampier 'volcan,' but this has not superseded 'vol-
cano ;' nor 'pagod' (Pope) 'pagoda ;' nor 'skelet'
(Holland) 'skeleton ;' nor 'stimule' (Stubbs) 'stimu-
lus.'   Bolingbroke wrote 'exode,' but we hold fast to
'exodus ;' Burton 'funge,' but we 'fungus ;' Henry
More 'enigm,' but we 'enigma ;' and 'analyse,' but
we 'analysis.'   'Superfice' (Dryden) has not put
'superficies,' nor 'sacrary' (Hacket) 'sacrarium,'·
nor 'limbeck' 'alembic,' out of use.   Chaucer's
'potecary' has given place to a more Greek formation, 'apothecary ;' so has 'ancre' to 'anchorite,'
'auntre' to 'adventure.'   Yet these are exceptions ;
the set of language is all in the other direction.

   Looking at this process of the reception of foreign
words, with their after assimilation in feature to our own,
we may trace a certain conformity between the genius
of our institutions and that of our language.   It is the
very character of our institutions to repel none, but
rather to afford a shelter and a refuge to all, from what-

ever quarter they come ; and after a longer or shorter while all the strangers and incomers have been incorporated into the English nation, within one or two generations have forgotten that they were ever extraneous to it, have retained no other reminiscence of their foreign extraction than some slight difference of name, and that often disappearing or having disappeared. Exactly so has it been with the English language. No language has shown itself less exclusive ; none has stood less upon niceties ; none has thrown open its doors wider, with a fuller confidence that it could make truly its own, assimilate and subdue to itself, whatever it received into its bosom ; and in none has this confidence been more fully justified by the result.

Such are the two great augmentations from without of our vocabulary. All other are minor and subordinate. Thus the Italian influence has been far more powerful on our literature than on our language. In Chaucer it makes itself very strongly felt on the former,* but very slightly upon the latter ; and, as compared with that of French, it may be counted as none at all. And this remained very much the condition of things for the whole period during which the star of Italy was in the ascendant here. When we consider how potent its influences were, and how long they lasted, it is only surprising that the deposit left in the language has not been larger. There was

---

* See Kessner, *Chaucer in seinen Beziehungen zur Italienischen Literatur*, Bonn, 1867.

a time when Italian was far more studied in England, and Italian books far more frequently translated, than they are at this present. Thus Ascham complains of the immense number of wicked Italian books, such as those of that 'poisonous Italian ribald,' Aretine, which were rendered into English ; * and it is not less abundantly evident that for a period extending from the reign of Henry the Eighth to the end of that of Elizabeth, it more concerned an accomplished courtier and man of the world to be familiar with Italian than with French.

Almost every page of Spenser bears witness to his intimate acquaintance with Ariosto, and with his own contemporary, Tasso. His sonnets are 'amoretti.' In the choice of names for persons in his *Fairy Queen*, such as Orgoglio, Archimago, Braggadocchio, Malbecco, Fradubio, Gardante, Parlante, Jocante, Fidessa, Duessa, Dispetto, Difetto, Speranza, Humiltà, and the like, he assumes the same familiarity with the language of Italy on the part of his readers. He introduces words purely Italian, as 'basciomani' (handkissings), 'capuccio' (hood), or only not Italian, because clipped of their final letter, as 'maltalent' for ill will, 'intendiment' for understanding, 'forniment' for furniture ; or words formed on Italian models, as 'to aggrate' (aggratare), and sometimes only intelligible when referred to their Italian source, as 'affret' (=encounter), from 'affrettare,' 'to affrap,' the Italian 'affrappare ;' or words

* *The Schoolmaster*, edited by Rev. J. E. Mayor, 1863, p. 82.

employed not in our sense, but altogether in an Italian, as 'to revolt' in that of 'rivoltare' (*F. Q.* iii. 11, 25).

Milton in his prose works frequently avouches the peculiar affection to the Italian literature and language which he bore, so that, next to those of Greece and of Rome, he was most addicted to these.* And his poetry without such declarations would itself attest the same. He too calls his poems by Italian names, '*L'Allegro,*' '*Il Penseroso.*' His diction is enriched with Italian words, as 'gonfalon,' 'libecchio,' or with words formed on Italian models, as ' to imparadise,' which beautiful word, however, was not of his invention ; he employs words in their Italian, not their English acceptation ; thus 'to assassinate,' in the sense not of to kill, but grievously to maltreat. His adjectival use of 'adorn,' as equivalent to 'adorned,' he must have justified by the Italian 'adorno ;' so too his employment of 'to force' in that of 'sforzare,' to vanquish or reduce (*S. A.* 1096). His orthography, departing from the usual, approximates to the Italian ; thus he writes 'ammiral' (ammiraglio) for admiral,' 'haralt' (araldo) for herald, 'gonfalon' for gonfanon,' sovran' (sovrano) for sovereign ; 'desertrice' (prose) where another would have written desertress. 'Soldan,' for sultan, he has in common with others who went before him ; so too

---

* Thus see his beautiful letter *Benedicto Bonmatthico, Florentino.*

'to 'sdeign,' a form no doubt suggested by the Italian 'sdegnare.'

Jeremy Taylor's acquaintance with Italian, even if it were not asserted in his *Funeral Sermon*, with his assumption of the same acquaintance on the part of his readers, is testified by his frequent use of Italian proverbs and Italian words. He sometimes gives these an English shape, as 'to picqueer' in the sense of to skirmish ; but oftener leaves them in their own. It would be easy to gather out of his writings a considerable collection of these ; such as 'amorevolezza,' 'grandezza,' 'sollevamento,' 'avisamente,' 'incurabili' (can it be that 'incurables,' was in his time wanting in our language?) ; while, scattered up and down our literature of the first half of the seventeenth century, we meet other Italian words not a few ; as 'farfalla' for butterfly (Dubartas) ; 'amorevolous,' 'mascarata,' 'gratioso' (=favourite), 'bugiard' (=liar), all in Hacket, 'leggiadrous,' in Beaumont's *Psyche* and elsewhere. A list, as complete as I could make it, of such as have finally obtained a place in the language was given in my first lecture ; * they are above a hundred, and doubtless many have escaped me.

There is abundant evidence that Spanish was during the latter half of the sixteenth and the first half of the seventeenth century very widely known in England, indeed far more familiar than it ever since has been. The wars in the Low Countries, in which so many of

---

* See p. 16.

our countrymen served, the probabilities at one period
of a match with Spain, the fact that Spanish was
almost as serviceable at Brussels, at Milan, at Naples,
and for a time at Vienna, not to speak of Lima
and Mexico, as at Madrid itself, and scarcely less
indispensable, the many points of contact, friendly
and hostile, of England with Spain for well-nigh a
century, all this had conduced to an extended knowledge of Spanish in England.   It was popular at
court.   Queen Mary and Queen Elizabeth were both
excellent Spanish scholars.   A passage in Howell's
Letters would imply that at the time of Charles the
First's visit to Madrid, his Spanish was imperfect,
and Clarendon affirms the same ; but at a later date,
that is in 1635, a Spanish play was acted by a Spanish
company before him.   The statesmen and scholars of
the time were rarely ignorant of the language.   We
might have confidently presumed Raleigh's acquaintance with it ; but in his *Discovery of Guiana* and
other writings there is abundant proof of this.   Lord
Bacon gives similar evidence, in the Spanish proverbs
which he quotes, and in the skilful employment
which he sometimes makes of a Spanish word.*   It was
among the many accomplishments of Archbishop
Williams, who, when the Spanish match was pending,
caused the English Liturgy to be translated under his
own eye into Spanish.   Whether Shakespeare's knowledge of the language was not limited to the few chance
words which occasionally he introduces, as ' palabras,'

---

* As for instance of ' desenvoltura ' in his Essay, *Of Fortune.*

'passado,' 'duello,' it is difficult to say. But Jonson's familiarity with it is evident. More than once, as in *The Alchemist* (Act iv. Sc. 2), he introduces so large an amount of Spanish that he must have assumed this would not be altogether strange to his audience. Of the Spanish words which have effected a settlement in English, so far as I know them, I have given a list already.* ⓑ

The introduction of French tastes by Charles the Second and his courtiers returning from their enforced residence abroad, rather modified the structure of our sentences than seriously affected our vocabulary ; yet it gave us some new words. In one of· Dryden's plays, *Marriage à la Mode*, a lady shows her affectation by constantly employing French idioms in .preference to English, French words rather than native. Curiously enough, of these, thus put into her mouth to render her ridiculous, several, as 'repartee,' 'grimace,' 'chagrin,' to be in the 'good graces' of another, are excellent English now, and have nothing far-sought or affected about them : for so it frequently proves that what is laughed at in the beginning, is by all admitted and allowed at the last. 'Fougue' and 'fraischeur,' which Dryden himself employed—being, it is true, a very rare offender in this line, and for 'fraischeur' having Scotch if not English authority— have not been justified by the same success.

Nor indeed can it be said that this adoption and naturalization of foreign words has ever wholly ceased.

---

* See page 17.

There are periods, as we have seen, when a language throws open its doors, and welcomes strangers with an especial freedom ; but there is never a time, when one by onē these foreigners and strangers are not slipping into it. The process by which they do this eludes for the most part our observation. Time, the greatest of all innovators, manages his innovations so dexterously, spreads them over periods so immense, and is thus able to bring them about so gradually, that often, while he is effecting the mightiest changes, we have no suspicion that he is effecting any at all. Thus how nearly imperceptible are the steps by which a foreign word is admitted into the full rights of an English one. Many Greek words, for example, quite unchanged in form, have in one way or another ended in obtaining a home and acceptance among us. We may in almost every instance trace step by step the stealthy naturalization of these. We may note them spelt for a while in Greek letters, and avowedly employed as Greek and not English vocables. Having .thus won a certain allowance, and ceased to be altogether unfamiliar, we note them next exchanging Greek for English letters, and finally obtaining recognition as words which, however drawn from a foreign source, are yet themselves English. Thus ' acme,' ' apotheosis,' ' euthanasia,' ' iota,' ' criterion,' ' chrysalis,' ' dogma,' ' encyclopædia,' ' metropolis,' ' ophthalmia,' ' phenomenon,' ' pathos,' are all English now, while yet South with many others always wrote ἀκμή, Jeremy Taylor ἀποθέωσις, εὐθανασία, ἰῶτα, Cudworth κριτήριον, Henry More χρυσαλίς; Ham-.

mond speaks of δόγματα, Ben Jonson of 'the knowledge of the liberal arts, which the Greeks call
ἐγκυκλοπαιδείαν,* Culverwell writes μητρόπολις
and ὀφθαλμια, Preston φαινόμενα, Sylvester ascribes
to Baxter not 'pathos,' but πάθος.† Ἦθος is at the
present moment preparing for this passage from
Greek characters to English, and certainly before
long will be acknowledged as English.   The only
cause which for some time past has stood in the way
of this is the misgiving whether it will not be read
'ethos,' and not 'ethos,' and thus not be the word
intended.

Let us endeavor to trace this same process in some
French word, which is at this moment gaining a footing among us.   For 'prestige' we have manifestly no
equivalent of our own.   It expresses something which
only by a long circumlocution we could express ;
namely, that real though undefinable influence on
others, which past successes, as the pledge and
promise of future ones, breed.   It has thus naturally

---

* He is not perfectly accurate here ; the Greeks spoke of
ἐν κύκλῳ παιδεία and ἐγκύκλιος παιδεία but had no
such compound word as ἐγκυκλοπαιδεία. We gather, however, from his statement, as from Lord Bacon's use of 'circle-
learning' (='orbis doctrinæ,' Quintilian), that 'encyclopædia'
did not exist in their time.   'Monomania' is in like manner
a modern formation, of which the Greek language knows
nothing.

† See the passages quoted in my paper, *On some Deficiencies
in our English Dictionaries*, p. 38, published separately and in
the *Transactions of the Philological Society*, 1857.

passed into frequent use. No one could feel that in employing it he was slighting as good a word of our own. At first all used it avowedly as French, writing it in italics to indicate this. Some write it so still, others do not ; some, that is, count it still as foreign, others consider that it is not so to be regarded any more.* Little by little the number of those who write it in italics will diminish ; and finally none will do so. It will then only need that the accent be shifted as far back as it will go, for such is the instinct of all English words, that for ' prestíge,' it should be pronounced ' préstige,' even as within these few years for ' depót ' we have learned to say ' dépot,' and its naturalization will be complete. I have no doubt that before many years it will be so pronounced by the majority of educated Englishmen,—some pronounce it so already,—and that the pronunciation common now will pass away, just as ' obleege,' once universal, has everywhere given place to ' oblige.'†

* We trace a similar progress in Greek words which were passing into Latin. Thus Cæsar (*B. G.* iii. 103), writes, quæ Græci ἄδυτα appellant ; but Horace (*Carm.* i. 16. 5), non *adytis* quatit. In like manner Cicero writes ἀντιποδες (*Acad.* ii. 39. 123), but Seneca (*Ep.* 122), ' antipodes ;' that is, the word for Cicero was still Greek, while in the period that elapsed between him and Seneca, it had become Latin. So too ·Cicero writes εἴδωλον, but the Younger Pliny ' idolon,' and ·Tertullian ' idolum ;' Cicero στρατήγημα (*N. D.* 3. 6), but Valerius Maximus ' strategema.'

† See in Coleridge's *Table Talk*, p. 3, the amusing story of John Kemble's stately correction of the Prince of Wales for adhering to the earlier pronunciation, ' obleege,'—' It will become your royal mouth better to say oblige.'

III. *Shifting of Accents.* 129

I observe in passing, that the process of throwing the accent of a word as far back as it will go, is one which has been constantly proceeding among us. In the time and writings of Chaucer there was much vacillation in the placing of the accent; as was to be expected, while the adoptions from the French were comparatively recent, and had not yet unlearned their foreign ways or made themselves perfectly at home among us. Some of his French words are still accented on the final syllable, thus ' honoúr,' ' creatúre,' ' senténce,' ' penánce,' ' beauté,' ' manére,' ' servíce ;' others, as ' trésour,' ' cólour,' ' cónseil,' on the first ; while this vacillation displays itself still more markedly in the fact that the same word is accented by him sometimes on the one syllable, and sometimes upon the other ; he writing at one time ' natúre' and at another nát.ure,' at one time ' vertúe' and at another ' vértue ;' so too ' vísage' and ' viságe,' ' fórtune' and ' fortúne ;' ' sérvice,' and ' servíce,' with many more. The same disposition to throw back the accent is visible in later times. Thus ' preságe,' ' captíve,' ' envy,' ' cruél,' ' trespáss,' ' forést,' in Spenser, and these, ' prostráte,' ' advérse,' ' aspéct,' ' procéss,' ' instínct,' ' insúlt,' ' impúlse,' ' pretéxt,' ' contríte,' ' surfáce,' ' prodúct,' ' upróar,' ' edíct,' ' contést,' in Milton, had all their accent once on the last syllable ; they have it now on the first. So too, ' acádemy' was ' académy ' for Cowley and for Butler ;* while ' théatre'

---

* In this great *académy* of mankind.'
To the Memory of Du Val.

was 'theátre' with Sylvester, this American pronunciation being archaic and not vulgar. 'Próduce'
was 'prodúce' for Dryden : 'éssay' was 'essáy' both
for him and for Pope; he closes heroic lines with both
these words; Pope does the same with 'barríer'* and
'effórt.' We may note the same process going forward still. Middle-aged men may remember that it
was a question in their youth whether it should be
'revénue' or 'révenue ;' it is always 'révenue' now.
'Contémplate' has in like manner given way to 'cón-
template.' Rogers bewailed the change which had
taken place in his memory from 'balcóny' to 'bálcony.' 'Bálcony,' he complains, 'makes me sick ;'
but it has effectually won the day. Nor is it, I think,
difficult to explain how this should be. The speaker,
conscious that somewhere or other the effort must be
made, is glad to have it over as soon as possible.
'Apostólic,' which in Dryden's use was 'apóstolic'
(he ends an heroic line with it), is a rare instance of
the accent moving in the opposite direction.

Other French words not a few, besides 'prestige'
which I instanced just now, are at this moment
hovering on the confines of English, hardly knowing
whether they shall become such altogether or not.
Such are 'ennui,' 'exploitation,' 'verve,' 'persiflage,'
'badinage,' 'chicane,' 'finesse,' 'mêlée' (Tennyson
already spells it 'mellay'), and others. All these are
often employed by us,—and it is out of such frequent
employment that adoption proceeds,—because ex-

---

* ' 'Twixt that and reason what a nice bar*rier*.'

pressing shades of meaning not expressed by any words of our own. Some of them will no doubt complete their naturalization; others will after a time retreat again, like some which were named just now, and become for us once more avowedly French. 'Solidarity,' which we owe to the French Communists,—it signifies a fellowship in gain and loss, in honour and dishonour, in victory and defeat, a being, so to speak, all in the same boat,—is so convenient that it would be idle to struggle against it. It has established itself in German, and in other European languages as well.

Or take an example of this progressive naturalization from another quarter. In an English glossary, of date 1671, I do not find 'tea,' but 'cha,' 'the leaf of a tree in China, which being infused into water, serves for their ordinary drink.' Thirteen years later the word is no longer a Chinese one, but already a French one for us; Locke in his *Diary* writing it 'thé,' Early in the next century the word is spelt in an entirely English fashion, in fact as we spell it now, but still retains a foreign pronunciation,—Pope rhymes it with 'obey,'—and this it has only lately altogether let go.

- Greek.and Latin words we still continue to adopt, although now no longer in troops and companies, but only one by one. The lively interest which always has been felt in classical studies among us, and which will continue to be felt, so long as Englishmen present to themselves a high culture of their faculties and powers as an object of ambition, so long as models of what is truest and loveliest in . art have any attraction for them, is itself a pledge that accessions from these quarters can never cease altogether. I refer not here to purely scientific terms; these, so long as they do not pass beyond the threshold of the science for whose use they were invented, have no proper right to be called words at all. They are a kind of shorthand, or algebraic notation of the science to which they belong ; and will find no place in a dictionary constructed upon true principles, but will constitute rather a technical dictionary by themselves. They are oftentimes drafted into a dictionary of the language ; but this for the most part out of a barren ostentation, and that so there may be room for boasting of the many thousand words by which it excels all its predecessors. But such additions are very cheaply made. Nothing is easier than to turn to modern treatises on chemistry or electricity, or on some other of the sciences which hardly existed, or did not at all exist, half a century ago, or which have been in later times wholly new-named—as botany, for example,—and to transplant new terms from these by the hundred and the thousand, with which to crowd and deform the pages of a dictionary. The labour is little more than that of transcription ; but the gain is nought ; or indeed is much less than nought ; for it is not merely that half a dozen genuine English words recovered from our old authors would be a truer gain, a more real advance toward the complete inventory of the wealth which we possess in words than a hundred or a thousand of these ; but additions of this kind are mere disfigurements of the work which they profess to complete.

When we call to mind the near affinity between English and German, which, if not sisters, are at any rate first cousins, it is remarkable that almost since the day when they parted company, each to fulfil its own destiny, there has been little further commerce, little giving or taking, between them. Adoptions on our part from the German have been extremely rare. The explanation of this lies no doubt in the fact that the literary activity of Germany did not begin till very late, nor our interest in it till later still, nor indeed till the beginning of the present century. Literature, however, is not the only channel by which words pass from one language to another; thus 'plunder' was brought back from Germany about the beginning of our Civil War by the soldiers who had served under Gustavus Adolphus and his captains; while 'trigger' ('tricker' in *Hudibras*), which reached us at the same time, and by the same channel, is manifestly the German 'drücker,' though none of our dictionaries have marked it as such. 'Crikesman' ('kriegsmann'), common enough in the *State Papers* of the sixteenth century, found no permanent place in the language; and 'brandshat' ('brandschatz'), being the ransom paid to an enemy for *not* burning down your house or your city, as little. 'Iceberg' we must have taken whole from the German, since a word of our own construction would have been not 'ice-*berg*,' but 'ice-*mountain*.' I have not met with it in our earlier voyagers. An English 'swindler' is not exactly a

German 'schwindler;' yet a subaudition of the knave, though more latent in German, is common to both; and we must have drawn the word from Germany (it is not in Johnson) late in the last century. Why, by the way, do we not adopt 'shwärmer'? 'Enthusiast' does not in the least supply its place. If '*life*guard' was originally, as Richardson suggests, '*leib*garde,' or '*body*-guard,' and from that transformed, by the determination of Englishmen to make in significant in English, into '*life*-guard,' or guard defending the *life* of the sovereign, this will be another word from the same quarter. Yet I have my doubts; 'leibgarde' would scarcely have found its way hither before the accession of the House of Hanover, or at any rate before the arrival of William with his memorable Guards; while 'life-guard,' in its present shape, is older in the language; we hear often of the 'life-guards' during our Civil War; and Fuller writes, 'The Cherethites were a kind of *lifegard* to king David.' *

There is only one province of words in which we are recent debtors to the Germans to any considerable extent. Of the terms used by the mineralogist many have been borrowed, and in comparatively modern times, from them; thus 'quartz,' 'felspar,' 'cobalt,' nickel,' 'zinc,' 'hornblend;' while other of the terms employed by us are a direct translation from the same; such for instance as 'fuller's earth' (walkererde), 'pipeclay' (pfeifenthon), 'pitchstone' (pechstein.)

---

* *Pisgah Sight of Palestine*, 1650, p. 217.

Of very recent importations I hardly know one˙; unless, indeed, we adopt the ingenious suggestion that ' to loaf ' and ' loafer,' which not very long ago arrived in England by way of America, are the German ' laufen ' and ' läufer.'

But if we have not imported, we have been somewhat given of late to the copying of, German words, that is to the forming of words of our own on the scheme and model of some, which having taken our fancy, we have thought to enrich our own vocabulary with the like.   I cannot consider that we have always been very happy in those thus selected for imitation.   Possessing ' manual,' we need not have called ' hand-book ' back from an oblivion of nine hundred years ; and one can only regret that ' standpoint' has succeeded in forcing itself on the language. ' Einseitig ' (itself modern, if I mistake not), is the pattern on which we have formed ' one-sided '—a word to which a few years ago something of affectation was attached ; none using it save those who dealt more or less in German wares ; it has however its manifest conveniences, and will hold its ground ; so too, as it seems, will ' fatherland,' though a certain note of affectation cleaves to it still.   The happiest of these compounded words, of which the hint has been taken from the German, is ' folk-lore ;' the substitution of · this for ' popular superstitions,' is an unquestionable gain.

It is only too easy to be mistaken in such a matter ; but, if I do not err, the following words have all been born during the present century, some within quite

the later decades of this century. A distribution of
them according to the languages from which they are
drawn will show that Greek and Latin are the languages from which at the present day our own is
mainly recruited ; 'abnormal,' 'acrobat,' 'æon,'
'æsthetics' (Tennyson has given allowance to 'æon ;'
but it and 'æsthetics' must both renounce their
initial diphthong, as 'either,' 'economy,' and other.
words have done, before they can be regarded as
quite at home with us) ;* 'bus,' 'cab,' 'clipper,'
'demonetize,' 'demoralize,' 'demoralization,' 'de-
plete,' 'depletion,' 'desirability,' 'dissimilation,' 'educational,' 'eurasian,' 'excursionist,' 'exploitation,' 'ex-
tradition,' 'fatherland,' 'flange,' 'flunkey,' 'folk-lore,'
'garotte,' 'garotter,' 'grandiose,' 'hymnal,' 'immi-
grant,' 'international,' 'linguistic,' 'loot,' 'myth,'
'neutralization,' 'normal,' 'oldster,' 'one-sided,'
'ornamentation,' 'outsider,' 'paraffin,' 'pérvert,'
'photograph,' 'prayerful,' 'pretentious,' 'realistic,'
'recoup,' 'reformatory,' 'reliable,' 'revolver,' 'san-
itary,' 'sensational,' 'shrinkage,' 'shunt,' 'solidarity,'
'squatter,' 'standpoint,' 'statistics,' 'stereotype' (the
word was invented by Didot), 'suggestive,' 'tele-
gram,' 'tourist,' 'transliteration,' 'utilize,' 'utiliza-
tion,' 'watershed.' It must be confessed of several

---

* A writer in the *Philological Museum*, so late as 1832,
p. 369, was doubtful whether 'æsthetics' would establish
itself in the language ; but this it must be confessed to have
done.

among these that we could want them (in the old
sense of 'to want') without the want being very
seriously felt ; others like the last in this list are manifest acquisitions of the language.

LECTURE IV.

GAINS OF THE ENGLISH LANGUAGE.

(CONTINUED.)

TAKING up the subject where in my last lecture I left off, I proceed to enumerate some other sources from which we have made additions to our vocabulary. Of course the period when absolutely new roots are generated will have passed away very long indeed before men begin by a reflective act to take notice of processes going forward in the language which they speak. That pure productive energy, creative we might call it, belongs to times quite out of the ken of history. It is only from materials already existing that it can enrich itself in the later, or historical stages of its development.

This it can do in many ways. And first, it can bring what it has already, two words or more, into new combinations, and form a new word out of these. Much more is wanted here than merely to link them together by a hyphen; they must really coalesce and grow together. Different languages, and even the same language at different epochs of its life, will possess this power in very different degrees. The eminent felicity of the Greek has been always acknowledged. 'The joints of her compounded words,' says Fuller, 'are so naturally oiled, that they run nimbly on the tongue, which makes them, though long, never tedious, because significant.'* Sir Philip Sidney makes the same claim for our English, namely that 'it is particularly happy in the composition of two or three words together, near equal to the Greek.' No one has done more than Milton to justify this praise, or to show what may be effected by this happy marriage of words. Many of his compound epithets, as 'grey-hooded even,' 'coral-paven floor,' 'flowry-kirtled Naiades,' 'golden-wingéd host,'

---

* *Holy State*, b. ii. c. 6. Latin promised at one time to display an almost equal freedom in forming new words by the happy marriage of old. But at the period of its highest culture it seemed possessed with a timidity, which caused it voluntarily to abdicate this with many of its own powers. In the Augustan period we look in vain for epithets like these, both occurring in a single line of Catullus : 'Ubi cerva *silvicultrix*, ubi aper *nemorivagus ;*' or again, as his 'fluenti· sonus' or as the 'imbricitor' of Ennius. Nay, of those compound epithets which the language once had formed, it let numbers drop : 'parcipromus,' 'turpilucricupidus,' and many more, do not extend beyond Plautus. Quintilian (i. 5. 70) : Res tota magis Græcos decet, nobis minus succèdit ; nec id, fieri naturâ puto, sed alienis favemus ; ideoque cum κυρταύχενα mirati sumus, *incurvicervicum* vix a risu defendimus. Elsewhere he complains of the little *generative* power of the Latin. its continual losses being compensated by no equivalent gains (viii. 6. 32) : Deinde, tanquam consummata sint omnia, nihil generare audemus ipsi, quum multa quotidie ab antiquis ficta moriantur. Still the silver age of the language did recover to some extent the abdicated energies of its earlier times, reas· serted among other powers that of combining words, with a certain measure of success.

'Night's drowsy-flighted steeds,' 'tinsel-slippered feet,' '.violet-embroidered vale,' 'dewy-feathered sleep,' 'sky-tinctured grain,' 'vermeil-tinctured lip,' 'amber-dropping hair,' 'night-foundered skiff,' are themselves poems in miniature. Not unworthy to be set beside these are Sylvester's 'opal-coloured morn,' Drayton's 'silver-sanded shore,' Marlowe's 'golden-fingered Ind,' Beaumont and Fletcher's 'golden-tressed Apollo,' Shakespeare's 'heavy-gaited toad,' and Chapman's (for Pope owed it to Chapman) 'rosy-fingered morn.' At the same time combinations like these remain to so great a degree fhe peculiar property of their first author, they so little pass into any further use, that they must rather be regarded as augmentations of its poetical wealth than its linguistic. Such words as 'international,' or as 'folk-lore,' instanced already, are better examples of real additions to our vocabulary. 'International' we owe to Jeremy Bentham, one of the boldest, yet, in the main, least successful among the coiners of new words. But strange and formless as is for the most part this progeny of his brain, he has given us here a word which does such excellent service, that it is difficult to understand how we contrived so long to do without it.

We have further increased our vocabulary by forming new words according to the analogy of formations which in parallel cases have been already allowed. Thus upon the substantives, 'congregation,' 'convention,' were formed 'congregational,' 'conventional;' yet these at a comparatively modern date; 'congregational' first rising up in the Assembly of Divines, or during the time of the Commonwealth.* These having found allowance, the process is repeated, not always with very gratifying results, in the case of other words with the same ending. We are now used to 'educational,' and the word is serviceable enough ; but I can remember when a good many years ago an '*Educational* Magazine' was started, one's first impression was, that a work having to do with education should not thus bear upon its front an offensive, at best a very questionable, novelty in the English language. These adjectives are now multiplying fast. We have 'inflexional,' 'seasonal,' 'denominational,' and on this, in dissenting magazines at least, the monstrous birth,' 'denominationalism ;' 'emotional' is creeping into books ; 'sensational,' name and thing, has found only too ready a welcome among us ; so that it is hard to say whether all words with this termination will not finally generate an adjective. Convenient as you may sometimes find these, you will do well to abstain from all but the perfectly well recognized formations. For as many as have no claim to be arbiters of the language Pope's advice is good, as certainly it is safe, that they be not among the last to use a word which is going out, nor among the first to employ one that is coming in.

'Its,' the anomalously formed genitive of 'it,' was created with the object of removing an inconvenience, which for a while made itself seriously felt in the lan-

---

* *Collection of Scarce Tracts*, edited by Sir W. Scott, vol. vii. p. 91.

guage. The circumstances of the rise of this little word, and of the place which it has secured itself among us, are sufficiently curious to justify a treatment which might seem out of proportion with the importance that it has ; but which none will deem so, who are at all acquainted with the remarkable facts of our language bound up in the story of the word.

Within the last few years attention has been drawn to the circumstance that 'its' is of comparatively recent introduction into the language. The earliest example which has yet been adduced is from Florio's *World of Words*, 1598 ; the next from the translation of Montaigne by the same author, 1603. You will not find it once in our English Bible, the office which it fulfils for us now being there fulfilled either by 'his' (Gen. i. 11 ; Exod. xxxvii. 17 ; Matt. v. 15) or 'her' (Jon. i. 15 ; Rev. xxii. 2), these applied as freely to inanimate things as to persons ; or else by 'thereof' (Gen. iii. 6 ; Ps. lxv. 10) or 'of it' (Dan. vii. 5). Nor may Lev. xxv. 5 be urged as invalidating this assertion, as there will presently be occasion to show. To Bacon 'its' is altogether unknown ; he too had no scruple about using 'his' as a neuter ; as in the following passage : 'Learning hath *his* infancy, when *it* is but beginning and almost childish ; then *his* youth, when *it* is luxuriant and juvenile ; then *his* strength of years, when *it* is solid and reduced ; and lastly *his* old age, when *it* waxeth dry and exhaust.'*
'Its' occurs very rarely in Shakespeare, in far the

* *Essay* 58.

larger number of his plays not once ; indeed, all counted, I do not believe more than ten times in the whole ; though singularly enough, three of these uses occur in one speech of twelve lines in *The Winter's Tale.** Milton for the most part avoids it ; yet we find it a few times in his poetry.†

It is not hard to trace the motives which led to the generation of this genitive, or the causes which have enabled it against much tacit opposition to hold its own. A manifest inconvenience attended the employment of 'his' both for masculine and neuter, or to speak more accurately, for persons and for things ; this namely, that the personifying power of 'his,' no unimportant power for the poet, was seriously impaired, almost destroyed thereby. It would be often difficult, nay impossible, to determine whether such a personification was intended or not ; and even where the context made perfectly evident that such *was* meant, the employment of the same form where

---

* Act 1. Sc. 2.

† As in *P. L.* i. 254 ; iv. 813. At the same time it is employed by him so rarely, that the use of it four times in the little poem which has been recently ascribed to him, seems to me of itself nearly decisive against his authorship. It is worth while, however, to see what has been said on the other side in Mr. Morley's *The King and the Commons*. Unluckily, neither Mrs. Cowden Clarke, to whom we owe so invaluable a Concordance of Shakespeare's *Plays* (but why not of his *Poems* as well ?) nor Mr. Prendergast, to whom we are indebted for one of Milton's *Poetical Works*, were aware of the importance of registering the very rare occurrences of 'its' in either author, and we look in vain for any notice of the word in them.

nothing of the kind was intended, contributed greatly to diminish its effect. Craik has noticed as a consequence of this that Milton prefers, wherever it is possible, the feminine to the masculine personification,* as if he felt that the latter was always obscure from the risk of 'his' being taken for the neuter pronoun. There was room too for other confusions. When we read of the Ancient of Days, that '*his* throne was like the fiery flame, and *his* wheels as burning fire' (Dan. vii. 9), who does not now refer the second 'his' as well as the first to 'the Ancient of Days'? It indeed belongs to the throne.

So strongly had these and other inconveniences made themselves felt, that there was already, and had been for a long while, a genitival employment of 'it,' whereby it was made to serve all the uses which 'its' served at a later day. In some dialects, in the West Midland for example, this dates very far back.† We have one example of 'it,' so used, in the Authorized Version of Scripture, Lev. xxv. 5 : 'That which groweth of *it* own accord thou shalt not reap'—which has silently been changed in later editions to '*its* own accord ;' but 'it' was the reading in the exemplar edition of 1611, and for a considerable time following. Exactly the same phrase, 'of *it* own accord,' occurs in the Geneva Version at Acts xii. 10.‡ There are

---

* Thus, see *P. L.* ii. 4, 175, 584; ix. 1103 ; *Comus,* 396, 468.

† See Guest, *Hist. of English Rhythms,* vol. i. p. 280.

‡ And also in Hooker, *Eccles. Pol.* i. 3, 5. In Keble's edition this is printed 'of *its* own accord.' Were this the

several examples, thirteen have been counted, of this
use of ' it ' in Shakespeare ; thus in *The Winter's Tale*,
iii. 2 : 'The innocent milk in *it* most innocent
mouth ;' and again in *King John*, ii. 3 : 'Go to *it*
grandame.' And they are by no means unfrequent
in other writers of the earlier half of the seventeenth
century. Thus in Rogers' *Naaman the Syrian*, published in 1642, but the lectures delivered some eight
years earlier, 'its' nowhere occurs, but a genitival
' it' often ; thus, 'I am at this mark, to withdraw the
soul from the life of *it* own hand' (*Preface*, p. 1) ;
and again, 'The power of the Spirit is such that it
blows at *it* own pleasure' (p. 441) ; and again, 'The
scope which mercy propounds to herself of the turning of the soul to God, even the glory of *it* own self'
(p. 442).*

No doubt we have here in this use of ' it' a step-
ping-stone by which the introduction of 'its' was
greatly aided. And yet for a long while the word
was very reluctantly allowed, above all in any statelier
style. It was evidently regarded as a distasteful
makeshift not always to be dispensed with, but to

original reading, then, as the book was first published in 1594,
we should have an earlier example of 'its' by four years than
that in Florio ;·but in all editions up to that of 1632, 'of *it*
own accord' is the reading.

* See upon this whole subject Craik, *On the English of
Shakespeare*, 2nd edit. p. 97 ; Marsh, *Manual of the English
Language*, Engl. edit. p. 278 ; *Transactions of the Philological
Society*, vol. i. p. 280; and Wright, *The Bible Wordbook*,
s. v. 'it.'

which recourse should be had only when this was
unavoidable. This feeling is not even now extinct.
I remember hearing Lord Macaulay say that he always
avoided '.its' when he could ; while to every writer of
English verse, who has any sense of melody, the
necessity of using it is often most unwelcome. It is
in fact a *parvenu*, which forced itself into good society
at last, but not with the good will of those who in the
end had no choice but to admit it.

There is indeed a very singular period in our
literature, extending over more than the first half of
the seventeenth century, during which the old grammatical usages, namely, 'his' applied to neuters as
freely as to masculines, or instead of this, 'thereof,'
or 'of it,' were virtually condemned—the first as
involving many possible confusions, the others as
clumsy and antiquated contrivances for escaping these
confusions, while yet at the same time the help of 'its'
is claimed as sparingly as possible, by some is not
claimed at all. Thus I have carefully examined large
portions of Daniel and Drayton—the first died in 1619,
the second in 1631—without once lighting upon the
word, and am inclined to believe that it occurs in
neither ; but, which is very much more noticeable, I
have done this without lighting upon more than one
or two passages where there was even the temptation,
if the poet shrunk from the employment of ' its,' to
employ any of the earlier substitutes ; so that it is
hardly too much to say that the whole fashion of their
sentences must have been often shaped by a conscious
or unconscious seeking to avoid the alternative neces-

sities either of using, or else evidently finding a substitute for, this unwelcome little monosyllable. Dryden, I suppose, had no conscious scruple about employing 'its,' and yet how rarely he did so, as compared with a modern writer under the same inducements, a fact like this remarkably attests, namely, that in his rendering of the second book of the *Æneid*, on which I made the experiment, 'its' occurs only three-times, while in Conington's translation of the same no fewer times than twenty-six. We may further note that many who employ the newly invented possessive, ever and anon fall back on 'his,' or 'her,' or 'thereof,' as though the other did not exist. It is thus continually with Fuller, and, though not so often, with Jeremy Taylor. Thus the former says of Solomon's Temple : 'Twice was *it* pillaged by foreign foes, and four times by *her* own friends before the final destruction *thereof.*' * He turns to 'thereof' for help ten times for once that 'its' finds allowance with him. And in Jeremy Taylor a construction such as the following is not unusual : 'Death hath not only lost the sting, but *it* bringeth a coronet in *her* hand.'

How soon, with all this, the actual novelty of 'its' was forgotten is strikingly evidenced by the fact that when Dryden, in one of his moods of fault-finding with the poets of the preceding generation, is taking Ben Jonson to task for general inaccuracy in his

---

* *Pisgah Sight of Palestine*, p. 40. Compare Marsh, *Lectures on the English Language.* New York, 1860, p. 399.

English diction, among other counts of his indict-
ment, he quotes this line from *Catiline.*

' Though heaven should speak with all *his* wrath at once,'

and proceeds, '*heaven* is ill syntax with *his ;*' and
this, while in fact till within forty or fifty years of the
time when Dryden began to write, no other syntax
was known ; and to a much later date was exceedingly rare. Curious, too, is it to note that in the
earnest controversy which followed on the publication
by Chatterton of the poems ascribed by him to the
monk Rowley, who should have lived in the fifteenth
century, no one appealed to the following line,

' Life and all *its* goods I scorn,'

as at once deciding that the poems were not of the
age which they pretended. Warton, who denied,
though with some hesitation, the antiquity of the
poems,* giving many and sufficient reasons for this
denial, failed to take note of this little word, which
betrayed the forgery at once.

Again, languages enrich their vocabulary, our own
has largely done so, by recovering treasures which
had escaped them for a while. Not that all which
drops out of use and memory *is* loss ; there are words
which it is gain to be rid of, and which none would
wish to revive ; words of which Dryden says truly,
though in a somewhat ingracious comparison—they
do ' not deserve this redemption, any more than the

---

* *History of English Poetry*, vol. ii. p. 463 sqq.

crowds of men who daily die, or are slain for sixpence
in a battle, merit to be restored to life, if a wish could
revive them.'* But there are others which it is a real
advantage to draw back again from the temporary oblivion into which they had fallen; and such recoveries
are more numerous than might at first be supposed.

You may remember that Horace, tracing in a few
memorable lines the fortune of words, and noting
that many, once current, were in his time no longer
in use, did not therefore count that of necessity their
race was for ever run. So far from this, he confidently anticipated a *palingenesy* or renewed existence
for many among them.† They had set, but they
should rise again : what seemed death was only sus-
pended animation. Such indeed is constantly the
fact. Words slip almost or quite as imperceptibly
back into use as they once slipped out of it. There
is abundant evidence of this. Thus in the contemporary gloss which an anonymous friend of Spenser
furnishes to his *Shepherd's Calendar*, first published
in 1579, 'for the exposition of old words,' as he de-
clares, he includes the following in his list : 'askance,'
'bevy,' 'coronal,' 'dapper,' 'embellish,' 'fain,'
'flowret,' 'forlorn,' 'forestall,' 'glee,' 'keen,'
'scathe,' 'seer,' 'surly,' 'welter,' 'wizard,' with
others quite as familiar as these. In Speght's *Chau-*

---

* Postcript to his *Translation of the Æneid.* For Gray's
judgment on the words recovered or recalled by Dryden see
Letter 43, to West.

† Multa renascentur, quæ jam cecidere.

Ars Poet, 46–72 ; cf. *Ep.* ii. 2. 115.

cer (1667), there is a long list of 'old and obscure
words in Chaucer explained ;' these 'old and obscure
words,' including 'anthem,' 'blithe,' 'bland,' 'chap-
let,' 'carol,' 'deluge,' 'franchise,' 'illusion,' 'problem,' 'recreant,' 'sphere,' 'tissue,' 'transcend,' with
very many easier than these. In Skinner's *Etymologicon* (1671), there is another such list of words which
have gone out of use,* and among these he includes
'to 'dovetail,' 'to interlace,' 'elvish,' 'encumbred,'
'phantom,' 'gawd,' 'glare,' 'malison,' 'masquerade,' (mascarade), 'oriental,' 'plumage,' 'pummel,'
(pomell), 'shapely.' Again, there is prefixed to
Thomson's *Castle of Indolence*, in which, as is well
known, he affects the antique, an 'explanation of the
obsolete words used in this poem.' They are not very
many, but they include 'appal,' 'aye,' 'bale,' 'bla-
zon,' 'carol,' 'deftly,' 'gear,' 'glee,' 'imp,' 'nurs-
ling,' 'prankt,' 'sere,' 'sheen,' 'sweltry,' 'thrall,'
'unkempt,' 'wight ;' many of which would be used
without scruple in the prose, the remainder belonging to the recognized poetical diction, of the present
day. West, a contemporary of Thomson, whose
works have found their way into *Johnson's Poets*, and
who imagined, like Thomson, that he was writing 'in
the manner of Spenser,' counts it necessary to explain
'assay,' 'astound,' 'caitiff,' 'dight,' 'emprise,'
'guise,' 'kaiscr,' 'palmer,' 'paragon,' 'paramour,'

---

* *Etymologicon vocum omnium antiquarum quæ usque a
Wilhelmo Victore invaluerunt et jam ante parentum ætatem
in usu esse desierunt.*

'paynim,' 'prowess,' 'trenchant,' 'welkin ;' with all which our poetry is familiar now.)
It is well-nigh incredible what words it has been sometimes proposed to dismiss from our English Bible on the plea that they 'are now almost or entirely obsolete.' Wemyss, writing in 1816, desired to get rid of 'athirst,' 'ensample,' 'garner,' 'haply,' 'jeopardy,' 'lack,' 'passion,' 'straightway,' 'twain,' 'wax,' with a multitude of other words not a whit more aloof from our ordinary use. Purver, whose *New and Literal Translation of the Old and New Testament* appeared in 1764, has an enormous list of expressions that are 'clownish, barbarous, base, hard, technical, misapplied, or new coined ;' and among these are ' beguile,' 'boisterous,' 'lineage,' 'perseverance,' 'potentate,' 'remit,' 'seducer,' 'shorn,' 'swerved,' 'vigilant,' 'unloose,' 'unction,' 'vocation.' And the same worship of the fleeting present, of the transient fashions of the hour in language, with the same contempt of that stable past which in all likelihood will be the enduring future, long after these fashions have passed away and are forgotten, manifests itself to an extravagant degree in the new Version of the American Bible Union. It needs only for a word to have the slighest suspicion of age upon it, to have ceased but for the moment to be the current money of the street and the market-place, and there is nothing for it but peremptory exclusion. ' To chasten' and 'chastening,' 'to better,' 'to faint,' 'to quicken,' 'conversation,' 'saints,' 'wherefore,' 'straitly,' 'wroth,' with hundreds more, are thrust out, avowedly upon this plea ; and modern

substitutes introduced in their room. I can fancy no
more effectual scheme for debasing the Version, nor,
if it were admitted as the law of revision, for the
lasting impoverishment of the English tongue. One
can only liken it to a custom of the Fiji islanders,
who, as soon as their relatives begin to show tokens
of old age, bury them alive, or by some other means
put them out of the way. They, however, might
plead this, that their old would grow older still, more
useless, more burdensome, every day. It is nothing
of the kind with the words which, on somewhat similar grounds, are forcibly dismissed. A multitude of
these, often the most precious ones, after a period of
semi-obsoleteness, of withdrawal from active service
for a while, obtain that second youth, pass into free
and unquestioned currency again. But nothing
would so effectually hinder this rejuvenescence as the
putting a ban upon them directly they have passed
out of vulgar use ; as this resolution, that if they
have withdrawn for ever so brief a time from the
every-day service of men, they shall never be per-
mitted to return to it again. A true lover of his native
tongue will adopt another course :

> Obscurata diu populo bonus eruet,

and valuable words which are in danger of disappearing, instead of bidding to be gone, he will do his best
to detain or recover.

Who would now affirm of the verb 'to hallow' that
it is even obsolescent ? yet Wallis two hundred years
ago observed—' it has almost gone out of use ' (fere

desuevit). It would be difficult to find an example
of the verb 'to advocate' between Milton and Burke.
Franklin, an admirable master of the homelier English style, considered the word to have sprung up
during his own residence in Europe. In this indeed
he was mistaken ; it had only during this period revived. Johnson says of 'jeopardy' that it is a 'word
not now in use ;' which certainly is not any longer
true.*

I am persuaded that in facility of being understood,
Chaucer is not merely as near, but much nearer, to
us than he was felt by Dryden and his contemporaries
to be to them. They make exactly the same sort of
complaints, only in still stronger language, about his
archaic phraseology and the obscurities which it in-
volves, which we still sometimes hear at the present
day. Thus in the *Preface* to his *Tales from Chaucer*,
having quoted some not very difficult lines from the
earlier poet whom he was modernizing, he proceeds :
'You have here a specimen of Chaucer's language,
which is so obsolete that his sense is scarce to be
understood.'† Nor did it fare thus with Chaucer

---

* In like manner La Bruyère (*Caractères*, c. 14) laments
the extinction of a large number of French words which he
names. At least half of these have now free course in the
language, as 'valeureux,' 'haineux,' 'peineux,' 'fructueux,'
'mensonger,' 'coutumier,' 'vantard,' 'courtois,' 'jovial,'
'fétoyer,' 'larmoyer,' 'verdoyer.' Two or three of these
may be rarely used, but every one would be found in a dictionary of the living language.

† But for all this Dryden thought him worth understanding.
Not so Addison. In a rapid review of English poets he ac-

only. These wits and poets of the Court of Charles the Second were conscious of a greater gulf between themselves and the Elizabethan æra, separated from them by little more than fifty years, than any of which *we* are aware, separated from it by two centuries more. It was not merely that they felt themselves more removed from its tone and spirit; their altered circumstances explain this;* but I am convinced that they found more difficulty and strangeness in the language of Spenser and Shakespeare than we find at this present; that it sounded more uncouth, more old-fashioned, more crowded with obsolete terms than it does in our ears at the present. Only so can one explain the tone in which they are accustomed to speak of these worthies of the near past. I must again cite Dryden, the truest representative for good and for evil of literary England during the later de-

counts 'the merry bard'—this is his characteristic epithet for the most pathetic poet in the language—as one the whole significance of whose antiquated verse has for ever passed away :

> But age has rusted what the poet writ,
> Worn out his language, and obscured his wit.
> In vain he jests in his unpolished strain,
> And tries to make his readers laugh in vain.'

* Addison takes credit for this inability of his own age to find any satisfaction in that which Spenser sung for the delight of his :

> ' But now the mystic tale, that pleased of yore,
> Can charm our understanding age no more ;
> The long-spun allegories fulsome grow,
> While the dull moral lies too plain below.'

cades of the seventeenth century. Of Spenser, whose death was separated from his own birth by little more than thirty years, he speaks as of one belonging to quite a different epoch, counting it much to say, 'notwithstanding his obsolete language, he is still intelligible; at least after a little practice.'* Nay, hear his judgment of Shakespeare himself, as far as language is concerned : 'It must be allowed to the present age that the tongue in general is so much refined since Shakespeare's time, that many of his words and more of his phrases are scarce intelligible. And of those which we understand, some are ungrammatical, others coarse ; and his whole style is so pestered with figurative expressions, that it is as affected as it is obscure.'†

Sometimes a word emerges from the lower strata of society, not indeed new, but yet to most seeming new, its very existence having been forgotten by the larger number of those speaking the language ; although it must have somewhere lived on upon the lips of men. Thus, since the gold-fields of California and Australia have been opened, we hear often of a ' nugget ' of gold ; being a lump of the pure metal ; and it has been debated whether the word is a new birth altogether, or a popular recasting of ' ingot.' It

* *Preface to Juvenal.*
† *Preface to Troilus and Cressida.* In justice to Dryden, and lest he should seem to speak poetic blasphemy, it should not be forgotten that ' pestered ' had in his time no such offensive a sense as it has now. It meant no more than inconveniently crowded. See my *Select Glossary*, s. v.

is most probably this last; and yet scarcely a recent one, framed for the present need, seeing that 'nugget,' or 'niggot' as it is spelt by them, occurs in our elder writers.* There can be little doubt of the identity of 'niggot' and 'nugget'; all the consonants, the *stamina* of a word, being the same; whilst that earlier form makes plausible the suggestion that 'nugget' is only 'ingot' a little disguised, since it wants nothing but the very common transposition of the first two letters to bring them to an almost absolute identity.

There is another very fruitful source of increase in the vocabulary of a language. What was once one word separates into two, takes two forms, or even more, and each of these asserts an existence independent of the other. The impulse and suggestion to this is in general first given by differences in pronunciation, which are presently represented by differences in spelling; or it will sometimes happen that what at first were no more than precarious and arbitrary variations in spelling come in the end to be regarded as words altogether distinct; they detach themselves from one another, not again to reunite; just as accidental varieties in fruits or flowers, produced at hazard,

---

* Thus in North's *Plutarch*, p. 499: 'After the fire was quenched, they found in *niggots* of gold and silver mingled together, about a thousand talents;' and again, p. 323: 'There was brought a marvellous great mass of treasure in *niggots* of gold.' The word has not found its way into our dictionaries or glossaries.

have permanently separated off, and settled into different kinds. They have each its own distinct domain of meaning, as by general agreement assigned to it ; dividing the inheritance between them, which before they held in common. No one who has not watched and catalogued these words as they have fallen under his notice, would believe how numerous they are.

Sometimes as the accent is placed on one syllable of a word or another, it comes to have different significations, and those so distinctly marked, that the separation may be regarded as complete. Examples of this are the following : 'dívers,' and divérse ; cónjure ' and ' conjúre ;' 'ántic' and 'antíque ;' 'húman ' and 'humáne ;' ' úrban ' and 'urbáne :' ' géntle ' 'géntile ' and ' gentéel ;' ' cústom ' and ' costúme ;' ' éssay ' and ' assáy ;' ' próperty ' and ' propríety.' Or again, a word is pronounced at full, or somewhat more shortly : thus ' spirit ' and ' sprite ;' ' blossom ' and ' bloom ;' ' courtesy ' and ' curtsey ;' ' chaloupe ' and ' sloop ; ' nourish ' and ' nurse ;' ' personality ' and ' personalty ;' ' fantasy ' and ' fancy;' ' triumph ' and ' trump ' (the *winning* card*) ; ' happily ' and ' haply ;' ' ordinance ' and ' ordnance ; ' shallop ' and ' sloop ;' ' brabble ' and ' brawl ;' ' syrup ' and ' shrub ;' ' balsam ' and ' balm ;' ' dame ' and ' dam ;' ' cape ' and ' cap ;' ' eremite ' and ' hermit ;' ' nighest ' and ' next ;' ' poesy ' and ' posy ;' ' achievement ' and ' hatchment ;' ' manœuvre ' and

---

* See Latimer's famous *Sermon on Cards*, where ' triumph ' and ' trump ' are interchangeably used.

'manure;' and, older probably than any of these, 'other' and 'or;'—or, with the dropping of the first letter or letters : 'history' and 'story;' 'harbour' and 'arbour; 'etiquette' and 'ticket;' 'escheat' and 'cheat;' 'estate' and 'state;'—or with a dropping of·the last syllable, as 'Britany' and 'Britain;' 'crony' and 'crone;'—or, without losing a syllable, with more or less stress laid on the close ; 'regiment' and 'regimen;' 'corpse' and 'corps;' 'bite' and 'bit;' 'sire' and 'sir;' 'land' or 'laund' and 'lawn; 'suite' and 'suit;' 'swinge' and 'swing;' 'gulph' and 'gulp.;' 'launch' and 'lance;' 'wealth' and 'weal;' 'stripe' and 'strip;' 'borne' and 'born;' 'glaze' and 'glass;' 'stave' and 'staff;' 'clothes' and 'cloths.' Or sometimes a slight internal vowel change finds place, as between 'dent' and 'dint;' 'rant' and 'rent' (a ranting actor tears or *rends* a passion to tatters) ; 'creak' and 'croak;' 'float' and 'fleet :' 'lill' (Spenser) and 'loll;' 'reel' and 'roll;' 'cross' and 'cruise;' 'sleek' and 'slick;' 'sheen' and 'shine;' 'shriek' and 'shrike;' 'pick' and 'peck :' 'peak' 'pique' and 'pike;' 'snip' 'snib' and 'snub;' 'plot' and 'plat;' 'weald' and 'wold;' 'drip' and 'drop; 'wreathe' and 'writhe;' 'spear' and 'spire' ('the least *spire* of grass,' South) ; 'trist' and 'trust;' 'band' 'bend' and 'bond;' 'cope' 'cape' and 'cap;' 'tip' and 'top;' 'slent' (now obsolete) and 'slant;' 'sweep' and 'swoop;' 'wrest' and 'wrist;' 'neb' and 'nib;' 'gad' (now surviving only in gadfly) and 'goad;' 'complement' and 'compliment;' 'spike' and 'spoke;' 'tamper' and 'temper;' 'flutter' and 'flatter;' 'ragged' and 'rugged;' 'gargle' and 'gurgle;' 'snake' and 'sneak' (both crawl); 'deal' and 'dole;' 'giggle' and 'gaggle' (this last is now commonly spelt 'cackle'); 'scribble' and 'scrabble;' 'flicker' and 'flacker' (now obsolete); 'gourmand' and 'gormand;' 'sip' 'sop' 'soup' and 'sup;' 'clack' 'click' and 'clock;' 'tetchy' and 'touchy; 'sauce' and 'souse;' 'spoil' and 'spill;' 'halt' and 'hold;' 'vendor' and 'vender;' 'visitor' and 'visiter;' 'neat' and 'nett;' 'stud' and 'steed;' 'then' and 'than;'* 'grits' and 'grouts;' 'spirt' and 'sprout;' 'prune' and 'preen;' 'mister' and 'master;' 'allay' and 'alloy;' 'ghostly' and 'ghastly;' 'person' and 'parson;' 'cleft' and 'clift' (now written 'cliff') 'travel' and 'travail;' 'truth' and 'troth;' 'pennon' and 'pinion;' 'quail' 'quell' and 'kill;' 'metal' and 'mettle;' 'ballad' and 'ballet;' 'chagrin' and 'shagreen;' 'can' and 'ken;' 'Francis' and 'Frances;'† 'chivalry' and 'cavalry;' 'oaf' and 'elf;' 'thresh' and 'thrash;' 'lose' and 'loose;' 'taint' and 'tint.' Sometimes the difference is mainly or entirely in the initial consonants, as between 'phial'

---

* On these words see a learned discussion in *English Retraced*, Cambridge, 1862.

† The appropriating of 'Frances' to women and 'Francis' to men is quite modern; it was formerly as often Sir Frances Drake as Sir Francis, while Fuller (*Holy State*, b. iv. c. 14) speaks of Francis Brandon, eldest *daughter* of Charles Brandon, Duke of Suffolk; and see Ben Jonson, *New Inn*, Act ii. Sc. i.

and 'vial ; 'pother' and 'bother ;' 'bursar' and 'purser ;' 'thrice' and 'trice ;' 'fitch' and 'vetch ; 'strinkle' (now obsolete) and 'sprinkle ; 'shatter' and 'scatter ;' 'chattel' and 'cattle ;' 'chant' and 'cant ;' 'champaign' and 'campaign ;' 'zealous' and 'jealous ;' 'channel' and 'kennel ;' 'quay' and 'key ;' 'thrill' 'trill' and 'drill ;'—or in the consonants in the middle of the word, as between 'cancer' and 'canker' 'nipple' and 'nibble ;' 'tittle' and 'title ;' 'price' and 'prize ;' 'consort' and 'concert ;'—or there is a change in both consonants, as in 'pipe' and 'fife.'

Or a word is spelt now with a final *k* and now with a final *ch* ; out of this variation two different words have been formed, with, it may be, other slight differences superadded ; thus is it with 'poke' and 'poach ; 'dyke' and 'ditch ;' 'stink' and 'stench ;' 'prick' and 'pritch' (now obsolete) ; 'milk' and 'milch ;' 'break' 'breach' and 'broach ;' 'lace' and 'latch ;' 'stick' and 'stitch ;' 'lurk' and 'lurch ;' 'bank' and 'bench ;' 'stark' and 'starch ;' 'wake' and 'watch.' So too *t* and *d* are easily exchanged ; as in 'clod' and 'clot ;' 'vend' and 'vent ;' 'brood' and 'brat ;' 'sad' and 'set ;' 'card' and 'chart ;' 'medley and 'motley.' Or there has grown up, beside the accurate pronunciation, a popular as well ; and this in the end has formed itself into another word ; thus it is with 'housewife' and 'hussey ;' 'grandfather' and 'gaffer ;' 'grandmother' and 'gammer ;' 'hanaper' and 'hamper ;' 'puisne' and 'puny ;' 'patron' and 'pattern ;' 'spital' (hospital)

and 'spittle' (house of correction) ; 'accompt' and
'account ;' 'polity' and 'policy ;' 'donjon' and
'dungeon ;' 'nestle' and 'nuzzle' (now obsolete) ;
'Egyptian' and 'gypsy ;' 'Bethlehem' and 'Bedlam ;'
'Pharaoh' and 'faro' (this last so called because the
winning card bore the likeness of the Egyptian king ;)
'exemplar' and 'sampler ;' 'procuracy' and 'proxy ;'
'dolphin' and 'dauphin ;' 'iota' and 'jot ;' 'synods-
man' and 'sidesman.'

Other changes cannot perhaps be reduced exactly
under any of these heads ; as between 'ounce' and
'inch ;' 'errant' and 'arrant ;' 'slack' and 'slake ;'
'twang' and 'tang ;' 'valet' and 'varlet ;' 'slow'
and 'slough ;' 'bow' and 'bough ;' 'hurl' and
'whirl ;' 'hew' and 'hough ;' 'dies' and 'dice'
(both plurals of 'die') ; 'plunge' and 'flounce ;'
'egg' and 'edge ;' 'staff' and 'stave ;' 'scull'
'school' and 'shoal ;' 'frith' and 'firth ;' 'benefit'
and 'benefice.'*   Or, it may be, the difference is in

* A singular characteristic trait of Papal policy once turned
upon the fact that 'beneficium' contained in itself both 'benefice' and 'benefit.' Pope Adrian the Fourth writing to
Frederic the First to complain of certain conduct of his, re-
minded the Emperor that he had placed the imperial crown
upon his head, and would willingly have conferred even
greater 'beneficia' upon him than this. Had this been allowed to pass, it would no doubt have been afterwards
appealed to as an admission on the Emperor's part, that he
held the Empire as a feud or fief (for 'beneficium' was then
the technical word for this, though the meaning has much
narrowed since) from the Pope—the very point in dispute
between them. The word was indignantly repelled by the

the spelling only, appreciable by the eye, but escaping altogether the ear. It is thus with 'draft' and 'draught ;' 'plain' and 'plane ;' 'coign' and 'coin ;' 'flower' and 'flour ;' 'check' and 'cheque ;' 'straight' and 'strait ;' 'ton' and 'tun ;' 'road' and 'rode ;' 'throw' and 'throe ;' 'wrack' and 'rack ;' 'gait' and 'gate ;' 'hoard' and 'horde ;' 'knoll' and 'noll ;' 'chord' and 'cord ;' 'drachm' and 'dram ;' 'license' and 'licence ;' 'sergeant' and 'serjeant ;' 'mask' and 'masque ;' 'villain' and 'villein.'

Now, if you will put the matter to proof, you will find, I believe, in every case that there has attached itself to the different forms of a word a modification of meaning more or less sensible, that each as won an independent sphere of meaning, which remains peculiarly its own. Thus 'divers' implies difference only, but 'diverse' difference with opposition ; thus the several Evangelists narrate the same event in 'divers' manners, but not in 'diverse.' 'Antique' is ancient, but 'antic' is this same anciént regarded as overlived, out of date, and so in our days grotesque, ridiculous ; and then, with a dropping of the reference to age, the grotesque, the ridiculous alone. 'Human' is what every man is, 'humane' is what every man ought to be ; for Johnson's suggestion that

---

Emperor and the whole German nation, whereupon the Pope appealed to the etymology, that ' beneficium ' was but ' bonum factum,' and protested that he meant no more than to remind the Emperor of the various ' benefits ' which he had done him (Neander, *Kirch. Geschichte*, vol. v. p. 318).

'humane' is from the French feminine 'humaine,' and 'human' from the masculine, is contrary to all the analogies of language. 'Ingenious' expresses a mental, 'ingenuous' a moral excellence. A gardener 'prunes' or trims his trees, properly indeed his *vines* (pro*vigner*), birds 'preen' or trim their feathers. We 'allay' wine with water; we 'alloy' gold with platina. 'Bloom' is a finer and yet more delicate efflorescence even than 'blossom;' thus the 'bloom,' but not the 'blossom,' of the cheek. It is now always 'clots' of blood and 'clods' of earth; a 'float' of timber, and a 'fleet' of ships; men 'vend' wares, and 'vent' complaints. 'A curtsey' is one, and that merely an external, manifestation of 'courtesy.' 'Gambling' may be, as with a fearful irony it is called, *play*, but it is nearly as distant from 'gambolling' as hell is from heaven. Nor would it be hard, in almost every pair or larger group of words which I have adduced, to detect shades of meaning which one word has obtained and not the other.*

---

* The same happens in other languages. Thus in Greek ἀνάθεμα and ἀνάθημα both signify that which is devoted, though in very different senses, to the higher powers; θάρσος, boldness, and θράσος, temerity, were at first but different spellings of the same word; so too γρῖπος and γρῖφος, ἔθος and ἦθος, βρύκω and βρύχω: and probably ὀβελός and ὀβολός, ὄορος and ὠρός. In Latin 'penna' and 'pinna' differ only in form, and signify alike a 'wing;' while yet 'penna' has come to be used for the wing of a bird, 'pinna' (its diminutive 'pinnaculum,' has given us 'pinnacle') for that of a building; so is it with 'Thrax' a Thracian, and 'Threx' a gladiator; with 'codex' and 'cau-

There is another very sensible gain which the
language has made, although of a different kind altogether. For a long time past there has been a
tendency to bring the component parts of a word into
linguistic harmony, so that it shall not any longer be
made up of a Saxon prefix or suffix, joined to a Latin
root, but shall be all homogeneous ; and if Latin in
the body of the word, then such throughout. This
evidently was not the case with 'unsatiable,' 'un-
glorious,' 'undiscreet,' 'uncredible,' 'unvisible,' 'un-
tolerable,' 'unreligious' (all in Wiclif) ; which have
now severally given place to 'insatiable,' 'inglorious,'
'indiscreet,' and the rest ; while 'untimely,' 'unwit-
ting,' and many more, in which there existed no such
discord between the parts, remain as they were. In

---

dex ;' 'forfex' and 'forceps ;' 'anticus' and 'antiquus ;'
'celeber' and 'creber ;' 'infacetus' and 'inficetus ;' 'mulgeo'
and 'mulceo ;' 'providentia,' 'prudentia,' and 'provincia ;'
'columen' and 'culmen ; 'coïtus' and 'cœtus ;' 'ægrimonia'
and 'ærumna ;' 'Lucina' and 'luna ;' 'cohors' and 'cors ;'
'navita' and 'nauta ;' in German with 'rechtlich' and
'redlich ;' 'schlecht' and 'schlicht ;' 'golden' and 'gulden ;'
'höfisch' and 'hübsch ;' 'ahnden' and 'ahnen' (see a very
, interesting notice in Grimm's *Woerterbuch*) ; 'biegsam' and
'beugsam ;' 'fürsehung' and 'vorsehung ;' 'deich' and
'teich ;' 'trotz' and 'trutz ;' 'born' and 'brunnen ;' 'athem'
and 'odem :' in French with 'harnois,' the armour or 'har-
ness' of a soldier, and 'harnais' of a horse ; with 'foible'
and 'faible ;' with 'Zéphire' and 'zéphyr ; with 'chaire'
and 'chaise,' the latter having been at the first nothing else
but a vicious and affected pronunciation of the former, and
with many more.

the same way ' unpure' (Barnes) has been replaced
by 'impure,' 'unfirm' (Shakespeare) by 'infirm,'
' unmoveable' (Coverdale) by 'immoveable,' 'un-
noble' (Drayton) by 'ignoble,' 'unmeasurable'
(North) by 'immeasurable,' 'uncapable' (Hooker)
by 'incapable,' 'unpatient' (Coverdale) by 'impa-
tient,' 'unpartial' (Jackson) by impartial,' 'unde-
cent' (Cowley) by 'indecent,'' unactive' (Milton) by
' inactive.' 'Unpossible,' which is the proper reading of our Authorized Version at Matt. xvii. 20 ; xix.
26, and, I believe, throughout, has been silently
changed into 'impossible.' Here and there, but very
rarely, the tendency has been in the opposite .direc-
tion—to create these anomalies, not to remove them.
Thus Milton's 'inchastity' (prose), 'ingrateful,'
have given place to the less correct ' unchastity,' ' un-
grateful.'

And as with the prefix, so also it has fared with the
suffix.   A large group of our Latin words for a long
while had not a Latin, but a Saxon termination.   We
have several of these in the Bible and in the Prayer
Book ; 'pureness,' for example, 'frailness,' 'dis-
quietness,' 'perfectness,' and 'simpleness.'   'Pureness' may perhaps still survive ; but for the others we
have substituted ' frailty' (recalled it, we may say, for
it was already in *Piers Ploughman*), 'disquietude,'
' perfection,' 'simplicity.'   The same has happened
with a multitude of others ; ' gayness' (*Piers Ploughman*) has given way to ' gaiety,' 'poverness (*ibid.*) to
' poverty,' ' subtleness' (Sidney) to 'subtlety,' 'able-
ness' (Spenser) to 'ability ;' 'ferventness' (Coverdale)

to 'fervency;' 'cruelness' (Golding) to 'cruelty;'
'desolateness' (Andrews) to 'desolation;' 'partial-
ness' (Frith) to 'partiality;' 'spiritualness,' 'vain-
ness,' 'realness,' 'vulgarness,' 'immoralness' (all in
Rogers), severally to 'spirituality,' 'vanity,' 'reality,'
'vulgarity,' 'immorality;' 'stableness' (Coverdale)
to 'stability;' 'dejectedness' (Bishop Hall) to 'de-
jection,' 'insensibleness' (Manton) to 'insensibility;'
'doubleness' (Hawes) to 'duplicity;' so too 'furi-
ousness,' 'terribleness,' 'valiantness,' have all been
felt to be words ill put together, and have silently
been dropped; nor would it be difficult to augment
this list. Thus too, though we have not at this day
altogether rejected words in which the French termination 'able' is combined with a Saxon root, as 'unspeakable' and the like, still there has been an evident disposition among us to diminish their number.
There were once far more of these, as 'findable,'
'unlackable,' 'ungainsayable' (all in Pecock),
'matchable' (Spenser), 'mockable' (Shakespeare),
'woundable' (Fuller), 'speakable' (Milton), than
there are now. 'The rejection of these hybrid words,'
as has been well said,* 'from the modern vocabulary
is curious, as an instance of the unconscious exercise
of a linguistic instinct by the English people. The
objection to such adjectives is their mongrel character,
the root being Saxon, the termination Romanic; and
it is an innate feeling of the incongruity of such al-

---

* Marsh, _Origin and History of the English Language_,
p. 475.

liances, not the speculative theories of philologists, which has driven so many of them out of circulation. But changes not unlike to those which I have just noted have come over words, where there was no such inducement arising from want of congruity in their component parts; where, on the contrary, they were already homogeneous in the quarters from which they were derived. In these instances the language seems, so to say, to have hesitated for a while before it made up its mind which suffix it would employ, and has often in later times rejected one which in earlier it appeared disposed to adopt, and in the stead of this adopted another. The termination ' ness,' which, as we just now saw, has lost its hold on a great many Latin words, with which it certainly had no right to be joined, has more than made good these losses by gains in other directions. Many words that ended for a while in ' ship,' now end in ' ness,' as ' gladship ' (*Ormulum*), ' mildship,' ' meekship,' ' idleship ' (all in *Hali Meidenhad*), ' guiltship ' (Geneva Bible) ; which are now severally ' gladness,' ' mildness,' ' meekness,' ' idleness,' and ' guiltiness.' More numerous are those which, terminating once in 'head' or ' hood,' have finally settled down with that same termination. I adduce a few, ' busihede,' ' wearihede,' ' holihede,' ' newhede,' ' godlihede,' 'swifthede,' ' greenhede,' 'vilehede,' 'blisedhede' (all in *The Ayenbite*); 'wickedhed,' ' pensivehed,' ' lowlihed ' (all in Chaucer) ; ' manlihed,' ' noblehed ' (both in *The Tale of Melusine*) ; ' onehed,' ' worldlihood ' (Pecock); 'fulsomehed,' ' fairhed ' (both in *King Horn*); ' sinfulhed,' 'rightwisehed,' 'tamehed,' (all in the *Story of Genesis*); 'wantonhed,' 'evenhood' (*Promptorium Parvulornm*); 'fulhed,' 'mightihed,' 'filthihed' 'drunkenhed' (all in Wiclif); 'headlesshood,' 'seem-lihed,' 'drearihed,' 'drowsihed,' 'livelihed,' 'goodli-hed' 'beastlihed,' (all in Spenser). In place of these we have 'business,' 'weariness,' 'holiness,' and so on with the rest.

Then again, words not a few, once ending in 'hood,' have relinquished this in favour of 'ship;' thus 'apostlehood,' 'disciplehood,' 'headhood' (all in Pecock), have done this. Others, but they are fewer, for 'hood' have taken 'dom;' thus 'Christen-hood' (Pecock) is 'Christendom' now; or for 'rick,' which survives only in 'bishoprick' ('hevenriche,' or kingdom of heaven, having long since disappeared), have taken the same; thus 'kingrick' (*Piers Plough-man*) or 'kunneriche' (*Proclamation of Henry III.*) is 'kingdom' now. As between 'head' and 'hood,' which are no more than variations of the same form, the latter has seriously encroached on the domain of words once occupied by the former. I quote a few instances, 'childhed,' 'manhed,' 'womanhed' 'bre-thered' (all in Chaucer); 'falsehed' (Tyndal), 'widowhed' (Sibbald's *Glossary*). I am unable to adduce any instances in which the opposite tendency, 'head' taking the place of 'hood,' has displayed itself. Then too many adjectives ending in 'ful' have changed this for 'ly' (= like); thus 'gastful,' 'loveful,' 'grisful' (all in Wiclif), are severally now 'ghastly,' 'lovely,' 'grisly.' I shall note elsewhere the extensive perishing of adjectives ending in 'some.' Many of these, however, still survive, but with some other suffix—often with one which brings their component parts into harmony with one another; thus 'humoursome' survives in 'humorous,' 'laboursome' in 'laborious,' 'clamoursome' in 'clamorous;' or sometimes where no such motive of making the word all of one piece can be traced, as in 'hatesum,' which is now 'hateful,' friendsome,' which is now 'friendly,' 'mirksome' (Spenser), which is now 'murky;' and 'thoughtsome,' which is now 'thoughtful.' This part of the history of our language has hitherto attracted almost no attention. No catalogues of these words, which I know of, have yet been so much as attempted.

Let me trace, before this lecture comes to an end, the history of the rise of some words in the language, noting briefly the motives which may have first induced their creation or adoption, the resistance which they may have met, the remonstrances against them which were sometimes made, the authors who first introduced them. It is a curious chapter in the history of the language, and even a few scattered contributions to it will not be without their value.

Sometimes a word has been created to supply an urgent want, to fill up a manifest gap in the language. For example, that sin of sins, the undue love of self, with the postponing of the interests of all others to our own, being a sin as old as the Fall, had yet for a long time no word to express it in English. Help

was first sought from the Greek, and 'philauty'
(φιλαυτία) more than once put forward by our
scholars ; but it found no popular acceptance. This
failing, men turned to the Latin ; one writer pro-
posing to supply the want by calling the sin 'suicism,'
and the man a 'suist,' as one seeking *his own* things
('sua'), but this with no better success ; and our
ethical terminology was here still incomplete, till
some of the Puritan divines, drawing on native resources, devised 'selfish' and 'selfishness,' words to
us seeming obvious enough, but which yet are little
more than two hundred years old. A passage in
Hacket's *Life of Archbishop Williams** marks the first
rise of 'selfish,' and the quarter in which it rose :
'When they [the Presbyterians] saw that he was not
selfish (it is a word of their own new mint),' &c. In
Whitlock's *Zootomia* (1654, p. 364), there is another
indication of its novelty : 'If constancy may be
tainted with this *selfishness* (to use our *new wordings*
of old and general actings).' It is he who in his
Grand Schismatic, or Suist Anatomized, puts forward
the words 'suist' and 'suicism.' 'Suicism' had not
in his time the obvious objection of resembling
'suicide' too nearly, and being liable to be con-
fused with it ; for 'suicide' did not exist in the language till some twenty years later. Its coming up is
marked by this protest in Phillips' *New World of
Words*, 3rd edit., 1671 : 'Nor less to be exploded is
the word "*suicide*," which may as well seem to par-

ticipate of *sus* a sow, as of the pronoun *sui.*' In the
Index to Jackson's *Works*, published two years later,
it is still '*suicidium*'—'the horrid *suicidium* of the
Jews at York.'*

I should greatly like to see a collection, as nearly
complete as the industry of the collectors could make
it, of all the notices in our literature, which serve as
dates for the first appearance of new words in the
language. These notices are of the most various
kinds. Sometimes they are protests and remonstrances, as that just quoted, against a new word's
introduction ; sometimes they are gratulations at the
same ; while many, neither approving nor disap-
proving, merely state, or allow us to gather, the fact
of a word's recent apparition. Many such notices
are brought together in Richardson's *Dictionary.*† Nor

---

* 'Suicide' is of later introduction into French. Génin
(*Récréations Philol.* vol. i. p. 194) places it about the year
1738, and makes the Abbé Desfontaines its first sponsor. He
is wrong, as we have just seen, in assuming that we borrowed
it from the French, and that it did not exist in English till the
middle of last century. The French complain that the fashion
of suicide was borrowed from England. It is probable that
the word was so.

† Thus one from Lord Bacon under 'essay ;' from Swift
under 'banter ;' from Sir Thomas Elyot under 'mansuetude ;'
from Lord Chesterfield under 'flirtation ;' from *The Spectator*,
No. 537, under 'caricature ;' from Davies and Marlowe's
Epigrams under 'gull ;' from Roger North under 'sham'
(Appendix) ; from Dryden under 'mob,' 'philanthropy,' and
'witticism,' which last word Dryden claims for his own ; from
Evelyn under 'miss ;' and from Milton under 'demagogue.'

are they wanting in *Todd's Johnson.* But the work is one which could only be accomplished by many lovers of their native tongue throwing into a common stock the results of their several studies.* Our Eliza-

* As a slight sample of what might be accomplished here by the joint contributions of many, let me throw together references to a few such passages, which I do not think have found their way into our dictionaries. Thus add to that which Richardson has quoted on 'banter' another from *The Tatler*, No. 230, marking the disfavor with which it was regarded at the first. On 'plunder' there are two instructive passages in Fuller's *Church History*, b. xi. §§ 4, 33 ; and b. ix. § 4 ; and one in Heylin's *Animadversions* thereupon, p. 196 ; on 'admiralty' see a note in Harrington's *Ariosto*, b. xix. ; on 'maturity' Sir Thomas Elyot's *Governor*, i. 22 ; and on 'industry' the same, i. 23 ; on 'neophyte,' which made its first appearance in the Rheims Bible, a notice in Fulke's *Defence of the English Bible*, Parker Society's edition, p. 586, where he says 'neophyte is neither Greek, Latin, nor English ;' on 'fanatic' a passage in Fuller, *Mixt Contemplations in Better Times*, p. 212, ed. 1841, and another in Clarendon's *History of the Rebellion;* and on 'panorama,' and marking its recent introduction (it is not in Johnson), a passage in Pegge's *Anecdotes of the English Language*, first published in 1803, but my reference is to the edition of 1814, p. 306 ; on 'accommodate,' and supplying a date for its first coming into popular use, see Shakespeare's 2 *Henry IV.* Act 3, Sc. 2 ; on 'shrub,' Junius' *Etymologicon*, s. v. 'syrup ;' on 'sentiment' and 'cajole,' Skinner, s. vv., in his *Etymologicon* ('vox nuper civitate donata ') ; and on 'opera,' Evelyn's *Memoirs and Diary*, 1827, vol. i. pp. 189, 190 ; on 'umbrella,' Torriano's *Italian Proverbs*, 1666, p. 58 : 'ombrella is a certain canopy that in Italy we use to shelter ourselves with from the sun and the rain.' 'Starvation' may have been an old word in Scotland, but it was unknown in England until used by Mr. Dundas, the

bethan dramatists would yield much ; even the worthless plays of Charles the Second's time might prove
of some service here.   Early classical scholars like
Sir Thomas Elyot, who wrote when Latin words, good,
bad, and indifferent, were pouring into the language
like a flood, and who from time to time passed their
judgment on these ; the early translators, Protestant
and Roman Catholic, of the Bible, who when they
had exhausted more serious invective, fell foul of one
another's English, and charged each other with bringing in new and un-English words ; the *Spectator*, the
Tatler, the *Guardian*, and even the second and third-
rate imitations of these, might all be consulted with
advantage.   Indeed it is hard beforehand to say in
what unexpected quarter notices of the kind might
not occur.

Let me observe that in such a collection should
be included passages which supply *implicit* evidence
for the non-existence of a word up to a certain date.
It may be urged that it is difficult, nay impossible,

first Lord Melville, therefore called ' Starvation Dundas,' in
a debate on American affairs in 1775 (see *Letters of Horace
Walpole and Mann*, vol. ii. p. 396, and Pegge's *Anecdotes of
the English Language*, 1814, p. 38).   We learn from a protest in *The Spectator*, No. 165, that ' pontoon,' ' fascine,' ' to
reconnoitre,' were in 1704 novelties, which under the influence
of the frequent bulletins were creeping into English.   In Bar-
low's *Columbiad*, published in 1807, we on this side of the
Atlantic first made acquaintance with the verb ' to utilize.'   In
a review of the poem which appeared shortly after in the
Edinburgh Review, there is an earnest, but as it has proved an
ineffectual, remonstrance against the word.

to prove a negative; yet when Bolingbroke wrote as follows, it is certain that 'isolated' did not exist in our language : 'The events we are witnesses of in the course of the longest life, appear to us very often original, unprepared, signal and *unrelative* : if I may use such a word for want of a better in English. In French I would say *isolés.*'* Compare Lord Chesterfield in a letter to Bishop Chenevix, of date March 12, 1767 : 'I have survived almost all my contemporaries, and as I am too old to make new acquaintances, I find myself *isolé.*' Fuller would have scarcely spoken of a 'meteor of foolish fire,'† if 'ignis fatuus,' which has now quite put out 'firedrake,' the older name for these meteors, had not been, when he wrote, still strange to the language. So too when Sir Walter Raleigh spoke of 'strange visions which are also called *panici terrores,*'‡ it is tolerably plain that 'panic' was not yet recognized among us. In like manner when Holland, translating Pliny's long account of the sculptors and sculpture of antiquity, never once uses the word 'sculptor,' but always 'imager' in its room, I feel tolerably sure that 'sculptor' had not yet come into existence. The use of 'noctambulones' by Donne makes me pretty certain that in his time 'somnambulist' had not been invented. When Hacket§ speaks of 'the *cimici* in our bedsteads,' these unsavoury creatures had scarcely gotten the

---

* *Notes and Queries,* No. 226. † *Comm. on Ruth,* p. 38.
‡ *Hist. of the World,* iii. 5, 8.
§ *Life of Archbishop Williams,* vol. ii. p. 182.

name which now they bear. So, too, it is pretty certain that 'amphibious' was not yet English, when one writes (in 1618) : 'We are like those creatures called αμφίβια, which live in water or on land.' Ζωο-λογία, as the title of an English book published in 1649, makes it clear that 'zoology' was not yet in our vocabulary, as ζωόφυτον (Jackson) proves the same for 'zoophyte,' ἐκλεκτικοί † for 'eclectics,' θεο-κρατία (Jeremy Taylor) for 'theocracy,' ἄθεοι (Ascham) for 'atheist,' and πολυθειόμος (Gell, it is a word of his own invention) for polytheism.'‡

It is not merely new words, but new uses of old ones, which should thus be noted, with the time of their first appearing. Thus take the two following

---

* Rust, *Funeral Sermon on J. Taylor.*

† One precaution, let me observe, would be necessary in the collecting, or rather in the adopting, of any statements about the newness of a word—for the passages themselves, even when erroneous, should not the less be noted—namely, that no one's affirmation ought to be accepted simply and at once as to this novelty, seeing that all here are liable to error. Thus more than one which Sir Thomas Elyot indicates as new in his time, 'magnanimity' for example (*The Governor*, ii. 14), are frequent in Chaucer. 'Sentiment,' which. Skinner affirmed to have only recently obtained the rights of English citizenship from the translators of French books, continually recurs in the same. Wotton, using 'character,' would imply that it was a novelty in the language (*Survey of Education*, p. 321) ; it is of constant recurrence in Spenser, and is used by Wiclif. In *Notes and Queries*, No. 225, there is a useful catalogue of recent neologies in our speech, while yet at least half a dozen in the list have not the smallest right to be so considered.

quotations, in proof that the modern use of 'edify' and 'edification' began among the Puritans ; and first this from Oldham :

> ' The graver sort dislike all poetry,
> Which does not, as they call it, *edify ;* '

and this from South : ' All being took up and busied, some in pulpits and some in tubs, in the grand work of preaching and holding forth, and that of *edification,* as the word then went,' &c. Here too the evidence may not be positive, but negative. Thus when I read in Fuller of ' that beast in the Brazile which in fourteen days goes no further than a man may throw a stone, called therefore by the Spaniards *pigritia,*' I am tolerably certain that the aï, as the natives call it, had not yet found among us the name ' sloth,' which now it bears. .

A few observations in conclusion on the deliberate introduction of words to supply felt omissions in a language, and the limits within which this or any other conscious interference with it is desirable or possible. Long before the time when a people begin to reflect upon their language, and to give an account to themselves either of its merits or defects, it has been fixed as regards structure in immutable forms ; the sphere in which any alterations or modifications, addition to it, or subtraction from it, deliberately devised and carried out, are possible, is very limited indeed. The great laws that rule it are so firmly established that almost nothing can be taken from it, which it has got ; almost nothing added to it,

which it has *not* got.   It will travel indeed in certain
courses of change ; but it would be almost as easy
for us to alter the course of a planet as to alter these.
This is sometimes a subject of regret with those who
see what appear to them manifest defects or blemishes
in their language, and at the same time ways by which,
as they fancy, these could be remedied or removed.
And yet this is well ; since for once that these re-
dressers of real or fancied wrongs, these suppliers of
things lacking, would mend, we may be tolerably
confident that ten times, probably a hundred times,
they would mar ; letting go that which would better
have been retained ; retaining that which was overlived and out of date ; and in manifold ways interfer-
ing with those processes of a natural logic, which in
a living language are evermore working themselves
out.   The genius of a language, unconsciously pre-
siding over all its transformations, and conducting
them to definite issues, will prove a far truer and far
safer guide, than the artificial wit, however subtle, of
any single man, or of any association of men.   For
the genius of a language is the sense and inner conviction entertained by all who speak it, of what it
ought to be, and of the methods by which it will
most nearly approach its ideal of perfection ; and
while a pair of eyes, or two or three pairs of eyes,
may see much, a million of eyes will certainly see
more.

It is only with the words, and not with the forms
and laws of a language, that any interference is
possible.   Something, indeed much, may here be

accomplished by wise masters, in the rejecting of that
which deforms or mars, the allowing and adopting of
that which will complete or enrich. Those who have
set such objects before them, and who, knowing the
limits of the possible, have kept within these, have
often effected much. No language affords a better
proof and illustration of this than the German. When
the patriotic Germans began to wake up to a consciousness of the enormous encroachments which
foreign languages, Latin, French, and Italian, had
made on their native tongue, the lodgements which
they had therein effected, and the danger which lay
so near, that it should cease to be a language at all,
but only a mingle-mangle, a variegated patchwork of
many tongues, without any unity or inner coherence,
various Societies were instituted among them, at the
beginning and during the course of the seventeenth
century, for the recovering of what was lost of their
own, for the expelling of that which had intruded
upon it from abroad ; and these with excellent results.

But more effectual than these learned Societies
were the efforts of single writers, who in this merited
eminently well of their country.* Numerous words
now accepted by the whole nation are yet of such
recent introduction that it is possible to designate the
writer who first substituted them for some affected

---

* There is an admirable Essay by Leibnitz with this view
(*Opera*, vol. vi. part 2, pp. 6-51) in French and German, with
this title, *Considérations sur la Culture et la Perfection de la
Langue Allemande.*

Gallicism or pedantic Latinism. Thus to Lessing his
fellow-countrymen owe the substitution of 'zartge-
fühl' for ' délicatesse,' of ' wesenheit ' for ' essence.' It
was he who suggested to the translator of Sterne's *Sentimental Journey*, ' empfindsam ' as a word which would
correspond to our ' sentimental ;' he too who recalled
' bieder,' with which every schoolboy is familiar now,
from the forgetfulness of centuries.   Voss (1786) first
employed 'alterthümlich' for 'antik,' Winkelmann
' denkbild' for 'idée.' Wieland was the author or
reviver of a multitude of excellent words, for some of
which he had to do earnest battle at the first ; such
were 'seligkeit,' 'anmuth,' ' entzückung,' 'festlich,'
'entwirren,' with many more. But no one was so
jealous for the cleansing of the temple of German
speech from unworthy intruders as Campe, the author
of the Dictionary.   For 'maskerade,' he was fain to
substitute 'larventanz,' for 'ballet' 'schautanz,' for
'lauvine' 'schneesturz,' for 'detachement' 'abtrab,' for
'electricität' 'reibfeuer.' It was a novelty when
Büsching called his great work on geography ' Erd-
beschreibung' (1754) instead of ' Geographie ;' while
' schnellpost' for ' diligence,' ' zerrbild' for ' carricatur,'
are almost of recent introduction. Of 'wörterbuch'
itself Jacob Grimm tells us he can find no example
dating earlier than 1719.

Some of these reformers, it must be owned, proceeded with more zeal than knowledge, while others
did what in them lay to make the whole movement absurd—even as there ever hang on the skirts of a noble
movement, be it in literature or politics or higher

things yet, those who by extravagance and excess
contribute their little all to bring ridicule and contempt upon it. Thus in the reaction against foreign
interlopers, and in the zeal to rid the language of them,
some would have disallowed words consecrated by
longest use ; thus Campe, who in the main did such
good service here, desired to replace 'apostel' by
' lehrbote ;' or they understood so little what words
deserved to be called foreign, that they would fain
have gotten rid of such words as these, ' vater,' ' mutter,' ' wein,' ' fenster,' ' meister,' ' kelch ;'* the three
former belonging to the Gothic dialects by exactly
the same right as they do to the Latin and the Greek ;
while the other three have been naturalized so long
that to propose at this day to expel them is as though
having passed an Alien Act for the banishment of
all foreigners, we should proceed to include under
that name, and drive from the kingdom, the descen-
dants of the French Protestants who found refuge
here when Rochelle was taken, or even of the Flem-
ings who came over in the time of our Edwards. One
notable enthusiast proposed to create an entirely new
nomenclature for all the mythological personages of
the Greek and Roman pantheons, although these, one
would think, might have been allowed, if any, to
retain their Greek and Latin names. Cupid was to
be ' Lustkind,' Flora ' Bluminne,' Aurora ' Röthin ;'

* Fuchs, *Zur Geschichte und Beurtheilung der Fremdwoerter
im Deutschen*, Dessau, 1842, pp. 85-91. Compare Jean Paul,
Æsthetik, §§ 83-85.

instead of Apollo schoolboys were to speak of
'Singhold ;' instead of Pan of 'Schaflieb ;' instead
of Jupiter of 'Helfevater,' with other absurdities to
match. We may well beware (and the warning extends much further than to the matter in hand) of
making a good cause ridiculous by our manner of
supporting it, by taking for granted that exaggerations
on one side are best redressed by equal exaggerations
upon the other.

LECTURE V.

DIMINUTION OF THE ENGLISH LANGUAGE.

I OBSERVED in my latest lecture but one that it is the essential character of a living language to be in flux and flow, to be gaining and losing ; and indeed no one who has not given some attention to the subject, would at all imagine the enormous amount of these gains, and not less the enormous amount of these losses—or, for reasons already stated, and because all that comes is not gain, and all is not loss that goes, let us say the enormous additions and diminutions which in a few centuries find place in the vocabulary of a people.   It is not indeed with a language altogether as it is with a human body, of which the component parts are said to be in such unceasing change, with so much taken from it, and so much added to it, that in a very few years no particle of it remains the same.   It is not, I say, exactly thus. There are stable elements, and so to speak, constant quantities in a language which secure its identity, and attest its continuity ; but at the same time the fluctuating element in it, that is in its vocabulary, is much in excess of aught which most of us beforehand would have supposed.   Of acquisitions which our language has made something has been said already.   Of the diminutions it is now our business to speak.

It is certain that all languages must, or at least all languages do in the end, perish. They run their course ; not all at the same rate, for the tendency to change is different in different languages, both from internal causes (mechanism and the like), and also from causes external to the language, and laid in the varying velocities of social progress and social decline ; but so it is, that, sooner or later, they have all their youth, their manhood, their old age, their decrepitude, their final dissolution. Not indeed that they disappear, leaving no traces behind them, even when this last has arrived. On the contrary, out of their death a new life comes forth ; they pass into other forms, the materials of which they were composed are organized in new shapes and according to other laws of life. Thus, for example,' the Latin perishes as a living language ; and yet perishes only to live again, though under somewhat different conditions, in the four daughter languages, French, Italian, Spanish, Portuguese ; or the six, if we count the Provençal and Wallachian. Still in their own proper being they pass away. There are dead records of what they were in books ; not living men who speak them any more. Seeing then that they thus perish, the possibilities of this decay and death must have existed in them from the beginning.

Nor is this all ; but in such strong-built fabrics as these, the causes which thus bring about their final dissolution must have been actually at work very long before the results are so visible as that they cannot any longer be mistaken. Indeed, very often it is with them as with states, which, while in some respects they are knitting and strengthening, in others are already unfolding the seeds of their future and, it may be, still remote dissolution. Equally in these and those, in states and in languages, it would be a serious mistake to assume that all up to a certain point and period is growth and gain, while all after is decay and loss. On the contrary, there are long periods during which growth in some directions is going hand in hand with decay in others; losses in one kind are being compensated, or more than compensated, by gains in another ; during which a language changes, but only as the bud changes into the flower, and the flower into the fruit. A time indeed arrives when the growth and gains, becoming ever fewer, cease to constitute any longer a compensation for the losses and the decay, which are ever becoming more ; when the forces of disorganization and death at work are stronger than those of life and order. But until that crisis and turning-point has arrived, we may be quite justified in speaking of the losses of a language, and may esteem them most real, without in the least thereby implying that its climacteric is passed, and its downward course begun. This may yet be far distant : and therefore when I dwell on certain losses and diminutions which our own has undergone or is undergoing, you will not suppose that I am presenting it to you as now travelling that downward course to dissolution and death. I have no such intention. If in some respects it is losing, in others it is gaining. Nor is everything which it lets go, a loss; for this too,

the parting with a word in which there is no true
help, the dropping of a cumbrous or superfluous form,
may itself be sometimes a most real gain. English is
undoubtedly becoming different from what it has
been ; but only different in that it is passing into
another stage of its development ; only different, as
the fruit is different from the flower, and the flower
from the bud ; not having in all points the same
excellencies which it once had, but with excellencies
as many and as real as it ever had ; possessing, it
may be, less of beauty, but more of usefulness ; not,
perhaps, serving the poet so well, but serving the
historian and philosopher better than before.

With one observation more I will enter on the
special details of my subject. It is this. The losses
or dimiuntions of a language differ in one respect
from the gains or acquisitions—namely, that those
are of two kinds, while these are only of one. The
gains are only in words ; it never puts forth in the
course of its later evolution a new power ; it never
makes for itself a new case, or a new tense, or a new
comparative. But the losses are both in words and
in powers. In addition to the words which it drops,
it leaves behind it, as it travels onward, cases which
it once possessed ; renounces the employment of
tenses which it once used ; forgets its dual ; is content with one termination both for masculine and
feminine, and so on. Nor is this a peculiar feature
of one language, but the universal rule in all. ' In
all languages,' as has been well said, 'there is a constant tendency to relieve themselves of that precision

which chooses a fresh symbol for every shade of meaning, to lessen the amount of nice distinction, and detect as it were a royal road to the interchange of opinion.' For example, a vast number of languages had at an early period of their development, besides the singular and plural, a dual number, some even a trinal, which they have let go at a later. But what I mean by a language renouncing its powers I hope to make clearer in my next lecture. This much I have here said on the matter, to explain and justify a division which I propose to make, considering first the losses of the English language in *words*, and then in *powers*, the former constituting my theme in the present lecture, and the latter in one that will succeed it.

And first, there is going forward a continual extinction of the words in our language—as indeed in every other. When we ask ourselves what are the causes which have led to this, why in that great struggle for existence which is going on here as in every other domain of life, this still makes part of the living army of words, while that has fallen dead, or been dismissed to drag out an obscure provincial existence ; why oftentimes one word has been displaced by another, as it seems to us not better but worse ; or, again, why certain families of words, or words formed after certain schemes and patterns, seem exposed to more than the ordinary chances of mortality, it is not always easy to give a satisfactory answer to these questions. Causes no doubt in every case there are. We can ascribe

little, if indeed anything here, to mere hazard or
caprice. Hazard might cause one man to drop the
use of a word, but not a whole people to arrive at
a tacit consent to employ it no more : while without
this tacit consent it could not have become obsolete.
Caprice, too, is an element which may be eliminated
when we have to do with multitudes ; for in such case
the caprice of one will traverse and defeat the caprice
of another, leaving matters very much where they
were. But the causes oftentimes are hard to discover ;
they lie deep-hidden in the genius of the language
and in the tendencies of it at particular periods, these
affecting speakers and writers who are quite unconscious of the influence thus exercised upon them.*
Much here must remain unexplained : but some suggestion may be offered, which shall account for some,
though by no means all, of the facts which here come
under the eye.

And first, men do not want, or fancy that they do
not want certain words, and so suffer them to drop out
of use. A language in the vigorous acquisitive periods

---

* Dwight (_Modern Phonology_, 2nd series, p. 208) : 'Great,
silent, yet determinative laws of criticism, and so, of general
acceptance or condemnation, are ever at work upon words,
deciding their position among mankind at large, as if before a
court without any appeal. Their action is certain, though
undefinable to our vision, like the seemingly blind laws of the
weather ; which yet, however multiplied in their sources, or
subtle in their action, rule infallibly not only the questions of
human labour and of human harvests, but also, to a great extent, those of human health, power, and enjoyment.

of its existence has generated, or has otherwise got together from different quarters, a larger number of words, each, it may be, with its separate shade of meaning, at all events with its separate etymology, to connote some single object, than can be taken into actual use, more at any rate than the great body of the speakers of a language, with their lazy mental habits, are prepared to take up. Thus we speak at this day of a 'miser,' and perhaps in popular language of a 'hunks' and a 'skinflint;' but what has become of a 'gripe,' a 'huddle,' a 'snudge,' a 'chinch,' a 'pinch-penny,' a 'pennyfather,' a 'nip-cheese,' a 'nipscreed,' a 'nipfarthing,' a 'clutch-fast,' a 'kumbix' (κίμβιξ)? They have all or nearly all quite dropped out of the living language of men, and, as I cannot doubt, for the reason just suggested, namely, that they were more and more various than men would be at pains to discriminate, and having discriminated, to employ.*

Let me indicate another cause of the disappearance of words. Arts, trades, amusements in the course of time are superseded by others. These had each more or less a nomenclature peculiarly its own. But with

---

* Diez (*Gram. d. Roman. Sprachen,* vol. i. p. 53) traces to the same cause the disappearance in the whole group of Romanic languages, of so many words which from their wide use in Latin we might have expected to remain ; thus 'arx' was rendered unnecessary by 'castellum,' 'equus' by 'caballus,' 'gramen' by 'herba,' 'janua' by 'ostium' and 'porta,' 'sidus' by 'astrum,' 'magnus' by 'grandis,' 'pulcher' by 'bellus,' 'sævus' by 'ferox,' and have thus vanished out of the languages descended from the Latin.

these a large number of words, which in the first instance were proper and peculiar to them, will have vanished likewise. Archery in all its more serious aspects is now extinct ; and the group of words is by no means small, which with it have ceased to belong to our living language any more. How many readers would need to turn to a glossary, if they would know so much as what a ' fletcher ' is.* Or turn to any old treatise on hawking. How many terms are there assumed as familiar to the reader, which have quite dropped out of our common knowledge. Nor let it be urged that these can have constituted no very real loss, seeing that they were only used within the narrow circle, and comparatively narrow it must have always been, of those addicted to this sport. This is not the case. Words travel beyond their proper sphere ; are used in secondary senses, and in these secondary senses are everybody's words, while in their primary sense they may remain the possession only of a few.

When I spoke a little while ago of the extinction of such a multitude of words, I did not, as you will have observed already, refer merely to *tentative* words, candidates for admission into the language, offered to, but never in any true sense accepted by it, such as those of which I quoted some in an earlier lecture ; but to such as either belonged to its primitive stock, or, if not this, had yet been domiciled in it so long, that they seemed to have found there a lasting home.

* Marsh, *Lectures on the English Language*, 1860, p. 267.

The destruction has reached these quite as much as those. Thus not a few words of the purest old English stock, some having lived on into the Elizabethan period or beyond it, have finally dropped out of our vocabulary; sometimes leaving a gap which has never since been filled; but their places oftener taken by others which have come up in their room. That beautiful word 'wanhope,' hope, that is, which has wholly *waned,* or despair, long held its ground; it occurs in Gascoigne; being the latest survivor of a whole family of words which continued much longer in Scotland than with us; of which some perhaps continue there still. These are but a few of them : 'wanthrift' for extravagance; 'wanluck' or 'wanhap,' misfortune; 'wanlust,' languor; 'wanwit,' folly; 'wangrace,' wickedness; 'wantrust' (Chaucer), suspicion; 'wantruth' (*Metrical Homilies*), 'falsehood.' 'Skinker' (no very graceful word), for cupbearer, is used by Shakespeare, and lasted to Dryden's time and beyond it. Spenser uses often 'to welk' (welken) as to fade, 'to sty' as to mount, 'to hery' as to glorify or praise, 'to halse' as to embrace,' 'teene' as vexation or grief; Shakespeare 'to tarre' as to provoke, 'to sperr' as to enclose or bar in. Holland has 'specht' for woodpecker, or tree-jobber as it used oftener to be called; 'reise' for journey, 'frimm' for lusty or strong. 'To tind,' surviving in 'tinder,' occurs in Bishop Sanderson; 'to nimm' (nehmen) in Fuller. 'Nesh,' soft through moisture, good Saxon-English once, still lives on in some of our provincial dialects, with not a few of the other words which I have just named. Thus 'leer' for empty, and 'heft,' that which only by an effort can be heaved up (used by Shakespeare), 'to fettle' (the verb is employed by Swift), are common on the lips of our southern peasantry to this day.

A number of vigorous compounds we have lost and let go. Except for Shakespeare we might have quite forgotten that young men of hasty fiery valour were once named 'hotspurs;' and this even now is for us rather the proper name of one than the designation of all.* Austere old men, such as, in Falstaff's words, 'hate us youth,' were 'grimsirs' or 'grimsires' once (Massinger); a foe that wore the semblance of a friend was a 'heavy friend;' a mischief-maker a 'coal-carrier;' an impudent railer a 'saucy jack;' pleasant drink 'merrygodown' (all these in Golding); a cockered favorite was a 'whiteboy' (Fuller); a drunkard an 'aleknight,' a 'maltworm;' an old woman an 'old trot;' an ill-behaved girl a 'naughty pack;' a soldier who of evil will ('malin gré') shirked his share of duty and danger a 'malingerer'—the word is familiar enough to military men, but not in our dictionaries;—a sluggard a 'slowback;' an ignoble place of refuge a 'creephole' (Henry More); entertainments of song or music were 'earsports' (Holland); a hideous assemblage of all most discordant sounds a 'black-sanctus;' well-merited punishment 'whipping-cheer' (Stubbs).

---

*.See Holland, *Livy*, p. 922; Baxter, *Life and Times*, p. 39; Rogers, *Matrimonial Honour*, p. 233.

'Double-diligent' (Golding) was as much as needlessly officious; 'snoutfair' an epithet applied to a woman who, having beauty, had no other gifts mental or moral to commend her; 'mother-naked' (revived by Carlyle) finds its explanation at Job i. 21; 1 Tim. vi. 7. Who too but must acknowledge the beauty of such a phrase as 'weeping-ripe' (Shakespeare), ready, that is, to burst into tears, the ἀτίδαχρυ5 of Euripides?

And as words, so also phrases are forgotten. 'From the teeth outward' to express professions which have no root in the heart of him who speaks them, has so approved itself to Carlyle that he has called it back into use. How expressive too are many other of the proverbial phrases which we have suffered to fall through; as for instance 'to make a coat for the moon,' to attempt something in its nature every way impossible; 'to tread the shoe awry,' to make a *faux pas;* 'to play rex,' to domineer; 'to weep Irish,' to affect a grief which is not felt within, as do the hired mourners at an Irish wake. But these are legion, and quite impossible to enumerate, so that we must content ourselves with the examples here given.

An almost unaccountable caprice seems often to preside over the fortunes of words, and to determine which should live and which die. Of them quite as much as of books it may be affirmed, *habent sua fata.* Thus in instances out of number a word lives on as a verb, but has perished as a noun; we say 'to embarrass,' but no longer an 'embarrass;' 'to revile,'

but not, with Chapman and Milton, a 'revile;' 'to
dispose,' but not a 'dispose;' 'to retire,' but not a
'retire' (Milton) ; 'to wed,' but not a 'wed;' 'to
'infest,' but use no longer the adjective 'infest.' Or
with a reversed fortune a word lives on as a noun,
but has perished as a verb ; thus as a noun substantive, a 'slug,' but no longer 'to slug,' or render sloth-
ful ; a 'child,' but no longer 'to child' ('*childing*
autumn,' Shakespeare) ; a 'rape,' but not 'to rape'
(South) ; a 'rogue,' but not 'to rogue ;' 'malice,' but
not 'to malice ;' a 'path,' but not 'to path ;' or as a
noun adjective, 'serene,' but not 'to serene,' a beautiful word, which we have let go, as the French have
'sereiner ;'* 'meek,' but not 'to meek' (Wiclif) ;
'fond,' but not 'to fond' (Dryden) ; 'dead,' but not
'to dead ;' 'intricate,' but 'to intricate' (Jeremy
Taylor) no longer. So too we have still the adjective
'plashy,' but a 'plash,' signifying a wet place, no
more.

Or again, the affirmative remains, but the negative
is gone ; thus 'wisdom,' 'bold,' 'sad,' but not any
more 'unwisdom,' 'unbold,' 'unsad' (all in Wiclif);

---

* How many words modern French has lost which are most
vigorous and admirable, the absence of which can only now
be supplied by a circumlocution or by some less excellent
word—'Oseur,' 'affranchisseur' (Amyot), 'mépriseur,' 'mur-
murateur,' 'blandisseur' (Bossuet), 'abuseur' (Rabelais),
'désabusement,' 'rancœur,' are all obsolete at the present ;
and so 'désaimer,' to cease to love ('disamare' in Italian),
'guirlander,' 'stériliser,' 'blandissant,' 'ordonnément' (Mon-
taigne), with innumerable others.

'cunning,' but not 'uncunning ;' 'manhood,' ' wit,'
'mighty,' 'tall,' but not 'unmanhood,' 'unwit,' 'un-
mighty,' 'untall' (all in Chaucer) ; 'tame,' but not
'untame' (Jackson) ; 'buxom,'but not 'unbuxom'
(Dryden) ; 'hasty,' but not 'unhasty' (Spenser) ;
'blithe,' but not 'unblithe ;' 'idle,' but not 'unidle'
(Sir P. Sidney) ; 'base,' but not ' unbase ' (Daniel);
'ease,' but not ' unease ' (Hacket) ; 'repentance,'
but not 'unrepentance ;' 'remission,' but not 'irre-
mission' (Donne) ; 'science,' but not ' nescience'
(Glanvill) ; 'to know,' but not 'to unknow' (Wiclif);
'to give,' but not 'to ungive ;' 'to hallow,' but not
'to unhallow' (Coverdale).   Or, with a curious
variation from this, the negative survives, while the
affirmative is gone ; thus 'wieldy' (Chaucer) survives only in 'unwieldy;' 'couth' and 'couthly'
(both in Spenser), only in 'uncouth'and 'uncouthly;'
'speakable' (Milton), in 'unspeakable;' 'ruly'
(Foxe), in 'unruly;' 'gainly' (Henry More), in
'ungainly;' these last two were serviceable words,
and have been ill lost ; 'gainly' is still common in
the West Riding of Yorkshire ; 'exorable' (Holland)
and ' evitable' survive only in 'inexorable' and 'inevitable ;' 'faultless' remains, but hardly 'faultful'
(Shakespeare) ; 'semble' (Foxe), except as a technical law term, has disappeared, while 'dissemble'
continues ; 'simulation' (Coverdale) in like manner
is gone, but 'dissimulation remains. So also of
other pairs one has been taken, and one left ; 'height,'
or 'highth,' as Milton better spelt it, remains, but
'lowth' (Becon) is gone ; 'underling' remains, but

'overling' has perished. 'Exhort' continues, but 'dehort,' a word whose place 'dissuade' does not exactly supply, has escaped us; 'righteousness,' or 'rightwiseness,' as once more accurately written, remains, but '-wrongwiseness' has been taken; 'inroad' continues, but 'outroad' (Holland) has disappeared; 'levant' lives, but 'ponent' (Holland) has died; 'to extricate' continues, but, as we saw just now, 'to intricate' does not; 'parricide,' but not 'filicide' (Holland); 'womanish,' but not 'mannish' (Shakespeare). Again, of whole groups of words formed on some particular scheme it may be only a single specimen will survive. Thus 'gainsay' (=againsay) survives; but 'gainstrive' (Foxe), 'gainstand,' 'gaincope' (Golding), and other similarly formed words exist no longer. 'Praiseworthy,' 'trustworthy,' 'noteworthy,' are the only survivors of a family that numbered once 'shameworthy' (Wiclif), 'japeworthy' (Chaucer), 'kissworthy' (Sidney), 'thankworthy' (English Bible), 'crownworthy' (Ben Jonson), 'painworthy' (Spenser), 'deathworthy' (Shakespeare), and very probably more. In like manner 'foolhardy' alone remains out of at least five adjectives formed on the same pattern; thus 'foollarge,' as expressive a word as prodigal, occurs in Chaucer, and 'foolhasty,' found also in him, lived on to the time of Holland; while 'foolhappy' is in Spenser, and 'foolbold' in Bale. 'Laughing-stock' we still use; but 'gazing-stock' (English Bible), 'wondring-stock,' 'jesting-stock' (both in Coverdale), 'mocking-stock' (Latimer), 'playing-stock'

(North), have all disappeared. 'Steadfast' remains, but 'shamefast,' 'rootfast,' 'bedfast' (=bed-ridden), 'homefast,' 'housefast,' 'masterfast,' or engaged to a master (Skelton), 'weatherfast,' or detained by stress of weather (Cleaveland dialect), 'trothfast' (Cumbrian), 'handfast' (=betrothed), with others, are all gone. We have 'twilight,' but 'twibil' (=bipennis, Chapman), 'twifight' (=duel), are extinct.

It is a real loss that the comparative 'rather' should now stand alone, having dropped alike the positive, 'rathe,' and the superlative, 'rathest'. 'Rathe,' or early, though a graceful word, and not fallen quite out of popular remembrance, being embalmed in the *Lycidas* of Milton,

> 'And the *rathe* primrose, which forsaken dies,'

might be suffered to share the common lot of so many others which have perished, though worthy to live ; but the disuse of 'rathest' is a real loss to the language, and the more so, that 'liefest' is gone too. 'Rather' expresses the Latin 'potius ;' but 'rathest' being obsolete, we have no word, unless 'soonest' may be accepted as such, to express 'potissimum,' or the preference not of one way over another or over certain others, but of one over all ; which we therefore effect by aid of various circumlocutions. Nor has' 'rathest' been so long out of use, that it would be hopeless to attempt to revive it. Sanderson, in his beautiful sermon on the text, 'When my father and my mother forsake me, the Lord taketh me up,' puts the consideration, 'why father and mother are named the *rathest*, and the rest to be included in them.' *

I observed just now that words formed on certain patterns had a tendency to fall into desuetude, and are evidently exposed to more than the ordinary chances of mortality. It has been thus with adjectives ending in 'some,' the Anglo-Saxon and early English 'sum,' the German 'sam' ('friedsam,' 'seltsam') ; and reappearing as an independent word in 'same.' It is true that of these many survive, as 'gladsome,' 'handsome,' 'wearisome,' 'buxom' ('bucksome,' in our earlier writers, the German 'beugsam' or 'biegsam,' bendable, complaint) ; but of these far more than a rateable proportion are nearly or quite extinct. Thus 'wansum,' or sorrowful, is in the *Story of Genesis ;* while in Wiclif's Bible you may note 'lovesum,' 'hatesum,' 'lustsum,' 'gilsum' (guilesome), 'wealsum,' 'heavysum,' 'lightsum,' 'delightsum ;' of these 'lightsome' survived long, and indeed still survives in provincial dialects ; but of the others all save 'delightsome' are gone ; while that, although used in our Authorized Version (Mal. iii. 12), is now only employed in poetry. So too 'mightsome' (see Herbert Coleridge's *Glossarial Index*), 'willsome' (*Promptorium*), 'hearsome' (=obedient), 'needsome,' 'wantsome,' 'brightsome,' (Marlowe), 'wieldsome,' 'unwieldsome' (Golding), 'unlightsome' (Milton), 'thoughtsome,' 'growth-

---

* For other passages in which 'rathest' occurs see the *State Papers*, vol. ii. pp. 92, 170.

some' (both in Fairfax), 'healthsome' (*Homilies*),
'ugsome,' 'ugglesome' (both in Foxe), 'laboursome' (Shakespeare),' 'friendsome,' 'longsome'
(Bacon),' 'quietsome,' 'mirksome' (both in Spenser), 'toothsome' (Beaumont and Fletcher), 'glee-
some' 'joysome' (both in Browne's *Pastorals*),
'gaysome' (*Mirror for Magistrates*), 'likesome'
(Holinshed), 'roomsome,' 'bigsome,' 'awsome,'
'timersome,' 'winsome,' 'viewsome,' 'dosome'
(=prosperous), 'flaysome' (=fearful), 'aunter-
some' (=adventurous), 'drearisome,' 'dulsome,'
'doubtsome,' 'wranglesome,' 'clamorsome' (all
these still surviving in the North), 'playsome' (employed by the historian Hume), 'lissome,' 'meltsome,'
'heedsome,' 'laughsome,' 'clogsome,' 'fearsome,'
have nearly or quite disappeared from our English
speech. More of them have held their ground in
Scotland than in the south of the Island.*

Nor can it be mere accident that of a group of words,
almost all of them depreciatory and contemptuous,
ending in 'ard,' the German 'hart,' the Gothic
'hardus,'† more than one half should have dropped

---

* Thus see in Jamieson's *Dictionary* 'bangsome,' 'freak-
some,' 'drysome,' 'grousome,' with others out of number.

† This, though a German form, reached *us* through the
French ; having been early adopted by the Neo-latin languages.
In Italian words of this formation are frequent, 'bugiardo,'
'falsardo,' 'leccardo,' 'testardo,' 'vecchiardo ;' and certainly
not less so in French : 'goliart,' 'pifart,' 'bavard,' 'fuyard,'
with many more ; and in these languages, no less than our
own, they have almost always, as Diez observes (*Gram. d.*

out of use; I refer to that group of which 'dotard,' 'laggard,' 'braggart,' 'sluggard,' 'buzzard,' 'bastard,' 'wizard,' may be taken as surviving specimens ; while 'blinkard' (*Homilies*), 'dizzard' (Burton), 'dullard' (Udal), 'musard' (Chaucer), 'trichard' (*Political Songs*), 'haskard,' 'shreward' (Robert of Gloucester), 'ballard' (a bald-headed man, Wiclif) ; 'palliard,' 'pillard,' 'snivelard' (*Promptorium Parvulorum*) ; 'bosard,' 'puggard,' 'stinkard' (Ben Jonson), 'haggard' (a worthless hawk), are extinct. There is a curious province of our vocabulary, in which we were once so rich, that extensive losses have failed to make us poor. I refer to those double words which either contain within themselves a strong rhyming modulation, such, for example, as 'willy-nilly,' 'hocus-pocus,' 'helter-skelter,' 'tag-rag,' 'namby-pamby,' 'pell-mell,' 'hab-nab,' 'hodge-podge,' 'hugger-mugger,' 'hurly-burly ;'* or, with

---

Rom. Sprachen, vol. ii. p. 359), 'eine ungünstige Bedeutung.' Compare Mätzner, vol. i. p. 439.

* The same pleasure in a swiftly recurring rhyme has helped to form such phrases as these : 'scot and lot,' 'top and lop,' 'creep and leap,' 'rape and scrape,' 'draff and chaff,' 'shame and blame.' Fairly numerous in English, there are far more of them in German ; thus 'gut und blut,' 'lug und trug,' 'steg und weg,' 'hülle und fülle,' 'hege und pflege,' 'saus und braus,' 'rath und that,' 'tritt und schritt,' 'schutz und trutz,' 'sack und pack,' 'weit und breit,' 'band und rand,' 'dach und fach,' 'sichten und richten,' 'handel und wandel,' 'schalten und walten,' 'leben und weben.' For some earlier and mainly juristic forms of the like kind see Grimm, *Deutsche Rechtsalterthumer*, p. 13.

a slight difference from this, those whose characteristic
feature is not this internal likeness with initial unlikeness, but initial likeness with internal unlikeness ;
not rhyming, but strongly alliterative, and in every
case with a change of the interior vowel from a weak
into a strong, generally from ' i ' into ' a ' or ' o ' ; as
' shilly-shally,' ' mingle-mangle,' ' tittle-tattle,' ' prittle-
prattle,' ' riff-raff,' ' see-saw,' ' slip-slop.'   No one
who is not quite out of love with the homelier portions of·the language, but will acknowledge the life
and strength which there is often in these and in
others still current among us.   But of this sort what
vast numbers have fallen out of use, some so fallen
out of all remembrance that it may be difficult to find
credence for them.   Thus take of rhyming the following : ' kaury-maury,' ' trolly-lolly ' (*Piers Ploughman*), ' tuzzie-muzzie ' (*Promptorium*), ' kicksy-wick-
sy ' (Shakespeare) ; ' hibber-gibber,' ' rusty-dusty,'
' horrel-lorrel,' ' slaump-paump ' (all in Gabriel Harvey), ' royster-doyster ' (*Old Play*), ' hoddy-doddy,'
(Ben Jonson) ; while of alliterative might be instanced these : ' skimble-skamble,' ' bibble-babble '
(both in Shakespeare), ' twittle-twattle,' ' kim-kam '
(both in Holland), ' trim-tram,' ' trish-trash,' ' swish-
swash ' (all in Gabriel Harvey), ' whim-wham '
(Beaumont and Fletcher), ' mizz-mazz ' (Locke),
' snip-snap ' (Pope,) ' flim-flam ' (Swift,) ' tric-trac,'
and others.*

---

* *A Dictionary of Reduplicated Words in the English Language*, by Henry B. Wheatley, published as an appendix to
The Transactions of the Philological Society, 1865, contains

Again, there is a whole family of words,—many of
them are now under ban,—which were at one time
formed almost at pleasure, the only condition being·
that the combination should be a happy one. I refer
to those singularly expressive words formed by a combination of verb and substantive, the former governing
the latter ; as 'telltale,' 'scapegrace,' 'turncoat,'
'turntail,' 'skinflint,' 'spendthrift,' 'spitfire,' 'lick-
spittle,' 'daredevil' (=wagehals), 'makebate' (=stö-
renfried), 'marplot,' 'killjoy.' These, with some
others, have held their ground, and are current still ;
but how many are forgotten ; while yet, though not
always elegant, they preserved some of the most genuine and vigorous idioms of·the language.* Nor is

nearly six hundred of these words, and the collector believes
that there are some hundreds more which he has not ingathered.
I very much doubt whether he has left any such gleaning to
those who follow him. I have lighted upon several, in what
seemed to me out of the way corners of English literature, but
have invariably found them duly registered by him. Words
constructed on a similar scheme are to be found in the Romance
languages ; but are less numerous there, and not indigenous ;
their existence in these being rather the result of Germanic
influences, which the Neo-latin languages did not altogether
escape (Diez, *Gram. d. Rom. Sprachen*, vol. i. p. 71).

* Many languages have groups of words formed upon the
same scheme, although, singularly enough, they are altogether
absent from the Anglo-Saxon (Grimm, *Deutsche Gram.* vol. ii.
p. 976). Thus in Spanish a vaunting braggart is a 'mata-
moros,' a slaymoor ; he is a 'matasiete,' a slayseven (the
'ammazzasiete' of the Italians) ; a 'perdonavidas,' a spare-
lives. Others may be added to these, as 'azotacalles,'
'picapleytos,' 'saltaparedes,' 'rompeesquinas,' 'ganapan,'
'cascatreguas.' So in French, 'attisefeu,' 'coupegorge,'

this strange ; they are almost all words of abuse or contempt, and these are invariably among the most picturesque and imaginative which a language possesses. The whole man speaks out in them, and often the man under the influence of passion and excitement, which always lend force and fire to his speech. Let me of these recount a few : 'smellfeast' (Davies),—it may remind us of the Greek τρεχεδειπνος,—if not a better, is a more graphic, word than our foreign parasite ; 'clawback' (Hacket) is stronger, if not more graceful, than flatterer or sycophant ; 'tosspot' (Fuller), it is sometimes 'reelpôt' (Middleton), or 'swillpot' (Cotgrave), tells its tale as well as drunkard ; and 'pinchpenny' (Holland), or 'nipfarthing' (Drant), as well or better than miser. 'Spintext,' 'lacklatin,' 'mumblematins,' were all applied to ignorant clerics ; 'bitesheep' (a favourite word with Foxe), to bishops who were rather wolves tearing, than shepherds feeding, the flock ; 'slipstring' (Beaumont and Fletcher, =pendard), 'slipgibbet,' 'scapegallows,' were all names given to those who, however they might have escaped, were justly owed to the gallows, and might still, as our common people say, 'go up stairs to bed.'

How many of these words occur in Shakespeare. The following list makes no pretence to completeness : 'martext,' 'carrytale,' 'pleaseman,' 'sneakcup,' 'mumblenews,' 'wantwit,' 'lackbrain,'

'fainéant,' 'vaurien,' 'troublefête.' In Italian 'accattapane,' 'cercabrighe,' 'rubacuori' (Diez, *Gram. d. Rom. Sprachen*, vol. ii. p. 410).

'lackbeard,' 'lacklove,' 'ticklebrain,' 'cutpurse,' 'cutthroat,' 'crackhemp,' 'tearsheet, 'breedbate,' 'swingebuckler,' 'pickpurse,' 'pickthank,' 'picklock,' 'scarecrow,' 'breakvow,' 'breakpromise,' 'findfault,' 'choplogic,' 'makepeace '—this last and 'telltruth' (Fuller) being the only two in the whole collection, wherein reprobation or contempt is not implied. Nor is the list exhausted yet ; there are further 'dingthrift' (=prodigal, Herrick), 'wastegood,' 'spendall' (both in Cotgrave), 'stroygood' (Golding), 'scattergood,' 'wastethrift' (Beaumont and Fletcher), 'scapethrift,' 'swashbuckler' (both in Holinshed), 'rushbuckler,' 'shakebuckler,' 'rinsepitcher' (both in Becon), 'drawlatch' (Awdeley), 'crackrope' (Howell), 'waghalter,' 'wagfeather' (both in Cotgrave), 'blabtale' (Hacket), 'getnothing' (Adams), 'tearthroat' (Gayton), 'spitpoison' (South), 'spitvenom,' 'marprelate,' 'nipcheese,' 'nipscreed,' 'killman' (Chapman), lackland,' 'pickquarrel,' 'pickfault,' 'pickpenny' (Henry More), 'makefray' (Bishop Hall,) 'makedebate (Richardson's *Letters*), 'quenchcoal' (an enemy to all zeal in religion, Rogers,) 'kindlecoal,' 'kindlefire' (both in Gurnall), 'turntippet' (Cranmer), 'swillbowl' (Stubbs), 'smellsmock' (=mulierarius), 'cumberworld' (Drayton), 'curryfavor,' 'pinchfist,' 'suckfist,' 'hatepeace' (Sylvester), 'hategood ' (Bunyan), 'clusterfist' (Cotgrave), 'clutchfist,' 'sharkgull' (both in Middleton), 'makesport' (Fuller), 'hangdog' ('Herod's *hangdogs* in the tapestry,' Pope), 'catchpoll,' 'makeshift' (used not imperson-

ally, as now), 'pickgoose' ('the bookworm was
never but a *pickgoose'*), 'killcow' (these three last in
Gabriel Harvey), 'frayboggard' (=scarecrow, Coverdale), 'letgame' (=spoilsport, Chaucer), 'rake-
shame' (Milton, prose), with others which it will be
convenient to omit. 'Rakehell,' which used to be
spelt 'rakel' or 'rakle' (Chaucer), a good English
word, would be wrongly included in this list, although
Cowper, when he writes 'rakehell' ('*rake-hell* baronet'),* must evidently have regarded it as belonging
to this family of words.†

There is another frequent cause of the disuse of
words. In some inexplicable way there comes to be
attached something of ludicrous, or coarse, or vulgar
to them, out of a sense of which they are no longer
used in earnest writing, and fall out of the discourse

---

* I regret by too much brevity to have here led astray Dr.
G. Schneider, who has written a *History of the English Language*, Freiburg, 1863, and done me the honour to transfer
with slight acknowledgment whatever he found useful in my
little book to his own. He has at p. 159, this wonderful para-
graph : 'Rakehell bedeutete ehemals baronet ; bald verband
sich damit der Begriff von " wohllebender Mensch ;" und da
derjenige, welcher mehr an's Wohlleben denkt, leicht ein
Wohllüstling wird, ging die anfangs gute Bedeutung in diese
letztere über ; der Ausdruck ward desshalb aufgegeben, um
nicht mit dem Gedanken an baronet stets die Idee von einem
ausschweifenden wohllüstigen Menschen zu verbinden.'

† The mistake is far earlier ; long before Cowper wrote the
sound suggested first this sense, and then this spelling. Thus
Stanihurst, *Description of Ireland*, p. 28 : 'They are taken
for no better than *rakehels*, or *the devil's black guard ;*' and
often elsewhere.

of those who desire to speak elegantly.* Not indeed
that this degradation which overtakes words is in all
cases inexplicable. The unheroic character of most
men's minds, with their consequent intolerance of
that heroic which they cannot understand, is constantly at work, too often with success, in taking down
words of nobleness from their high pitch ; and, as the
most effectual way of doing this, in casting an air of
mock-heroic about them. Thus 'to dub,' a word
resting on one of the noblest uses of chivalry, has
now something of ludicrous about it ; so too has
'doughty.' · They belong to that serio-comic, mock-
heroic diction, the multiplication of which, as of all
parodies on greatness, is evermore a sign of evil
augury for a nation that receives it with favor, is at
present such a sign of evil augury for our own.

'Pate' is now comic or ignoble; it was not so
once ; else we should not meet it in the Psalms
(vii. 17) ; as little was 'noddle,' which occurs in one
of the few poetical passages in Hawes. The same
may be affirmed of 'sconce,' of 'nowl' or 'noll'
(Wiclif); of 'slops' for trousers (Marlowe's *Lucan*) ;
of 'cocksure' (Rogers), of 'smug,' which once meant
adorned ('the *smug* bridegroom,' Shakespeare). 'To
nap' is now a word without dignity ; while in Wiclif's
Bible we read, 'Lo He schall not *nappe*, neither slepe
that kepeth Israel' (Ps. cxxi. 4). 'To punch,' 'to
thump,' both occurring in Spenser, could not now
obtain the same serious use ; as little 'to wag' (Matt.
xxvii. 39), or 'to buss' (Shakespeare). Neither would
any one now say with Wiclif that at Lystra Barnabas

and Paul 'rènt their clothes and *skipped out* among
the people' (Acts xiv. 14); nor with Coverdale, 'My
beloved cometh *hopping* upon the mountains' (Cant.
ii. 8); nor yet that 'the Lord *trounced* Sisera and
all his host,' as it stands in the Bible of 1551. 'A *sight*
of angels' (as Tyndale has it at Heb. xii. 22), would
be felt to be a vulgarism now. 'A *blubbered* face'
(Spenser) would scarcely appeal to our pity. We
should not call now a delusion of Satan a '*flam* of the
devil' (Henry More); nor our Lord's course through
the air to the pinnacle of the temple 'his aery *jaunt*'
(Milton). 'Verdant' is no longer a name which
Spenser could give to one of the knights of Fairyland.
It is the same with phrases. 'Through thick and
thin' (Spenser), 'cheek by jowl' (Dubartas), do not
now belong to serious literature. In the glorious
ballad of *Chevy Chase*, a noble warrior whose legs are
hewn off, is 'in doleful dumps;' just as, in Holland's
Livy, the Romans are 'in the dumps' after their
disastrous defeat at Cannæ. In Golding's *Ovid*, one
fears that he will 'go to pot.' In one of the beautiful
letters of John Careless, preserved in Foxe's *Martyrs*,
he announces that a persecutor, who expects a recan-
tation from him, is 'in the wrong box.' And in the
sermons of Barrow, who certainly did not seek familiar,
still less vulgar, expressions, we constantly meet such
terms as 'to rate,' 'to snub,' 'to gull,' 'to pudder,'
'dumpish,' and the like; words, we may be sure, not
vulgar when he used them.

Then too the advance of refinement causes words
to be dismissed, which are felt to speak too plainly.

It is not here merely that one age has more delicate ears than another; and that subjects are freely spoken of at one period which at another are withdrawn from conversation. There is something of this; but even if this delicacy were at a standstill, there would still be . 'a continual disallowing of words, which for a certain while have been employed to designate coarse or disagreeable facts or things ; or, where not a disallowing, a relinquishing of them to the lower classes of society, with the adoption of others in their stead. The former words being felt to have come by long use into too direct and close relation with what they designate, to summon it up too distinctly before the mind's eye, they are thereupon exchanged for others, which, at first at least, indicate more lightly and allusively the offensive thing, rather hint and suggest than paint and describe it: although by and by these new will in their turn be discarded, and for exactly the same reasons which brought about the dismissal of those which they themselves superseded. It lies in the necessity of things that I must leave this part of my subject, curious as it is, without illustration ;* but no one even moderately acquainted with

---

* As not, however, turning on a *very* coarse matter, and illustrating the subject with infinite wit and humour, I might refer the Spanish scholar to the discussion between Don Quixóte and his squire on the dismissal of ' regoldar ' from the language of good society, and the substitution of ' erutar ' in its room (*Don Quixote,* 4. 7. 43). In a letter of Cicero to Pætus (*Fam.* ix. 22) there is a subtle and interesting disquisition on the philosophy of these forbidden words.

the early literature of the Reformation can be ignorant of words having free course therein, which now are not merely coarse, and as such under ban,. but which no one would employ who did not mean to speak impurely and vilely.*

I spoke in a former lecture of the many words which have come back to us after a temporary absence, and of the extent to which the language has been reinforced and recruited· by these. For there is this difference between words and flexions, that of the last what is once gone is gone for ever ; they are irrevocable ; no human power could ever recall them. A poet indeed may use 'pictaï' for 'pictæ' (Virgil), or 'glitterand' ·for glittering (Spenser) ; but it is not in their power to call these back, even if they would ; and when a German writer suggests that to abate the too great sibilation of our language we should recover the plurals in *n*, 'eyne,' 'housen,' and the like, he betrays his ignorance of the inexorable laws of language, and of the impossibility of controlling these. But it is not so with words ; and I cannot but think, in view of this disposition of theirs to return, in view also of the havoc which, as we have seen, various causes are evermore effecting in the ranks of a language, that much might be done by writers of authority and influence in the way of bringing back deserters, where they are capable of yielding good service still, and placing them in the ranks again ; still more

* See Grimm's *Deutsches Woerterbuch*, s. v. *Koth*, for some good remarks on this matter. ·

in that of detaining words, which, finding no honourable employment, seem more or less disposed to be
gone, though they have not as yet actually disappeared. This would be less difficult from the fact
that in almost every instance these words, obsolete or
obsolescent, which our literary English knows, or is
about to know, no more, live on, as has been already
noted, in one or more of our provincial dialects ;
they need not therefore, as dead, that life should be
breathed into them anew; but only, as having retired into obscurity for a while, some one to draw
them forth from this óbscurity again. Of these there
are multitudes. If I instance a very few, it is not as
specially recommending them for rehabilitation,
though some of them are well worthy of it, and capable
of good service still ; but as showing to what kind of
work I invite.

It is indeed to the poet that mainly, although not
exclusively, this task must be committed. ' That
high-flying liberty of conceit' which is proper to him
will justify liberties on his part which would be
denied to the writer of less impassioned prose.* It
is felt by all that with the task which is before him, he

---

* Jean Paul (*Æsthetik*, § 83) : Ueberhaupt bildet und nährt
die Prose ihre Sprachkraft an der Poesie, denn diese muss immer mit neuen Federn steigen, wenn die alten, die ihren
Flügeln ausfallen, die Prose zum Schreiben nimmt. Wie diese
aus Dichtkunst entstand, so wächst sie auch an ihr.

Ewald *(Die poet. Bucher des Alten Bundes*, p. 55) : ' End-
lich aber ist der Dichter nicht bloss so der freieste Herrscher
und Schöpfer im Gebiete der Sprache seiner Zeit, er spricht

has a right to all the assistance which the language trained to the uttermost is capable of yielding. Whatever resources it offers, he has a claim to draw upon them all. This liberty Tennyson has used. Thus 'to burgeon' had pretty nearly disappeared from the language since the time of Dryden, but has by him on several occasions been employed. But not to the poet only is such a privilege conceded. The verb 'to hearten' was as good as dead till Mr. Grote, by his frequent employment of it in his *History of Greece*, gave it life again. ' To sagg,' a Shakespéarian word, and one too good to lose, is alive everywhere in England, except in our literary dialect; thus a tired horse 'saggs' his head; an ill-hung gate 'saggs' on its hinges. ' To gaster ' and ' to flayte,'—they are synonyms, but the first is rather to terrify, and the second to scare,—are frequent in the Puritan writers of East Anglia ; so is 'to fellow-feel ;' the two former

---

auch am wärmsten und frischesten aus der Zeit und dem Orte, woran seine Empfindungen zunächst geknüpft sind ; seine Sprache ist bei aller Wurde und Höhe zugleich die heimischste und eigenthümlischste, weil sie am reinsten und anspruchlosesten aus dem ganzen menschlichen Sein des Einzelnen fliesst. Der Dichter kann also freier und leichter abweichende Farben und Stoffe der Sprache seiner nächsten Heimath und seiner eigenen Zeit einfliessen lassen, und während die Prosa eine einmal festgewordene Form schwer ändert, bereichert und verjüngt sich die Dichtersprache beständig durch Aufnahme des Dialectischen, welches in die herrschende Prosa nicht übergegangen, und durch den Eindrang von Stoffen der Volkssprache, welche doch immer mannigfältiger ist, weil die unerschöpfliche Quelle lebendiger Sprache auch unvermerkt sich immer verändert und fortbildet.

are still alive upon the lips of the people. Perhaps
'to fleck' is not gone; nor yet 'to shimmer;' but
both are certainly in danger of going. Coleridge
supposed that he had invented 'aloofness;' it is well
worthy of acceptance; but if it has been accepted,
which is not yet perfectly clear, he only revived a
word which was in use two hundred years ago.
'Litherness,' as expressing a want of moral backbone
in the character, has gone without leaving a substitute behind it. 'Elfish' and 'elfishness,' these last
expressing a certain inborn and mischievous way-
wardness, have done the same.

'Damish' (Rogers) applied in blame to proud im-
perious women, 'wearish' in the sense of small,
weak, shrunken (thus, 'a wearish old man,' (Burton), 'masterous' or 'maistrous,' as Milton spells it,
in that of overbearing, 'kittle,' an epithet given to
persons of a certain delicate organization, and thus
touchy and easily offended, 'birdwitted,' or incapable
of keeping the attention fixed for long on any single
point (Bacon), 'afterwitted,' applied by Tyndale to
one having what the French now call *l'esprit de
l'escalier*, who always remembers what he should have
said when, having left the room, it is too late to say
it, with numberless others, may each of them singly
be no serious loss, but when these losses may be
counted by hundreds and thousands, they are no
slight impoverishment of our vocabulary; and assuredly it would not be impossible to win some of
these back again. There are others, such as Baxter's
'wordwarriors,' strivers, that is, about words, as Lord

Brooke's ' bookhunger,' as a ' little-ease,' or place of
discomfortable restraint, as 'realmrape'(=usurpation,
Mirror for Magistrates) as ' to witwanton' (Fuller
warns men that they do not 'witwanton with God')
' to cankerfret' ('sin cankerfrets the soul,' (Rogers),
which, though never popular, seem to me happier
than that they should be allowed to die.

We have to thank the American branch of the
English-speaking race that we have not lost 'freshet'
(an exquisite word and used by Milton), ' snag,'
'bluff,' 'kedge,' ' slick,'* 'to whittle,' 'to cave in,'
'to rile,' 'to snarl' that is, to entangle). They are
counted as American inventions, but are indeed
nothing of the kind. There is scarcely one of them,
of which examples could not be found in our earlier
literature, and in provincial dialects they are current
every one to this present day.† Even 'the fall.' as
equivalent to the autumn is not properly American ;
being as old as Dryden,‡ and older.

---

* 'Slick ' is indeed only another form of 'sleek.' Thus
Fuller (*Pisgah Sight of Palestine*, vol. ii. p. 190) : ' Sure I am
this city [the New Jerusalem] as presented by the prophet, was
fairer, finer, *slicker*, smoother, more exact, than any fabric the
earth afforded.'

† See Nall, *Dialect and Provincialisms of East Anglia,*
s. vv.

‡ ' What crowds of patients the towndoctor kills,
     Or how last *fall* he raised the weekly bills.'

So in the answer to Marlowe's *Passionate Pilgrim*, ascribed
to Raleigh :

       ' A honey tongue, a heart of gall,
        Is fancy's *spring*, but sorrow's *fall*.'

But besides these deserters, of which some at least might with great advantage be recalled to the ranks, there are other words, which have never found a place in our literary English, that yet might be profitably adopted into it. A time arrives for a language, when, apart from the recoveries I have been speaking of just now, its own local and provincial dialects are almost the only source from which it can derive additions, such as shall really constitute an increase of its wealth ; while yet such additions from one quarter or another are most needful, if it is not daily to grow poorer, if it is to find any compensation for the waste which is evermore going forward of the wealth that in time past it possessed. We have seen how words wear out, become unserviceable, how the glory that clothed them once disappears, as the light fades from the hills ; how they drop away from the stock and stem of the language as dead leaves from their parent tree ; so that others, a later growth, must supply their place, if the foliage is not to grow sparser and thinner every day.

Before, however, we turn to the dialects as likely to yield here any effectual help, we must form a juster estimate of what these really are, than is commonly entertained ; they must be redeemed in our minds from that unmerited contempt and neglect with which they are by too many regarded. We too often

On this matter of American-English compare a very interesting paper, with the title, ' Inroads upon English,' in *Blackwood's Magazine*, Oct. 1867, p. 399, sqq.

think of a dialect, as of a degraded, distorted, and vulgarized form of the classical language ; all its departures from this being for us violations of grammar, or wrongs which in one kind or another it has suffered from the uneducated and illiterate by whom mainly it is employed. But it is nothing of the kind. It may not have our grammar, but it has a grammar of its own. If it have here and there a distorted or mutilated word, much oftener what we esteem such embodies some curious fact in the earlier history of the language. A dialect is one of the many forms in which a language once existed ; but one, as an eminent French writer has expressed it, which has had misfortunes ;* or which at any rate has not had the good fortune that befell High-German in Germany, Castilian in Spain, Tuscan in Italy, that namely of being

---

* Sainte-Beuve : Je définis un patois, une ancienne langue qui a eu des malheurs. Littré (*Hist. de la Langue Française,* vol. ii. p. 93) : Les faits de langue abondent dans les patois. Parce qu'ils offrent parfois un mot de la langue littéraire estropié ou quelque perversion manifeste de la syntaxe régulière, on a été porté à conclure que le reste est à l'avenant, et qu'ils sont, non pas une formation indépendante et originale, mais une corruption de l'idiome cultivé qui, tombé en des bouches mal apprises, y subit tous les supplices de la distorsion. Il n'en est rien ; quand on ôte ces taches peu nombreuses et peu profondes, on trouve un noyau sain et entier. Ce serait se faire une idée erronée que de considérer un patois comme du français altéré ; il n'y a eu aucun moment où ce que nous appelons aujourd'hui le français ait été uniformément parlé sur toute la surface de la France ; et, par conséquent, il n'y a pas eu de moment non plus où il ait pu s'altérer chez les paysans et le peuple des villes pour devenir un patois. Elsewhere the same writer says

elevated above its compeers and competitors to the
dignity of the classical language of the land. As a
consequence it will not have received the development, nor undergone the elaboration, which have been
the portion of its more successful rival ; but for these
very reasons will have often retained a freedom, a
freshness, and a *naïveté* which the other has in good
measure forgone and lost.*

(vol. ii. p. 150) : Sauf l'usage des bons écrivains et de la
société polie, sauf l'élaboration grammaticale (double avantage
que je suis loin de vouloir atténuer), la langue littéraire n'est,
non plus, qu'un patois ou dialecte élevé à la suprématie, et
elle a, comme les autres, ses fautes et ses méprises.

* Littré (*Hist. de la Langue Française*, vol. ii. p. 130) : Un
patois n'a pas d'écrivains qui le fixent, dans le sens où l'on dit
que les bons auteurs fixent une langue ; un patois n'a pas les
termes de haute poésie, de haute éloquence, de haut style, vu
qu'il est placé sur un plan où les sujets qui comportent tout cela
ne lui appartiennent plus. C'est ce qui lui donne une apparence de familiarité naïve, de simplicité narquoise, de rudesse
grossière, de grâce rustique. Mais, sous cette apparence, qui
provient de sa condition même, est un fonds solide de bon et
vieux français, qu'il faut toujours consulter. Compare Ampère,
La Formation de la Langue Française, p. 381 ; and Schleicher
(*Die Deutsche Sprache*, p. 110) : Die Mundarten nun sind die
natürlichen, nach den Gesetzen der sprachgeschichtlichen
Veränderungen gewordenen Formen der deutschen Sprache,
im Gegensatze zu der mehr oder minder gemachten und schul-
meisterisch geregelten und zugestutzten Sprache der Schrift.
Schon hieraus folgt der hohe Werth derselben für die wissen-
schaftliche Erforschung unserer Sprache ; hier ist eine reiche
Fülle von Worten und Formen, die, an sich gut und echt, von
der Schriftsprache verschmäht würden ; hier finden wir
manches, was wir zur Erklärung der älteren Sprachdenkmale,

Of its words, idioms, turns of speech, many which
we are ready to set down as vulgarisms, solecisms of
speech, violations of the primary rules of grammar, do
no more than attest that those who employ them
have from some cause or another not kept abreast
with the advances which the language has made. The
usages are only local in the fact that, having once
been employed by the great body of a people, they
have now receded from the lips of all except those in
some certain country districts, who have been more
faithful than others to the traditions of the past.
Thus there are districts of England where for ' we
sing' ' ye sing' 'they sing,' they decline their plurals,
'we singen ' ' ye singen ' 'they singen.' This was
not indeed the original plural, but was that form of it
which, coming up about Chaucer's time, was dying
out in Spenser's. He indeed constantly employs it,*

---

ja zur Erkenntniss der jetzigen Schriftsprache verwerthen können, abgesehen von dem sprachgeschichtlichen, dem lautphy-
siologischen Interesse, welches die überaus reiche Mannigfal-
tigkeit unserer Mundarten bietet.

* It must be owned that Spenser does not fairly represent
the language of his time, or indeed of any time, affecting as
he does a certain artificial archaism both of words and forms.
Some call in question the justice of this charge, and will fain
have it that he does but write the oldest English of his time.
I cannot so regard it. Jonson, born only twenty years later,
could not have been mistaken ; and with all its severity there
is a truth in his observation, 'Spenser, in affecting the ancients,
writ no language.' And Daniel, born some ten years later,
implicitly repeats the charge :

> ' Let others sing of knights and Paladins
> In *aged* accents and *untimely* words.'

but after him it becomes ever rarer in our literary English. In the *Homilies* I have met it once, in Drayton,* and even so late as in Fuller ; but in his time it quite disappears.

Now of those who retain such forms you should esteem not that they violate the laws of the language, but that they have taken their *permanent* stand at that which was only a point of transition for it, and which it has now left behind. A countryman will nowadays say, 'He made me *afeard*,' or 'The price of corn *ris* last market-day,' or 'I will *axe* him his name ;' or 'I tell *ye*,' and you will be tempted to set these phrases down as barbarous English. They are not such at all. 'Afeard' is the regular participle of an Anglo-Saxon verb ' a-færan,' as 'afraid' of ' to affray ;'

See too the remarkable Epistle prefixed by the anonymous Editor to his *Shepherd's Calendar*, where the writer glories in the archaic character of the author, on whom he is annotating. In the matter, however, which is treated above, Ben Jonson was at one with him, himself expressing a strong regret that these flexions had not been retained. ' The persons plural,' he says (*English Grammar*, c. xvii.), ' keep the termination of the first person singular. In former times, till about the reign of King Henry VIII., they were wont to be formed by adding *en ;* thus, *loven, sayen, complainen.* But now (whatsoever is the cause) it hath quite grown out of use, and that other so generally prevailed, that I dare not presume to set this afoot again ; albeit (to tell you my opinion) I am persuaded that the lack hereof, well considered, will be found a great blemish to our tongue. For seeing *time* and *person* be as it were the right and left hand of a verb, what can the maiming bring else, but a lameness to the whole body ? '

*   ' The happy shepherds *minsen* on the plain.'

'ris' or 'risse' is an old preterite of 'to rise;' 'to axe' is not a mispronunciation of 'to ask,' but the constant form which in earlier English the verb assumed. Even such a phrase as 'Put *them* things away,' is not bad, but only antiquated English.* 'Ourn,' which our rustics in the South of England so freely employ (cf. Gen. xxvi. 20, Wiclif), has been disallowed by those classes with which rests the final decision as to what shall stand in a language, and what shall not; but it is in itself as correct, it would hardly be too much to say, more correct than 'ours,' You are not indeed therefore to conclude that these

* Génin (*Récréations Philologiques*, vol. i. p. 71) says to the same effect : Il n'y a guères de faute de français, je dis faute générale, accréditée, qui n'ait sa raison d'être, et ne pût au besoin produire ses lettres de noblesse ; et souvent mieux en règle que celles des locutions qui ont usurpé leur place au soleil. The French Academy, in the Preface to the last edition of the *Dictionnaire Historique de la Langue Française*, p. xv., has some excellent remarks in respect of acts of similar injustice, into which in our judgment of old authors, and trying the past by the rules of the present, we are in danger of falling : Ces écrivains y seront quelquefois défendus contre d'indiscrètes critiques, qui leur ont reproché comme des fautes de langage ce qui n'était que l'emploi légitime de la langue de leur temps. À chaque époque s'établissent des habitudes, des conventions, des règles même, auxquelles n'ont pu assurément se conformer par avance les écrivains des époques antérieures, et qu'il n'est ni juste ni raisonnable de leur opposer, comme s'il s'agissait de ces premiers principes dont l'autorité est absolue et universelle. C'est pourtant en vertu de cette jurisprudence rétroactive qu'ont été condamnées, chez d'excellents auteurs, des manières de parler alors admises, et auxquelles un long abandon n'a pas toujours enlevé ce qu'elles avaient de grâce et de vivacité.

forms are open to you to employ, or that they would
be good English now.   They would not; being departures from that present use and custom, which must
be our standard in what we speak and write ; just as
in our buying and selling we must use the current
coin of the realm, not attempt to pass that which
long since has been called in, whatever intrinsic value
it may possess.

The same may be asserted of certain ways of pronouncing words, not now in use, except among the
lower classes ; thus, 'contráry,' 'mischiévous,' 'blasphémous,' instead of 'cóntrary,' 'míschievous,' 'blás-
phemous.'   It would be easy to show by quotations
from our poets that these are no mispronunciations,
but only the retention of an earlier pronunciation by
the people, after the higher classes have abandoned
it.*   And let me here say how well worth your while
it will prove to watch for provincial words and inflections, local idioms and modes of pronunciation.
Count nothing in this kind beneath your notice.   Do
not at once ascribe any departure from what you have
been used to, either in grammar, or pronunciation,
or meaning ascribed to words, to the ignorance or
stupidity of the speaker.   If you hear 'nuncheon,'†
do not at once set it down for a malformation of

* A single proof may in each case suffice :
'Our wills and fates do so *contráry* run.'—*Shakespere.*
'Ne let *mischiévous* witches with their charms.'—*Spenser.*
'O argument *blasphémous*, false and proud.'—*Milton.*

† This form, which our country people in Hampshire always
employ, either retains the original pronunciation, our received

'luncheon,' nor 'yeel'* of 'eel.' Lists and collections of provincial usage, such as I have suggested,
always have their value. If you cannot turn them to
profit yourselves, and they may not stand in close
enough connection with your own studies for this,
there always are those who will thank you for them ;
and to whom the humblest of these collections, care-

one being a modern corruption ; or else, as is more probable,
we have confounded two different words, from which confusion
they have kept clear. In Howell's *Vocabulary*, 1659, and in
Cotgrave's *French and English Dictionary*, both words occur :
'nuncion or nuncheon, the afternoon's repast,' (cf. *Hudibras*,
i. 1. 346 : 'They took their breakfasts or their *nuncheons*'),
and 'lunchion, a big piece,' *i.e.* of bread ; both giving 'cari-
bot,' which has this meaning, as the French equivalent ; and
compare Gay :

> ' When hungry thou stood'st staring like an oaf,
>   I sliced the *luncheon* from the barley loaf ;'

and Miss Baker (*Northamptonshire Glossary*) explains 'lunch'
as a large lump of bread, or other edible ; " He helped himself to a good *lunch* of cake." ' This 'nuntion ' may possibly
help us to the secret of the word. Richardson notes that it is
spelt 'noon-shun ' in Browne's *Pastorals*, which must suggest
as plausible, if nothing more, that the 'nuntion' was originally the labourer's slight meal, to which he withdrew for the
shunning of the heat of *noon :* above all when in Lancashire
we find 'noon-scape,' and in Norfolk 'noon-miss,' for the time
when labourers rest after dinner. The dignity at which
'lunch ' or 'luncheon ' has now arrived, as when we read in
the newspapers of a 'magnificent *luncheon*,' is quite modern ;
the word belonged a century ago to rustic life, and in literature
had not travelled beyond the 'hobnailed pastorals' which
professed to describe that life.

* Holland (*Pliny*, vol. ii. p. 428, and often) writes it so.

fully and conscientiously made, will be in one way or
other of real assistance.* There is the more need to
urge this at the present, because, notwithstanding the
tenacity with which our country folk cling to their old
forms and usages, still these must now be rapidly
growing fewer ; and there are forces, moral and
material, at work in England, which will probably
cause that of those which now survive the greater
part will within the next fifty years have disappeared.
Many of them even now are only to be gleaned from
such scattered and remote villages as have not yet
been reached by the ravages of the schoolmaster, or
the inroads of the railway.

What has been just now said of our provincial
English, namely, that it is often *old* English rather
than *bad* English, is not less true of many so-called
Americanisms.† There are parts of America where
'het' is still the participle of 'to heat ;' if our Authorized Version had not been meddled with, we should
so read it at Dan. iii. 19 to this day ; where 'holp'
still survives as the perfect of 'to help ;' 'pled' (as
in Spenser) of 'to plead.' Longfellow uses 'dove'
as the perfect of 'to dive ;' nor is this a poetical

---

* An article *On English Pronouns Personal* in the *Transactions of the Philological Society*, vol. i. p. 277, will attest the
excellent service which an accurate acquaintance with provincial usages may render in the investigation of perplexing
phenomena in English grammar.   Compare Guest, *Hist. of
English Rhythms*, vol. ii. p. 207.

† See Bartlett, *Dictionary of Americanisms*, passim.

license, for I lately met the same in a well-written
book of American prose.

The dialects then are worthy of respectful attention
—and if in their grammar, so in their vocabulary no
less. If the sage or the scholar were required to
invent a word which should designate the slight meal
claimed in some of our southern counties by the
labourer before he begins his mowing in the early
morning, they might be sorely perplexed to·do it.
The Dorsetshire labourer, who demands his 'dew-
bit,' has solved the difficulty. In the same dialect
they express in a single word that a house has a
northern aspect; it is 'backsunned.' You have
marked the lighting of the sky just above the horizon
when clouds are about to break up and disappear.
Whatever name you gave it you would hardly improve
on that of the 'weather-gleam,' which in some of our
dialects it bears. And this is what we find continually, namely that the true art of word-making,
which is hidden from the wise and learned of this
world, is revealed to the husbandman, the mechanic,
the child. Spoken as the dialects are by the actual
cultivators of the soil, they will often be inconceivably
rich in words having to do with the processes of
husbandry; thus ripe corn blown about, or beaten
down by rain or hail, may in East Anglia be said
either to be 'baffled,' or 'nickled,' or 'snaffled,' or
'shuckled,' or 'wilted,'* each of these words having

---

* See Nall, *Dialect of East Anglia*, s. vv. 'To wilt,' provincial with us, is not so in America (Marsh, *Lectures*, 1860,
p. 668).

its own shade of meaning. Spóken by those who are in constant and close contact with external nature, the dialects will often possess a fat richer and more varied nomenclature to set forth the various and changing features of this than the literary language itself. Max Müller has said in a passage of singular eloquence on the subject of ' dialectical regeneration,'* and of dialects as the true feeders of a language, ' We can hardly form an idea of the unbounded resources of dialects. When literary languages have stereotyped one general term, these dialects will supply fifty, each with its own special shade of meaning. If new combinations of thought are evolved in the progress of society, dialects will readily supply the required names from the store of their so-called superfluous words.' † Thus a brook, a streamlet, a rivulet are all very well, but what discriminating power do they possess as compared with a ' beck,' a ' burn,' a ' gill,' a ' force,' North-country words, with each a special signification of its own ?

Words from the local dialects are continually slipping into the land's language. ' Poney,' a northern word, has crept into English during the last century ; ' gruesome,' which has always lived in Scotland, is creeping back into English, being used by Browning ; and with it not a few other words from the same quarter, as ' blink,' ' canny,' ' douce,' ' daft,' ' feckless ' ' eerie ' ' foregather,' ' glamour,' ' gloaming,'

---

* *On the Science of Language,* 1st part, p. 60.
† Compare Heyse, *System der Sprachwissenschaft,* p. 229.

'glower,' 'uncanny,' all excellent in their kind. Wordsworth has given allowance to 'force,' which I just now cited as the North-country name for a water-fall; and, if my memory do not err, to 'beck,' and 'burn' as well.* 'Clever,' is an excellent example of a low-born word which almost without observation has passed into general allowance. Sir Thomas Browne noted it two centuries ago as an East Anglian provincialism, and Ray as dialectic. Johnson protests against it as 'a low word, scarcely ever used but in burlesque or conversation.' The facts of the case do not quite bear his statement out, but there can be no doubt that it is a *parvenu*, which has little by little been struggling up to the position which it has now obtained.† 'Fun' too, a word not to be found in

* What use Luther made of the popular language in his translation of the Bible he has himself told us, and here is one secret of its epoch-marking character. These are his words: 'Man muss nicht die Buchstaben in der lateinischen Sprache fragen, wie man soll deutsche reden; sondern man muss die Mutter im Hause, die Kinder auf den Gassen, den gemeinen Mann auf dem Markte darum fragen, und denselben auf das Maul sehen, wie sie reden.' Montaigne, who owes not a little of his reputation to his wonderful style, pleads guilty to the charge brought in his lifetime against him, that he employed not a few words and idioms which, till he gave them a wider circulation, belonged to his native Gascony alone. Goethe too has given general currency to words not a few, which were only provincial before him.

† Nisard (*Curiosités de l'Etymol. Franç.* p. 90): Les patois sont à la fois l'asile où s'est réfugiée en partie l'ancienne langue française et le dépôt où se gardent les éléments de la nouvelle.

our earlier Dictionaries, was 'a low cant word' in Johnson's time and in his estimation.

So much has been done in this matter, the language has been so largely reinforced, so manifestly enriched by words which either it has received back after a longer or shorter absence, or which in later days it has derived from the dialects and enlisted for the first time, as to afford abundant encouragement for attempting much more in the same direction. But these suggestions must for the present suffice. I reserve for my lecture which follows the other half of a subject which is very far from being half exhausted.

LECTURE VI.

DIMINUTIONS OF THE ENGLISH LANGUAGE.

(CONTINUED.)

WHAT in my last preceding lecture has been said must suffice in respect of the words, and the character of the words, which we have lost or let go. Of these, indeed, if a language, as it travels onwards, loses some, it also acquires others, and probably many more than it loses; they are leaves on the tree of language, of which if some fall away, a new succession takes their place. But it is not so, as I already observed, with the *forms* or *powers* of a language, that is, with the various inflections, moods, duplicate or triplicate formation of tenses. These the speakers of a language come gradually to perceive that they can do without, and therefore cease to employ; seeking to suppress grammatical intricacies, and to obtain grammatical simplicity and, so far as possible, a pervading uniformity, sometimes even at the cost of letting go what had real worth, and contributed to the more lively, if not to the clearer, setting forth of the inner thought or feeling of the mind.* Here there is only loss, with no com-

---

* It has been well said, 'There is nothing more certain than this, that the earlier we can trace back any one language, the

pensating gain ; or, at all events, diminution only, and never addition. In this region no creative energy is at work during the later periods of a language, during ‘any, indeed, but quite the earliest, and such as are withdrawn from our vision altogether. These are not as the leaves, but may be likened to the stem and leading branches of a tree, whose shape, mould, and direction are determined at a very early stage of its growth ; and which age, or accident, or violence may make fewer, but which cannot become more numerous than they are. I have already slightly referred to a notable example of this, namely, to the dropping within historic times of the dual in Greek. And not in Greek only has it been felt that this was not worth

more full, complete, and consistent are its forms : that the later we find it existing, the more compressed, colloquial and businesslike it has become. Like the trees of our forests, it grows at first wild, luxuriant, rich in foliage, full of light and shadow, and flings abroad in its vast branches the fruits of a youthful and vigorous nature ; transplanted to the garden of civilisation and trained for the purposes of commerce, it becomes regulated, trimmed, pruned—nature indeed still gives it life, but art prescribes the direction and extent of its vegetation. Always we perceive a compression, a gradual loss of fine distinctions, a perishing of forms, terminations, and conjugations in the younger state of the language. The truth is, that in a language up to a certain period, there is a real indwelling vitality, a principle acting unconsciously, but pervasively in every part : men wield their forms of speech as they do their limbs—spontaneously, knowing nothing of their construction or the means by which these instruments possess their power. It may be even said that the commencement of the age of self-consciousness is identical with the close of that of vitality in language.’

preserving, or at all events that no serious inconvenience would follow from its dismissal. There is
no such number in the modern German, Danish, or
Swedish; in the old German and Norse there was.·
In other words, the stronger logic of a later day has
'found no reason for splitting the idea of *moreness*
into *twoness* and *muchness*,' as Mommsen has quaintly
put it.

How many niceties, delicacies, subtleties of language, *we*, speakers of the English tongue, in the
course of centuries have got rid of; how bare (whether
too bare is another question) we have stripped ourselves; what simplicity, for better or for worse, reigns
in the present English, as compared with the earlier
forms of the language. Once it had six declensions,
our present English has but one; it had three genders,
English as it now is, if we except one or two words,
has none; and the same fact meets us, at what point
soever we compare the grammar of the past with that
of the present. Let me here repeat, that in an estimate of the gain or loss, we must not put certainly to
loss everything which a language has dismissed, any
more than everything to gain which it has acquired.
Unnecessary and superfluous forms are no real wealth.
They are often an embarrassment and an encumbrance
rather than a help. The Finnish language has fifteen
cases.* Without pretending to know exactly what it
can effect by them, I feel confident that it cannot
effect more with its fifteen than the Greek is able to

---

* Barnes, *Philological Grammar*, p. 106.

do with five. The half here may indeed be more
than the whole. It therefore seems to me that some
words of Otfried Müller, in many ways admirable,
exaggerate the disadvantages consequent on a reduc-
tion of the forms of a language. ' It may be observed,' he says, ' that in the lapse of ages, from the
time that the progress of language can be observed,
grammatical forms, such as the signs of cases, moods
and tenses, have never been increased in number, but
have been constantly diminishing. The history of the
Romance, as well as of the Germanic, languages
shows in the clearest manner how a grammar, once
powerful and copious, has been gradually weakened
and impoverished, until at last it preserves only a few
fragments of its ancient inflections. Now there is no
doubt that this luxuriance of grammatical forms is not
an essential part of a language, considered merely as
a vehicle of thought. It is well known that the
Chinese language, which is merely a collection of
radical words destitute of grammatical forms, can express even philosophical ideas with tolerable precision ;
and the English, which from the mode of its formation by a mixture of different tongues, has been
stripped of its grammatical inflections more completely
than any other European language, seems, nevertheless, even to a foreigner, to be distinguished by its
energetic eloquence. All this must be admitted by
every unprejudiced inquirer ; but yet it cannot be
overlooked, that this copiousness of grammatical
forms, and the fine shades of meaning which they
express, evince a nicety of observation, and a faculty

of distinguishing, which unquestionably prove that
the race of mankind among whom these languages
arose was characterized by a remarkable correctness
and subtlety of thought. Nor can any modern
European, who forms in his mind a lively image of
the classical languages in their ancient grammatical
luxuriance, and compares them with his mother
tongue, conceal from himself that in the ancient languages the words, with their inflections, clothed as it
were with muscles and sinews, come forward like
living bodies, full of expression and character, while
in the modern tongues the words seem shrunk up
into mere skeletons.'*

Whether languages are as much impoverished by
this process as is here assumed, may be fairly ques-
tioned. I will endeavor to give you some materials
which shall assist you in forming your own judgment
in the matter ;† not bringing before you forms which

---

* *Literature of Greece*, p. 5.

† I will also append the judgment of another scholar (Renan,
Les Langues Sémitiques, p. 412) : Bien loin de se représenter
l'état actuel comme le développement d'un germe primitive
moins complet et plus simple que l'état qui a suivi, les plus
profonds linguistes sont unanimes pour placer à l'enfance de
l'esprit humain des langues synthétiques, obscures, compliquées,
si compliquées même que c'est le besoin d'un langage plus
facile qui a porté les générations postérieures à abandonner la
langue savante des ancêtres. Il serait possible, en prenant
l'une après l'autre les langues de presque tous les pays où
l'humanité a une histoire, d'y vérifier cette marche constante
de la synthèse à l'analyse. Partout une langue ancienne a
fait place à une langue vulgaire, qui ne constitue pas, à vrai

the language has relinquished long ago, but mainly such as it is relinquishing at the present instant; these, touching us so nearly, will have more than a merely archaic interest for us. Thus the words which retain the Romance female termination in 'ess,'* as 'heir,' which makes 'heiress,' and 'prophet' 'prophetess,' are every day becoming fewer. This has already fallen away in so many instances, and is evidently becoming of unfrequent use in so many more, that, if we may augur of the future frcm the analogy of the past, it will one day wholly vanish from our tongue. Thus all these occur in Wiclif's Bible: 'techeress' (2 Chron. xxxv. 25); 'friendess' (Prov. vii. 4); 'servantess' (Gen. xvi. 2); 'leperess' (=saltatrix, Ecclus. ix. 4); 'daunceress' (Ecclus. ix. 4); 'neighboress' (Exod. iii. 22); 'sinneress' (Luke vii. 37); 'purpuress' (Acts xvi. 14); 'cousiness' (Luke i. 36); 'slayeress' (Tob. iii. 9); 'devouress' (Ezek. xxxvi. 13); 'spousess' (Prov. v. 19); 'thralless'

dire, un idiome nouveau, mais plutôt une transformation de celle qui l'a précédée : celle-ci, plus savante, chargée de flexions pour exprimer les rapports infiniment délicats de la pensée, plus riche même dans son ordre d'idées, bien que cet ordre fût comparativement moins étendu, image en un mot de la spontanéité primitive, où l'esprit accumulait les éléments dans une confuse unité, et perdait dans le tout la vue analytique des parties ; le dialecte moderne, au contraire, correspondant à un progrès d'analyse, plus clair, plus explicite, séparant ce que les anciens assemblaient, brisant les mécanismes de l'ancienne langue pour donner à chaque idée et à chaque relation son expression isolée.

* Diez, *Rom. Gram.* vol. iii. pp. 277, 326, 344.

(Jer. xxxiv. 16); 'dwelleress' (Jer. xxi. 13); 'waileress' (Jer. xix. 17); 'cheseress' (=electrix, Wisd. viii.
4); 'singeress' (2 Chron. xxxv. 25); 'breakeress,'
'waiteress,' this last indeed having recently come up
again. Add to these 'souteress' (*Piers Ploughman*),
'chideress,' 'constabless,' 'moveress,' 'jangleress,
'vengeress,' 'soudaness' (=sultana), 'guideress,'
'charmeress' (all in Chaucer). Others reached to far
later periods of the language; thus 'vanqueress'
(Fabyan), 'Ethiopess' (Raleigh), 'exactress' (Isai.
xiv. 4, margin), 'inhabitress' (Jer. x. 17); 'poisoner-
ess' (Greneway); 'knightess' (Udal); 'pedleress,'
'championess,' 'vassaless,' 'avengeress,' 'warriour-
ess,' 'victoress,' 'creatress,' 'tyranness,' 'Titaness,'
'Britoness' (all in Spenser); 'offendress,' 'fornica-
tress,' 'cloistress,' 'jointress' (all in Shakespeare);
'vowess' (Holinshed); 'ministress,' 'flatteress' (both
in Holland); 'captainess' (Sidney); 'treasuress'
(*The Golden Boke*); 'saintess' (Sir T. Urquhart);
'leadress' (F. Thynne); 'heroess,' 'dragoness,' 'but-
leress,' 'contendress, 'waggoness,' 'rectress' (all in
Chapman); 'shootress' (Fairfax); 'archeress' (Fan-
shawe); 'architectress' (Sandys); 'clientess,' 'pan-
dress' (both in Middleton); 'papess,' 'Jesuitess'
(Bishop Hall); 'incitress' (Gayton); 'mediatress'
(H. More); 'fautress,' 'herdess' (both in Browne);
'neatress' (=neat-herdess, Warner); 'soldieress,'
'guardianess,' 'votaress' (all in Beaumont and Fletcher); 'comfortress,' 'fosteress' (Ben Jonson); 'fac-
tress' (Ford); 'soveraintess' (Sylvester); 'preser-
veress' (Daniel; 'hermitress' (Drummond); 'emula-

tress' (Skelton) ; 'solicitress,' 'impostress,' 'build-
ress,' 'intrudress' (all in Fuller) ; 'favouress' (Hake-
well) ; 'commandress' (Burton) ; 'monarchess,'
'discipless' (Speed) ; 'auditress,' 'cateress,' 'chant-
ress,' 'prelatess' (all in Milton) ; 'saviouress'
(Jeremy Taylor) ; 'citess,' 'divineress' (both in
Dryden) ; 'deaness' (Sterne) ; 'detractress' (Addison) ; 'hucksteress' (Howell) ; 'tutoress,' 'legisla-
tress' (both . in Shaftesbury) ; 'farmeress' (Lord
Peterborough, *Letter to Pope*) ; 'suitress' (Rowe) ;
'nomenclatress' (*Guardian*) ; 'pilgrimess,' 'laddess,'
still surviving in the contracted form of 'lass ;' with
others which, I doubt not, a completer catalogue
would contain.'*

The same has happened with another feminine
suffix, with the Saxon 'ster,' which takes the place of
'er,' where a female doer is intended.† 'Spinner'
and 'spinster' are the only pair of such words which
still survive. There were formerly many such ; thus
'baker' had 'bakester,' being the female who baked ;
'brewer' had 'brewster' (*Piers Ploughman*, 3087) ;
'sewer' 'sewster ;' 'reader', 'readster ;', 'seamer'
'seamster ;' 'weaver' 'webster' (Golding, *Ovid*,
p. 77) ; 'hopper' 'hoppester ;' 'fruiterer' 'fruitester ;'
'tumbler' 'tumblester' (all in Chaucer) ; 'host'

---

* In Cotgrave's *Dictionary* I note 'praiseress,' 'com-
mendress,' 'fluteress,' 'possesseress,' 'loveress,' 'regentess,'
but have never met them in use.

† On this termination see J. Grimm, *Deutsche Gram.*, vol.
ii. p. 134 ; vol. iii. p. 339 ; Donaldson, *New Cratylus*, 3rd
edit. p. 419.

'hotestre' (*Ayenbite*); 'knitter' 'knitster' (the word still lives in Devon) : 'harpster' I have never met in use ; but I have seen it quoted. Add to these 'whitster' (a female bleacher, Shakespeare), 'bandster,' the woman who binds up the sheaves (Cleveland dialect), 'wafrester,' the woman who made wafers for the priest (*Piers Ploughman*); 'kempster' (pectrix), 'dryster' (siccatrix), 'brawdster' (=embroideress), and 'salster' (salinaria).* It is a singular evidence of the richness of a language in forms at the earlier stages of its existence, that not a few of the words which had, as we have just seen, a feminine termination in 'ess,' had also a second in 'ster.' Thus, 'daunser,' beside 'daunseress,' had also 'daunster' (Ecclus. ix. 4) ; 'wailer,' beside 'waileress,' had 'wailster' (Jer. ix. 17) ; 'dweller' 'dwelster' (Jer. xxi. 13) ; and 'singer' 'singster' (2 Kin. xix. 35) ; so too, 'chider' had 'chidester' (Chaucer), as well as 'chideress,' 'slayer' 'slayster' (Tob. iii. 9), as well as 'slayeress,' 'chooser' 'chesister' (Wisd. viii. 4), as well as 'cheseress,' with others that might be named.

It is impossible then to subscribe to Marsh's statement, high as his authority on a matter of English scholarship must be, when he affirms, 'I find no positive evidence to show that the termination "ster" was ever regarded as a feminine termination in English.'† It has indeed been urged that the existence

---

* I am indebted for these last four to a *Nominale* in the *National Antiquities*, vol. i. p. 216.

† Mätzner, *Engl. Gram.* p. 243.

of such words as 'seamst*ress*,' 'songstr*ess*,' is decisive
proof that the ending 'ster' or 'estre,' of itself was
not counted sufficient to designate persons as females ;
since if 'seam*ster*' and 'song*ster*' had been felt to be
already feminine, no one would have thought of
doubling on these, and adding a second female termination ; seam*stress*,' 'song*stress*.' But all which
this proves is, that when the final 'ess' was superadded to these already feminine forms, and all examples of it belong to a comparatively late period of the
language, the true significance of this ending had
been lost sight of and forgotten.*   The same may be
affirmed of such other of these feminine forms as are
now applied to men, such as 'gamester,' 'youngster,'
' oldster,' ' drugster ' (South), ' huckster,' ' hackster '
(=swordsman, Milton, prose), 'teamster,' 'throwster,'
'rhymester,' 'punster' (*Spectator*), 'tapster, 'malster,'
' whipster,' ' lewdster ' (Shakespeare), ' trickster.'
Either like ' teamster,' and ' punster,' the words did .
not come into being till the force of this termination
was altogether forgotten ; † or like ' tapster,' which

---

* Richardson's earliest example of 'seamstress' is from Gay,
of 'songstress,' from Thomson. I find however ' sempstress '
in Olearius' *Voyages and Travels*, 1669, p. 43. As late as
Ben Jonson, ' seamster ' and 'songster' expressed the *female*
seamer and singer ; in his *Masque of Christmas*, one of the
children of Christmas is ' Wassel, like a neat *sempster* and
songster : her page bearing a brown bowl.' Compare a passage from *Holland's Leaguer*, 1632 : ' A *tyre-woman* of
phantastical ornaments, a *sempster* for ruffes, cuffes, smocks
and waistcoats.'
    † This was about the time of Henry VIII. In proof of the

was still female in Skelton's time ('a *tapster* like a lady bright'), as it is now in Dutch and Frisian, and distinguished from 'tapper,' the *man* who has charge of the tap, or as 'bakester,' at this day used in Scotland for 'baker,' as 'dyester,' for 'dyer,' the word did originally belong of right and exclusively to women ; * but with the gradual transfer of the occupation to men, and an increasing forgetfulness of what this termination implied, there went also a transfer of the name,† just as in other words, and out of

---

confusion which reigned on the subject in Shakespeare's time, see his use of 'spinster' as == 'spinner,' the *man* spinning, *Henry VIII.*, Act i. Sc. 2 ; and doubtless too in *Othello*, Act i. Sc. 1. And a little later in Howell's *Vocabulary*, 1659, 'spinner' and 'spinster' are *both* referred to the male sex, and the barbarous 'spinstress' invented for the female.

* The Latin equivalent for 'malster' in the *Promptorium Parvulorum* is 'brasia*trix*.'

† In the *Nominale* referred to, p. 234, the words, 'hæc auxiatrix, a *hukster*,' occur. That the huckster is properly the *female* pedlar is sufficiently plain. 'To hawk' was formerly 'to huck '—it is so used by Bishop Andrews, and the 'hucker' or hawker (the German 'höker' or 'höcker ') is the *man* who 'hucks,' 'hawks,' or peddles, the 'huckster' the *woman* who does the same. Howell then and others employing 'huckster*ess*,' fall into the same barbarous excess of expression, whereof we are all guilty in 'seamstress' and 'songstress.' I take the opportunity of noting another curious excess of expression that has succeeded in establishing itself in the language. In books of two or three hundred years ago, we find 'adulter' (Tyndale), 'poulter' (Shakespeare), 'cater' (Drayton), 'royster' (Gascoigne), 'upholster' (Strype), 'embroider' (Holland) ; and these all sufficiently justify themselves ; 'adulter,' a transfer of a Latin word into English, 'poulter'

the same causes, the converse finds place; and
'baker' or 'brewer,' not 'bakester' or 'brewster,'
would be now applied to the woman baking or brew-
ing. So entirely has this power of the language
died out, that it survives more apparently than really
even in 'spinner' and 'spinster;' seeing that 'spinster' has now quite another meaning than that of a
woman spinning ; whom, as well as the man, we
should call, not a 'spinster,' but a 'spinner.'*   It
would be hard to believe, but for the constant experience we have of the fact, how soon and how easily
the true law and significance of some form, which
has never ceased to be in everybody's mouth, may
yet be lost sight of by all.   No more curious chapter

one dealing in poults, 'cater,' in cates, and so on ; but the
sense of this final 'er,' the remnant of the Anglo-Saxon 'wer,'
a man, and of what it indicates, namely the habitual doer of a
thing, is so strong, that men have not been content without
adding it a second time to all these words ; and they are severally now 'adulterer,' 'poulterer,' 'caterer,' 'roysterer,' 'up-
holsterer,' 'embroiderer.'   'Launder' in like manner became
'launderer,' though both one and the other have now given
way to 'laundress.'   That this superaddition has its root in the
linguistic instinct of our people is evident from the fact that
the same has been attempted in other words, though without
the same success ; thus 'fisherer' (it occurs in Cotgrave) is in
provincial usage for 'fisher' (see Forby and other local glossaries) ; and the same has extended to words of a different
formation as to 'burglarer' for 'burglar' (Butler's *Hudibras*) ;
to 'musicianer,' 'physicianer,' 'masoner' (all in Forby) ; to
'politicianer,' a vulgar Americanism ; to 'poeter,' a vulgar
Anglicism, and to others.
* *Notes and Queries*, No. 157.

in the history of language could be written than one
which should trace the transgressions of its most
primary laws, the violations of analogy and the like,
which follow hereupon ; the plurals, as 'chicken,'*
which are dealt with as singulars, the singulars, like
' riches ' (richesse),† 'pease.' (pisum, pois),‡ 'alms'
('almesse ' in Coverdale,) ' eaves,' ' summons '
(summoneas), ' Cyclops,' which on the score of the
final 's' are assumed to be plurals.

One example of the kind is familiar to us all ; to
which yet it may be worth adverting as a signal
example of this forgetfulness which may overtake a
whole people, of the true meaning of a grammatical
form which they have never ceased to employ. I
refer to the mistaken assumption that the 's' of the

---

* When Wallis wrote, it was only beginning to be forgotten
that 'chick' was the singular, and 'chicken' the plural:
' *Sunt qui dicunt* in singulari " chicken," et in plurali
"chickens ;" and even now the words are in many country
parts correctly employed. In Sussex, a correspondent writes,
they would as soon think of saying ' oxens ' as 'chickens.'

† See Chaucer, *Romance of the Rose*, 1032, where Richesse,
'an high lady of great noblesse,' is one of the persons of the
allegory. In Tyndale's Version of the Bible we read at
James v. 2, 'Your riches *is* corrupte ;' in the Geneva ' is '
gives place to ' are,' which stands in our Version. This has so
entirely escaped Ben Jonson, English scholar as he was, that
in his *Grammar* he cites ' riches as an example of an English
word wanting a singular ; and at a later day Wemyss (*Biblical
Gleanings*, p. 212) complains of a false concord at Rev. xviii.
17 : ' For in one hour so great riches *is* come to nought.'

‡   ' Set shallow brooks to surging seas,
         An orient pearl to a white *pease.—Puttenham.*

genitive, as, the king's countenance,' was merely a more rapid way of pronouncing 'the king *his* countenance,' and that the final 's' in king's was in fact an elided 'his.' This explanation for a long time prevailed almost universally; I believe there are many who accept it still. It was in vain that here and there one more accurately acquainted with the past history of our tongue protested against this 'monstrous syntax,' as Ben Jonson justly calls it.* It was in vain that Wallis, another English scholar of the seventeenth century, pointed out that the slightest examination of the facts revealed the untenable character of this explanation, seeing that we do not merely say 'the *king's* countenance,' but 'the *queen's* countenance,' where 'the queen *his* countenance cannot be intended ;† we do not say merely 'the *child's* bread,' but 'the *children's* bread,' where it is no less impossible to resolve the phrases into 'the children his bread.‡ Notwithstanding these protests, the error

---

* It is curious that, despite this protest, one of his plays has for its name, *Sejanus his Fall.*

† Even this does not startle Addison, or cause him any misgiving ; on the contrary he boldly asserts (*Spectator*, No. 135), 'The same single letter "s" on many occasions does the office of a whole word, and represents the "his" *or* "*her*" of our forefathers.'

‡ Wallis excellently well disposes of this scheme, although less successful in showing what this 's' does mean than in showing what it cannot mean (*Gram. Ling. Anglic.*, c. v.) : Qui autem arbitrantur illud s, loco *his* adjunctum esse (priori scilicet parte per aphæresim abscissâ), ideoque apostrophi notam semper vel pingendam esse, vel saltem subintelligendam,

held its ground. This much indeed of a plea it could
make for itself, that such an actual employment of
'his' *had* found its way into the language, as early as
the fourteenth century, and had been in occasional,
though rare use, from that time downward.* Yet
this, which has only been elicited by the researches of
recent scholars, does not in the least justify those who
assumed that in the ordinary ' s ' of the genitive were
to be found the remains of 'his'—an error from which
the books of scholars in the seventeenth, and in the
early decade of the eighteenth century are ·not a
whit clearer than those of others. Spenser, Donne,
Fuller, Jeremy Taylor, all fall into it; Dryden more
than once helps out his verse with an additional
syllable in this way gained. It has forced itself into
our Prayer Book where the ' Prayer for all sorts and
conditions of men,' added by Bishop Sanderson to the
last revision of the Liturgy in 1661, ends with these
words, 'and this we beg for Jesus Christ his sake.'†

omnino errant. Quamvis enim non negem quin apostrophi
nota commode nonnunquam affigi possit, ut ipsius litteræ s usus
distinctius, ubi opus est, percipiatur ; ita tamen semper fieri
debere, aut etiam ideo fieri quia vocem *his* innuat, omnino
nego. Adjungitur enim et fœminarum nominibus propriis, et
substantivis pluralibus, ubi vox *his* sine solœcismo locum
habere non potest : atque etiam in possessivis *ours, yours,
theirs, hers,* ubi vocem *his* innui nemo somniaret.

   * See the proofs in Marsh, *Manual of the English Language,*
English Edit., pp. 280, 293.

   † It would not exceed the authority of our University Presses,
if this were removed from the Prayer Book. Such a liberty
they have already assumed with the Bible. In all earlier edi-

I need hardly tell you that this 's' is in fact the one remnant of flexion surviving in the singular number of our English noun substantives; it is in all the Indo-European languages the orignal sign of the genitive, or at any rate the earliest of which we can take cognizance; and just as in Latin 'lapis' makes 'lapidis' in the genitive, so 'king,' 'queen,' 'child,' make severally 'kings,' 'queens,' 'childs,' the apostrophe, an apparent note of elision, being a mere modern expedient, 'a late a refinement,' as Ash calls it,* to distinguish the genitive singular from the plural cases.†

I will call to your notice another example of this willingness to dispense with inflection, of this endeavour to reduce the forms of a language to the fewest possible, consistent with the accurate communication of thought. Of our adjectives in 'en,' formed on substantives, and expressing the material or substance of a thing, the Greek *ινος*, a vast number have

tions of the Authorized Version it stood at 1 Kin. xv. 14: 'Nevertheless *Asa his* heart was perfect with the Lord;' it is '*Asa's* heart' now. In the same way '*Mordecai his* matters' (Esth. iii. 4) has been silently changed into '*Mordecai's* matters;' while 'by Naomi *her* instruction Ruth lieth at Boaz *his* feet,' in the heading of Ruth iii. has been as little allowed to stand.

* In a good note on the matter, p. 6, in the *Comprehensive Grammar* prefixed to his *Dictionary*, London, 1775.

† See Grimm, *Deutsche Gram.*, vol. ii. pp. 609, 944; and on the remarkable employment of it not merely as the sign of the genitive singular, but also of the plural, Loth, *Angelsachsisch-Englische Grammatik*, p. 203.

gone, many others are going, out of use ; we having
learned to content ourselves with the bare juxtaposi-
tion of the substantive itself, as sufficiently expressing
our meaning. Thus instead of '*golden* pin ' we say
'*gold* pin ;' instead of '*earthen* works' we say '*earth-
works*.' 'Golden' and 'earthen,' it is true, still
belong to our living speech, though mainly as part of
our poetic diction, or of the solemn and thus stereotyped language of Scripture ; but a whole company of
such words have nearly or quite disappeared ; some
recently, some long ago. 'Steelen,' 'flowren,'
'thornen,' 'clouden,' 'rocken,' 'firen,' belong, so
far as I know, only to a very early period of the language. 'Rosen' also went early ; Chaucer is my
latest authority for it ('*rosen* chapelet') ; as also for
'iven,' or of ivy ; 'hairen' is in Wiclif and in Chaucer ; 'stonen' in the former (John ii. 6).* 'Silvern'
stood originally in Wiclif's Bible ('*silverne* housis to
Diane,' Acts viv. 24) ; but already in the second re-
cension this was exchanged for 'silver ;' 'hornen,'
still in our dialects, he also employs, with 'clayen'
(Job iv. 19), and 'iverene' (Cant. vi. 4) or made of
ivory. 'Tinnen' occurs in Sylvester's *Du Bartas ;*
in Bacon it is never 'the *Milky* Way' but 'the *Milken*.'
In the coarse polemics of the Reformation the phrase,
'*breaden* god,' provoked by the Romish doctrine of

---

* The existence or 'stony' (=lapidosus, steinig) does not
make 'stonen' (=lapideus, steinern) superfluous any more
than 'earthy' makes 'earthen' and 'earthly.' That part
of the field in which the good seed withered so quickly (Matt.
xiii. 5) was 'stony ;' the vessels which held the water turned
into wine (John ii. 6) were 'stonen.'

transubstantiation, is of frequent recurrence, and is
found as late as in Oldham. '*Mothern* parchments
is in Fulke ;· '*twiggen* bottle' and '*threaden* sail' in
Shakespeare ; '*yewen*' or '*ewghen* bow,' in Spenser ;
'*cedarn* alley' and '*azurn* sheen' in Milton ; '*boxen*
leaves' in Dryden ; '*a corden* ladder' in Arthur
Brooke ; 'a *treen* cup' in Jeremy Taylor ; '*eldern*
popguns' in Sir Thomas Overbury ; 'a *glassen* breast'
in Whitlock ; 'a *reeden* hat' in Coryat ; 'a *wispen*
garland' in Gabriel Harvey ; 'yarnen' occurs in
Turberville ; 'fursen' in Holland ; while 'bricken,'
'papern,' 'elmen,' appear from our provincial glossaries to be still in use.*

It is true that some of these adjectives still hold
their ground ; but the roots which sustain even these
are being gradually cut away from beneath them.
Thus 'brazen' might at first sight seem as strongly
established in the language as ever ; but this is very
far from the case.   Even now it only lives in a tropical and secondary sense, as 'a *brazen* face ;' or if in
a literal, in poetic diction or in the consecrated language of Scripture, as 'the *brazen* serpent ;' otherwise
we say 'a *brass* farthing,' 'a *brass* candlestick.'   It is
the same with 'oaten,' 'oaken,' 'birchen,' 'beechen,'
'strawen,' and many more, whereof some are obsolescent, some obsolete, the language manifestly
tending now, as it has tended for centuries past, to
the getting quit of all these, and to the satisfying of

---

* For a long list of words of this formation which never
passed from the Anglo-Saxon into the English, see Loth,
Angelsachsisch-Englische Grammatik, p. 332.

itself with an adjectival apposition of the substantive instead.

There are other examples of the manner in which a language, as it travels onward, simplifies itself, approaches more and more to a grammatical and logical uniformity, seeks to do the same thing always in the same manner ; where it has two or more ways of conducting a single operation, disuses, and so ·loses, all save one ; and thus becomes, no doubt, easier to be mastered, more handy and manageable ; for its very riches were to many an embarrassment and a perplexity ; but at the same time limits and restrains its own freedom of action, and is in danger of forfeiting elements of strength, variety and beauty, which it once possessed. Take for instance the tendency of our verbs to let go their strong preterites, and to substitute weak ones in their room ; or, where they have two or three preterites, to retain only one of these, and that almost invariably the weak.

But before proceeding further let me trace the steps by which it has come to pass that of our preterites some are strong and some weak, and explain what these terms, objected to by some, but as I think wrongly, severally mean. The Indo-European languages at the earliest period that we know formed their preterites by reduplication ; of which not inconsiderable traces still remain in the Latin, as in 'cano' 'cecini,' 'tundo' 'tutudi,' and though not so clearly in 'vĭdeo' 'vīdi' (='vĕvĭdi'), while the same is a regular part of the Greek conjugation. But this reduplication only survived in one of the Gothic languages. From the Anglo-Saxon it had died out, and, if leaving any, yet certainly the very faintest traces behind it, long before it comes within the scope of our vision. With the perishing of this, the internal vowel-change, or variation of the radical vowel (we want some good equivalent for the German 'ablaut') which appears to have been properly no more than an euphonic process, was adopted as a means of marking flexion, and as the sign of the past; thus 'grow' 'grew,' 'cleave' 'clove,' 'dive' 'dove.' At the same time there must have been that of indeterminate and capricious about this which caused the language-speakers to seek for some plainer and more obvious sign, and as often as new verbs were introduced into the language, they marked the preterite in these by adding to the verb in its crude state the auxiliary 'did;' thus 'I love,' in the perfect, 'I love did,' or when the words had grown together, 'I loved;' leaving in most instances the radical vowel unchanged. It will follow from this that the strong verbs are invariably the older, the weak the newer, in the language.*

---

* J. Grimm (*Deutsche Gram.*, vol. i. p. 1040) : Dass die starke Form die ältere, kräftigere, innere ; die schwache die spätere, gehemmtere und mehr äusserliche sey, leuchtet ein. Elsewhere, speaking generally of inflections by internal vowel change, he characterizes them as a 'chief beauty' (hauptschön-heit) of the Teutonic languages. Marsh (*Manual of the English Language*, p. 233, English ed.) protests, though, as it seems to me, on no sufficient grounds, against these terms 'strong' and 'weak,' as themselves fanciful and inappropriate.

But for all this the battle is not to the strong.
Multitudes of these have already disappeared, many
more are in process of disappearing. For example,
'shape' has now a weak preterite, 'shaped,' it had
once a strong one, 'shope' (Coverdale) ; 'bake' has
now a weak preterite, 'baked,' it had once a strong
one, 'boke ;' the preterite of 'glide' is now 'glided ;'
it was once 'glodè' or 'glid ;' 'help' makes now
'helped,' it made once 'halp' and 'holp.' 'Creep'
made 'crope,' still current in the north of England,
and 'crep' (*Story of Genesis*) ; 'weep' 'wope' and
'wep ;' 'yell' 'yoll ;' 'starve' 'storve ;' 'washe'
'wishe' (all in Chaucer) ; 'seethe' 'soth' or 'sod'
(Gen. xxv. 29) ; 'sheer' once made 'shore ;' as
'leap' made 'lep' and 'lope' (Spenser) ; 'snow'
'snew ;' 'thaw' 'thew ;' 'gnaw' 'gnew ;' 'sow'
'sew ;' 'delve' 'dalf' and 'dolve ;' 'sweat' 'swat ;'
'yield' 'yold' (both in Spenser) and also 'yald ;'
'reach' 'raught ;' 'melt' 'molt ;' 'wax' 'wex' and
'wox ;' 'squeeze' 'squoze ;' 'laugh' 'leugh ;'
'knead' 'kned ,' 'beat' 'bet' (Coverdale) ; with
others more than can be enumerated here.* A very

---

* The entire ignorance as to the past historic evolution of
the language, with which some have undertaken to write about
it, is curious. Thus the author of *Observations upon the English Language*, without date, but published about 1730, treats
all these strong preterites as of recent introduction, counting
'knew' to have lately expelled 'knowed,' 'rose' to have
, acted the same part·toward 'rised,' and of course esteeming
them so many barbarous violations of the laws of the language ;
and concluding with the warning that 'great care must be
taken to prevent their increase.' ! !—p. 24. · Cobbett does not

large number of these still survive in our provincial dialects.

Observe further that where verbs have not actually · renounced their strong preterites, and contented themselves with weak in their room, yet, once possessing two, perhaps three of these strong, they now retain only one. The others they have let go. Thus 'chide' had once 'chid' and 'chode,' but though 'chode' is in our Bible (Gen. xxxi. 36), it has not maintained itself in our speech ; 'sling' had 'slung' and 'slang' (1 Sam. xvii. 49) ; only 'slung' remains ; 'fling' had once 'flung' and 'flang ;' 'strive' had 'strove' and 'strave' (Holland) ; 'smite' had 'smote' and 'smate ;' 'stick' had 'stuck' and 'stack ;' 'tread' had 'trod' and 'trad ;' 'choose' had 'chose' and 'chase' (Elyot) ; 'give' had 'gove' and 'gave ;' 'spin' 'spun' and 'span ;' 'steal' 'stole' and 'stale ;' 'lead' had 'lode' 'led' and 'lad ;' 'write' 'writ' 'wrote' and 'wrate.'   In these instances, and in many more, only one preterite remains in use.

Observe too that wherever a struggle is now going forward between weak and strong forms, which at the present shall continue, the weak are carrying the day : 'climbed' is gaining the upper hand of 'clomb,'

fall into this absurdity, yet proposes in his *English Grammar*, that they should all be abolished as inconvenient.   There are two letters in *The Spectator*, Nos. 78 and 80, on the relations between 'who,' 'which,' and 'that,' singularly illustrative of the same absolute ignorance of the whole past of the language. The writers throughout assume 'that' to have recently displaced 'which,' as a relative pronoun !

'swelled' of 'swoll,' 'hanged' of 'hung.' There are, it is true, exceptions to this; and these not quite so few as at first one might suppose. Thus 'they have *digged* a pit' stands in our Bibles; we should now say 'dug.' 'Shaked' 'shined' and 'shrinked' in like manner are there; while we only admit 'shook' 'shone' and 'shrunk' or 'shrank;' 'to catch' had 'catched' (Bacon) as well as 'caught;' 'to stick' makes 'sticked' in Coverdale's Bible; it has only 'stuck' for a preterite now; in the same 'to swim' had 'swimmed;' it has now only 'swum' or 'swam.' 'Growed' and not 'grew' is in *Piers Ploughman* the perfect of 'to grow;' 'spended' and not 'spent' of 'to spend' in Wiclif. But these are the exceptions; and we may anticipate a time, though still far off, when all English verbs will form their preterites weakly; not without serious detriment to the fulness, variety, and force, which in this respect the language even now displays, and once far more signally displayed.*

It is found in practice that men care very little for a grammatical right or wrong, if by the ignoring of this they can procure a handier implement of use. The consideration of convenience will override for them every other. Our English verbs formed on the passive participle past of the Latin verb, as for instance 'to devote,' 'to corrupt,' 'to circumcise,' have

---

† J. Grimm, *Deutsche Gram.*, vol. i. p. 839): Die starke Flexion stufenweise versinkt and ausstirbt, die schwache aber um sich greift. Cf. i. 994, 1040; ii. 5; iv. 509.

in a large number of instances been preceded by verbs which formed themselves more correctly from the present tense active; thus 'to devove' (Holland) preceded 'to devote ;' 'to corrump' (Wiclif, Mal. iii. 11) 'to corrupt ;' 'to circumcide' (Coverdale, Ezek. xvi. 30) 'to circumcise ;' though these with others like them, 'to compromit' (Capgrave), 'to suspeck,' 'to correck,' 'to instruck' (all in Coverdale), have been unable to make good their footing in the language, having every one given place to those which we now employ. We need not look far for the motive which led to the taking of the participle past of the Latin verb as that on which to form the English. In many cases it was difficult, in some apparently impossible, to form this on the Latin present. ' To devove,' 'to corrump,' 'to circumcide' might pass ; but 'to suspeck,' 'to correck,' 'to instruck,' did not commend themselves much, while yet nothing better could be done with 'suspicio,' 'corrigo,' 'instruo ;' not to say that other verbs out of number, as 'accipio,' 'exhaurio,' 'addico,' 'macero,' 'polluo,' lent themselves hardly or not at all to the forming in the same way of an English verb upon them. But all was easy if the participle past were recognized as the starting-point ; and thus we have the verbs, 'to accept,' 'to exhaust,' 'to addict,' 'to macerate,' 'to pollute,' with a multitude of others. It is true that these words could not all at once forget that they were already participles past ; and thus side by side with that other usage they continued for a long while to be employed as such ; and instead of 'instructed,' 'dejected,' 'accepted,' 'exhausted,' and the rest, as now in use, we find 'instruct' ('elephants *instruct* for war,' Milton), 'exhaust' (Bacon), 'distract' (the fellow is *distract*,' Shakespeare), 'attaint' (Holland), 'addict' (Frith), 'convict' (Habington), 'infect' (Capgrave), 'pollute,' 'disjoint' (both in Milton), with many more. Little by little, however, it passed out of men's consciousness that these were past participles already ; and this once forgotten, no scruple was then made of adding to them a second participial sign, and ·we thus have them in their present shape and use ; 'instruct*ed*,' 'exhaust*ed*,' and the like.

I return to the subject from which these last remarks have a little led away ; and will urge another proof of the manifest disposition in our language to drop forms and renounce its own inherent powers ; though here also the renunciation, however it may threaten one day to be complete, is only partial at the present. I refer to the formation of our comparatives and superlatives ; and will ask you to observe once more that ever-recurring law of language, namely, that wherever two or more methods of attaining the same result exist, there is always a disposition to drop and dismiss all of these but one, so that the alternative, or choice of ways, once existing shall not exist any more. If only a language can attain a greater simplicity, it seems to grudge no self-impoverishment by which this result may be brought about. We have two ways of forming our comparatives and superlatives, one inherent in the word itself, and derived from our old Gothic stock, thus 'bright,'

'brighter,' 'brightest; the other supplementary to
this, by aid of the auxiliaries 'more' and 'most.'
The first, organic we might call it, the indwelling
power of the word to mark its own degrees, must
needs be esteemed the more excellent way; which
yet, already disallowed in almost all adjectives of
more than two syllables in length, is daily becoming
of more restrained application. Compare in this matter our present position with our past. Wiclif forms
without scruple such comparatives as 'grievouser,'
'gloriouser,' 'patienter,' 'profitabler,' such superlatives
as 'grievousest,' 'famousest,' 'preciousest.' We
meet in Tyndale, 'excellenter,' 'miserablest;' in
Roger Ascham, 'inventivest,' 'shiningest;' in Shakespeare, 'ancientest,' 'violentest;' in Gabriel Harvey,
'vendiblest,' 'substantialest,' 'insolentest;' in Rogers, 'insufficienter,' 'goldenest;' in Beaumont and
Fletcher, 'valiantest;' in Bacon, 'excellentest;' in
Sylvester, 'infamousest;' in North, 'unfortunatest.'
Milton uses 'sensualest,' 'resolutest,' 'exquisitest,'
'virtuosest,' and in prose 'vitiosest,' 'elegantest,'
'artificialest,' 'servilest,' 'sheepishest,' 'moralist;'
Fuller has 'fertilest;' Baxter 'tediousest;' Butler
'dangerouser,' 'preciousest,' 'intolerablest,' 'prepos-
terousest;' Burnet 'copiousest;' Gray 'impudentest.'
Of these forms, and it would be easy to adduce almost
any number, we should hardly now employ one. In
participles and adverbs in 'ly' these organic comparatives and superlatives hardly survive at all. We do not
say 'willinger' or 'lovinger,' and still less 'flourish-
ingest,' or 'shiningest,' or 'surmountingest,' all which

Gabriel Harvey, a foremost master of the English of his time, employs ; ' plenteouslyer,' ' charitablier (Barnes), ' amplier ' (Milton), ' easliest ' (Fuller), ' plainliest ' (Dryden), ' fulliest ' (Baxter), would be all inadmissible at present.

In the evident disposition of English at the present moment to reduce the number of words in which this more vigorous scheme of expressing degrees is allowed, we must recognize an evidence that youthful energies in the language are abating, and the stiffness of advancing age making itself felt. Still it fares with us here only as it fares with all languages, in which at a certain stage of their existence auxiliary words, leaving the main word unaltered, are preferred to inflections of this last. Such preference makes itself ever more strongly felt ; and, judging from analogy, I cannot doubt that a day, however distant now, will arrive, when the only way of forming comparatives and superlatives in the English language will be by prefixing ' more ' and ' most ;' or, if the other survive, it will be in poetry alone. Doubtless such a consummation is to be regretted ; for our language is too monosyllabic already ; but it is one which no regrets will avert.

It will not fare otherwise, as I am bold to predict, with the flexional genitive, formed in ' s ' or ' es.' This too will finally disappear, or will survive only in/ the diction of poetry. A time will arrive, when it will no longer be free to say as now, either ' *the king's sons,*' or ' *the sons of the king,*' but when the latter will be the only admissible form. Tokens of this are already evident. The region in which the alternative forms are equally good is daily narrowing. We should not now any more write, 'when *man's son* shall come' (Wiclif), but 'when *the Son of man* shall come ;' nor yet, '*the hypocrite's hope* shall perish' (Job viii. 13), but '*the hope of the hypocrite* shall perish ;' nor '*the Philistines' land*' (Gen. xxi. 34), but '*the land of the Philistines ;*' not with Barrow, 'No man can be ignorant of *human life's brevity and uncertainty,*' but 'No man can be ignorant *of the brevity and uncertainty of human life.*' Already in our Authorized Version the more modern form displaces in passages out of number the earlier. Thus at John xviii. 15, it is 'the palace of the High Priest ;' but in Coverdale,' 'the High Priest's palace ;' at Heb. ii. 17, 'the sins of the people,' but in earlier Versions 'the people's sins ;' at 1 Pet. iv. 13, 'partakers of the sufferings of Christ,' but in earlier Versions 'partakers of Christ's passions.' This change finds place in cases innumerable, but never, so far as I have observed, the converse. The consummation which I have here anticipated may be centuries off, but with other of a like character will assuredly arrive.*

---

* Schleicher in his masterly treatise, *Die Deutsche Sprache*, 1860, p. 69, notes the same as going forward in German : Das Schwinden der Casus und ihren Ersatz durch Präpositionen können wir in unsrer jetzigen deutschen Sprache recht deutlich beobachten. Anstatt süssen Weines voll u. dgl. pflegen wir im gewöhnlichen Leben schon zu sagen, voll von süssem Weine ja manche deutsche Volksmundarten haben den Genitiv fast spurlos verloren, und sagen z. B. anstatt ' meines Bruders

Then too diminutives are fast disappearing. If we desire to express smallness, we prefer to do it by an auxiliary word ; thus, a little fist, and not a ' fistock ' (Golding), a little lad, and not a ' ladkin,' a little drop, and not a ' droplet' (Shakespeare), a little worm, and not a ' wormling ' (Sylvester). It is true that of diminutives a good many still survive, in all our four terminations of such, as ' hillock,' ' stream-let,' ' lambkin,' ' gosling ;' but they are few as com- pared with those which have perished, and are every day becoming fewer. Where now is ' kingling' (Holland), ' friarling ' (Foxe), ' twinling ' (=gemel- lus, *Old Vocabulary*, ' beamling ' (Vaughan), ' whim- ling ' (Beaumont and Fletcher), 'popeling' (Hacket), ' streamling,' ' godling,' ' loveling,' ' dwarfling,' ' shepherdling ', (all in Sylvester), ' chasteling' (Be- con), ' niceling ' (Stubbs), ' poetling,' ' fosterling ' (both in Ben Jonson), and ' masterling '? Where now 'porelet' (=paupercula, Isai. x. 30, Vulg.), ' bundelet' (both in Wiclif) ; ' chastilet' or little cas- tle (*Piers Ploughman*), 'cushionet' (Henry More), ' riveret ' (Drayton), ' closulet,' ' orphanet,' ' lionet' (all in Phineas Fletcher), ' herblet' (Shakespeare), ' dragonet' (Spenser),' ' havenet' or little haven, ' pistolet, ' bulkin ' (Holland), ' thumbkin,' ' cana- kin,' ' bodikin' (both in Skakespeare), ' ladykin,' ' slamkin ' (a slovenly girl), ' pillock ' a little pill (Levins), ' laddock;' ' wifock,' and a hundred more ? Even of those remaining to us still many are putting

Sohn ' entweder ' der Sohn von meinem Bruder,' oder ' meinem Bruder sein Sohn.'

off, or have long since put off, their diminutive sense ; a ' pocket' being no longer a *small* poke, nor a 'latchet' a *small* lace, nor a 'trumpet a *small* trump, as formerly they were.

Once more—in the entire dropping among the higher classes, and in some parts of England among all classes, of ' thou,' except in poetry or in addresses to the Deity, and, consequent on this, in the dropping of the second singular of the verb with its strongly marked flexion, as ' lovest,' 'lovedst,' we have another example of a power which has been allowed to expire. In the seventeenth century 'thou' in English, as at the present ' du' in German, 'tu' in French, was the sign of familiarity, whether that familiarity was of love or of contempt.* It was not unfrequently the latter. Thus at Sir Walter Raleigh's trial (1603), Coke, when argument and evidence failed him, insulted, and meant to insult, the illustrious prisoner by applying to him the term 'thou' :—' All that Lord Cobham did was at *thy* instigation, *thou* viper l for I *thou* thee, *thou* traitor l' And when Sir Toby Belch in *Twelfth Night* is urging Sir Andrew Aguecheek to send a sufficiently provocative challenge to Viola, he suggests ' that he taunt him with the licence of ink ; if thou *thou'st* him some thrice, it shall not be amiss.' To keep this in mind will throw much· light on one peculiarity of the Quakers, and give a certain dignity to it, as once maintained, which at present it is very

---

* Thus Wallis (*Gramm. Ling. Anglic.*, 1654) : Singulari numero siquis alium compellet, vel dedignantis illud esse solet, vel familiariter blandientis.

far from possessing. However needless and unwise
their determination to 'thee' and 'thou' the whole
world, this was not then, as it seems now to us, and,
through the silent changes which language has undergone, as now it indeed is, a gratuitous departure from
the ordinary usage of society. Right or wrong, it
meant something, and had an ethical motive : being
indeed a testimony upon their parts, however mis-
placed, that they would not have high or great or rich
men's persons in admiration ; nor render the obser-
vance to some which they withheld from others. It
was a testimony too which cost them something. At
present we can very little understand the amount of
courage which this 'thou-ing' and 'thee-ing' of all
the world demanded on their parts, nor yet the
amount of indignation and offence which it stirred up
where men were not aware of, or would not allow for,
the scruples which, as they considered, obliged them
to this.*   It is, however, in its other aspect that we

---

* What the actual position of the compellation 'thou' was
at that time, we learn from Fuller (*Church History*, *Dedication
of Book* vii.) : 'In opposition whereunto [*i.e.* to the Quaker
usage] we maintain that *thou* from superiors to inferiors is
proper, as a sign of command ; from equals to equals is passa-
ble, as a note of familiarity ; but from inferiors to superiors,
if proceeding from ignorance, hath a smack of clownishness ;
if from affection, a tone of contempt. See a brief but instructive disquisition in Skeat's edition of *The Romance of
William of Palerne*, p. xli., in proof that in early English
Literature the distinction between 'thou' and 'ye,' as here
laid down, was accurately observed. There is a most interesting and exhaustive treatment of the past relation between
'thou' and 'you' in *Guesses at Truth*, 1866, pp. 120–133.

must chiefly regret the dying out of the use of 'thou'
—that is as the pledge of peculiar intimacy and
special affection, as between husband and wife,
parents and children, and such others as might be
knit together by bands of more than a common love.

I have more than once remarked that nothing can
be imagined more stealthy, more calculated to elude
observation, than the disappearance of an old form,
and the usurpation of its place by a new.   Take for
instance the getting rid of the plural in 'n' or 'en.'
This, originally the Saxon plural in 'an' of the first
declension, had, during the anarchical period of the
language, spread over a much larger group of words;
but, as we all know, has long since given way to 's,'
which, with a few exceptions, is now the universal sign
of the plural.*   By steps so slow as to be almost imperceptible, diffused as they have been over large
spaces of time, this dismissing of one and adopting of
another has been effected.   Long before Chaucer,
already in the *Rhymed Chronicle* of Robert of Gloucester, written before 1300, it is evident that the
termination in 'n' or 'en' is giving way, and that in
's' has virtually won the day; but we do not the less
meet in this 'arwen' (arrows), 'steden,' 'sterren,'
'ameten' (emmets), 'chyrchen,' 'massen,' 'been,'
'heveden' (heads), 'applen,' 'candlen,' 'honden,'
'soulen,' 'unclen,' 'lancen,' and others ; as in *The
Romance of King Alexander* of the same date we have
'crabben,' 'hawen,' 'slon' (sloes), 'noten' (nuts).

* See Mätzner, p. 220.

In Chaucer's time they are very far fewer, while yet
he has 'doughteren,' 'sistren,' 'fone,' 'ashen,' 'been,'
'schoon,' 'eyne ;' but all these side by side with our
present 'daughters,' 'sisters,' 'foes,' 'ashes,' 'bees,'
'shoes,' 'eyes ;' now one and now the other. Thus
the plural in 'n' has narrowed still further the region
which it occupies, but still is holding a certain ground
of its own. Two centuries later 'sistern' is still alive,
it is frequent in Coverdale's Bible and in our early
Reformers ; 'hosen' too appears in our English
Version (Dan. iii. 21), with 'fone' and 'schoon' and
'eyne' in the diction of poetry, but chiefly in that of
poets who, like Spenser, affect the archaic. At the
present day, setting aside four or five words which
have preserved and will now probably preserve to the
end the termination in 'en,' as 'oxen,' 'chicken,'
'kine' (kyen), 'brethren,' perhaps 'eyne' is the only
one of these plurals which even the poets would feel
at liberty to employ ; while a few others, as 'housen,'
'fuzzen' (furzes), 'cheesen' (Dorsetshire), and possibly one or two more, maintain a provincial existence.

A history very nearly similar might be traced of the
process by which the southern termination of the
participle present in 'ing' has superseded and displaced the northern in 'and,' so that we say now .
'doing,' 'sitting,' 'leaping,' not 'doand,' 'sittand,'
'leapand.' We have here, it is true, a further circumstance helping to conceal and keep out of sight the
progress of the change ; namely, the only gradual
melting, through intermediate steps, of the one form
into the other, of 'and' into 'end,' into 'ind,' and

finally into 'ing,' examples of all these four forms
sometimes occurring side by side in the same poem ;
for example in *The Romance of William of Palerne,*
of date about 1350.   Spenser's 'glitterand' (*F. Q.* i.
7, 29) is about the last surviving specimen of the
northern form, that is in English ; in Scotch it maintained its ground to a far later day, in some sort
maintains it still.

It is thus, and by steps such as these, that a change
is brought about.   That which ultimately is to win all
comes in, it may be, at first as an exception ; it then
just obtains a footing and allowance ; it next exists
side by side and on equal terms with the old ; then
overbears it ; and finally, it may be, claims the whole
domain of the language as its own ; so that sometimes
a single isolated word, like the 'paterfamilias' of the
Latins, keeps record of what was once the law of all
the words of some certain class in a language.

I will not conclude this lecture without one further
illustration of the same law, which, as I have sought to
show, is evermore working, and causing this and that
to be dismissed from a language, so soon as ever the
speakers feel that it is not absolutely indispensable,
that they can attain their end, which is, to convey
their meaning, without it ; though having dwelt on the
subject so fully, I shall do little more than indicate
this.   I refer not here to any change in English
now going forward, but to one which completed
its course several centuries ago ; namely, to the
renouncing upon its part, of any distribution of nouns
into masculine, feminine, and neuter, as in German,

or even into masculine and feminine, as in French : and with this, and as a necessary consequence of this, the dropping of any flexional modification of the adjectives in regimen with them. It was the boldest step in the way of simplification which the language has at any time taken ; and, after what has lately been said, I need not observe was one which it took centuries to accomplish. Natural *sex*, of course, remains, being inherent in all language ; but grammatical *gender*, with the exception of 'he,' 'she,' and 'it,' and perhaps one or two other fragmentary instances, the languge has altogether forgone. An example will make clear the distinction between these. Thus it is not the word 'poetess' which is *feminine*, but the person indicated who is *female*. So too 'daughter,' 'queen,' are in English not *feminine* nouns, but nouns designating *female* persons. Take on the contrary 'filia,' or 'regina,' 'fille' or 'reine,' there you have *feminine* nouns as well as *female* persons. We did not inherit this simplicity from others, but, like the Danes, in so far as they have done the like, have made it for ourselves. Whether we turn to the Latin, or, which is for us more important, to the old Gothic, we find gender ; and in all the daughter languages which were born of the Latin, in most of those which have descended from the ancient Gothic stock, it is fully established to this day. The practical businesslike character of the English mind asserted itself in the rejection of a distinction, which in a vast proportion of words, that is, in all which are the signs of *inanimate* objects, and as such incapable of sex, rested upon a fiction, and had no ground in the real nature of things. It is only by an act and effort of the imagination that sex, and thus gender, can be attributed to a table, a ship, or a tree ;* and there are aspects, this being one, in which the English is among the least imaginative of all languages, even while it has been employed in some of the mightiest works of imagination which the world has ever seen. †

What, it may be asked, is the meaning and explanation of all this ? It is that at certain earlier periods of a nation's life its genius is synthetic, and at later becomes analytic. At earlier periods the imagination is more than the understanding ; men love to contemplate the thing and the mode of the thing

---

* Compare Pott, *Etymologische Forschungen*, part 2, p. 404. The entirely arbitrary character of the attribution of gender to sexless things is illustrated well by the way in which different genders are ascribed in the same book to one and the same thing ; thus in our Authorized Version, 'the tree *his* fruit' (Dan. iv. 14), 'the tree *her* fruit' (Rev. xxii. 1) ; and the different Versions vary, thus 'the vine *her* roots' (Ezek. xvii. 7, E. V.), 'the vine *his* roots' (ibid. Coverdale, 'the salt *his* savour' (Matt. v. 13, E. V.), 'the salt *her* saltness' (ibid. Tyndale). But at a much earlier date it had become to a great extent a matter of subjective individual feeling whether *his* (masculine and neuter) or *her* (feminine should be employed. The two recensions of Wiclif frequently differ from one another ; thus at Job xxxix. 14, the first, 'the ostridge *her* eggs,' the second, 'the ostridge *his* eggs ;' so too at Gen. viii. 9, the first, 'the culver *his* foot,' the second, 'the culver *her* foot.'.

† Compare Chasles, *Etudes sur l'Allemagne*, p. 25.

together, as a single idea, bound up in one. But a time arrives when the intellectual obtains the upper hand of the imaginative, when the inclination of those that speak a language is to analyse, to distinguish between these two, and not only to distinguish, but to divide, to have one word for the thing itself, and another for the quality or manner of the thing ; and this, as it would appear, is true not of some languages only, but of all.

LECTURE VII.

CHANGES IN THE MEANING OF ENGLISH WORDS.

I PROPOSE in my present lecture a little to consider those changes which have found or are
now finding place in the meaning of English words ;
so that, whether we are aware of it or not, we employ
them at this day in senses very different from those in
which our forefathers employed them of old. You
will observe that it is not *obsolete* words, such as have
quite fallen out of present use, which I propose to
consider ; but such, rather, as are still on the lips of
men, although with meanings more or less removed
from those which once they possessed. My subject
is far more practical, has far more to do with your
actual life, than if I were to treat of words at the
present day altogether out of use. These last have
an interest indeed, but so long as they remain what
they are, and are to be found only in our glossaries,
it is an interest of an antiquarian character. They
constitute a part of the intellectual money with which
our ancestors carried on the business of their lives ;
but now they are rather medals for the cabinets and
collections of the curious than current money for the
service of all. Their wings are clipped ; they are

'*winged* words' no more ; the spark of thought or feeling, kindling from mind to mind, no longer runs along them, as along the electric wires of the soul. And then, besides this, there is little danger that any should be misled by them. They are as rocks which, standing out from the sea, declare their presence, and are therefore easily avoided ; while those other are as hidden rocks, which are the more dangerous, that their very existence is unsuspected. A reader lights for the first time on some word which has now passed out of use, as 'frampold,' or 'garboil,' or 'brangle ;' he is at once conscious of his ignorance ; he has recourse to a glossary, or if he guesses from the context at the signification, still his guess is a guess to him, and no more.

But words that have changed their meaning have often a deceivableness about them ; a reader not once doubts but that he knows their intention ; he is visited with no misgivings that they possess for him another force than that which they possessed for the author in whose writings he finds them, and which they conveyed to *his* contemporaries. He little dreams how far the old life may have gone out of them, and a new life entered in. Let us suppose a student to light on a passage like the following (it is from the *Preface* to Howell's *Lexicon*, 1660) : 'Though the root of the English language be *Dutch*, yet it may be said to have been inoculated afterwards on a French stock.' He may know that the Dutch is a sister dialect to our own ; but this that it is the mother or root of it will certainly perplex him, and he

will hardly know what to make of the assertion ;
perhaps he ascribes it to an error in his author, who
is thereby unduly lowered in his esteem. But presently in the course of his reading he meets with the
following statement, this time in Fuller's *Holy War*,
being a history of the Crusades : 'the French,
Dutch, Italian, and English were the four elemental
nations, whereof this army [of the Crusaders] was
compounded.' If the student has sufficient historical
knowledge to know that in the time of the Crusades
there were no Dutch, in our use of the word, this
statement would merely startle him ; and probably
before he had finished the chapter, having his attention once roused, he would perceive that Fuller with
the writers of his time used 'Dutch' for German ;
even as it was constantly so used up to the end of
the seventeenth century,—what we call now a Dutch-
man being then a Hollander,—and as the Americans
use it to this present day. But a young student
might very possibly want that amount of previous
knowledge, which should cause him to receive this
announcement with misgiving and surprise ; and thus
he might carry away altogether a wrong impression,
and rise from a perusal of the book, persuaded that
the Dutch, as we call them, played an important part
in the Crusades, while the Germans took little or no
part in them at all.

And as it is here with an historic fact, so still more
often will it happen with the subtler moral and
ethical transformations which words have undergone.
Out of these it will continually happen that words

convey now much more reprobation, or convey now
much less, or of a different kind, than once they did;
and a reader not aware of the altered value which
they now possess, may be in constant danger of mis-
reading his author, of misunderstanding his intention,
and this, while he has no doubt whatever that he
perfectly apprehends and takes it in.   Thus when
Shakespeare makes the gallant York address Joan of
Arc as a 'miscreant,' how coarse a piece of invective
this sounds; how unlike what the chivalrous soldier
would have uttered; or what one might have supposed that Shakespeare, even with his unworthy
estimate of the holy warrior-maid, would have put into
his mouth.   But the 'miscreant' of Shakespeare's time
was not the 'miscreant' of ours.   He was simply, in
agreement with the etymology of the word, a misbe-
liever, one who did not believe rightly the articles of the
Catholic Faith.   This I need not remind you was the
constant charge which the English brought against the
Pucelle,—namely, that she was a dealer in hidden
magical art, a witch, and as such had fallen from the
faith.   On this plea they burnt her, and it is this which
York intends when he calls her a 'miscreant,' and
not what we should intend by the name.

In poetry above all what beauties are often missed,
what forces lost, through this assumption that the
present meaning of a word accurately represents the
past.   How often the poet is wronged in our estimation; that seeming to us now flat and pointless, which
would assume quite another aspect, did we know how
to read into some word the emphasis which it once had,

but which now has departed from it. For example,
Milton ascribes in *Comus* the '*tinsel-slippered*' feet to
Thetis, the goddess of the sea. How comparatively
poor an epithet this 'tinsel-slippered' sounds for those
who know of 'tinsel' only in its modern acceptation of
mean and cheap finery, affecting a splendour which it
does not really possess. But learn its earlier use by
learning its derivation, bring it back to the French
'étincelle,' and the Latin 'scintillula;' see in it as
Milton and the writers of his time saw, 'the spark-
ling,' and how exquisitely beautiful a title does this
become applied to a sea-goddess; how vividly does
it call up before our mind's eye the quick glitter and
sparkle of the waves under the light of sun or moon.*
It is the 'silver-footed' (ἀργυρόπεζα) of Homer; but
this is not servilely transferred, rather reproduced and
made his own by the English poet, dealing as one
great poet will do with another; who will not disdain
to borrow, yet to what he borrows will add often a
further grace of his own.

Or, again, do we keep in mind, or are we even
aware, that whenever the word 'influence' occurs in
our English poetry, down to comparatively a modern
date, there is always more or less remote allusion to
invisible illapses of power, skyey, planetary effects,
supposed to be exercised by the heavenly luminaries
upon the dispositions and the lives of men? The ten

* So in Herrick's *Electra :*
　　' More white than are the whitest creams,
　　Or moonlight *tinselling* the streams.'

occasions on which the word occurs in Shakespeare do
not offer a single exception. How many a passage
starts into a new life and beauty and fulness of allusion,
when this is present with us ; even Milton's

> ' store of ladies, whose bright eyes
> Rain *influence*,'

as spectators of the tournament, gain something,
when we regard them—and using this language, he
intended we should—as the luminaries of this lower
sphere, shedding by their propitious presence strength
and valour into the hearts of their knights.

A word will sometimes even in its present acceptation yield a convenient and even a correct sense ;
the last I have cited would do so ; we may fall into no
positive misapprehension about it ; and still, through
ignorance of its past history and of the force which it
once possessed, we may miss much of its significance. We are not *beside* the meaning of our author, but we are *short* of it. Thus in Beaumont
and Fletcher's *King and no King* (Act iii. Sc. 2), a
cowardly braggart of a soldier describes the treatment
he experienced, when, like Parolles, he was at length
found out, and stripped of his lion's skin :—' They
hung me up by the heels and beat me with hazel
sticks, . . . that the whole kingdom took notice of
me for a *baffled* whipped fellow.' Were you reading
this passage, there is probably nothing which would
make you pause ; you would attach to 'baffled' a
sense which sorts very well with the context—' hung
up by the heels and beaten, all his schemes of being

thought much of were *baffled* and defeated.' But
'baffled' implies far more than this; it contains allusion to a custom in the days of chivalry, according to
which a perjured or recreant knight was either in
person, or more commonly in effigy, hung up by the
heels, his scutcheon blotted, his spear broken, and he
himself or his effigy made the subject of all kinds of
indignities; such a one being said to be 'baffled.'*
Twice in Spenser recreant knights are so treated. I
can only quote a portion of the shorter passage in
which this infamous punishment is described : .

> ' And after all, for greater infamy
> He by the heels him hung upon a tree,
> And *baffled* so, that all which passèd by
> The picture of his punishment might see.' †

Probably when Beaumont and Fletcher wrote, men
were not so remote from the days of chivalry, or at
any rate from the literature of chivalry, but that this
custom was still fresh in their minds. How much
more to them than to us, so long as we are ignorant
of the same, must their words just quoted have conveyed ?

There are several places in the Authorized Version
of Scripture, where those who are not aware of the
changes which have taken place during the last two
hundred and fifty years in our language, can hardly
fail of being to a certain extent misled as to the

---

* See Holinshed, *Chronicles*, vol. iii. pp. 827, 1218 : Ann.
1513, 1570.
† *Fairy Queen*, vi. 7, 27 ; cf. v. 2, 37.

intention of our Translators ; or, if they are better
acquainted with Greek than with early English, will
be tempted to ascribe to them, though unjustly, an
inexact rendering of the original. Thus the altered
meaning of 'religion' may very easily draw after it a
serious misunderstanding in that well-known statement of St. James, ' Pure *religion* and undefiled before
God and the Father is this, to visit the fatherless and
widows in their affliction.' ' There !' exclaims one who
wishes to set up St. James against St. Paul, that so he
may escape the necessity of obeying either, ' listen to
what St. James says ; there is nothing mystical in
what he requires ; instead of harping on faith as a
condition necessary to salvation, he makes all religion
to consist in deeds of active well-doing and kindness
one to another.' But let us pause for a moment.
Did ' religion,' when our Version was made, mean
godliness ? did it mean the *sum total* of our duties
towards God ? for, of course, no one would deny that
deeds of charity are a necessary part of our Christian
duty, an evidence of the faith which is in us. There
is abundant evidence to show that ' religion ' did not
mean this ; that, like the Greek θρησκεία, for which
it here stands, like the Latin 'religio,' it meant the
outward forms and embodiments in which the inward
principle of piety arrayed itself, the *external service*
of God : and St. James is urging upon those to whom
he is writing something of this kind : ' Instead of the
ceremonial services of the Jews, which consisted in
divers washings and in other elements of this world,
let our service, our θρησκεία, take a nobler shape,

let it consist in deeds of pity and of love '—and it was
this which our Translators ihtended, when they used
' religion ' here and ' religious ' in the verse preceding.
How little ' religion' was formerly in meaning co-
extensive with godliness, how predominantly it was
used for the *outward* service of God, is plain from
many passages in our *Homilies*, and from other contemporary literature.

You remember the words in the Sermon on the
Mount, ' *Take no thought* for your life, what ye shall
eat or what ye shall drink' (Mat. vi. 25). They have
been often found fault with ; and, to quote one of the
fault-finders, 'most English critics have lamented the
inadvertence of our Authorized Version, which in
bidding us *take no thought* for the necessaries of life
prescribed to us what is impracticable in itself, and
would be a breach of Christian duty even if possible.'*
But there is no 'inadvertence' here. When our
Translation was made, 'Take no thought' was a
perfectly correct rendering of the words of the original.
' Thought' was then constantly used for painful soli-
citude and care. Thus Bacon writes, ' Harris an
alderman was put in trouble and died of *thought* and
and anxiety before his business came to an end ; and
in one of the *Somers Tracts* (its date is of the reign
of Elizabeth) these words occur : 'In five hundred
years only two queens have died in childbirth. Queen
Catherine Parr died rather of *thought.*' A still better
example occurs in Shakespeare's *Julius Cæsar*—' *take*

* Scrivener, *Notes on the New Testament*, vol. i. p. 162.

thought, and die for Cæsar'—where 'to take thought is to take a matter so seriously to heart that death ensues.

Again, there are some words in our Liturgy which are not unfrequently misunderstood. In the Litany we ask of God that it would please Him 'to give and preserve to our use the *kindly* fruits of the earth.' What is commonly understood by these '*kindly* fruits of the earth'? The fruits, if I mistake not, in which the *kindness* of God or of nature towards us finds its expression. This is no unworthy meaning to give to the words, but still it is not the right one. The '*kindly* fruits' are the '*natural* fruits,' those which the earth according to its *kind* should naturally bring forth, which it is appointed to produce. To show you how little 'kindly' meant once benignant, as it means now, I will instance an employment of it from Sir Thomas More's *Life of Richard the Third.* He tells us that Richard calculated by murdering his two nephews in the Tower to make himself accounted 'a *kindly* king'—not certainly a 'kindly' one in our present usage of the word; but, having put them out of the way, that he should then be lineal heir of the Crown, and should thus be reckoned as king *by kind* or natural descent; and such was of old the constant use of the word. And Bishop Andrews, preaching on the Conspiracy of the Gowries, asks concerning the conspirators, 'Where are they? Gone to their own place, to Judas their brother; as is most *kindly*, the sons to the father of wickedness, there to be plagued with him forever.'

A phrase in one of our occasional Services, 'with my body I thee *worship*,' has perplexed and sometimes offended those who were unacquainted with the early uses of the word, and thus with the intention of the actual framers of that Service. Clearly in our modern sense of 'worship,' this language would be inadmissible. But 'worship' or 'worthship' meant 'honour' in our early English, and 'to worship' to honour, this meaning of 'worship' still very harmlessly surviving in 'worshipful,' and in the title of 'your worship' addressed to the magistrate on the bench. So little was it restrained of old to the honour which man is bound to pay to God, that it is employed by Wiclif to express the honour which God will render to his faithful servants and friends. Thus our Lord's declaration, 'If any man serve Me, him will my Father *honour*,' in Wiclif's translation reads thus: 'If any man serve Me, my Father shall *worship* him.' I do not mean that the words, 'with my body I thee *worship*,' might not profitably be changed, if only it were possible to touch things indifferent in the Prayer Book without giving room for a meddling with things which could not be touched without extremest hazard to the peace of the Church. I think they would be very well changed, liable as they are to misconstruction now ; but for all this they did not mean at the first, and therefore do not now really mean, any other than, 'with my body I thee *honour*,' and so you may reply to any gainsayer here.

Take another example of a misapprehension, which lies very near. Fuller, our Church historian, praising some famous divine that was lately dead, exclaims, ' Oh the *painfulness* of his preaching ! ' How easily we might take this for an exclamation wrung out at the recollection of the tediousness which he inflicted on his hearers. It is nothing of the kind ; the words are a record not of the *pain* which he caused to others, but of the *pains* which he bestowed himself; and I cannot doubt, if we had more 'painful' preachers in the old sense of the word, that is, who *took* pains themselves, we should have fewer 'painful' ones in the modern sense, who *cause* pain to their hearers. So too Bishop Grosthead is recorded as 'the *painful* writer of two hundred books'—not meaning hereby that these books were 'painful' in the reading, but that he was laborious and 'painful' in their composing.

Here is another easy misapprehension. Swift wrote a pamphlet, or, as he called it, a *Letter to the Lord Treasurer*, with this title, 'A proposal for correcting, improving, and *ascertaining* the English Tongue.' Who that brought a knowledge of present English, and no more, to this passage, would doubt that '*ascertaining* the English Tongue,' meant arriving at a certain knowledge of what it was? Swift, however, means something quite different from this. ' *To ascertain* the English tongue ' was not with him to arrive at a subjective certainty in our own minds of what that tongue is, but to give an objective certainty to that tongue itself, so that henceforth it should not change any more. For even Swift himself, with all his masculine sense, entertained a dream of this kind, fancied that the growth of a language might be ar-

rested, as is more fully declared in the work itself.*

In other places unacquaintance with the changes in
a word's usage may leave you sorely perplexed and
puzzled as to your author's meaning. It is evident
that he has a meaning, but what it is you are unable
to divine, even though all the words he employs are
familiarly employed to the present day. Thus 'courtly
Waller,' congratulating Charles the Second on his
return from exile, and describing how men, once his
bitterest enemies, were now the most earnest to offer
themselves to his service, writes thus :

> ' Offenders now, the chiefest, do begin
> To strive for grace, and expiate their sin :
> All winds blow fair that did the world embroil,
> *Your vipers treacle yield*, and scorpions oil.'

Readers not a few before now will have been perplexed at the poet's statement that '*vipers treacle yield*'
—who yet have been too indolent, or who have not
had the opportunity, to search out what his meaning
was. There is in fact allusion here to a curious piece
of legendary lore. 'Treacle,' or 'triacle,' as Chaucer
wrote it, was originally a Greek word, and wrapped up
in itself the once popular belief (an anticipation, by
the way, of homœopathy), that a confection of the
viper's flesh was the most potent antidote against the
viper's bite.* Waller serves himself of this old legend,

---

* *Works* (Sir W. Scott's edition), vol. ix. p. 139.

† Θηριακἠ from θηρίον, a designation given to the
viper (Acts xxviii. 4). 'Theriac' is only the more rigid form

familiar enough in his time, for Milton speaks of 'the sovran *treacle* of sound doctrine,'* while 'Venice treacle,' or 'viper-wine,' was a common name for a supposed antidote against all poisons; and he would say that regicides themselves began to be loyal, vipers not now yielding hurt any more, but rather a healing medicine for the old hurts which they themselves had inflicted.   'Treacle,' it may be observed, designating first this antidote, came next to designate any antidote, then any medicinal confection or sweet syrup, and lastly that particular syrup, namely, the sweet syrup of molasses, to which alone we restrict it now.

I will draw on Fuller for one more illustration.   In his *Holy War*, having enumerated the rabble rout of fugitive debtors, runaway slaves, thieves, adulterers, murderers, of men laden for one cause or another with heaviest censures of the Church, who swelled the ranks, and helped to make up the army, of the Crusaders, he exclaims, 'A lamentable case, that the devil's *black guard* should be God's soldiers!'   What does

---

of the same word, the scholarly, as distinguished from the popular, adoption of it.   Augustine (*Con. duas Epp. Pelag.* iii. 7) : Sicut fieri consuevit antidotum etiam de serpentibus contra venena serpentum.   See the *Promptorium Parvulorum*, s. v., Way's edition.

* And Chaucer, more solemnly still :

> 'Christ, which that is to every harm *triacle*.'

The *antidotal* character of treacle comes out yet more in those lines of Lydgate :

> ' There is no *venom* so parlious in sharpnes,
>   As whan it hath of *treacle* a likenes.'

he mean, we may ask, by 'the devil's *black guard'?*
The phrase does not stand here alone ; it is, on the
contrary, of frequent recurrence in the early dramatists
and others down to the time of Dryden ; in whose
Don Sebastian, 'Enter the captain of the rabble, with
the *Black guard,'* is a stage direction.   What is this
'black guard'?   Has it any connection with a word
of our homeliest vernacular?   None which is very
apparent, and yet such as may very clearly be traced.
In old times, the palaces of our kings and seats of our
nobles were not so well and completely furnished as
at the present day : and thus it was customary, when
a royal progress was made, or when the great nobility
exchanged one residence for another, that at such a
removal all kitchen utensils, pots and pans, and even
coals, should be also carried with them where they
went.   Those who accompanied and escorted these,
the meanest and dirtiest of the retainers, were called
'the black guard ;'* then any troop or company of
ragamuffins ; and lastly, when the word's history was
obscured and men forgot that it properly belonged to
a company, to a rabble rout, and not to a single
person, one would compliment another, not as belonging to, but as himself being, 'the black guard.'

These examples are sufficient to prove that it is not
a useless and unprofitable study, nor yet one altogether
without entertainment, to which I invite you.   It is a

* 'A slave, that within these twenty years rode with the
black guard in the Duke's carriage, 'mongst spits and dripping
pans ' (Webster, *White Devil,* Act i. Sc. 1).

study indeed so far from unprofitable, that any one
who desires to read with accuracy, and thus with
advantage and pleasure, our earlier classics, who
would not often fall short of, and often go astray from,
their meaning, must needs bestow some attention on
the altered significance of English words. And if
this is so, we could not more usefully employ what
remains of this present lecture than in seeking to
indicate those changes which words most frequently
undergo; and to trace as far as we can the causes,
moral and material, which bring these changes about,
with the good and the evil out of which they have
sprung, and to which they bear witness. For indeed
these changes are not changes at random, but for
the most part are obedient to certain laws, are capable of being distributed into certain classes, being
the outward transcripts and attestations of mental and
moral processes which have inwardly gone forward in
those who bring them about. Many, it is true, will
escape any classification of ours ; will seem to us the
result of mere caprice, and not to be accounted for
by any principle to which we can appeal. But all this
admitted freely, a majority will remain which are
reducible to some law or other, and with these we
will occupy ourselves now.

And first the meaning of a word oftentimes is
gradually narrowed. It was once as a generic name,
embracing many as yet unnamed species within itself,
which all went by its common designation. By and
by it is found convenient that each of these should

have its own more special sign allotted to it.* It is
here just as in some newly enclosed country, where a
single household will at first loosely occupy a whole
district ; this same district being in the course of time
parcelled out among twenty proprietors, and under
more accurate culture employing and sustaining them
all. Thus all food was once called 'meat ;' it is so in
our Bible, and 'horse-meat' for fodder is still no
unusual phrase ; yet 'meat' is now a name given
only to flesh. Any little book or writing was a
'libel' once ; now only such a one as is scurrilous
and injurious. Every leader was a 'duke' (dux) ;
thus '*duke* Hannibal' (Sir Thomas Elyot), '*duke*
Brennus' (Holland), '*duke* Theseus' (Shakespeare),
'*duke* Amalek,' with other 'dukes' in Scripture (Gen.
xxxvi.) Every journey, by land as much as by sea,
was a 'voyage.' 'Fairy' was not a name restricted,
as now, to the *Gothic* mythology ; thus 'the *fairy*
Egeria' (Sir J. Harrington). A 'corpse' might
quite as well be a body living as one dead. In each
of these cases, the same contraction of meaning, the
separating off and assigning to other words of large
portions of this, has found place. 'To starve ' (the
German 'sterben,' and generally spelt 'sterve' up to
the middle of the seventeeth century), meant once to
die any manner of death ; thus Chaucer says, Christ

---

* Génin (*Lexique de la Langue de la Molière*, p. 367) says
well : En augmentant le nombre des mots, il a fallu restreindre
leur signification, et faire aux nouveaux un apanage aux dépens
des anciens.

'*sterved* upon the cross for our redemption ;' it now
is restricted to the dying by cold or by hunger.
Words not a few were once applied to both sexes alike,
which are now restricted to the female. It is so even
with 'girl,' which was once, as in *Piers Ploughman,* a
young person of either sex ; * while other words in
this list, such for instance as 'hoyden' (Milton,
prose), 'shrew,' 'harlot,' 'leman' (all in Chaucer),
'coquet' (Phillips, *New World of Words*), 'witch'
(Wiclif), 'slut' (Gower), 'termagant' (Bale),
'scold,' 'jade,' 'hag' (Golding), must, in their
present exclusive appropriation to the female sex, be
regarded as evidences of men's rudeness, and not of
women's deserts.

The necessities of an advancing civilization demand
more precision and accuracy in the use of words
having to do with weight, measure, number, size.
Almost all such words as 'acre,' 'furlong,' 'yard,'
'gallon,' 'peck,' were once of a vague and unsettled
use, and only at a later day, and in obedience to the
necessities of commerce and social life, exact mea-
sures and designations. Thus every field was once
an 'acre ;' and this remains so still with the German
'acker,' and with us when we give the name of 'God's
acre' to ground where we lay our dead ; it was not
till about the reign of Edward the First that 'acre'

---

* And no less so in French with 'dame,' by which form not
'domina' only, but 'dominus,' was represented. Thus in
early French poetry, '*Dame* Dieu' for '*Dominus* Deus' continually occurs.

was commonly restricted to a determined measure and
portion of land. Here and there even now a glebe-
land will be called 'the acre ;' and this, though it
should contain not one but many of our measured
acres. A 'furlong' was a 'furrowlong,' or length of
a furrow.* Any pole was a 'yard,' and this vaguer
use survives in 'sail*yard*,' 'hal*yard*,' and in other
sea-terms. Every pitcher was a 'galon' (Mark xiv. 13,
Wiclif), while a 'peck' was no more than a 'poke'
or bag. And the same has taken place in all other
languages. The Greek 'drachm' was at first a hand-
ful.† The word which stood at a later day for ten
thousand (μύριοι), implied in Homer's time any
great multitude ; and, differently accented, retained
this meaning in the later periods of the language.

Opposite to this is a counter-process by which words
of narrower intention gradually enlarge the domain of
their meaning, becoming capable of much wider application than any which once they admitted. Instances in this kind are fewer than in the last. The
main stream and course of human thoughts and
human discourse tends the other way, to discerning,
distinguishing, dividing ; and then to the permanent
fixing of the distinctions gained, by the aid of desig-

---

* 'A *furlong*, quasi *furrowlong*, being so much as a team
in England plougheth going forward, before they return back
again' (Fuller, *Pisgah Sight of Palestine*, p. 42).

† Δραχμή = 'manipulus,' from δράσσομαι, to grasp as
much as one can hold in the fingers.

nations which shall keep apart for ever in word that
which has been once severed and sundered in thought.
Nor is it hard to perceive why this process should be
the more frequent. Men are first struck with the
likeness between those things which are presented to
them ; on the strength of which likeness they men-
tally bracket them under a common term. Further
acquaintance reveals their points of unlikeness, the
real dissimilarities which lurk under superficial resem-
blances, the need therefore of a different notation for
objects which are essentially different. It is comparatively much rarer to discover real likeness under
what at first appeared as unlikeness; and usually
when a word moves forward, and from a special acquires a general significance, it is not in obedience to
any such discovery of the true inner likeness of things,
—the steps of successful generalizations being marked
and secured in other ways—but this widening of a
word's meaning is too often a result of quite other
causes. Men forget a word's history and etymology ;
its distinctive features are obliterated for them, with
all which attached it to some thought or fact which
by right was its own. All words in some sort are
faded metaphors, but this is one of which the fading
has become absolute and complete. Appropriated
and restricted once to some striking speciality which
it vigorously set out, it can now be used in a wider,
vaguer, more indefinite way. It can be employed
twenty times for once when it would have been
possible formerly to employ it. Yet this is not gain,
but pure loss. It has lost its place in the disciplined

army of words, and become one of a loose and dis-
orderly *mob.**

Let me instance 'preposterous.' It is now no
longer of any practical service at all in the language,
being merely an ungraceful and slipshod synonyn
for absurd.   But restore and confine it to its old use ;
let it designate that one peculiar branch of absurdity
which it designated once, namely the reversing of the
true order of things, the putting of the last first, and,
by consequence, of the first last, and whàt excellent
service it would yield. · Thus it is 'preposterous' to
put the cart before the horse, to expect wages before
the work is done, to hang a man first and try him
afterwards ; and in this stricter sense 'preposterous'
was always used by our elder writers.

In like manner ' to prevaricate ' was never employed
by good writers of the seventeenth century without
nearer or more remote allusion to the uses of the
word in the Roman law courts, where a 'prævarica-
tor' (properly a straddler with distorted legs) did not
mean generally and loosely, as now with us, one who
shuffles, quibbles, and evades ; but one who played
false in a particular manner ; who, undertaking, or
being by his office bound, to prosecute a charge, was
in secret collusion with the opposite party ; and,
betraying the cause which he affected to support, so

---

* The exact opposite of this will sometimes take place.
Beaucoup de mots, qui du temps de Corneille se pliaient à
plusieurs significations, se sont, de la façon la plus bizarre,
immobilisés et pétrifiés, si l'on ose le dire, dans des sens étroits
et restreints (*Lexique de la Langue de Corneille*, p. xxii.).

managed the accusation as to obtain not the condemnation, but the acquittal, of the accused ; a 'feint
pleader,' as in our old law language he would have
been termed.   How much force would the keeping of
this in mind add to many passages in our elder
divines.

Or take 'equivocal,' 'equivocate,' 'equivocation.'
These words, which belonged at first to logic, have
slipped into common use, and in so doing have lost
all the precision of their first employment.   'Equivocation ' is now almost any such ambiguous dealing in
words with the intention of deceiving, as falls short of
an actual lie ; but according to etymology and in
primary use 'equivocation,' this fruitful mother of so
much error, is the calling by the same name of things
essentially diverse, hiding intentionally or otherwise
a real difference under a verbal resemblance.*   Nor
let it be urged in defence of the present looser use,
that only so could it serve the needs of our ordinary
conversation ; so far from this, had it retained its
first use, how serviceable an implement of thought
might it have been in detecting our own fallacies, or
those of others ; all which it can now be no longer.

What now is 'idea' for us !   How infinite the fall
of this word since the time when Milton sang of the
Creator contemplating his newly created world,

> 'how it showed,
> Answering his great *idea*,'

---

* Thus Barrow : 'Which [courage and constancy] he that
wanteth is no other than *equivocally* a gentleman, as an image
or a carcass is a man.'

to the present use, when this person 'has an *idea* that
the train has started,' and the other 'had no no *idea* that
the dinner would be so bad.'   But 'idea' is perhaps
the worst treated word in the English language.
Matters have not mended since the times of Dr. Johnson ; who, as Boswell tells us, 'was particularly indig-
nant against the almost universal use of the word *idea*
in the sense of *notion* or *opinion*, when it is clear that
idea can only signify something of which an image can
be formed in the mind.'   There is perhaps no word in
the whole compass of the language so seldom employed with any tolerable correctness ; in none is the
distance so immense between what properly it means,
and the slovenly uses which popularly it is made to
serve.

   This tendency in words to lose the sharp, rigidly
defined outline of meaning which they once possessed,
to become of wide, vague, loose application instead of
fixed, definite, and precise, to mean almost anything,
and so really to mean nothing, is among the most
fatally effectual which are at work for the final ruin of
a language, and, I do not fear to add, for the demoralization of those that speak it.   It is one against
which we shall all do well to watch ; for there is none
of us who cannot do something in keeping words
close to their own proper meaning, and in resisting
their encroachments on the domain of others.

   The causes which bring this mischief about are not
hard to trace.   We all know that when a piece of our
silver money has for a long time been fulfilling its
part as 'pale and common drudge 'tween man and

man,' whatever it had at first of sharper outline and livelier impress is in the end nearly or altogether worn away. So it is with words, above all with words of science and theology. These, getting into general use, and passing often from mouth to mouth, lose the 'image and superscription' which they had before they descended from the school to the market-place, from the pulpit to the street. Being now caught up by those who understand imperfectly and thus incorrectly their true value, who will not be at the pains of learning what that is, or who are incapable of so doing, they are obliged to accommodate themselves to the lower sphere in which they circulate, by laying aside much of the precision and accuracy and· fulness which once they had ; they become weaker, shallower, more indistinct ; till in the end, as exponents of· thought and feeling, they cease to be of any. service at all.

Sometimes a word does not merely narrow or extend its meaning, but altogether changes it ; and this it does in more ways than one. Thus a secondary figurative sense will quite put out of use and extinguish the literal, until in the entire predominance of that it is altogether forgotten that it ever possessed any other. In 'bombast' this forgetfulness is nearly complete. What 'bombast' now means is familiar to us all, namely inflated words, 'full of sound and fury,' but 'signifying nothing.' This, at present the sole meaning, was once only the secondary and superinduced ; 'bombast' being properly the cotton plant,

and then the cotton wadding with which garments were
stuffed out and lined.   You remember perhaps how
Prince Hal addresses Falstaff, ' How now, my sweet
creature of *bombast;*' using the word in its literal
sense ; and another early poet has this line :

'Thy body's bolstered out with *bombast* and with bags.'

' Bombast ' was then transferred in a vigorous image
to the big words .without strength or solidity where-
with the discourses of some were stuffed out, and has
now quite forgone any other meaning.   So too 'to
garble' was once 'to cleanse from dross and dirt, as
grocers do their spices, to pick or cull out.'*   It is
never used now in this its primary sense, and has
indeed undergone this further change, that while once
' to garble ' was to sift for the purpose of selecting the
best, it is now to sift with a view of picking out the
worst. †   ' Polite ' is another word which in the figurative
sense has quite extinguished the literal.   We still speak
of 'polished' surfaces ; but not any more, with Cudworth, of '*polite* bodies, as looking glasses.'   Neither
do we now ' exonerate'a ship (Burton); nor ' stigma-
tize,' otherwise than figuratively, a ' malefactor' (the
same) ;   nor 'corroborate' our health (Sir Thomas
Elyot) any more.

Again, a word will travel on by slow and regularly
progressive courses of change, itself a faithful index

* Phillips, *New World of Words*, 1706.

† ' But his [Gideon's] army must be *garbled*, as too great for
God to give victory thereby ; all the fearful return home by
proclamation' (Fuller, *Pisgah Sight of Palestine*, b. ii. c 8).

of changes going on in society and in the minds of men, till at length everything is changed about it. The process of this it is often very curious to observe ; being one which it is possible to watch as step by step it advances to the final consummation.   There may be said to be three leading phases which the word successively presents, three stages in its history.   At first it grows naturally out of its own root, is filled with its own natural meaning.   Presently it allows another meaning, one foreign to its etymology, and superinduced on the earlier, to share possession with this, on the ground that where one exists, the other commonly exists with it.   At the third step, the newly introduced meaning, not satisfied with a moiety, with dividing the possession of the word, has thrust out the original and rightful possessor altogether, and reigns henceforward alone.   The three successive stages may be represented by a, ab, b; in which series b, which was wanting altogether at the first stage, and was only admitted as secondary at the second, does at the third become primary, and indeed remains in sole and exclusive possession.

We must not suppose that in actual fact the transitions from one signification to another are so strongly and distinctly marked, as I have found it convenient to mark them here.   Indeed it is hard to imagine anything more gradual, more subtile and imperceptible, than the process of change.   The manner in which the new meaning first insinuates itself into the old, and then drives out the old, can only be compared to the process of petrifaction, as rightly understood—the water not gradually turning what has fallen into it to stone, as we generally take the operation to be ; but successively displacing each several particle of that which is brought within its power, and depositing a stony particle in its stead, till, in the end, while all appears to continue the same, all has in fact been thoroughly changed. It is precisely thus, by such slow, gradual, and subtle advances that the new meaning filters through and pervades the word, little by little displacing entirely that which it formerly possessed.

No word would illustrate this process better than that old example, familiar probably to us all, of ' villain.' The ' villain ' is, first, the serf or peasant, ' villanus,' because attached to the ' villa ' or farm. He is, secondly, the peasant who, it is further taken for granted, will be churlish, selfish, dishonest, and generally of evil moral conditions, these having come to be assumed as always belonging to him, and to be permanently associated with his name, by those higher classes of society, the καλοι κάλαθοι, who in the main commanded the springs of language. At the third step, nothing of the meaning which the etymology suggests, nothing of ' villa,' survives any longer ; the peasant is wholly dismissed, and the evil moral conditions of him who is called by this name alone remain ;* so that the name would now in this its final

---

* Epigrams and proverbs like the following, and they are innumerable in the middle ages, sufficiently explain the successive phases of meaning through which ' villain ' has passed :

stage be applied as freely to peer, if he deserved it, as to peasant. 'Boor' has had exactly the same history; being first the cultivator of the soil; then secondly, the cultivator of the soil, who, it is assumed, will be coarse, rude, and unmannerly; and then thirdly, any one who is coarse, rude, and unmannerly. So too 'pagan; which is first villager, then heathen villager, and lastly heathen.* You may trace the same progress in 'churl,' 'clown,' 'antic,' and in numerous other words. The intrusive meaning might be likened in all these cases to the egg which the cuckoo lays in the sparrow's nest; the young cuckoo first sharing the nest with its rightful occupants, but not resting till it has dislodged and ousted them altogether.

I will illustrate by the aid of one word more this part of my subject. I called your attention in my last lecture to the true character of several words and forms in use among our country people, and claimed for them to be in many instances genuine English, although English now more or less antiquated and overlived. 'Gossip' is a word in point. This name is given by our Hampshire peasantry to the sponsors in baptism, the godfathers and godmothers. We have here a perfectly correct employment of 'gossip,' in fact its proper and original one, one involving moreover a very curious record of past beliefs. 'Gossip' or 'gossib,' as Chaucer spelt it, is a compound word,

---

Quando mulcetur villanus, pejor habetur :
Ungentem pungit, pungentem rusticus ungit.
† See my *Study of Words,* 13th edit., p. 119.

made up of the name of 'God,' and of an old Anglo-
Saxon word, 'sib,' still alivé in Scotland, as all
readers of Walter Scott will remember, and in some
parts of England, and which means, akin ; they
being 'sib,' who are related to one another.   But
why, you may ask, was the name given to sponsors ?
Out of this reason :—in the Middle Ages it was the
prevailing belief (and the Romish Church still affirms
it), that those who stood as sponsors to the same
child, besides contracting spiritual obligations on
behalf of that child, also contracted spiritual affinity
one with another ; they became *sib*, or akin, in *God*,
and thus 'gossips ;' hence 'gossipred,' an old word,
exactly analogous to 'kindred.'   Out of this faith
the Roman Catholic Church will not allow (unless
by dispensation), those who have stood as sponsors
to the same child, afterwards to contract marriage with
one another, affirming them too nearly related for
this to be lawful.

Take 'gossip' however in its ordinary present use,
as one addicted to idle tittle-tattle, and it seems to
bear no relation whatever to its etymology and first
meaning.   The same three steps, however, which we
have traced before will bring us to its present use.
'Gossips' are, first, the sponsors, brought by the act of
a common sponsorship into affinity and near familiarity
with one another ;   secondly, these sponsors, who
being thus brought together, allow themselves with
one another in familiar, and then in trivial and idle,
talk ; thirdly, they are any who allow themselves in
this trivial and idle talk,—called in French 'com-

mérage,' from the fact that 'commère' has run through exactly the same stages as its English equivalent.

It is plain that words which designate not things and persons only, but these as they are contemplated more or less in an ethical light, words which are tinged with a moral sentiment, are peculiarly exposed to change ; are constantly liable to take a new colouring or to lose an old. The gauge and measure of praise or blame, honour or dishonour, admiration or abhorrence, which they convey, is so purely a mental and subjective one, that it is most difficult to take accurate note of its rise or of its fall, while yet there are causes continually at work to bring about the one or the other. There are words not a few, ethical words above all, which have so imperceptibly drifted away from their former moorings, that although their position is now very different from that which they once occupied, scarcely one in a hundred of casual readers, whose attention has not been specially called to the subject, will have observed that they have moved at all. Here too we observe some words conveying less of praise or blame than once, and some more ; while some have wholly shifted from the one to the other. Some were at one time words of slight, almost of offence, which have altogether ceased to be so now. Still these are rare by comparison with those which once were harmless, but now are harmless no more ; which once, it may be, were terms of honour, but which now imply a slight or even a scorn. It is only too easy to perceive why these should exceed those in number.

Let us take an example or two. To speak now of royal children as 'royal *imps*,' would sound, and according to our present usage would be, impertinent ; and yet 'imp' was once a name of dignity and honour, and not of slight or of undue familiarity. Thus Spenser addresses the Muses,

> ' Ye sacred *imps* that on Parnasso dwell ;'

and 'imp' was especially used of the scions of royal or illustrious houses. More than one epitaph, still existing, of our ancient nobility might be quoted, beginning in such language as this, ' Here lies that noble *imp*.' Or what should we say of a poet who commenced a solemn poem in this fashion,

> ' Oh Israel, oh household of the Lord,
> Oh Abraham's *brats*, oh brood of blessed seed ' ?

Could we conclude but that he meant, by using low words on lofty occasions, to turn sacred things into ridicule? Yet this was very far from the intention of Gascoigne, the poet whose lines I have just quoted. 'Abraham's *brats*' was used by him in perfect good faith, and without the slightest feeling that anything ludricous or contemptuous adhered to 'brat,' as indeed in his time there did not, any more than now adheres to 'brood,' which is another form of the same word now.

Call a person 'pragmatical,' and you now imply not merely that he is busy, but *over*-busy, officious, self-important and pompous to boot. But it once meant nothing of the kind, and a man 'pragmatical' (like πραγματικός) was one engaged in affairs, and the title an honourable one, given to a man simply and industriously accomplishing the business which properly concerned him.* So too to say that a person 'meddles' or is a 'meddler' implies now that he interferes unduly in other men's matters, without a call mixing himself with them. This was not insinuated in the earlier uses of the word. On the contrary three of our earlier translators of the Bible have, '*Meddle* with your own business' (1 Thes. iv.' 11); and Barrow in one of his sermons draws at some length the distinction between 'meddling' and 'being *meddlesome*,' and only condemns the latter.

Or take again the words, 'to prose' or a 'proser. It cannot indeed be affirmed that they involve any *moral* condemnation, yet they certainly convey no compliment now; and are almost among the last which any one would desire should with justice be applied either to his talking or his writing. For 'to prose,' as we all now know too well, is to talk or write heavily and tediously, without spirit or animation; but once it was simply the antithesis of to versify, and a 'proser' the antithesis of a versifier or a poet. It will follow that the most rapid and liveliest writer who ever wrote, if he did not write in verse would have 'prosed' and been a 'proser,' in

---

* 'We cannot always be contemplative, or *pragmatical* abroad: but have need of some delightful intermissions, wherein the enlarged soul may leave off awhile her severe schooling' (Milton, *Tetrachordon*).

the language of our ancestors. Thus Drayton writes of his contemporary Nashe :

> ' And surely Nashe, though he a *proser* were,
> A branch of laurel yet deserves to bear ;'

that is, the ornament not of a 'proser' but of a poet. The tacit assumption that vigour, animation, rapid movement, with all the precipitation of the spirit, belong to verse rather than to prose, and are the exclusive possession of it, must explain the changed uses of the word.

Still it is according to a word's present signification that we must employ it now. It would be no excuse, having applied an insulting epithet to any, if we should afterwards plead that, tried by its etymology and primary usage, it had nothing offensive or insulting about it ; although indeed Swift assures us that in his time such a plea was made and was allowed. 'I remember,' he says, 'at a trial in Kent, where Sir George Rooke was indicted for calling a gentleman "knave" and "villain," the lawyer for the defendant brought off his client by alledging that the words were not injurious ; for "knave" in the old and true signification imported only a servant ; and "villain" in Latin is villicus, which is no more than a man employed in a country labour, or rather a baily.' The lawyer may have deserved his success for the ingenuity and boldness of his plea ; though, if Swift reports him aright, not certainly on the ground of the strict accuracy either of his Anglo-Saxon or his Latin.

The moral sense and conviction of men is often at work upon their words, giving them new turns in

obedience to these convictions, of which their changed
use will then remain a permanent record. The history
of 'sycophant' will illustrate this. You probably are
acquainted with the story which the Greek scholiasts
invented by way of explaining a word of whose history
they knew nothing,—namely that the 'sycophant' was
a 'manifester of figs,' one who detected and denounced others in the act of exporting figs from
Attica, an act forbidden, they asserted, by the
Athenian law ; and accused them to the people. Be
this explanation worth what it may, the word obtained
in Greek a more general sense ; any accuser, and
then any *false* accuser, was a 'sycophant ;' and when
the word was first adopted into English, it was in
this meaning : thus an old poet speaks of 'the railing
route of *sycophants ;*' and Holland : ' The poor man
that hath nought to lose, is not afraid of the *sycophant.*'
But it has not kept this meaning ; a 'sycophant' is
now a fawning flatterer ; not one who speaks ill of
you behind your back ; rather one who speaks good
of you before your face, but good which he does not
in his heart believe. Yet how true a moral instinct
has presided over this changed signification. The
calumniator and the flatterer, although they seem so
opposed to one another, how closely united they
really are. They grow out of the same root. The
same baseness of spirit which shall lead one to speak
evil of you behind your back, will lead him to fawn
on you and flatter you before your face. There is a
profound sense in that Italian proverb, ' Who flatters
me before, spatters me behind.'

But it is not the moral sense only of men which is thus at work, modifying their words ; but the immoral as well. If the good which men have and feel, penetrates into their speech, and leaves its deposit there, so does also the evil. Thus we may trace a constant tendency—in too many cases it has been a successful one—to empty words employed in the condemnation of evil, of the depth and earnestness of the moral reprobation which they once conveyed. Men's too easy toleration of sin, the feebleness of their moral indignation against it, brings this about, namely that the blame which words expressed once, has in some of them become much weaker now than once, from others has vanished altogether. 'To do a *shrewd* turn,' was once to do a *wicked* turn ; Chaucer employs 'shrewdness' to render the Latin 'improbitas;' nay, two murderers he calls two 'shrews,'—for there were, as has been already noticed, male 'shrews' once as well as female. But 'a *shrewd* turn' now, while it implies a certain amount of sharp dealing, yet implies nothing more ; and 'shrewdness' is applied to men rather in their praise than in their dispraise. And not these only, but a multitude of other words,—I will only instrance 'prank,' 'flirt,' 'luxury,' 'luxurious,' 'peevish,' 'wayward,' 'loiterer,' 'uncivil,'—involved once a much more earnest moral disapprobation than they do at this present.

But I must bring this lecture to a close. I have but opened to you paths, which you, if you are so minded, can follow up for yourselves. We have learned lately to speak of men's 'antecedents ;' the phrase is newly come up ; and it is common to say that if we would know what a man really now is, we must know his 'antecedents,' that is, what he has been and what he has done in time past. This is quite as true about words. If we would know what they now are, we must know what they have been ; we must know, if possible, the date and place of their birth, the successive stages of their subsequent history, the company which they have kept, all the road which they have travelled, and what has brought them to the point at which now we find them ; we must know in short their antecedents.

And let me say, without attempting to bring back school into these lectures which are out of school, that, seeking to do this, we might add an interest to our researches in the lexicon and the dictionary which otherwise they could never have ; that taking such words for example as ἐκκλησία, or παλιγγενεσία, or εὐτραπελία, or σοφιστής, or σχολαστικός in Greek ; as 'religio,' or 'sacramentum,' or 'imperator,' or 'urbanitas,' or 'superstitio,' in Latin ; as 'casuistry,' or 'good-nature,' or 'humorous,' or 'danger,' or 'romance,' in English, and endeavoring to trace the manner in which one meaning grew out of and superseded another, and how they arrived at the use in which they have finally rested (if indeed before these English words there be not a future still), we shall derive, I believe, amusement, I am sure, instruction ; we shall feel that we are really getting something, increasing the moral and intellectual stores of our minds ; furnishing ourselves with that which may hereafter be of service to ourselves, may be of service to others—than which there can be no feeling more pleasurable, none more delightful.*

* For a fuller treatment of the subject of this lecture, see my *Select Glossary*, 3rd ed., 1865.

LECTURE VIII.

CHANGES IN THE SPELLING OF ENGLISH WORDS.

THE subject of my lecture to-day will be English orthography, and it will be mainly taken up with notices of some changes which this has undergone. You may think perhaps that a weightier, or at all events a more interesting, subject might have claimed our attention to-day. But it is indeed one wanting neither in importance nor in interest. Unimportant it is not, having often engaged the attention of the foremost scholars among us. Uninteresting it may be, through faults in the manner of its treatment; but would never prove so in competent hands.* Let me hope that even in mine it may yield some pleasure and profit.

It is Hobbes who has said, ' The invention of printing, though ingenious, compared with the invention of letters is no great matter.' Use and familiarity had not obliterated for him the wonder of that, at which we probably have long ceased to wonder, if

---

* Let me refer in proof, to a paper, *On Orthographical Expedients*, by Edwin Guest, Esq., in the *Transactions of the Philological Society*, vol. iii. p. 1.

indeed the marvel of it ever presented itself to our minds at all—the power, namely, of representing sounds by written signs, of reproducing for the eye what existed at first only for the ear. Nor was the estimate which he formed of the relative value of these two inventions other than a just one. Writing stands more nearly on a level with speaking, and deserves better to be compared with it, than with printing ; which last, with all its utility, is yet of quite another and inferior type of greatness : or, if this be too much to claim for writing, it may at all events be affirmed to stand midway between the other two, and to be as much superior to the one as it is inferior to the other.

The intention of the written word, the end whereto it is a mean, is by aid of signs agreed on beforehand, to represent to the eye with as much accuracy as possible the spoken word. This intention, however, it never fulfils completely. There is always a chasm between these two, and much going forward in a language to render this chasm ever wider and wider. Short as man's spoken word often falls of his thought, his written word falls often as short of his spoken. Several causes contribute to this. In the first place, the marks of imperfection and infirmity cleave to writing, as to every other invention of man. · It fares with most alphabets as with our own. They have superfluous letters, letters which they do not want, because others already represent their sound ; thus ' q ' in English is perfectly useless,' ' c ' ' k ' and ' s ' have only two sounds between them ; they have

dubious letters, such, that is, as say nothing certain
about the sounds they stand for, because more than
one sound is represented by them, our own 'a' for
example; they are deficient in letters, that is, the
language has elementary sounds such as our own 'th'
which have no corresponding letters appropriated to
them, and can only be represented by combinations
of letters. This then, being, as one called it long ago,
'an apendix to the curse of Babel,' is one reason of
the imperfect reproduction of the spoken word by the
written. But another is, that the human voice is so
wonderfully fine and flexible an organ, is able to mark
such subtle and delicate distinctions of sound, so
infinitely to modify and vary these sounds, that were
an alphabet complete as human art could make it, did
it possess twice as many letters as our own possesses,
—the Sanscrit, which has fifty, very nearly does so,—
there would soon remain a multitude of sounds which
it could only approximately give back.

But there is a further cause for the divergence which
little by little becomes apparent between men's spoken
words and their written. What men do often, they
will seek to do with the least possible trouble. There
is nothing which they do oftener than repeat words;
they will seek here then to save themselves pains;
they will contract two or more syllables into one;
'vuestra merced' will become 'usted;' and 'topside
the other way,' 'topsy-turvy;'* or draw two or
three syllables together,' 'itiner' will become 'iter,'

---

* See *Stanihurst's Ireland*, p. 33, in Holinshed's *Chronicles*.

'hafoc' 'hawk,' 'cyning' 'king,' and 'almesse' 'alms;'
they will assimilate consonants; 'subfero' will become
'suffero;' they will slur over, and thus after a while
cease to pronounce certain letters, especially at the
close of words, where the speaking effort has in a
manner exhausted itself; for hard letters they will
substitute soft; for those which require a certain
effort to pronounce, they will substitute those which
require little or almost none.*   Under the operation
of these causes a gulf between the written and spoken
word will not merely exist; but it will have the
tendency to grow ever wider and wider.   This ten-

---

* Schleicher (*Die Deutsche Sprache*, p. 49) : Alle Veränd-
erung der Laute, die im Verlaufe des sprachlichen Lebens
eintritt, ist zunächst und unmittelbar Folge des Strebens,
unseren Sprachorganen die Sache leicht zu machen.   Bequem-
lichkeit der Aussprache, Ersparung an Muskelthätigkeit ist
das hier wirkende Agens.   Who does not feel, for instance,
how much the *méteres* of Greek, with its thrice recurring ' e,'
has gained in facility of being spoken over the earlier *mataras*,
with its thrice recurring ' a,' of the Sanscrit ?   Ampère (*Formation de la Langue Française*) describes well the forces, and
this among the rest, which are ever at work for the final
destruction of a language : Les mots en vieillissent, tendent
à remplacer les consonnes fortes et dures par des consonnes
faibles et douces, les voyelles sonores, d'abord par des voyelles
muettes.   Les sons pleins s'éteignent peu à peu et se perdent.
Les finales disparaissent et les mots se contractent.   Par suite,
les langues deviennent moins mélodieuses ; les mots qui
charmaient et remplissaient l'oreille n'offrent plus qu'un signe
mnémonique, et comme un chiffre.   Les langues en général
commencent par être une musique et finissent par être une
algèbre.

dency indeed will be partially traversed by approxi-
mations which from time to time will by silent consent
be made of the written word to the spoken ; absolutely superfluous letters will be got rid of; as the
final 'k' in 'civic,' 'politic,' and such like words ;
the 'Engleneloande' of Henry the Third's famous
proclamation (1258) will become the England 'which
we now write, seven letters instead of thirteen ; here
and there a letter dropped in speech will be dropped
also in writing, as the 's' in so many French words,
where its absence is marked by a circumflex ; a new
shape, contracted or briefer, which a word has taken
on the lips of men, will find its representation in their
writing ; as 'chirurgeon' will not merely be pronounced, but also spelt, 'surgeon,' 'squinancy'
'quinsey,' and 'Euerwic' 'York.' Still, notwithstanding these partial readjustments of the relations
between the two, the anomalies will be infinite ; there
will be a multitude of written letters which have
ceased to be sounded letters ; words not a few will
exist in one shape upon our lips, and in quite
another in our books.   Sometimes, as in such proper
names as 'Beauchamp' and 'Belvoir,' even the pretence of a consent between the written word and
the spoken will have been abandoned.

It is inevitable that the question should arise—Shall
these anomalies be meddled with? shall it be attempted to remove them, and to bring writing and
speech into harmony and consent—a harmony and
consent which never indeed in actual fact at any
period of the language existed, but which yet may be

regarded as the object of written speech, as the idea
which, however imperfectly realized, has, in the re-
duction of spoken sounds to written, floated before
the minds of men ?   If the attempt is to be made, it
is clear that it can only be made in one way.   There
is not the alternative here that either Mahomet shall
go to the mountain, *or* the mountain to Mahomet.
The spoken word is the mountain ; it will not stir ; it
will resist all attempts to move it.   Conscious of
superior rights, that it existed the first, that it is, so to
say, the elder brother, it will never consent to become
different from what it has been, that so it may more
closely conform and comply with the written word.
Men will not be persuaded to pronounce 'wou*l*d' and
'de*b*t,' because they write these words severally with
an 'l' and with a 'b' : but what if they could be
induced to write 'woud' and 'det,' because they so
pronounce ; and to adopt the same course wherever a
discrepancy existed between the word as spoken, and
as written ?   Might not the gulf between the two be
in this way made to disappear?

Here we have the explanation of that which in the
history of almost all literatures has repeated itself
more than once, namely, the endeavour to introduce
phonetic writing.   It has certain plausibilities to rest
on ; it appeals to the unquestionable fact that the
written word was intended to picture to the eye what
the spoken word sounded to the ear.   For all this I
believe that it would be impossible to introduce it ;
and, even if possible, that it would be most unde-

sirable, and this for two reasons ; the first being that the losses consequent upon its introduction would far outweigh the gains, even supposing those gains as large as the advocates of the scheme promise ; the second, that these promised gains would themselves be only very partially realized, or not at all.

I believe it to be impossible. It is clear that such a scheme must begin with the reconstruction of the alphabet. The first thing that the phonographers have perceived is the necessity for the creation of a vast number of new signs, the poverty of all existing alphabets, at any rate of our own, not yielding a several sign for all the several sounds in the language. Our English phonographers have therefore had to invent ten of these new signs or letters, which are henceforth to take their place with our *a*, *b*, *c*, and to enjoy equal rights with them. Rejecting two (*q*, *x*), and adding ten, they have raised their alphabet from twenty-six letters to thirty-four. But to procure the reception of such a reconstructed alphabet is simply an impossibility, as much an impossibility as would be the reconstitution of the structure of the language in any points where it was manifestly deficient or illogical. Sciolists or scholars may sit down in their studies, and devise these new letters, and prove that we need them, and that the introduction of them would be a manifest gain ; and this may be all very true : but if they imagine that they can persuade a people to adopt them, they know little of the ways in which its alpha-bet is entwined with the whole innermost life of a

people.*   One may freely own that most present
alphabets are redundant here, are deficient there ;
our English perhaps is as greatly at fault as any, and
with that we have chiefly to do.   Unquestionably it
has more letters than one to express one and the
same sound ; it has only one letter to express two or
three sounds ; it has sounds which are only capable
of being expressed at all by awkward and roundabout
expedients.   Yet at the same time we must accept
the fact, as we accept any other which it is out of our
power to change—with regret, indeed, but with a
perfect acquiescence : as one accepts the fact that
Ireland is not some thirty or forty miles nearer to
England—that it is so difficult to get round Cape
Horn—that the climate of Africa is so fatal to European life.   A people will no more quit their alphabet
than they will quit their language ; they will no more
consent to modify the one at a command from without than the other.   Cæsar avowed that with all his
power he could not introduce a new word, and

---

* Of course it is quite a different thing when philologers,
for their own special purposes, endeavour to construct an
alphabet which shall cover all sounds of human speech, and
shall enable them to communicate to one another in all parts
of the world what is the true pronunciation, or what they
believe to be true pronunciation, of the words with which they
are dealing. But alphabets like these are purely scientific and
must remain such. A single fact will sufficiently prove this.
The *Standard Alphabet* of the German scholar Lepsius, intended, it is true, to furnish written equivalents for sounds, not
of one human speech, but of all, has two hundred and eighty-
six signs, every one of them having a distinct phonetic value.

certainly Claudius could not introduce a new letter. Centuries may bring about and sanction the introduction of a new one, or the dropping of an old. But to imagine that it is possible suddenly to introduce a group of ten new letters, as these reformers propose— they might just as feasibly propose that the English language should form its comparatives and superlatives on some entirely new scheme, say in Greek fashion, by the terminations ' oteros ' and ' otatos ;' or that we should agree to set up a dual ; or that our substantives should return to our Anglo-Saxon declensions. Any one of these or like proposals would not betray a whit more ignorance of the eternal laws which regulate human speech, and of the limits within which deliberate action upon it is possible, than does this of increasing our alphabet by ten entirely novel signs.

But grant it possible, grant our six and twenty letters to have so little sacredness in them that Englishmen would endure a crowd of upstart interlopers to mix themselves on an equal footing with them, still this could only arise from a sense of the greatness of the advantage to be derived from this introduction. Now the vast advantage claimed by the advocates of the system is, that it would facilitate the learning to read, and wholly save the labor of learning to spell, which 'on the present plan occupies,' as they assure us, 'at the very lowest calculation from three to five years.' Spelling, it is said, would no longer need to be learned at all ; since whoever knew the sound, would necessarily know also the spelling, these being in all cases in perfect conformity with one an-

other.   The anticipation of this gain rests upon two
assumptions which are tacitly taken for granted, but
both of them erroneous.

The first of these assumptions is, that all men pronounce all words alike, and thus that whenever they
come to spell a word, they will exactly agree as to
what the outline of its sound is.   Now we are sure
men will not do this from the fact that, before there
was any fixed and settled orthography in our language,
when therefore everybody was more or less a phono-
grapher, seeking to write down the word as it sounded
to him, (for he had no other law to guide him,) the
variations of spelling were infinite.   Take for instance
the word 'sudden ;' which does not seem to promise
any great scope for variety.   I have myself met with
this word spelt in the following sixteen ways among
our early writers : 'sodain,' 'sodaine,' 'sodan,' 'so-
dane,' 'sodayne,' 'sodden,' 'sodein,' 'sodeine,'
'soden,' 'sodeyn,' 'suddain,' 'suddaine,' 'suddein,'
'suddeine,' 'sudden,' 'sudeyn.'   Shakespeare's name
is spelt I know not in how many ways, and Raleigh's
in hardly fewer.   The same is evident from the spelling of uneducated persons in our own day.   They
have no other rule but the sound to guide them.
How is it that they do not all spell alike ; erroneously,
it may be, as having only the sound for their guide,
but still falling all into exactly the same errors ?   What
is the actual fact.   They not merely spell wrongly,
which might be laid to the charge of our perverse
system of spelling, but with an inexhaustible diversity
of error, and that too in the case of simplest words.

Thus the town of Woburn would seem to give small
room for caprice in spelling, while yet the postmaster
there has made, from the superscription of letters that
have passed through his hands, a collection of two
hundred and forty-four varieties of ways in which the
place has been spelt.*   It may be replied that these
were all or nearly all collected from the letters of the
ignorant and uneducated.   Exactly so ;—but it is for
their sakes, and to place them on a level with the
educated, or rather to accelerate their education by
the omission of a useless yet troublesome discipline,
that the change is proposed.   I wish to show you that
after the change they would be just as much, or
almost as much, at a loss in their spelling as now.

   Another reason would make it quite as necessary
then to learn orthography as now.   Pronunciation, as
I have already noticed, is oftentimes far too subtle a
thing to be more than approximated to, and indicated
in the written letter.   Different persons would attempt
by different methods to overcome the difficulties which
the reproduction of it for the eye presented, and thus
different spellings would arise ; or, if not so, one must
be arbitrarily selected, and would have need to be
learned, just as much as spelling at present has need
to be learned.   I .will only ask you, in proof of this
which I affirm, to turn to any Pronouncing Dictionary.
That absurdest of all books, a Pronouncing Dictionary,
may be of some service to you in this matter ; it will
certainly be of none in any other.   When you mark

---

* *Notes and Queries*, No. 147.

the elaborate and yet ineffectual artifices by which it
toils after the finer distinctions of articulation, seeks
to reproduce in letters what exists, and can only
exist, as the spoken tradition of pronunciation, acquired from lip to lip by the organ of the ear, capable
of being learned, but incapable of being taught ; or
when you compare two of these Dictionaries with one
another, and note the entirely different schemes and
combinations of letters which they employ for representing the same sound to the eye ; you will then
perceive how idle the attempt to make the written in
language commensurate with the sounded ; you will
own that not merely out of human caprice, ignorance,
or indolence, the former falls short of and differs from
the latter ; but that this lies in the necessity of things,
in the fact that man's *voice* can effect so much more
than ever his *letter* can.*   You will then perceive that
there would be as much, or nearly as much, of arbitrary in spelling which calls itself phonetic as there is
in our present. We should be as little able to dismiss
the spelling card then as now.   But to what extent
English writing would be transformed—whether for
the better or the worse each may judge for himself—
a single specimen will prove.   Take as the first sample
which comes to my hand these four lines of Pope,
which hitherto we have thus spelt and read,

> ' But errs not nature from this gracious end,
> From burning suns when livid deaths descend,

---

* See Boswell, *Life of Johnson*, Croker's edit., 1848,
p. 233.

> When earthquakes swallow, or when tempests sweep
> Towns to one grave, whole nations to the deep ? '

Phonetically written, they present themselves to us in
the following fashion :

> ' But ſ erz not netiur from ðis grecus end,
> from burniŋ sunz when livid debs disend,
> when erðkweks swolo, or when tempests swip
> tounz tu wun grev, hol neconz tu ðe dip.'

The scheme would not then fulfil its promises. The
gains which it vaunts, when we come to look closely at
them, disappear. And now for the losses. There are
in every language a vast number of words, which the
ear does•not distinguish from one another, but which
are at once distinguishable to the eye by the spelling.
I will only instance a few which are the same parts of
speech ; thus ' sun ' and ' son ;' ' virge' ('virga,' now
obsolete) and ' verge ;' ' reign,' ' rain,' and ' rein ;'
' hair' and ' hare ;' ' plate' and ' plait ;' ' moat' and
' mote ;' ' pear ' and ' pair ;' ' pain' and ' pane ;'
' raise' and ' raze ;' ' air' and ' heir ;' ' ark' and
' arc ;' ' mite' and 'might ;' ' pour' and 'pore ;' 'tail'
and ' tale ;' ' veil ' and 'vale ;' ·'knight' and 'night ;'
' knave' and ' nave ;' ' pier' and ' peer ;' ' rite' and
' right.;' ' site' and 'sight ;' ' aisle' and 'isle ;' ' con-
cent' and ' consent ;' ' signet' and ·' cygnet.' Now,
of course, it is a real disadvantage, and may be the
cause of serious confusion, that there should be words
in spoken language of entirely different origin and
meaning, which yet cannot in sound be differenced
from one another. The phonographers simply pro-

pose to extend this disadvantage already cleaving to our spoken language, to the written language as well. It is fault enough in the French language, that 'mère' a mother, 'mer' the sea, 'maire' a mayor of a town, should have no perceptible difference between them in the spoken tongue; or again that there should be nothing to distinguish 'sans,' 'sang,' 'sent,' 'sens,' 's'en,' 'cent;' and as little 'ver,' 'vert,' 'verre' and 'vers.' Surely it is not very wise to propose gratuitously to extend the same imperfection to the written language as well.

This loss in so many instances of the power to discriminate between words, which, however liable to confusion now in our spoken language, are liable to none in our written, would be serious enough ; but more serious still would be the loss which would constantly ensue, of all which visibly connects a word with the past, which tells its history, and indicates the quarter from which it has been derived. In how many English words a letter silent to the ear, is yet most eloquent to the eye—the 'g' for instance in 'deign,' 'feign,' 'reign,' 'impugn,' telling as it does of 'dignor,' 'fingo,' 'regno,' 'impugno;' even as the 'b' in 'debt,' 'doubt,' is not idle, but tells of 'debitum' and 'dubium.'

It is urged indeed as an answer to this, that the scholar does not need these indications to help him to the pedigree of the words with which he deals, that the ignorant is not helped by them ; that the one knows without, and that the other does not know with them ; so that in either case they are profitable for nothing. Let it be freely granted that this in both these cases is true ; but between these two extremes there is a multitude of persons, neither accomplished scholars on the one side, nor yet wholly without the knowledge of all languages save their own on the other ; and I cannot doubt that it is of great value that these should have all helps enabling them to recognize the .words which they are using, whence they came, to what words in other languages they are nearly related, and what is their properest and strictest meaning.

At present it is the written word which in all languages constitutes their conservative element. In it is the abiding witness against the mutilations or other capricious changes in shape which affectation, folly, laziness, ignorance, and half-knowledge would introduce. Not seldom it proves unable to hinder the final adoption of these corrupter forms, but it does not fail to oppose to them a constant, and often a successful, resistance. In this way for example the 'cocodrill' of our earlier English has given place to the 'crocodile' of our later. With the adoption of phonetic spelling, this witness would exist no longer. Whatever was spoken would have also to be written, were it never so barbarous, never so wide a departure from the true form of the word. Nor is it merely probable that such a barbarizing process, such an adopting and sanctioning of a vulgarism, might take place, but among phonographers it has taken place already. There is a vulgar pronunciation of the word 'Eu*rope*,' as though it were 'Eu*rup*.' Now it is quite possible that a larger number of persons in England may pronounce the word in this manner than in the right ; and therefore the phonographers are only true to their principles when they spell it 'Eurup,' or, indeed, omitting the first letter, 'Urup,' the life of the first syllable being assailed no less than that of the second. What are the consequences? First, all connection with the old mythology is entirely broken off; secondly, its most probable etymology from two Greek words, signifying 'broad' and 'face,'—Europe being so called from the *broad* line or *face* of coast which it presented to the Asiatic Greek,—is totally obscured. * But so far from the spelling servilely following the pronunciation, I should be bold to affirm that if ninety-nine out of every hundred persons in England chose to call Europe 'Urup,' this would be a vulgarism still, against which the written word ought to maintain its protest, not lowering itself to their level, but rather seeking to elevate them to its own.†

---

* Ampère has well said, Effacer les signes étymologiques d'une langue, c'est effacer ses titres généalogiques et gratter son écusson.

† Quintilian has expressed himself with the true dignity of a scholar on this matter (*Inst.* I. 6. 45) : Consuetudinum sermonis vocabo *consensum eruditorum ;* sicut vivendi consensum bonorum.—How different from innovations like this the changes in German spelling which J. Grimm, so far as his own example may reach, *has* introduced ; and the still bolder which in the *Preface* to his *Deutsches Woerterbuch,* pp. liv.-lxii., he avows his desire to see introduced ;—as the employment of *f,* not merely where at present used, but wherever *v* is now employed ; the substituting of the *v,* which would be thus dis-

Then too, if there is much in orthography which is
unsettled now, how much more would be unsettled
then! Inasmuch as the pronunciation of words is
continually altering, their spelling would of course
have continually to alter too. What I here assert,
namely, that pronunciation is undergoing constant
changes, although changes for the most part unmarked,
or marked only by a few, it would be abundantly easy
to prove. Take a *Pronouncing Dictionary* of fifty or a
hundred years ago ; in almost every page, you will
observe schemes of pronunciation there recommended
which are now merely vulgarisms, or which have been
dropped altogether. We gather from a discussion in
Boswell's *Life of Johnson,** that in his time 'great' was
by some of the best speakers of the language pronounced 'greet,' not 'grate ; Pope usually rhymes it
with 'cheat,' 'complete,' and the like; thus in the
Dunciad :

> ' Here swells the shelf with Ogilby the *great*,
> There, stamped with arms, Newcastle shines com*plete ;*'

while Spenser's constant use a century and a half
earlier, leaves no doubt that such was the established
pronunciation of his time. Again, Pope rhymes
'obliged' with 'besieged ;' and it has only ceased to

---

engaged, for *w*, and the entire dismissal of *w*. These may be
advisable, or they may not ; it is not for strangers to offer an
opinion ; but at any rate they all rest on a deep historic study
of the language, and of its true genius ; and are not a seeking
to give permanent authority to the fleeting accidents of the
present hour.

* Croker's edit., 1848, pp. 57, 61, 233.

be 'oblæged' almost in our own time. 'Key' in our Elizabethan literature always rhymes with such words as 'survey' (Shakespeare, *Sonnets*). Who now drinks a cup of 'tay'? yet it is certain that this was the fashionable pronunciation in the first half of the last century. This couplet of Pope's is one proof out of many.:

> ' Here thou, great Anna, whom three realms *obey*,
> Dost sometimes counsel take, and sometimes *tea*.'

Rhyme is a great detector of changes like these, which but for the help that it affords we should fail to detect, which indeed we should often have no means of detecting, which not seldom we should not suspect in the least. Thus when 'should' rhymes with 'cooled' (Shakespeare), with 'hold' (Daniel), with 'cold' (Ben Jonson), 'would' with 'bold' (Ford), with 'mould' (Chapman), with 'old' (Fletcher), 'could' with 'gold' (Ben Jonson), it is plain that our 'shou'd,' 'wou'd,' 'cou'd,' had not yet established themselves in the language. And how little our words ending in 'ough' are pronounced now as they were once we gather from the fact that Golding in his translation of *Ovid's Metamorphoses* rhymes 'tough' and 'through,' 'trough' and 'through,' 'rough' and 'plough.' Or a play on words may inform us how the case once stood. Thus there would be no point in the complaint of Cassius that in all *Rome* there was *room* but for a single man,

> 'Now is it *Rome* indeed, and *room* enough,'

if Rome had not been pronounced in Shakespeare's

time, as some few pronounce it still, as I believe John Kemble pronounced it to the last, but as the educated classes of society have now consented not to pronounce it any more. Samuel Rogers assures us that in his youth 'everybody said "Lonnon," not "London ;" that Fox said "Lonnon" to the last.'.

Swift long ago urged the same objection against the phonographers of his time : 'Another cause which has contributed not a little to the maiming of our language, is a foolish opinion advanced of late years that we ought to spell exactly as we speak : which, besides the obvious inconvenience of utterly destroying our etymology, would be a thing we should never see an end of. Not only the several towns and counties of England have a different way of pronouncing, but even here in London they clip their words after one manner about the court, another in the city, and a third in the suburbs ; and in a few years, it is probable, will all differ from themselves, as fancy or fashion shall direct ; all which, reduced to writing, would entirely confound orthography.'*

Let this much suffice by way of answer to those who would fain revolutionize our English orthography altogether. Dismissing them and their rash innovations, let me call your attention now to those changes in spelling which are constantly going forward, at some periods more rapidly than at others, but which never wholly cease ; while at the same time I en-

* *A proposal for correcting, improving and ascertaining the English Tongue,* 1711, *Works,* vol. ix. pp. 139-159.

deavor to trace, where this is possible, the motives and inducements which bring them about. It is a subject which none can neglect, who desire to obtain an accurate acquaintance with their native tongue. Some principles have been laid down in the course of what has been said already,· that may help us to judge whether these changes are for better or for worse. We shall find, if I mistake not, of both kinds.

There are alterations in spelling which are for the worse. Thus an altered spelling will sometimes obscure the origin of a word, concealing it from those who would else at once have known whence and what it was, and would have found both pleasure and profit in this knowledge. In all those cases where the earlier spelling revealed the secret of the word, told its history, which the latter defaces or obscures, the change has been injurious, and is to be regretted ; while yet, where this is thoroughly established, any attempt to undo it would be absurd. Thus, when 'grocer' was spelt 'gro*ss*er,' it was comparatively easy to see that he first had his name, because he sold his wares not by retail, but in the *gross*. 'Co*x*comb' tells us nothing now ; but it did when spelt 'co*ck*comb,' the *comb* of a *cock* being an ensign or token which the fool was accustomed to wear. In 'grogra*m*' we are entirely to seek for the derivation ; but in 'grogra*n*' or 'grogra*in*,'. as earlier it was spelt, one could scarcely miss 'grosgrain,' the stuff of a *coarse grain* or woof. What a mischievous alteration in spelling is 'd*i*vest' instead of 'd*e*vest.' The change here is so recent that surely it would not be impossible to return to the only intelligible spelling.

'P*i*gmy' used once to be spelt 'p*y*gmy,' and no Greek scholar could then fail to perceive that by 'pigmies' were indicated manikins of no greater height than that of a man's arm from the elbow to the closed fist.*   Now he may know this in other ways ; but the word itself tells him nothing.   Or again, the old spelling, 'diam*ant*,' was preferable to the modern 'diam*ond*.'   It was so, because it told more of the past history of the word.   'Diamant' and 'adamant' are in fact no more than different adoptions by the English tongue, of one and the same Greek, which afterwards became a Latin, word.   The primary meaning of 'adamant' is, as you are aware, the indomitable, and it was a name given at first to steel as the hardest of metals ; but afterwards transferred† to the most precious among all the precious stones, as that which in power of resistance surpassed everything besides.

Neither are new spellings to be commended, which

---

* Pygmæi, quasi *cubitales* (Augustine).

† First so used by Theophrastus in Greek, and by Pliny in Latin.   The real identity of the two words explains Milton's use of 'diamond' in *Paradise Lost*, b. vi. ; and also in that sublime passage in his *Apology for Smectymnuus :* 'Then Zeal, whose substance is ethereal, arming in complete *diamona* ascends his fiery chariot.'—Diez (*Woerterbuch d. Roman. Sprachen*, p. 123) supposes, not very probably, that it was under a certain influence of 'd*i*afano,' the translucent, that 'adamante' was in the Italian, from whence we have derived the word, changed into '*dia*mante.'

obliterate or obscure the relationship of a word with others to which it is really allied ; separating from one another, for those not thoroughly acquainted with the subject, words of the same family. Thus when '*jaw*' was spelt '*chaw*,' no one could miss its connection with the verb 'to chew.' Now probably ninety-nine out of a hundred are unaware of any relationship between them. It is the same with 'cousin' (consanguineus), and 'to cozen.' I do not say which of these should conform to the spelling of the other. The spelling of both was irregular from the first ; while yet it was then better than now, when a permanent distinction has established itself between them, keeping out of sight that 'to cozen' is in all likelihood to deceive under show of affinity ; which if it be so, Shakespeare's words,

> ' *Cousins* indeed, and by their uncle *cozened*
>   Of comfort,' *

will contain not a pun, but an etymology. The real relation between 'bliss' and to 'bless' is in like manner at present obscured.

The omission of a letter, or the addition of a letter, may each effectually work to keep out of sight the true character and origin of a word. Thus the omission of a letter. When for 'bran-new,' it was 'bran*d*-new' with a final 'd,' how vigorous was the image here. The 'brand' is the fire, and 'brand-new,' equivalent to 'fire-new' (Shakespeare), is that which is fresh and bright, as being newly come from

---

* *Richard III.* Act iv. Sc. 4.

the forge and fire.   As now spelt, it conveys to us no
image at all.   Again, you have the word 'scrip'—as
a 'scrip' of paper, government 'scrip.' Is this the
Saxon 'scrip,' a wallet, which has in some strange
manner obtained these meanings so different and so
remote?   Have we here only two different applica-
tions of one and the same word, or two homonyms,
wholly different words, though spelt alike?   It is
sufficient to note how the first of these 'scrips' used
to be written, namely with a final 't,' not 'scrip' but
'scrip*t*,' and the question is answered.   This 'scrip'
is a Latin, as the other is an Anglo-Saxon, word, and
meant at first simply a *written* (scripta) piece of paper
—a circumstance which since the omission of the final
't' may easily escape our knowledge.   'Afraid' was
spelt much better in old times with the double 'ff,'
than with the single 'f' as now.   It was then clear
that it was not another form of 'afeared,' but wholly
separate from it, the participle of the verb 'to affray,'
'affrayer,' or, as it is now written, 'effrayer.'

   In these cases it has been the omission of a letter
which has clouded and concealed the etymology.
The intrusion of a letter sometimes does the same.
Thus in the early editions of *Paradise Lost*, and in the
writings of that age, you will find 'scent,' an odour,
spelt 'sent.'   It was better so ; .there is no other noun
substantive 'sent,' with which it is in danger of being
confounded ; while its relations with 'sentio,' with
're*sent*,'* 'dis*sent*,' 'con*sent*,' and the like, is put out

---

* How close the relationship was once, not merely in respect

of sight by its novel spelling; the intrusive 'c' serving
only to mislead. The same thing was attempted with
'site,' 'situate,' 'situation,' spelt for for a time by
many, 'scite, 'scituate,' 'scituation ;' but it did not
continue with these. Again, 'whole,' in Wicliff's
Bible, and indeed much later, sometimes as far down
as Spenser, is spelt 'hole,' without the 'w' at the
beginning. The present orthography may have the
advantage of at once distinguishing the word to the
eye from any other ; but at the same time the initial
'w' hides its relation to the verb 'to heal.' The
'whole' man is he whose hurt is 'healed' or covered
(we say of the convalescent that he 'recovers') ;
'whole' being closely allied to 'hale' (integer),
from which also by its modern spelling it is divided.
'Wholesome' has naturally followed the fortunes of
'whole :' it was spelt 'holsome' once.

Of 'island' too our present spelling is inferior to
the old, inasmuch as it suggests a hybrid formation, as
though the word were made up of the Latin 'insula,'
and the Saxon 'land.' It is quite true that 'isle' is
in relation with, and descent from 'insula,' 'isola,'
'ile ;' and hence probably the misspelling of 'island.
This last however has nothing to do with 'insula,'

of etymology, but also of significance, a passage like this will
prove : 'Perchance, as vultures are said to smell the earthiness
of a dying corpse ; so this bird of prey [the evil spirit which,
according to Fuller, personated Samuel, 1 Sam. xxviii. 14]
resented a worse than earthly savor in the soul of Saul, as
evidence of his death at hand ' (Fuller, *The Profane State,*
b. v. c. 4).

being identical with the German ʿeiland,' the Anglo-
Saxon ' ealand,' and signifying either the land apart,*
or land girt round with the sea. And it is worthy of
note that this ' s ' is of quite modern introduction.
In the earlier Versions of the Scriptures, and in the
Authorized Version as first set forth it is 'iland ;'
which is not accidental, seeing that ' isle ' has the ' s,'
which ' iland ' has not (see Rev. i. 9) ; and the correct spelling obtained far down into the seventeenth
century.

One of the most frequent causes of alteration in
the spelling of a word is a wrongly assumed derivation ; as has been the case with the word which we
dealt with. It is then sought to bring the word into
harmony with, and to make it by its spelling suggest,
this derivation, which has been erroneously thrust
upon it. Here is a subject which, followed out as it
deserves, would form an interesting and instructive
chapter in the history of language. Very remarkable
is the evidence which we have here to the way in
which learned and unlearned alike crave to have a
meaning in the words which they employ, to have
these not body only, but body and soul. Where for
the popular sense the life has died out from a word,
men will put into it a life of their own devising, rather
than that it should henceforth be a mere dead and
inert sign for them. Much more will they be tempted
to this in the case of foreign words, which have been
adopted into the language, but which have not

---

* ʿEiland ' for 'einlant,' see Grimm, *Woerterbuch*, s. v.

brought with them, at least for the popular mind, the secret of their origin. These shall tell something about themselves ; and when they cannot tell what is true, or when that true is not intelligible any more, then, rather than that they should say nothing, men compel them to suggest what is false, moulding and shaping them into some new form, until at least they shall appear to do this.*

There is probably no language in which such a process has not been going forward ; in which it is not the explanation, in a vast number of instances, of changes in spelling and even in form, which words have undergone.   I will offer a few examples of it from foreign tongues, before adducing any from our own.   'Pyramid' is a word, whose spelling was affected in the Greek by an erroneous assumption of its derivation ; the consequences of this error surviving to the present day.   It is spelt by us with a 'y' in the first syllable, as it was spelt with the corresponding letter in the Greek.   But why was this ?   It was because the Greeks assumed that the pyramids were so named from their having the appearance of *flame* going up into a point,† and so they spelt 'pyramid,' that they might find πῦρ or 'pyre' in it ; while in fact 'pyramid' has nothing to do with flame or fire at all ; being, as those best qualified to speak on the

---

* Ammianus Marcellinus, xxii. 15, 28.

† Diez looks with much favour on this process, and calls it, ein sinnreiches Mittel Fremdlinge ganz heimisch zu machen. Compare Schleicher, *Die Deutsche Sprache*, pp. 114-117; Mätzner, *Engl. Grammatik*, vol. i. p. 483.

matter declare to us, an Egyptian word of quite a
different signification, and the Coptic letters being
much better represented by the diphthong 'ei' than
by the letter 'y,' as no doubt, but for this mistaken
notion of what the word was intended to mean, they
would have been.

Once more—the form 'Hierosolyma,' the Greek
reproduction of the Hebrew 'Jerusalem,' was intended in all probability to express that the city so
called was the *sacred* city of the *Solymi.** At all
events the intention not merely of reproducing the
Hebrew word, but also of making it significant in
Greek, of finding ἱερόν in it, is plainly discernible.
For indeed the Greeks were exceedingly intolerant of
foreign words, till these had laid aside their foreign
appearance,—intolerant of all words which they could
not quicken with a Greek soul; and, with a very
characteristic vanity and an ignoring of all other
tongues but their own, assumed with no apparent
misgivings that all words, from whatever quarter derived, were to be explained by Greek etymologies.†

---

* Tacitus, *Hist.* v. 2.

† Let me illustrate this by further instances in a note. Thus
βούτυρον, from which, through the Latin, our 'butter' has
reached us, is borrowed (Pliny, *H. N.* xxviii. 9) from a Scythian
word, now to us unknown : yet it is sufficiently plain that the
Greeks so shaped and spelt it as to contain apparent allusion to
cow and *cheese ;* there is in βούτυρον an evident feeling after
βοῦς and τυρόν. Bozra, meaning citadel in Hebrew and
Phœnician, and the name, no doubt, which the citadel of
Carthage bore, becomes Βυρσα on Greek lips ; and then the

'Tartar' is another word, of which it is at least possible that a wrongly assumed derivation has modified the spelling, and not the spelling only, but the very shape in which we now possess it. To many among us it may be known that the people designated by this appellation are not properly 'Tartars,' but 'Tatars ;' and you may sometimes have noted the omission of the 'r' on the part of some who are

---

well-known legend of the ox-hide was invented upon the name ; not having suggested, but being itself suggested by it. Herodian (v. 6) reproduces the name of the Syrian goddess Astarte in a shape significant for Greek ears—'Αστροάρχη, The Star-ruler or Star-queen. When the apostate hellenizing Jews assumed Greek names, 'Eliakim' or 'Whom God has set,' became 'Alcimus' (ἄλκιμος) or The Strong (1 Macc. vii. 5). Latin examples in like kind are 'comissatio,' spelt continually 'comessatio,' and 'comessation' by those who sought to naturalize it in England, as though connected with 'comedo,' to eat, being indeed the substantive from the verb 'comissari' (=κωμάζειν), to revel; as Plutarch, whose Latin is in general not very accurate, long ago correctly observed ; and 'orichalcum,' spelt often 'aurichalcum,' as though it were a composite metal of mingled *gold* and brass ; being indeed the *mountain* brass (ὀρείχαλκος). The miracle play, which is 'mystère' in French, whence our English 'mystery,' was originally written 'mistère,' being derived from 'ministère,' and having its name because the clergy, the *ministerium* or *ministri* Ecclesiæ, conducted it. This was forgotten, and it then became 'mystery,' as though so called because the mysteries of the faith were in it set out. The mole in German was 'moltwurf,' our English 'moldwarp,' once, one that cast up the mould ; but 'molte' faded out of the language, and the word became, as it now is, 'maulwurf,' one that casts up with the 'maul' or mouth ;—which indeed the creature does not.

curious in their spelling. How then, it may be asked, did the form 'Tartar' arise? When the terrible hordes of middle Asia burst in upon civilized Europe in the thirteenth century, many beheld in the ravages of their innumerable cavalry a fulfilment of that prophetic word in the Revelation (chap. ix.) concerning the opening of the bottomless pit; and from this belief ensued the change of their name from 'Tatars' to 'Tartars,' which was thus put into closer relation with 'Tartarus' or hell, whence their multitudes were supposed to have proceeded.*

Another good example in the same kind is the German word 'sündflut,' the Deluge, which is now so spelt as to signify a 'sinflood,' the plague or *flood* of waters brought on the world by the *sins* of mankind; and some of us may before this have admired the pregnant significance of the word. Yet the old High German word had originally no such intention; it was spelt 'sinfluot,' that is, the great flood; and as late as Luther, indeed in Luther's own translation of the Bible, is so spelt as to make plain that the notion of a '*sin*-flood' had not yet found its way into, as it had not affected the spelling of, the word.†

---

* We have here, in this bringing of the words by their supposed etymology together, the explanation of the fact that Spenser (*Fairy Queen*, i. 7, 44), Middleton (*Works*, vol. v. pp. 524, 528, 538), and others employ 'Tartary' as equivalent to 'Tartarus' or hell.

† For a full discussion of this matter and fixing of the period at which 'sinfluot' became 'sündflut,' see the *Theol. Stud. u. Krit.*, vol. ii. p. 613; and Delitzsch, *Genesis*, 2nd ed. vol. ii. p. 210.

But to look nearer home for our examples : 'Ceiling' was always 'sealing,' that which seals or closes the roof, in our early English ; but, as is easy to explain, cœlum (ciel) made itself unconsciously felt, intruded into the word and changed the spelling to our present. The little raisins brought from Greece, which play so important a part in one of our national dishes, the Christmas plum-pudding, used to be called 'corinths ;' and this name they bear in mercantile lists of a hundred years ago : either that for the most part they were shipped from Corinth, the principal commercial city in Greece, or because they grew in large abundance in the immediate district round about it. Their likeness in shape and size and general appearance to our own currants, working together with the ignorance of the great majority of English people about any such place as Corinth, soon transformed 'corinths' into 'currants,' the name which now with a certain unfitness they bear ; being not currants at all, but dried grapes, though grapes of diminutive size.

'*Court*-cards,' that is, the king, queen, and knave in each suit, were once '*coat*-cards ;'* having their name from the long splendid 'coat' with which they were arrayed. Probably 'coat' after a while did not perfectly convey its original meaning and intention ; being no more in common use for the long garment (the vestis talaris) reaching down to the heels ; and then 'coat' was easily exchanged for 'court,' as the

---

* Ben Jonson, *The New Inn*, Act i. Sc. i.

word is now both spelt and pronounced, seeing that nowhere so fitly as in a Court should such splendidly arrayed personages be found. A public house in the neighbourhood of London having a few years since for its sign 'The George *Canning*,' is already 'The George and *Cannon*,'—so rapidly do these transformations proceed, so soon is that forgotten which we suppose would never be forgotten. 'Welsh *rarebit*' becomes 'Welsh *rabbit*; and '*farced*' or stuffed 'meat' becomes '*forced* meat.' Even the mere determination to make a word *look* English, to put it into an English shape, without thereby so much as seeming to attain any result in the way of etymology, is often sufficient to bring about a change in its spelling, and even in its form.* It is thus that 'sipahi' has become 'sepoy; and only so could 'weissager' have taken its present form of 'wiseacre;'† or 'hausenblase' become 'isinglass.'

---

* 'Leghorn' is sometimes quoted as an example of this ; but erroneously ; for, as Admiral Smyth has shown (*The Mediterranean*, p. 409), 'Livorno' is itself rather the modern corruption, and 'Ligorno' the name found on the earlier charts.

† Exactly the same happens in other languages ; thus, 'armbrust,' a crossbow, *looks* German enough, and yet has nothing to do with 'arm' or 'brust,' being a contraction of 'arcubalista,' but a contraction under these influences. As little has abenteuer' anything to do with 'abend' or 'theuer,' however it may seem to be connected with them, being indeed the Provençal 'adventura.' And 'weissagen' in its earlier forms had nothing in common with 'sagen.' On this subject see Schleicher, *Die Deutsche Sprache*, p. 116.

Not uncommonly a word, derived from one word, will receive a certain impulse and modification from another. This extends sometimes beyond the spelling, and where it does so, would hardly belong to our present theme. Still I may notice an instance or two. Thus our 'obsequies' is the Latin 'exequiæ,' but formed under a certain impulse of 'obsequium,' and seeking to express and include the observant honour implied in that word. 'To refuse' is 'recusare,' while yet it has derived the 'f' of its second syllable from 'refutare ; it is a medley of the two. The French 'rame,' an oar, is 'remus,' but that modified by an unconscious recollection of 'ramus.' The old French 'candel*arbre*' is 'candelabrum,' but with 'arbre' seeking to intrude itself into the word. So too the French has adopted the German 'sauerkraut,' but in the form of '*chou*-croute,' of which the explanation is obvious. The Italian 'convitare' is the Latin 'invitare,' but with 'convivium' making itself felt in the first syllable. 'Orange·' is a Persian word, which has reached us through the Arabic, and which the Spanish 'naranja' more nearly represents than the form existing in other languages of Europe. But what so natural as to contemplate the orange as the *golden* fruit, especially when the '*aurea* mala' of the Hesperides were familiar to all antiquity? In this way 'aurum,' 'oro,' 'or,' made itself felt in the various shapes which the word assumed in languages of the West, and we have here the explanation of the change in the first syllable, as in the low Latin 'aurantium,'

in 'orangia,' in the French 'orange,' and in our
own.*

It is foreign words, or words adopted from foreign
languages, as already has been said, which are especially subjected to such transformations as these.
The soul which they once had in their own language,
having, for as many as do not know that language,
departed from them, men will not rest till they have
put another soul into them again. Thus—to take
first one or two popular and familiar instances, than
which none serve better to illustrate the laws which
preside over human speech,—the Bellerophon becomes for our sailors the ' Billy Ruffian,' for what can
they know of the Greek mythology, or of the slayer
of Chimæra? an iron steamer, the Hirondelle, which
plied on the Tyne, was the ' Iron Devil.' ' *Contredanse*,' or dance in which the parties stand *face to face*
with one another, and which ought to have appeared
in English as ' *counter* dance,' becomes ' *country*
dance,'† as though it were the dance of the country

---

* See Mahn, *Etym. Untersuch.* p. 157.

† On this word De Quincey (*Life and Manners*, p. 70,
American Ed.) says well : ' It is in fact by such corruptions,
by off-sets upon an old stock, arising through ignorance or
mispronunciation originally, that every language is frequently
enriched ; and new modifications of thought, unfolding themselves in the progress of society, generate for themselves con-
currently appropriate expressions. . . . It must not be
allowed to weigh against a word once fairly naturalized by all,
that originally it crept in upon an abuse or a corruption.
Prescription is as strong a ground of legitimation in a case of
this nature, as it is in law. And the old axiom is applicable—

folk and rural districts, as distinguished from the
quadrille and waltz and more artificial dances of the
town.* A well-known rose, the rose of the four
seasons, or 'rose des quatre saisons,' becomes on
the lips of our gardeners, the 'rose of the *quarter
sessions*,' though here the eye must have misled, rather
than the ear. The cherry of Médoc becomes presently a 'may-duke.' 'Dent de lion' (it is spelt
'dentdelyon' in our early writers) becomes 'dande-
lion,' *chaude* mêlée,' or an affray in *hot* blood,
'*chance*medley,' 'causey' (chaussée, or via calceata)
becomes 'causeway,' 'rachitis' 'rickets,' 'mandra-
gora' in French 'main de gloire,' and 'hammock'
(a native Indian word) is in Dutch 'hangmat.'

'Necromancy' for a long time was erroneously
spelt, under the influence of an erroneous derivation;
which, perhaps even now, has left traces behind it in
our popular phrase, 'the *Black* Art.' Prophecy by
aid of the dead, as I need not tell you, is the proper
meaning of the word ; assuming as it does that these
may be raised by potent spells, and compelled to give
answers about things to come.   Of such 'necromancy'

Fieri non debuit, factum valet. Were it otherwise, languages
would be robbed of much of their wealth.'

* Unless indeed according to the rights of the case it should
prove the exact converse of this, and the French 'contredanse'
be derived from our country dance : see Chappell's argument
to prove this in his *Popular Music*, vol. ii. p. 627, with his
reference to the *Encyclopédie Méthodique* of 1791. Whether
we derived from the French, or the French from us, the
illustration of the matter in hand remains equally good.

we have a very awful example in the story of the witch of Endor, and a very horrid one in Lucan.* But the Latin medieval writers, whose Greek was either little or none, spelt the word, '*nigro*mantia,' while at the same time getting round to the original meaning, though by a wrong process, they understood the dead by these 'nigri,' or blacks, whom they had brought into the word.† Down to a late day we find '*negro*mancer' and '*negro*mancy' frequent in English.

'Pleurisy' used often to be spelt (it is hardly so now) without an 'e' in the first syllable, evidently on the tacit assumption that it was from *plus pluris*. When Shakespeare falls into an error, he 'makes the offence gracious;' yet, I think, he would scarcely have written,

> ' For goodness growing to a *plurisy*
> Dies of his own *too much*,'

but that *he* too derived 'plurisy' from *pluris*. This, even with the 'small Latin and less Greek,' which Ben Jonson allows him, he scarcely would have done, had the word presented itself in that form, which by right of its descent from πλευρά (being a pain, stitch, or sickness *in the side*) it ought to have possessed. Those who for 'crucible' wrote 'chrysoble' (Jeremy Taylor does so), must evidently have assumed that

---

* *Phars.* vi. 720-830.

† Thus in a *Vocabulary*, 1475 : Nigromansia dicitur divin-atio facta *per nigros.*

the Greek for *gold*, and not the Latin for *cross*, lay at
the foundation of the word.   'Anthymn' instead of
'anthem' (Barrow so spells it), rests plainly on a
wrong etymology, even as this spelling clearly betrays what that wrong etymology is.   'Lanthorn'
(Fuller) for 'lantern,' not less clearly does the same.
'Rhyme' with a 'y' is a modern misspelling ; and
would never have been but for the undue influence
which the Greek 'rhythm' has exercised upon it.
Spenser and his contemporaries spelt it 'rime.'
'Abominable' was not unfrequently in the seventeenth century spelt 'ab*h*ominable,' as though it were
that which departed from the human (*ab homine*) into
the bestial or devilish.   'Posthumous' owes the 'h'
which has found its way into it to the notion that,
instead of being a superlative of 'posterus,' it has
something to do with 'post humum.'

In all these instances but one the correct spelling
has in the end resumed its sway.   Not so however
'frontisp*ie*ce,' which ought to be spelt 'frontisp*i*ce,'
(it was so by Milton and others,) being the low Latin
'frontispicium,' from 'frons' and 'aspicio,' the forefront of the building, that side which presents itself
to the view.   The entirely ungrounded notion that
'piece' constitutes the last syllable, has given rise to
our present orthography.*

---

* As 'orthography' itself means '*right* spelling,' it might
be a curious question whether it is permissible to speak of an
*incorrect oth*ography, that is, of a *wrong right*-spelling.   The
question thus started is one of frequent recurrence, and it is

You may, perhaps, wonder that I have dwelt so
long on these details of spelling ; but I have bestowed
on them so much of my own attention, that I have

---

worthy of note how often his *contradictio in adjecto* is found to
occur. Thus the Greeks, having no convenient word for rider,
apart from rider *on a horse*, did not scruple to speak of the
*horse*man (ἱππεύς) upon an *elephant*. They are often as inaccurate and with no necessity ; as in using ἀνδριάς of the statue of a *woman ;* where εἰκων or ἄγαλμα would have
served as well. So too their table (τράπεζα = τετράπεζα)
involved probably the *four* feet which commonly support one ;
yet they did not shrink from speaking of a *three*-footed table (τρίπους τράπεζα), in other words, a '*three*-footed *four*-
footed ;' much as though we should speak of a '*three*-footed
*quadru*ped.' Homer's ' hecatomb ' is not of a *hundred*, but
of twelve, oxen ; and elsewhere of Hebe he says, in words not
reproducible in English, νέκταρ ἐωνοχόει. His ἰκτιδέη
κυνέη, a helmet of weasel-skin, but more strictly a weaselskin
dogskin, contains a like contradiction. Ἄκρατος, the unmingled, had so come to stand for wine, that St. John speaks
of ἄκρατος κεκερασμένος (Rev. xiv. 10), or the mingled
unmingled. Boxes to hold precious ointments were so commonly of alabaster, that they bore this name whether they were
so or not ; and Theocritus celebrates '*golden* alabasters ;' as
one might now speak of a ' silver pyx,' that is a silver *box*wood,
or of an iron box. Cicero has no choice but to call a water-
clock a *water-sun*-dial (solarium ex aquâ) ; Columella speaks
of a ' *vintage* of honey ' (vindemia mellis), and Horace invites
his friend to im*pede*, not his *foot*, but his head, with myrtle
(*caput* imped ire myrto). A German who should desire to tell
of the golden shoes with which the folly of Caligula adorned
his horse, could scarcely avoid speaking of *golden* hoof-*irons*.
Ink in some German dialects is ' blak,' but red ink is ' rood
blak,' or red black. The same inner contradiction is involved
in such language as our own, a '*false ver*dict,' a ' *steel pen* '

claimed for them so much of yours; yet in truth I cannot regard them as unworthy of our very closest heed. For indeed of how much beyond itself is accurate or inaccurate spelling the certain indication. Thus when we meet 'syren,' for 'siren,' as so strangely often we do, almost always in newspapers, and often where we should hardly have expected (I met it lately in the *Quarterly Review*, and again in Gifford's *Massinger*), how difficult it is not to be 'judges of evil thoughts,' and to take this slovenly misspelling as the specimen and evidence of an inaccuracy and ignorance which reaches very far wider than the single word which is before us. But why is it that so much significance is ascribed to a wrong spelling? Because ignorance of a word's spelling at once argues ignorance of its origin and derivation. I do not mean that one who spells rightly may not be ignorant of it too, but he who spells wrongly is certainly so. We are quite sure that he who for 'siren' writes 'syren,' knows nothing of the magic knots and entanglements (σειραί) of song, by which those fair enchantresses were supposed to draw those that heard them to their ruin; and from which they most probably had their name.

Correct or incorrect orthography being, then, this note of accurate or inaccurate knowledge, we may

---

(penna), a '*steel cuirass*' ('coriacea' from corium, leather), '*antics new*' (Harington's *Ariosto*), 'looking-*glasses* of *brass*' (Exod. xxxviii. 8), a '*sweet sauce*' (salsa), an '*erroneous etymology*,' '*rather late*,' 'rather' being the comparative of 'rathe;' and in others.

confidently conclude where two spellings of a word
exist, and are both employed by persons who generally write with precision, that there must be something to account for this. It will be worth your while
to inquire into the causes which enable both spellings
to hold their ground and to find their supporters, not
ascribing either one or the other to mere carelessness
or error. You will commonly find that two spellings
exist, because two views of the word's origin exist,
which those two spellings severally express. The
question therefore which way of spelling should continue, and wholly supersede the other, and which, so
long as both are allowed, we should ourselves employ,
can only be settled by determining which of these
etymologies deserves the preference. It is thus with
'chymist' and 'chemist,' neither of which has obtained in our common use a complete ascendancy
over the other. It is not here, that one mode is certainly right, the other certainly wrong : but they
severally represent two different etymologies of the
word, and each is correct according to its own. When
we spell 'chymist' and 'chymistry,' we implicitly
affirm the words to be derived from the Greek χυμός,
sap ; and the chymic art will then have occupied itself
first with distilling the juice and sap of plants, and
will from this have drawn its name. Many however
object to this, that it was not with the distillation of
herbs, but with the amalgamation of metals, that
chemistry occupied itself at the first, and find in the
word a reference to Egypt, the land of Ham or

'Cham,'* in which this art was first practised with success. In this case 'chemist,' and not 'chymist,' would be the only correct spelling.

Of how much confusion the spelling which used to be so common, 'satyr' for 'satire,' is at once the consequence, the expression, and again the cause. Not indeed that this confusion first began with us ; † 'satyricus' in the Latin was no less continually written for 'satiricus'; and this out of an assumed identity of the Roman *satire* and the Greek *satyric* drama ; while in fact satire was the only form of poetry which the Romans did *not* borrow from the Greeks. The Roman 'satira,'—I speak of things familiar to many of my hearers,—is properly a *full* dish (lanx being understood)—a dish heaped up with various ingredients, a 'farce,' or hodge-podge ; the name being

---

* Xημία, the name of Egypt ; see Plutarch, *De Is. et Os.* c. 33. For reasons against this, the favorite etymology at present, see Mahn, *Etymol. Untersuch.* p. 81. There is some doubt about the spelling of 'hybrid.' If from ὕβρις, this would of course at once settle the question.

† We have a notable evidence how deeply rooted this error was, of the way in which it was shared by the learned as well as the unlearned, in Milton's *Apology for Smectymnuus*, sect. 7, which everywhere presumes the identity of the 'satyr' and the 'satirist.' It was Isaac Casaubon who first effectually dissipated it even for the learned world. The results of his investigations were made popular by Dryden, in a. very instructive *Discourse on Satirical Poetry*, prefixed to his translations from Juvenal ; but the confusion still survives, and 'satyrs' and 'satires,' the Greek 'satyric' drama, the Latin 'satirical' poetry, are still assumed by many to have something to do with one another.

transferred from this to a form of poetry which at first
admitted the utmost variety in the materials of which
it was composed, and the shapes into which these
materials were wrought up. Wholly different from
this, having no one point of contact with it in form,
history, or intention, is the 'satyric' drama of Greece,
so called because Silenus and the 'satyrs' supplied
the chorus; and in their naive selfishness, and mere
animal instincts, held up before men a mirror of what
they would be, if only the divine, which is also the
truly human, element of humanity, were withdrawn;
what man, all that properly constituted him such
being withdrawn, would prove.

And then what light, as we have already seen, does
the older spelling often cast upon a word's etymology;
how often clear up the mystery, which would otherwise have hung about it, or which *had* hung about it
till some one had noticed and turned to profit this its
earlier spelling. Thus 'dirge' is always spelt 'dirige'
in early English. Now this 'dirige' *may be* the first
word in a Latin psalm or prayer once used at funerals;
there is a reasonable likelihood that the explanation
of 'dirge'.is here; at any rate, if it is not here, it is
nowhere. The derivation·of 'midwife' is uncertain,
and has been the subject of discussion; but when we
find it spelt 'medewife' and 'meadwife,' in Wiclif's
Bible, this leaves hardly a doubt that it is the *wife* or
woman who acts for a *mead* or reward. In cases too
where there was no mystery hanging about a word,
how often does the early spelling make clear to all
that which was before only known to those who had

made the language their special study. Thus if an early edition of Spenser should come into your hands, or a modern one in which the early spelling is retained, what continual lessons in English might you derive from it. Thus 'nostril' is always spelt by him and his contemporaries 'nosethrill ;' a little earlier it was ' nosethirle.' Now 'to thrill ' is the same as to drill or pierce ; it is plain then here at once that the word signifies the orifice or opening with which the *nose* is *thrilled*, drilled, or pierced. We might have read the word for ever in our modern spelling without being taught this. ' Ell ' gives us no clue to its own meaning ; but in ' eln,' used in Holland's translation of Camden, we recognize ' ulna' at once. Again, the ' morris' or ' morrice-dance,' of which in our early poets we hear so much, as it is now spelt tells us nothing about itself ; but read ' *moriske* dance,' as Holland and his contemporaries spell it, and you will scarcely fail to perceive, that it was so called either because it was really, or was supposed to be, a dance in use among the *moriscoes* of Spain, and from Spain introduced into England.* Once more, we are told that our 'cray-fish,' or 'craw-fish,' is the French 'écrevisse.' This is quite true, but it is not self-evident. Trace it however through these successive spellings, ' krevys' (Lydgate), 'crevish' (Gascoigne), 'craifish' (Holland), and the chasm between ' cray-fish ' or

---

* I have seen him
Caper upright, like a wild *Morisco*,
Shaking the bloody darts, as he his bells.'
Shakespeare, 2 *Henry VI*. Act iii. Sc. 1.

'craw-fish' and 'écrevisse' is by aid of these three intermediate spellings bridged over at once; and in the fact of our Gothic 'fish' finding its way into this French vocable we see one example more of a law, which has been already abundantly illustrated in this lecture.*

---

* In the reprinting of old books it is often hard to determine how far the earlier spelling of words should be retained, how far they should be conformed to present usage. It is comparatively easy to lay down as a rule that in books intended for popular use, wherever the form of the word is not affected by the modernizing of the spelling, there it shall take place ; (who, for example, would wish our Bibles to be now printed letter for letter after the edition of 1611, or Shakespeare with the orthography of the first folio ?) but wherever the shape, outline, and character of the word have been affected by the changes which it has undergone, there the earlier form shall be held fast. The rule is a judicious one ; but in practice it is not always easy to determine what affects the form and essence of a word, and what does not. About some words there can be no doubt ; and therefore when a modern editor of Fuller's *Church History* complacently announces that he has changed ' dirige ' into ' dirge,' ' barreter ' into ' barrister,' ' synonymas ' into ' synonymous ' !, ' extempory ' into ' extemporary,' ' scited ' into ' situated,' ' vancurrier ' into ' avant-courier,' and the like, he at the same time informs us that for all purposes of the study of English (and few writers are for this more important than Fuller), his edition is worthless. Or again, when modern editors of Shakespeare print, giving at the same time no intimation of the fact,

' Like quills upon the fretful *porcupine*,'

the word in his first folio and quarto standing,

' Like quills upon the fretful *porpentine*,'

In other ways also an accurate taking note of the
successive changes which words have undergone, will
often throw light upon them.   Thus we may know,
others having assured us of the fact, that 'emmet'
and 'ant' were originally only two different spellings
of the same word ; but we may be perplexed to
understand how two forms, now so different, could
ever have diverged from a single root.   When however we find the different spellings, 'emmet,' 'emet,'
'amet,' 'amt,' 'ant,' the gulf which appeared to separate 'emmet' from 'ant' is bridged over at once, and
we not merely accept on the assurance of others that
these two are identical, but we perceive clearly in
what manner they are so.

Even apart from any close examination of the
matter, it is hard not to suspect that 'runagate' is
another form of 'renegade,' this being slightly transformed, as so many words, to put an English signification into its first syllable ; and then the meaning
gradually modified under the influence of the new
derivation, which was assumed to be its original and
true one.   Our suspicion of this is strengthened (for
we see how very closely the words approach one
another), by the fact that 'renegade' is constantly
spelt 'renegate' in our old authors, while at the same
time the denial of faith, which is now a necessary

and this being in Shakespeare's time the current form of the
word, they have taken an unwarranted liberty with his text ;
and no less, when they substitute 'Kenilworth' for 'Killing-
worth,' which was his, Marlowe's, and generally the earlier
form of the name.

element in 'renegade,' and one differencing it inwardly from 'runagate,' is altogether wanting in early use—the denial of *country* and of the duties thereto owing being all that is implied in it. Thus it is constantly employed in Holland's *Livy* as a rendering of 'perfuga;'* while in the one passage where 'runagate' occurs in the Prayer Book Version of the Psalms (Ps. lxviii. 6), a reference to the original will show that the Translators could only have employed it there on the ground that it also expressed rebel, revolter, and not runaway merely.

I might easily occupy your attention much longer, so little barren or unfruitful does this subject of spelling appear likely to prove ; but all things must have an end ; and as I concluded my first lecture with a remarkable testimony borne by an illustrious German scholar to the merits of our English tongue, I will conclude my last with the words of another, not indeed a German, but still of the great Germanic stock ; words resuming in themselves much of which we have been speaking upon this and upon former occasions : 'As our bodies,' he says, 'have hidden resources and expedients, to remove the obstacles which the very art of the physician puts in its way, so language, ruled by an indomitable inward principle, triumphs in some degree over the folly of grammarians. Look at the English, polluted by Danish

---

* 'The Carthaginians shall restore and deliver back all the *renegates* [perfugas] and fugitives that have fled to their side from us.'—p. 751.

and Norman conquests, distorted in its genuine and
noble features by old and recent endeavours to mould
it after the French fashion, invaded by a hostile
entrance of Greek and Latin words, threatening by
increasing hosts to overwhelm the indigenous terms.
In these long contests against the combined power
of so many forcible enemies, the language, it is true,
has lost some of its power of inversion in the structure
of sentences, the means of denoting the difference of
gender, and the nice distinctions by inflection and
termination—almost every word is attacked by the
spasm of the accent and the drawing of consonants to
wrong positions ; yet the old English principle is not
overpowered.   Trampled down by the ignoble feet of
strangers, its springs still retain force enough to
restore itself.   It lives and plays through all the veins
of the language ; it impregnates the innumerable
strangers entering its dominions with its temper, and
stains them with its colour, not unlike the Greek,
which, in taking up Oriental words, stripped them of
their foreign costume, and bid them to appear as
native Greeks.' *

---

* Halbertsma, quoted by Bosworth, *Origin of the English
and Germanic Languages*, p. 39.

INDEX OF WORDS.

Index of Words. 349

CPSIA information can be obtained
at www.ICGtesting.com
Printed in the USA
LVHW112317171022
730904LV00008B/376